D1740659

JINX TOWN

To Neil,

JINX TOWN

Sam Stone

Hope you enjoy the journey!

The Jinx Chronicles
Book 1

Love
Sam Stone
x

First published in 2015 by Telos Publishing Ltd
5A Church Road, Shortlands, Bromley, Kent, BR2 0HP

www.telos.co.uk

Telos Publishing Ltd values feedback. Please e-mail us with any comments
you may have about this book to: feedback@telos.co.uk

Jinx Town: The Jinx Chronicles Book 1 © 2015 Sam Stone

ISBN: 978-1-84583-096-0

Cover Art: © 2015 Jim Burns
Cover Design: David J Howe

British Library Cataloguing in Publication Data. A catalogue record for this
book is available from the British Library.

In Memory of Dorothy Lumley

PART ONE

Earth Falls

1

Jasmine Regis noted the progress of her students while they ran through the test to identify protein. This was her first term in the school, and half-way through, with only a week to go to the first half-term break, Jas was already exhausted from the sheer volume of her workload. She couldn't wait for the holiday. At least then she might catch up a little on the marking.

Jas was attractive and athlete slender. Her long brunette hair was pulled back in the regulation bun, and she wore her teacher's uniform, a bland tweed suit in dark grey, with a plain white shirt that had the Heathmoor Academy emblem on the pocket. The emblem matched the one on the blazer pocket: the Latin phrase, *Servitus Defendi Doceo*, stood out in bold red against the grey as though to remind her she had to Serve, Protect and Teach in that order. Jas detested the uniform. Mostly it was itchy and uncomfortable, but what it represented was that which she hated: it made each teacher look the same, and this meant that staff were treated very much like the students. Outrageous hairstyles and colours weren't permitted for the teachers any more than they were for the students. The uniform was like the curriculum in its rigidity; there was no allowance made for personality or flair, and personal creativity was restricted to making the bland lessons more engaging. If that was possible. Even so, Jas loved her job, and if she saw one small spark of understanding or enjoyment in the eyes of her students then she felt she was doing well. Unlike most of her colleagues she wasn't cynical, despite the strictness of the regime she had to work within.

'That's fantastic work, Andrew,' Jas said as she looked down at her pupil's experiment. It was perfect and controlled – just as it should be.

Andrew Carpenter was the ideal student. He was smart and he always produced beautifully neat work in his exercise book. He was only a first year and the youngest in the group and Jas thought he still had the air of primary school about him. Particularly when he sat quietly, looking wide-eyed at the Smartboard. Unlike some of the other boys, Andrew was sensible and always listened to instructions carefully.

The problem was that Andrew had the misfortune to be seated next to

Ray Steinberg: the worst-behaved pupil in the class. Generally Jas didn't enjoy teaching the younger end of the school. The boys were annoying; always giggling and tittering over every Biology lesson that involved the exploration of the human body. Andrew Carpenter, however, sat as silent and controlled as his experiment.

'Now remember, class,' said Jas, 'sodium hydroxide needs to be handled with extreme care. It dissolves clothing and skin and will also damage the bench tops. Therefore you must wash your hands *immediately* if you get any of it on you.'

Steinberg picked up the jar of sodium hydroxide and pretended to throw it in the direction of a group of girls working together on a nearby bench. One of the girls screamed, and Jas turned quickly to find Steinberg fooling around. Again.

'Steinberg. What are you doing?'

Steinberg put the jar down and nudged it toward Andrew.

'It's 'im miss. He's always messing with the experiments.'

'Steinberg,' Jas said firmly, 'either stop clowning around or I will ban you from taking part during these experiments. In fact you can go over there and sit in the corner.'

'You can't do that to me,' Steinberg replied. 'It's against the law and I'll tell me mam you're picking on me.'

'Get out!' said Jas, firmly but calmly. There was no way she was getting into a debate with this obnoxious child.

'I'm going to report you. She 'it me, didn't she?' Steinberg said, nudging Andrew again.

Andrew said nothing.

'If I had hit you, Steinberg, you wouldn't be conscious, because I pack a mean punch. Now get outside. Right now!'

'She's just threatened to 'it me! You all heard that, didn't you?'

Jas marched Steinberg out into the hallway. It was children like him that made working in schools so much more hard work than it should be.

Jas hadn't been teaching long. This was her first permanent job and she was trying hard to maintain discipline. Her old tutor had warned her never to smile during the first term. Jas was trying to follow that advice, but it was difficult for her to remain serious and stern all the time. Occasionally when funny things happened in the class, she would erupt into fits of laughter along with the students. Like the time when they had dissected frogs and one of them had still been alive. The amphibian had jumped all over the lab while a few of the boys chased it, until eventually the frog had escaped through an open window, out onto the playing field. One or two of the girls had screamed as though they were being murdered, a habit Jas found particularly irritating, but that day she had laughed so much at the comedy of the moment that eventually the whole class had seen the funny side.

Leaving Steinberg outside, Jas returned to her desk and picked up the internal phone. After a few rings, the school secretary answered.

'Steinberg is outside again,' Jas said. 'Can someone come and pick him up?'

Within minutes security had Steinberg and were marching him down the corridors to the isolation rooms. His parents would be called – again – but Jas didn't think anything much would happen to the boy. He was a nuisance, but his mother indulged him to the point of making him impossible to control.

'Continue with your experiments everyone. Then fill in the results charts and glue them into your books.'

Jas sat down behind her desk and began to fill in an incident report form on the school's internal system. Steinberg was a nightmare, and if it wasn't for her self-control, she *might* have punched him.

Strange how kids do that to you, she thought. *I'd never hurt anyone, but that little bastard totally winds me up.*

'Miss Regis?'

Jas looked up to find Andrew stood in front of her desk.

'Yes, An … Carpenter?' Jas said, catching herself just in time. The school did not approve of teachers addressing students by their first name. It was deemed politically incorrect. Even so, Jas couldn't bring herself to think of this kind-natured boy in such a cold and indifferent way.

'I've finished,' Andrew said, holding out his book.

Jas took the exercise book and rapidly read and marked the beautiful work the boy had produced. She reached inside her drawer and pulled out her 'special' stamp. Then she pressed it onto the page. It said 'Excellent Work' and had a smiley face under the words. Andrew looked down at the page and smiled widely. For every one of these stamps, he would get merits from his form tutor that equalled prizes at the end of the term.

A few minutes later the bell sounded and Jas dismissed the class. She had a free period next, so she completed the report on Steinberg and sent it off. Then she opened up her lesson plans and began to tweak and change the work she had planned for the class for the following week. It had to be rethought as Steinberg would always spoil the practical lessons. She didn't want to punish the rest of the class for his sake, though, so she organised a session for the boy elsewhere in the Special Needs Department. There at least Steinberg would get the attention he was craving, in the form of one-on-one tuition. The only way to deal with his sort was to take him out of the classroom, denying him an audience for his bad behaviour.

'Jas?' said Brian Maitland, her department head, poking his head around the doorway. 'I believe Steinberg was acting up again.'

'Yes. I just sent the report.'

'His mother just rang and put in a complaint about you. He apparently called her while he was waiting for security. She says you threatened to punch the boy in the face.'

'*What*? I wouldn't say anything like that.'

'Let's be honest,' Maitland said. 'We all *want* to punch Steinberg. He's a little shit. But what exactly did you say that could have been misinterpreted as that?'

Jas shook her head and thought back through the conversation. 'Well, he threatened to say I'd hit him. The whole class heard him.'

'He's pulled that stunt before,' said Maitland. 'His mother is in here at least once a week complaining about something the school's done. It's ridiculous really, but the system says the parent has rights and we have none.'

'Am I in trouble, Brian?' Jas asked. 'Only I know how these things work.'

'You have a lot of support and we've documentary evidence about the boy, Jas. Shame the days of permanent expulsion are now gone. Ten years ago we still had some power over the kids in our care. Now they just see us as a joke.'

'Andrew Carpenter was a witness if we need one. He saw how Steinberg was acting, and Andrew is a reliable boy.'

'Okay. I'll go and talk to him.'

Maitland left and Jas returned her gaze to the computer screen, but her mind was no longer on the task. The law had changed so much in the last few years. Teachers really did have little power. The schools employed 'qualified' bouncers, but they were there to avoid infractions, and pupils were escorted by them for *their* safety, even if they were the ones causing the problem. It had all started with the government initiative called Every Child Matters, but the new charters and regulations drawn up to ensure that every child got a proper education didn't take into account that some of them just wouldn't be taught. The failing was seen as the teachers'. It was their job to teach and protect, and the law assumed that every pupil wanted to be taught and protected. You couldn't lay hands on the students in any way, never mind use reasonable force, even if they were beating up other kids. You couldn't even touch them to console them if they were crying. If a child really got out of hand then the bouncers did the uplifting. Even the worst pupils wouldn't go up against one of those, because they did have the right to use reasonable force – but only because they were 'trained'.

Jas knew that Steinberg was always going to be a problem and his time at school would be spent causing trouble. This was because his mother encouraged his disobedience. Parents had rights – which was a good thing, of course – but this meant that they were the only ones truly allowed to punish their children. If the parents didn't care to teach their child manners and good behaviour, then the teachers couldn't do anything to correct that position.

Jas idly searched the net and found some old legislation that made teachers *in loco parentis*. Once they had had the authority to act in place of the parent; but now those days were gone.

'Little bastard,' Jas murmured as her mind flicked back to Steinberg: his sort always knew the law too. They knew they were untouchable and they used it all the time to threaten and bully the teaching staff.

Jas went to her mailbox and saw the report from Brian sitting there. She knew he would support her as much as he could. *When did it become 'them and us'?* Jas wondered. She couldn't place the moment, just knew that when she had entered university to study for her science degree this was the way it had been.

Jas opened the e-mail and looked down at the report. Her eyes rapidly took in the accusations from Steinberg, the complaints and rants of his indulgent mother, and the confirmation from Andrew Carpenter that Steinberg had lied.

Jas expelled her breath, suddenly realising she had been holding it, and her heartbeat steadied. She needed this job and she didn't want to be in trouble in her first year. It would mean a permanent stain on her teaching record. It was a relief that Andrew hadn't been too scared of Steinberg to confirm her report.

Thanks kid! I owe you one, she thought.

Another e-mail arrived in her inbox from Maitland.

'Sorry about this,' it read. 'His mother is still kicking up a stink and has asked to see the head. I've sent Rose all the evidence. I'm hoping she will just give Steinberg's mother "the talk" and that will end it. I'll keep you informed.'

Jas felt sick. Her heart hurt with anxiety. *This is ridiculous!* She was amazed how quickly things went from good to bad. In the space of an hour she had been pulled through the rollercoaster of insecurity that her job always seemed to provide.

'I didn't sign up for this shit,' she murmured to the screen. Then she typed a rapid response to Maitland, thanking him for all his help.

Her inbox bleeped again and Jas looked at the new mail, For a moment her mind refused to accept what she was seeing. *Interview. Re: Raymond Steinberg. Rose Harper.* This couldn't be good.

The bell sounded, and as the next set of pupils lined up outside the classroom, Jas reflected on how the authorities were even planning to rid them of this one small piece of control too. The noise the bell created was pollution and *distressed* the pupils. Lining them up was *degrading*.

Jas stood up from her desk and walked to the door, putting her stern face back in place. *Next they'll be saying that coming to school is bad for education.*

2

A stream of pupils in burgundy sweaters poured into the theatre. Jas stood at the end of the aisle and watched the rows of boys and girls take their seats before sitting down herself. She was near Ray Steinberg and Andrew Carpenter. Steinberg always wangled his way close to the other boy. Jas wondered if he thought Andrew was an easy target; someone to torment mercilessly without being reported. Pupils couldn't hurt each other – that was one rule that had been sustained – and attacks on their peers were dealt with firmly by the authorities. It was only in these cases that students could be removed from one school and placed in another, rapidly becoming someone else's problem. Steinberg knew the law and never crossed the line when anyone was there to witness it, but Jas suspected that once the lights dimmed he would try to intimidate Andrew, and she was definitely going to be watching out for the boy.

She was on the trip as a punishment. Rose Harper had targets to hit, and fewer complaints to the school was one of them.

'I don't really care if you did threaten to hit him,' Rose had said. 'But his mother keeps making complaints, and I have to do something to get her to withdraw this one.'

'So punishing me is the answer?' Jas asked. 'Even though I did nothing wrong?'

'Yes. You apologise to the mother and that will end this matter.'

Jas had gone along with it although she really didn't appreciate being the fall guy. Fortunately Andrew's statement meant her record was kept clean. Everyone knew Steinberg lied. But Jas wasn't convinced that this was the best way to deal with his parents. Brian had said 'The world's gone mad,' and he was right. Jas really couldn't make sense out of a system that gave so much power to people who would abuse it. She also knew that this wouldn't be the end of it. Steinberg's mother loved stirring trouble, and Jas would be teaching her son for the rest of the year.

'They did this to prevent teachers abusing kids,' Brian said. 'Now the parents and kids abuse us. It's no wonder we constantly lose good teachers because of the system.'

Once, teaching had been a sought-after career, a vocation you bought into for life. Now more and more teachers were leaving and seeking lesser jobs than they deserved for their qualifications. The money was excellent though, and it was this that attracted Jas to the job as well as her passion for science. She enjoyed sharing her knowledge, and the money meant that even at the age of 22 she was able to afford her own house and have complete independence.

Jas glanced over at the two boys. Strangely, Andrew didn't look unhappy or uncomfortable and was whispering with Steinberg as they both looked down at the programme that Andrew had bought. They had come to see a performance of Shakespeare's *Macbeth* as part of a literary culture week, and the theatre was full of kids on school trips.

Popcorn and crisps weren't allowed in the main auditorium, but Steinberg and Andrew shared a bag of jelly sweets.

'It's a tragedy,' said Andrew.

'Yeah – the costumes *are* funny,' said Steinberg. Andrew nudged him, then offered another sweet.

'The costumes add to the atmosphere of the story,' said Jas.

Steinberg looked up and glared at her, his eyes so full of open hostility that Jas was taken aback. Then he turned his gaze back to the programme. Jas shook her head and resisted saying anything to him, but she felt anger and irritation rising up inside her. *He'll get his comeuppance one of these days, the little bastard.* It was all too easy for her to dislike Steinberg, despite her promise that she would care for all the children she taught. He just wasn't pleasant to be around, and he had a serious issue with teachers.

The lights dimmed, and music came out of the speakers around the theatre. Jas recognised it as 'O Fortuna' from *Carmina Burana*.

'*X-Factor*,' laughed Steinberg. 'Old man Cowell makes me laugh ...'

Jas glanced at the boys again, then as the curtain rose, turned her eyes toward the stage. The first act began.

They were just returning to their seats after the interval when the earthquake hit the theatre. It was as if a giant hand had tried to rip the building clean out of its foundations. As a collective gasp issued from the audience, a huge crack appeared across the ceiling and the central chandelier rocked and jerked against its thick chains. A large chunk of plaster plummeted down into the aisles, narrowly missing an old woman who was struggling from her seat.

Jas threw herself forward, propelling the back end of the line of pupils in front of her out into the hallway just as another piece of plaster fell. For a fleeting moment that ridiculous children's story about Chicken Licken and the sky falling down flashed through her mind. She pulled herself up off the floor, grabbing Andrew and Steinberg by the arms and dragging them down the corridor toward the emergency exit, just as the rest of the children ran screaming out of the theatre ahead of them.

There were people pushing and shoving behind them, and Jas glanced over her shoulder to see the cast of the performance, still dressed in Shakespearean costume, merging with the crowd as they poured into the theatre foyer. Jas and the boys were pulled along with the throng, and even though they were moving in the opposite direction to the rest of the class, they had no choice but to go along or be crushed.

A male theatre usher, dressed in a black pin-stripe uniform, stood at the doorway, trying to calm a group of American tourists as they pushed at the door.

'It's pull!' he said, but the small group of men and women were so panicked that they weren't listening.

Another group of schoolchildren barged into an elderly couple, knocking them over, then trampled on the old man as they pushed their way through to the main entrance and out into the street. The old man's wife struggled to her feet. 'For god's sake someone help us!' she sobbed, but the people pushed her out of the way. It was every man for himself, and they were all afraid to stay inside the tumbling building. The wife continued to scream as she saw blood pouring from a wound on her husband's forehead. Eventually a security guard pushed through and lifted the old man off the floor. The old man couldn't walk, so the guard half carried, half pulled him to safety as his wife followed.

'Thank you. Thank you ...' she repeated. Shock had turned her face a sickly yellow, and as the guard placed her husband on a sofa in the theatre bar, she sank down beside him, nursing his damaged head against her thin chest.

'We've called for police and ambulance,' the security guard said. 'Just stay here till the madness dies down.'.

Outside, the previously sunny day had given way to a hurricane blizzard. The wind was a howling mass of dust, leaves and rubbish. The noise of panic was deafening. The horde of people swarmed out around Jas and the two boys and hurried toward their cars in mass hysteria.

Still pulling her two charges, Jas headed for the car park. She couldn't see the school bus, but vaguely remembered where the driver had parked.

'Ouch!' complained Steinberg. 'Miss Regis, please. You're 'urting me arm.'

'That's "hurting", Steinberg,' she corrected automatically. *And I suppose you'll tell your mother about it later too!*

Jas let go of the boys as another tremor rocked the ground beneath them. She stumbled to her knees, motion nausea bringing burning bile up into her mouth, and she swallowed hard, fighting the sickness back down into her throat. She winced as a stone pierced the tweed, grazing her knee, but for once she was glad she was wearing sturdy trousers and sensible shoes. She lifted her head, looked around for the other teachers in their matching clothing, but could see no sign of any of the Heathmoor Academy staff or pupils.

'What the hell is going on?' she said. 'We don't have earthquakes in England.'

'There!' said Andrew, pointing toward the front entrance of the theatre.

A massive void, like a black hole, had appeared in the middle of the road. Air and dust swirled around the space as though they were being pushed aside to make room for this new anomaly. Jas tried to look closer, but the wind buffeted against her face, throwing grit into her eyes every time she tried to open them. She shielded her face with her hands, looking out through slightly parted fingers.

It looked like some kind of vortex. *Only those sorts of things usually occur in water due to varying tides,* Jas thought. This vortex was made predominantly of air. *Impossible!* It was like something out of a science fiction movie or one of the games the kids played in the console room during break times.

The vortex was widening and Jas could vaguely make out movement just inside of it.

Andrew and Steinberg huddled against the side of the theatre, scared to move as the hole in the atmosphere grew larger. More grit and rubbish were hurled about as the ground rocked backwards and forwards. It was almost impossible to stand, let alone walk. They were trapped, but still Jas managed to crawl back toward the boys.

Pressed against the theatre wall, Jas watched as one of the actors, the man who had played Macbeth, tried to stand, staggering away from the roaring hole in space, only to be flung to the ground again. His head smashed against the concrete, cracking open like an egg. Blood and brains seeped out, turning the grey flags red.

'Don't look!' she ordered, moving her body to block the awful sight from Andrew and Steinberg. True to form, Steinberg peeked around her. His small, mischievous face drained of colour, and at last Jas saw the child in him. *Maybe Steinberg is normal to a point after all? But it's typical of him to disobey me even now,* Jas thought.

Just as quickly as they had begun, the howling winds subsided. The ground beneath steadied and the vortex became still. Jas could feel a cold rush of air pouring out from the opening. It hung inexplicably in the thinning atmosphere and smelt *wrong*. It was reminiscent of when you visited a hot country: that first breath you take when you step outside into a new environment. The idea of a *cold* desert floated into her mind. She turned and looked once more at the vortex, and her mind tried to make sense of all she was seeing. The panic rising in her chest intensified as the air thickened. She sniffed: iron and decay. Cold sun. The grit and dirt tasted salty on her lips, just like sand.

Deep inside the vortex there was movement. The sides were spinning like a fairground ride, but despite this a plateau formed inside, and Jas could make out a smooth, sandy walkway.

Blurred spots of darkness appeared within the murky abyss.

'Run for the bus!' Jas yelled, but the remaining wind stole the sound and the two boys looked at her blank and terrified.

Jas stumbled to her feet.

'Come on!' she said, grabbing the arm of each boy once more.

Steinberg just stared at her, his eyes vacant, mouth slack, but Andrew had the presence of mind to attempt to stand as she pulled.

'We need to get out of here!'

Andrew nodded, and helped by linking Steinberg's other arm. Between them they tugged the shocked boy to his feet.

'Monsters …' he murmured.

'It's an earthquake,' Jas explained, staggering across the pitted and cracked ground, but even as the words came out of her mouth, she knew it wasn't true.

Another tremor hit and the ground exploded behind them, sending tarmac and concrete up into the air; but this time the wind acted to their advantage, propelling them forward into the road, and they ran with it. They reached the car park a few minutes later. Jas recognised the bus and saw the children stumbling up into it. Girls and boys in their matching burgundy sweaters were screaming aloud in equal measure.

Jas glanced back over her shoulder. The vortex was fully open. A huge mouth-like tunnel of white light, reflecting beige sand; and Steinberg had been right: there were monsters inside.

They reached the bus and Jas propelled Steinberg before her, pushing him rapidly toward the steps.

'Get on,' she ordered.

Steinberg stumbled forward, falling up the steps and tearing a hole in his new and pristine trousers. Blood seeped from a gash in his knee. He began to cry. Jas helped the boy up, but the usually automatic words of reassurance failed to come to her lips. She didn't like him and couldn't be false. Instead, she reached inside her jacket pocket and retrieved a wad of tissues to staunch the flow.

'We have to get away from here, fast,' Jas said, meeting the frightened eyes of the driver.

'What the fuck is that?' he gasped, looking beyond her.

'Miss Regis … Miss!' Andrew yelled behind her. 'Look!'

Jas turned around. It felt like slow motion. The theatre grounds resembled a battlefield after the bombardment of explosive weapons. Bits of earth, rock and concrete were bursting up from the ground as though the core contained dynamite. The vortex spun around like a worm, and from it stepped an army of what could only be described as ancient soldiers, all wearing polished armour and carrying short swords. Ancient but … somehow alien. They poured out of the spinning vortex and into the grounds of the theatre, moving with fluid and agile grace across to the doorways of the building.

A woman screamed as the ground ripped up before her. As she pitched forward, half falling into a giant hole in the pavement, one of the soldiers leapt towards her, somersaulting on one hand like a circus performer and catching hold of her with his other hand seconds before she could plummet to her death. It looked like a rescue mission. The agile soldier had saved her. He bounded through the air, almost weightless as he turned, still carrying the woman, her body flopping like a rag doll, and headed for the vortex, only to disappear back inside. Jas was certain that no human could move that way, except in the movies, and it reinforced her first thought that the soldiers were not from this world. The word 'alien' rang in her head again, and after that she couldn't think of them as anything else.

A group of the alien soldiers reached a cluster of men, women and children as they huddled against the theatre wall too afraid to move. The aliens towered over the men. Jas could see that they were at least a foot taller than the humans. Ornate, curved helmets covered their heads. They were a jumbled mass of metal and jewels. At this distance, she couldn't even make out if the aliens had faces at all, but she wondered what monstrosity was hidden behind the glittery masks.

The aliens began to pick out the women and female children from the group. A man stood up.

'Get your hands off my wife and kid, you freak!' he yelled, clutching his wife and daughter as one of the aliens caught hold of them by the arm. His voice echoed over the car park as the noise coming from the vortex suddenly ceased.

The alien let go, drew his bejewelled sword from the scabbard at his side and swung it in a neat arc. The man's head rolled away from his body along the cracked pavement and tumbled down into the abyss, leaving a bloody trail in its wake. His body crumpled and fell among the group, scattering them as arterial blood sprayed from his neck.

The crowd erupted with screams of fear as the soldier once again took hold of the shocked wife and crying daughter, dragging them effortlessly toward the vortex.

An elderly woman ran from the group holding a child against her chest as an alien soldier pursued her, cutting off her exit to the car park. She screamed and fought as the little girl was ripped from her arms, but was knocked back when the alien viciously backhanded her. As the woman fell to the ground, her nose and mouth pouring blood, another soldier arrived. The two aliens looked over the old woman as she cowered on the ground. They seemed to be arguing, and it crossed Jas's mind that they were debating whether the woman was worth taking or not. Eventually, they shrugged in a very human way, turned their backs and left her unharmed as the child in her care was passed to yet another alien. This one ran at inhuman speed back to the vortex and disappeared. The old woman staggered to her feet and gave chase.

'Elise ...' she yelled, but her distress and the battering wind made the cry incoherent. As the old woman reached the vortex, the soldier guarding the entrance turned on her and, with barely a swing, ruthlessly ran his sword through her. She hung, suspended and twitching, and then slowly slipped off the sword to the ground. The soldier wiped his blade on her dress, then kicked her body aside as more of the horde returned with captives.

A group of men and women came out of the theatre holding wrenches, iron bars and planks of wood. They had obviously been watching from inside and were ready to fight, but the invaders responded brutally. The first man, the security guard that Jas had seen help the old couple during the initial panic, ran forward holding an iron bar above his head, only to be cut down as an alien sword pierced his belly, spilling his intestines over the front steps. A woman yelled in a primal battle cry, rushing forward with insane blood lust, followed by two more men. One alien overpowered the woman as she swung her weapon – a piece of wood taken from a broken chair. The alien swirled and span, leaping upside down above her head like a stuntman on wires in a Japanese film. While he was in the air, his hand lashed out over the woman's neck, delivering a stunning blow. At the same time, the soldier withdrew his sword and, with barely a flick, cut through one of the men at her side, slicing him in two from the head downwards. The other men quickly died, despite the bravery of their fight, and the walls and steps of the theatre were splashed with blood and gore. The soldiers spared the women, but overwhelmed them; once subdued, they were passed down the line straight into the heart of the vortex.

Jas blinked in confusion and horror at what she was seeing, and found herself staring down the tunnel once more. The vortex was turning at a leisurely pace, but also getting closer to the bus, and in those split seconds of shock and realisation she knew without doubt that she herself would be taken, possibly to her death. Andrew still hadn't climbed the steps into the bus; instead he drew closer beside her. As the vortex turned, fear and disbelief paralysed his limbs.

'Get out of the bus ...' Jas said. 'Everyone. *Get off the bus!*'

As the vortex closed in on them, Jas stared down into the cold and inhuman sandy light coming from the heart of the impossible object. The soldiers were also drawing nearer, chasing down the few fleeing people left in their path. The theatre grounds had become a war zone, and hundreds of armoured bodies were marching headlong towards them in a continuing onslaught. She felt Andrew's hand grip hers and looked down into his terrified gaze. Andrew had seen what was happening and he knew they would kill him. There were too many to fight, and now the bus had become a trap for the teachers and the students. Jas looked around, stared at the terrified faces peering through the windows. She couldn't save all of them. No-one could. Jas glanced down at Andrew. He was a good kid and more deserving than most. Right then, his normally serious and sensible blue eyes were wide and scared, but his mouth was set in a line of resolve. There was strength there.

As though both of the same mind, they ran, out and away from the bus, leaving behind the other children, teachers and driver scrambling to get out and away. They didn't look back. They didn't see the vortex come to a halt. Nor did they see the swarm of aliens pour like ants in and over the bus, swords ready.

Screams echoed across the parking lot, carried by the winds. Jas wanted to cover her ears, but was afraid to let go of Andrew. They ran back toward the disintegrating theatre. Even if the roof was falling in, it was still the safest place to be right then: certainly safer than facing some unknown enemy and an even more uncertain future.

Jas heard more cries as she and Andrew crashed in through the front doors of the building and skidded on the fresh blood underfoot. The foyer was empty, and as soon as they regained their balance they picked up pace and didn't stop running until they reached the stairs that led up to the theatre boxes. Without thinking they began to climb, then threw themselves through the first open door.

'Lock the door,' Jas said, and Andrew quickly did as he was told.

Jas huddled with her back against the door, heaving in gulps of air as her lungs screamed. Andrew was hunched on the floor, eyes tightly closed, small body trembling. Jas closed her own eyes and tried to control her breathing. Her heart was beating in her ears and she couldn't tell if they had been followed.

Jas thought she heard the haunting scream of a police siren being silenced outside, but even if the police had arrived, she knew they wouldn't stand a chance against this new and violent enemy.

Sometime later, Jas looked down over the seats and onto the abandoned stage. The theatre was empty, the earthquake rumblings long since finished, and the walls had remained stable despite the earlier appearance that the building was collapsing. Even though the cries from outside couldn't penetrate the thick walls, Jas imagined she could still hear the children screaming. As she looked over at Andrew, who was rolled up in a tight ball on the floor of the box, his scared eyes darting from corner to corner, Jas knew that things would never be the same again. She closed her eyes again, but her mind's eye presented a vision of the other children, scared and alone, being brutalised outside.

'There was nothing you could do,' said Andrew, as though he could read her mind. His young voice sounded old.

Jas knew his words were true, but how would she ever forget that she had sacrificed them to save herself? She looked at Andrew and she focused her thoughts on his life, his safety. She could at least save one child entrusted to her care.

'I'm going to get you out of here. I'm going to save you if it's the last thing I do.'

Andrew didn't respond. Exhaustion outweighed his fear, and his mind and body had shut down. Jas listened to his breathing, then focused on the lack of sound coming from outside. She thought they were safe. She hoped the monsters had gone, but she was too afraid to check. They would stay there a bit longer: at least so far no-one had come inside looking for them.

Her heart thudded in her chest as she heard movement below. She wrapped her arms around herself and held her breath for fear of being heard. Then, as if her mind could take no more, she rested her head on her knees and slept.

3

Jas found the bodies of two paramedics lying in the back of an ambulance at the front of the theatre. One of them was wearing a bright yellow jacket, but the front was covered with dried blood in a crumbling black stain, like a watercolour paint left out in the sun. Jas couldn't see the other man clearly, as half of his body was crammed under the wheels of an ambulance trolley. Flies buzzed around the bodies. The air was rank with the smell of vomit, decay and blood. The decomposing carcases reeked like nothing Jas had ever smelt before. It was as if rotting faeces had been turned to dust and was now fouling the air. Jas blocked Andrew's view of the inside of the vehicle, but knew that the boy could guess that the dead occupied the space within.

'Don't look,' Jas said, slamming the back doors of the ambulance shut.

They hiked toward Manchester city centre in a feverish haze, half expecting to find people and shops and everyday life still ticking over. Hungry and dehydrated, they walked through the streets vaguely noticing the abandoned cars, the destroyed shop fronts and the earthquake-damaged pavements. Neither of them had any concept of the length of time they had spent hiding in the theatre too afraid to come out, but it seemed that days had passed before their need to find food and drink had forced them outside.

'What the hell?' Jas murmured as they passed a post box that looked as though it had spontaneously combusted, bleeding letters and small parcels all over the pavement.

Andrew was silent at her side; his usually bright and interested eyes were duller than she had ever seen them. *He'll be in therapy for years,* Jas thought.

Jas was too young to have witnessed the devastation that the IRA had wrought on Manchester years earlier, but she had seen footage of the destruction, and at the time parts of the city had been unrecognisable. She knew on sight that however bad it had been then, this was far worse. As in the theatre car park, bits of pavement and road had been hurled up as though the Earth's core had blown a volcano through the city. The centre of

Manchester no longer existed. Only rubble remained.

Andrew and Jas didn't know what to make of it. The two of them regarded the devastation for a moment, then turned back toward the outskirts. Even though Jas's feet hurt in her low-heeled court shoes and her legs ached badly, she still kept going, determined that she would find some civilisation for Andrew.

They circled back to the theatre, taking a different route.

'There's got to be someone left out there,' Jas said.

Andrew said nothing. His movements were sluggish, and Jas wondered briefly if he was still in shock after their initial experience. He barely lifted his head to look at the chaos.

'There has to be something left,' Jas said in a voice she hoped was reassuring.

Their efforts were rewarded as they drew farther away from the centre. Although shops, cafés and clothing stores were all abandoned, some still remained intact.

Andrew's dull eyes lit up when they came to a supermarket. He stopped and stared at the building, and waited for Jas to notice it too. Then, as he realised it wasn't an illusion, he ran straight across the empty street and right up to the doors. Jas followed; she feared letting him out of her sight.

The automatic doors opened silently inwards as though welcoming them inside. It was eerily quiet as they walked through. Not even the usual ambient music was playing through the speakers. It was as though everyone had been evacuated and the staff had forgotten to lock up when they left. They stood in the doorway for a moment – it felt like trespassing – then they entered.

Running off to the drinks aisle, Andrew guzzled half a bottle of Coke and then puked it back up before Jas caught up with him. His stomach couldn't take the liquid after days of him drinking nothing. Jas knelt down beside him and offered sips from a bottle of still water. Andrew was shaking and sweating, and he sat back against the soda bottles, his legs splayed out.

'Take it slow,' she said.

There was still some fresh produce, and Jas noted that the freezers were running.

'All we have to do is hold out here until the police come, or the army or something,' Jas said, not for the first time. 'They're probably on their way as we speak.'

She sipped water as Andrew settled. Then she opened a bar of chocolate. 'Piece at a time …' she warned, holding out the bar.

They were starving, but once faced with a whole supermarket full of food, Jas's appetite shrivelled and disappeared. She pulled her mobile phone from her pocket and pressed redial, and the emergency services number began to ring once more. She put it on speaker, then placed the phone down on a shelf as she stood. She pulled a trolley closer to the shelves and began to fill the first one with bottles of water.

The phone rang out for a few rings, then switched to a recorded message: 'This is the accident and emergency services, please hold the line and an operator will be with you shortly ... This is the ...'

The message repeated over and over.

'You're wasting your time,' Andrew said. 'No-one's answering. No-one's coming.'

'They have to,' Jas responded. 'One attack can't end the entire world.'

'How do we know that?' Andrew said. 'How do we know that other places weren't destroyed like this? What were those things?'

Jas fell quiet. Her automatic response of 'It's not possible' choked in her dry throat. She sipped more water. The message repeated over and over until Andrew turned and picked up the phone. He pressed Cancel and the voice was cut off mid-stream. Jas stopped loading the trolley and sighed.

'We have to keep trying.'

'No. We have to survive.' Andrew stood up. The trembling had left his body and he sipped more water cautiously. This time the liquid stayed in his stomach, and even though his head was still fuzzy from the lack of nutrition and fluids, the dizziness and nausea he had been feeling were slowly subsiding. Jas noted that the boy was showing remarkable strength and resilience. He was almost ready to accept that the world had ended and think about survival rather than wait for help.

Andrew stood, found a trolley of his own and started to fill it with cans of cola and lemonade.

'We'd be better off with water,' Jas said.

'Yeah, but I don't drink water usually.'

Jas shrugged. 'We also need food that will keep,' she said. 'I'll go and find some.'

At the rotisserie the chicken had turned rancid. Flies had buried their eggs in the flesh and the meat was swarming with maggots. Jas turned away. The water sloshed around in her stomach. She swallowed. She needed to rehydrate and was determined not to bring any of it up. She hurried down the fridge aisles to distract herself. All the fridges were working and the cheeses and cooked meats looked good. She took a box of eggs, picked some ham out and took a lump of cheese.

'As long as this stays okay, some of this stuff will last – especially the cheese.'

Andrew pulled his trolley beside her. 'I'm hungry.'

'I know. How about an omelette?'

'I think I could stomach that. How are we going to cook?'

In the household aisle, Jas picked up a set of pans. 'We'll build a fire, I guess.'

Andrew was dubious. He wandered down the aisle, pushing the trolley. The place was creepy because it was so empty, so he stayed near Jas, following her from aisle to aisle as she filled the trolley with food and drinks. Andrew had seen a few zombie movies and knew exactly what happened when the end of the world came. He was scared of being alone, but tried not to let it show. To distract himself from the morbid thoughts running through his head, he browsed the plates and cups, while slowly eating the bar of chocolate.

'Hey. What about this?'

It was a small electric hob.

'Good,' said Jas. 'That will do for now. At least while we have electricity.'

Andrew didn't like the idea that one day they may not have lighting and heating, but felt that it was probably inevitable. The theatre's electricity had already failed, and they had spent the last few nights huddled in the box in the dark and cold. It felt strange to be out of there. Andrew had felt safe in the theatre, even though he had been scared. The supermarket seemed alien and frightening, and he had never realised it was this big before.

'We could … go home?' Andrew said. 'My folks must be worried sick. In fact I don't know why I didn't think of it sooner.'

Jas looked up from her scrutiny of the hob. It hadn't occurred to her to return to her flat, or to seek out Andrew's parents. Her main objective had been to keep the boy safe. This practical suggestion should have come from her, but somehow it hadn't formed in her mind at all. She had felt it better to remain still and let the authorities find them. After days of trying this, though, starvation had become their potential future and had driven them from their hidey-hole.

'Okay,' Jas said. 'The authorities aren't coming to us, let's go to them. But first, we'll find your folks. They might at least know what happened.'

Outside, Jas found an abandoned car. The keys were still in the ignition and the door lay open. It was all too convenient.

'Check the back seat …' Andrew warned, remembering a scene in a movie where a zombie hid from the main protagonist.

Jas stared at him, then quickly looked in the back. It was empty. She climbed in the front seat, started the engine and discovered the car had a full tank of fuel.

'All seems okay. Let's load up.'

They filled the boot and back seat with the food and drinks. Then Andrew climbed into the passenger seat and opened a bag of crisps as he waited for Jas to get in.

'Where did you live?' she asked.

Andrew noted she was talking in past tense. He thought it odd but said nothing. 'Just outside of town. I'll direct you.'

The street was full of abandoned vehicles, and Jas had to weave in and out of them. It was like the *Mary Celeste*, or a ghost town. They had noticed it as they had walked, but had been so dazed that it had hardly registered then. It was as if their lack of water had even made them blind to all of the devastation.

'There really is no-one here,' Andrew said. His face was pinched and scared. 'Where did everyone go? D'you think my folks are okay?'

Jas said nothing. She didn't think Andrew's parents or anyone else in or around the city was even alive. As they drew to the outskirts they began to see more bodies. All male. It was an open-air charnel house, and Jas knew exactly who had done the damage: it was the aliens. The monsters. They had killed everyone. She rolled up the car windows as they turned into a particularly nasty street. The smell of the grave tainted the air and irritated her nose. She thought she was going to be sick – and she was not, as a rule, particularly squeamish.

'Don't look!' she ordered. 'Cover your eyes.'

But Andrew had to look. He had to see for himself that the situation was hopeless. Even so, Jas tried to take her own advice and kept her eyes only on the road.

Around the next corner they saw a fire engine. The crew lay in pieces around the vehicle and half spilled from the cabin. The headless torso of the driver still sat upright at the wheel, his hands gripping tightly, while his head lay on top of the bonnet, facing his body. It was macabre and looked to Jas as though it had been deliberately placed there as a warning.

'Murderous bastards,' she whispered.

'Stop the car,' said Andrew, but Jas didn't react quickly enough, and the boy threw up against the window before he could wind it all the way down. Jas pulled into the kerb and got out of the car. She came round, opened Andrew's door and wiped up the mess that dripped down over both sides.

'I'm sorry,' said Andrew, clearly embarrassed.

'It's fine,' she said. 'You feeling okay?'

Andrew nodded, and Jas swilled some water over the inside and outside of the door. After that the interior of the car smelt less, but still the vile sweetness of stomach bile and chocolate occasionally drifted over to the driver's seat. Jas left both windows open as they drove off again.

As they reached the suburbs they began to notice that the front doors of all the houses were open – smashed down in most cases – and the carnage of male bodies continued. It didn't seem to have mattered to the aliens that the males were sometimes children. A row of decapitated boys were laid out on the grass of one house, and it was the worst sight she had ever seen.

'Why?' asked Andrew.

'I don't know,' Jas said, but she wondered again if the displaying of the dead was somehow a warning to any survivors.

Despite having been sick, Andrew was once more eating from another bag of crisps. The massacre was devastating, but the boy was recovering and adapting to it all at a surprising rate.

Jas was worried about him, but said nothing. Her mouth was a thin line and her knuckles tightened on the steering wheel as they rounded another corner. There were fewer bodies on this street, so it became easier to ignore them.

'Second left,' said Andrew.

Jas turned the car into Andrew's street. She knew what to expect, but was afraid to say it. Even so, the situation looked promising, as the street was clear of debris and corpses. They drew up outside Andrew's house. It was a typical suburban house: not salubrious, not poor. The front garden had been well maintained, but already the grass was growing up and becoming wild. Jas thought that this was the first sign that no-one was home.

'Dad hates that,' Andrew said as he got out of the car. 'He likes the garden neat.'

'Let me go in first,' Jas said.

Andrew was shivering, as though the cold reality of further deaths was already reaching out to him. He nodded, waiting by the gate as Jas approached the house.

'Hello?' she called. 'Hello? Mrs Carpenter, are you home?'

The front door was closed, and one of the few still intact. Jas rapped lightly, then harder when there was no response. If Andrew's parents were inside, they were probably afraid to come out.

'Mrs Carpenter. It's Miss Regis here, from your son Andrew's school. He's here and safe with me. Please answer the door.'

There was no sound, no movement from within. Jas looked at Andrew. He came forward, fishing out a door key, held on a piece of elastic around his neck. Jas took the key and placed it in the lock. The door opened easily and she stepped inside.

'You should wait here,' she suggested.

'No,' said Andrew. The silence outside was worse than anything he might find inside, and he had to know, had to see what had happened to his family. Andrew stepped inside ahead of Jas.

The hallway was small, with a wide staircase leading upstairs. Andrew's mother liked chintz paper, and it covered the walls in a cheerful lilac pattern. In the living room the television was on but the volume was turned down low. The house looked undisturbed and tidy, but a fine layer of dust had already begun to settle on the glass coffee table. A sofa was positioned against the wall under a large bay window, and there was an armchair in front of the television. It was impossible to see whether or not the armchair was occupied, because the back was facing the door. Jas walked inside and hurriedly looked round the other side, her heart in her mouth for fear of discovering one of Andrew's parents dead there. However, she found the chair empty.

Andrew led the way into the kitchen, which was small and rustic but contained all of the usual modern conveniences. It too was neat, but a packet of biscuits had been left open on the kitchen table.

'Mum would never do that,' Andrew said, frowning.

Jas said nothing but followed him from the room and up the stairs. In his parents' bedroom the bed was unmade and appeared to have been just vacated.

'They must be here!' Andrew said. He ran through the remaining bedrooms, even his own, then drew to a halt as he stood in the doorway of the bathroom.

Mr Carpenter was dead. Jas could see him, razor in hand, dried blood blackening the cream tiles.

'Oh my god,' said Jas. Pulling Andrew away, she closed the bathroom door.

'Dad,' he said. 'Oh no. Dad ...'

Andrew didn't cry, but he sat silently on the bottom step as Jas checked over the body. Although she had only limited knowledge of medical matters, she guessed he had been dead a few days. She was relieved that he had died with his eyes closed. She couldn't imagine touching him while being watched by his dead and empty gaze. As it was, coming into such close quarters with the dead body made her feel anxious and sick.

'We'll bury him,' she said, sitting down next to Andrew.

'They took Mum,' Andrew said. 'Dad probably thought I was dead ...'

Jas said nothing, but she placed her arm around the boy's shoulders as he dropped his head and finally cried.

Later, when Andrew fell into a state of quiet shock, Jas flicked through the news channels on the television and learnt that the world had gone to shit.

'The Jinx are everywhere,' said an ashen-faced news reporter on a live feed from Sky News.

Even with the shaking camera, Jas recognised the vortex opening up behind the man. She turned off the television as the screen went blank.

'The Jinx,' said Andrew.

'Yes. That's what they're calling them.'

'Why?'

'I don't know.'

4

Captain Taylor Arch walked into the UK through military customs with his passport in his hand. He was armed to the teeth, but no-one questioned or searched him as his papers gave him special dispensation. As the customs officer briefly inspected his documents, Taylor studied the woman beside him. She was in her early forties, with pale blonde hair, a fake tan and serious blue eyes. She had been sent from the Embassy to make his passage through customs move quickly and smoothly. Taylor had seen women like her before. She reminded him of other female military assistants that worked in American embassies all over the world. They were chosen because they looked good, but were usually really smart and tough too. It was likely that his escort was a lawyer, and she would know the laws of this country well.

Taylor removed his hat and ran his hand over his shorn regulation haircut as the customs officer looked up at him. He was an all-American boy and had the good looks to go with it. His pale grey eyes looked open and honest, but they hid the cold strength and determination of his soldier's heart. The taupe uniform suited him and fitted his agile frame perfectly. This was because his less-than-average height made it necessary to have his uniform made to measure. He was six-foot-five: army regulation trousers only stretched to six-two.

Taylor was in a mood. He wasn't happy that he had been dragged away from his long-deserved leave. He had only been home in South Carolina for only a few days before his recall. He hadn't seen his parents and sister for 18 months prior to that, as his tour of duty had taken him on three succession six-month stints in various war zones.

Other Baptist farmers occasionally enlisted, but Taylor was the first in the community of Lyman to have broken the mould. He had taken to it like the proverbial duck to water, and the travel, excitement and lifestyle of a soldier suited him. Even so, Taylor knew that one day he would have to quit the army and return to the farm in South Carolina. As the only son in the family, it was expected of him. Taylor didn't know how he could go back to his old life though. Despite having all the modern conveniences, Lyman was still something of a hick town, and the people were transparent and uncomplicated. Intrigue went on in the parlours of the church-goers, where they enjoyed their speculation on the sins of others, but that was about as far as any excitement went.

Taylor took back the papers held by the customs officer.

'We're going straight to the embassy in Grosvenor Square,' said the aide, pushing the blonde hair back from her eyes as they left the airport. 'I'm Eileen. Is there anything you need, Captain?'

'No,' Taylor answered. 'Just take me to the Major.'

There was a black limo waiting at the pick-up point, and the driver, a young soldier in uniform, jumped out, saluted and opened the door for them as they walked toward the car.

Taylor was a little unnerved by the pomp and ceremony that seemed to be greeting his arrival. He was a soldier, not a diplomat, and yet here he was being treated like a VIP. He noted the special plates on the vehicle and the biked police escort. What most intrigued him, though, was why his presence here had been requested in the first place.

The driver took his bag, but Taylor held on to the briefcase containing the documents he was to deliver to Major Handley. He climbed into the back of the limo with Eileen and sat back against the leather upholstery with the briefcase resting across his lap. He was tired. Somehow he could never sleep on planes, and the flight had been a long one. Taylor relaxed back into the comfort of the limousine seats.

There was a small fridge in the back, and Eileen opened it. Taylor noticed a bottle of champagne and a plate full of small biscuits. Eileen picked up a small metal tin: caviar.

'Can I tempt you?' Eileen said.

'Surely that isn't for me?'

'We've been asked to make you as comfortable as possible, Captain.'

'Water would be good,' Taylor said. He never drank when wearing his uniform, and he hated caviar.

Eileen shrugged and pulled a bottle of still spring water from the bay in the fridge door. She twisted the top off and poured the liquid into a crystal glass. By the time she had placed it in the holder beside Taylor, his eyes were shut and he had drifted into what appeared to be a deep sleep.

'We're here,' said Eileen sometime later.

Taylor opened his eyes. He had no idea how long the nap had been, but he felt better for it. He rubbed his eyes and glanced down at the briefcase on his knees. He wondered what information was inside and what that might mean for him.

'The Major's waiting,' said Eileen.

Taylor pulled himself out of the limo.

In the reception area he was subjected to a body scan, and only then did security let Eileen whisk him through the doorway that led to the embassy's inner sanctum. She took him up some stairs, past a door labelled 'Security' and another marked 'Private', and finally into a large boardroom.

'Captain Arch,' said Major Handley as they entered. 'We're glad you've made it here so quickly. As you know, there's a major crisis happening.' Unlike Taylor, Handley was not in the peak of fitness. His physique showed over-indulgence. His hair was greying at the sides and Taylor could tell the man was more of a diplomat than a soldier these days.

Taylor saluted the Major, but Handley quickly dismissed the formality. 'No time for that, Captain.'

Taylor placed the briefcase on the desk and the Major turned it toward him and keyed in the security code. The briefcase opened with a loud click and Handley removed a thick wad of papers from inside.

'What are my orders, Major?' Taylor asked eventually.

'London has been hit hard by an unknown force,' Handley said. 'We know they are alien, and so far both the British and American forces stationed here have been unable to prevent the attacks.'

'What do they want?' asked Taylor.

'Women and female children. We don't know why, but we can imagine,' Major Handley said. 'We've made an attempt to negotiate with them, to see if we could come to some compromise.'

'What compromise could you possibly make?' Taylor asked. 'They can't have our wives and kids.'

'Well, not all of them, I agree,' said Handley.

'You're not planning on giving them *some*?'

Taylor wasn't surprised that Handley had tried to make deals with the enemy: he had seen the negotiation of innocents before, and the powers-that-be weren't above using women and children for their own political gain. However, he listened as Handley went on to explain that the attempt had been pointless: the aliens didn't converse, they fought – and their response to the white flag held by the arbitration team was etched in the minds of all those who had witnessed the slaughter.

'They're aliens,' Taylor pointed out. 'Jesus, how would they know what a white flag means?'

Handley ignored his comment.

'It sounds as though a lot of good men have died ...?' Taylor said. 'Do we know where they will hit next?'

'No. British and American forces are waiting at various vantage points,' Handley said.

'They must have been here before,' Taylor said. 'They appear to know too much about us.'

'Don't be ridiculous,' Handley said, but he wouldn't meet Taylor's eyes.

Taylor considered Handley's reaction. Perhaps the Major wasn't being totally honest with him? He had always been treated with respect and trusted with the most sensitive information, and it piqued him to feel that there were more secrets being kept than truths being told.

'Is there anything else I need to know, Major?' he asked.

'You know how these things work,' Handley said. 'Some information is just too sensitive.'

'They *have* been here before.'

Handley shook his head. 'Captain, I can't confirm that, as I'm not in possession of the full facts. But I would appreciate it if you don't say anything to your men about your suspicions.'

Taylor said nothing. He pulled up a chair at the conference table as a civilian man and woman entered the room.

'This is our physicist, Giles Manet,' Handley explained, 'and his assistant Petra Solomon.'

Taylor scrutinised the scientist and his assistant. Manet was of the typical geek variety, but Solomon was tall and willowy.

'Captain, Major,' nodded Manet. He took a seat on the other side of the table as Solomon plugged her laptop into the projector screen.

Taylor found himself staring at amateur video footage of a swirling vortex appearing somewhere in the centre of London.

'The first sighting,' said Solomon, sitting down beside Taylor. 'Although a few moments later Manchester was also hit.'

The camerawork was shaky – the cameraman had obviously been terrified by the sight of the anomaly – but Taylor could make out the vortex clearly and leaned forward in his seat as the first alien warriors poured from it.

What followed looked like something from a slash horror movie. Taylor, a seasoned soldier, had never seen such mindless violence. When the vortex first appeared, the ground shook and roared like a hungry wolf. Pavements cracked, people stumbled and screamed with the onslaught of the earthquake. The air was a mass of swirling grit.

'It looks like sand,' commented Taylor.

'It *is* sand,' Manet said.

Taylor watched the aliens taking the women through the vortex, heard their screams of anguish while husbands and sons were senselessly slaughtered. A black rage made his pulse race, but his expression gave nothing away.

'Their technology is beyond our comprehension,' said Manet. 'Somehow they are able to scramble our tracking devices, stop engines and make weapons backfire.'

Manet had been brought onto the team to try to make sense of what might be happening.

'I think what we are seeing is a wormhole,' the scientist went on. 'And if it is so, then somehow these people have learnt how to manipulate time-space.'

'There's no such thing,' Taylor said.

'True, until now it has only ever been hypothetical,' Solomon said.

'If this is correct and indeed even possible, and these beings have such advanced technology, then why do they just carry swords?' Taylor asked. 'Why are they wearing ancient-looking armour? If they are so tech-savvy, there are far more effective ways they could kill us.'

'That's what we need to find out,' Handley said. 'We want you to capture one of them.'

At that moment Taylor's mobile phone rang. He took it from his pocket, glanced at the number showing, and realised he had failed to keep his promise yet again. His mother was worried, but now wasn't the time to reassure her. He had no clue what to tell her. Taylor pressed Reject and his phone went silent.

'Sorry about that,' he said. 'Forgot to switch it off.'

5

'We call them the Jinx,' Lieutenant Donovan said as he met up with his Captain at the embassy.

Steve Donovan was a man in his mid-thirties, lean, dark-haired and cold-eyed. Donovan was what Taylor recognised as a 'career soldier' like himself. Donovan had been in the army since he was barely out of school, and Taylor knew he would be a soldier until he died or until they forced him into retirement. He was glad to see Donovan, and even more pleased to learn that most of his men had survived the initial attacks.

'How long have you been here?' Taylor asked.

'They drafted the entire platoon in the day after you went on leave. It was sudden. I didn't think they'd get you back so quickly.'

'According to Handley, I'm "essential" to the fight,' Taylor laughed.

'Ain't that the truth, Captain!' Donovan smiled.

'Brief me,' Taylor said, suddenly growing serious. 'What do you know about these Jinx?'

'Every time one of them gets wounded they back off,' Donovan said. 'That's when most of our machines and weapons start to act up. It's like the most extreme bad luck. Hence why we gave them the name. It somehow feels like our equipment is jinxed.'

'So, no luck in capturing one, dead or alive?' Taylor asked.

Donovan shook his head. 'No, sir. Last time we cornered one, their entire army turned on the hostage party and took them out clean. I've never seen a massacre like it. We couldn't recognise any of the bodies; they were hacked to pieces. Then they took their wounded and fled.'

'It's like being in the dark ages,' Donovan added. 'Men fighting hand to hand.'

Despite his years as a US army officer, Donovan had never seen so much bloodshed. The Jinx were everywhere, crawling like vermin from their mysterious vortex, and even though they fought with swords, they had the strength and stamina to sustain the physical fight longer than his men could.

Taylor studied all the footage available. The Jinx armour reminded him of ancient Chinese, maybe Han dynasty. It was ornate and dramatic, but somehow served to be functional; and if the breastplates and helmets were as heavy as they appeared, the Jinx gave no sign that the weight was a problem. If they had been able to capture some of the aliens, then maybe they would have a better idea, but so far all the Jinx casualties had been taken back through the vortex by their comrades. The Jinx were also extremely tall; the smallest among them was approaching seven feet.

For all this, though, Taylor still found the Jinx's supernatural speed and agility the hardest things to accept. He had trained hard for years, honing his body, learning a variety of martial arts, but no way could he move like they did, especially when covered in heavy armour. It was as if the laws of gravity didn't apply to them.

Over the next few weeks, the military team devised early warning systems, and Taylor's men took up temporary residence in the British Library buildings. This makeshift headquarters served as a central base for the army. Most of them slept outside in tents, but among the many thousands of books, the collaborative army stored their spare weapons and artillery. They ate in the large hall on tables that were once for the exclusive use of readers and researchers. They planned strategy in the microfiche file room, on the librarian's old desk. They had alarms set up in and around the building and specialists who could gauge the movement of the ground beneath them. There was no way that they could be caught unawares.

By the time Taylor found himself facing the enemy for the first time, the city was emptied of all life other than military. London was a ghost town, with pockets of undamaged shops dotted between ruined streets, and it was in these intact places that Taylor, his men and the British amalgamated task forces were positioned.

The men were wound up and spoiling for the fight. When the alarms sounded, they were ready. After that, the world descended into a bloody blur.

The attack started in the centre of London, not far from Waterloo Bridge – not that the city was recognisable anymore. The ground was cracked and collapsing in several places across the bridge, and it was no longer safe to cross. Taylor and his men were called out immediately the vortex appeared, and they spent the next few hours dying at the hands of the Jinx. On the front line, a tank exploded, throwing metal debris into the air, and Taylor's men were bombarded by shrapnel. The trucks carrying men into the conflict stopped working 50 feet away from the drop-off site.

'Get out!' ordered Donovan as he jumped from the truck and ran in a crouch out toward the battlefield.

'Motherfuckers!' Taylor yelled, rushing forward with a grenade. He threw the grenade at the vortex, but it swirled around, rearing like a cobra. It ended up blowing a hole in the concrete pavement, but that was all. The vortex spun against the explosion, throwing off the blast as if it were nothing more than a breeze stirring up autumn leaves.

Despite the promises made by their superiors, their weapons were useless. Tanks exploded for no reason. Guns and bazookas either failed to fire or else, when they did work, left the Jinx unharmed. It was as though the aliens were protected by some form of magic shield. Not that Taylor believed in such things, but he couldn't deny it was eerie. A full-scale war was erupting around the globe, and all of the technology and science in the world couldn't save them. The army, British and American, was getting its collective arse kicked, and they couldn't do a thing about it.

'They're like roaches,' said Handley chewing on the end of a Havana cigar. 'Almost impossible to kill.'

Taylor found himself in a circle of his own men fighting one-on-one with Jinx warriors, who mostly towered over them. Up close the enemy were even more terrifying. Each of the aliens stood over seven feet tall, and they wielded their short swords effortlessly. Their helmets covered their faces entirely, with only a slit to see through, and bizarrely were decorated with what Taylor believed to be precious jewels. They were like something from an earlier time period. Looking around the battlefield, Taylor saw that all the armour was the same and none of the aliens stood out as the apparent leader. In his college days, in science lessons, Taylor had studied the breeding patterns of ant colonies. Soldier ants were bred to fight: all looked the same, and they fought until they were dead, mindless of their individual existence. The Jinx reminded him of that. But who was controlling them? Where was the queen – or king? There had to be a general of some sort; someone who directed the soldiers. The aliens were too organised; they worked together like parts of a well-oiled machine. It was almost as though they were of one mind; and they didn't seem to feel pain.

As the fighting raged at the end of the bridge, the vortex spun toward Taylor's men and more of the impossible soldiers streamed from its glowing innards. Taylor came face to face with one of the aliens and fired into its face and chest, but the bullets did nothing, barely even denting the breastplate.

The Jinx threw back its head and gave a guttural laugh that seemed to rumble from its expansive chest. Taylor wasted no time; he pulled out a grenade, removed the pin and threw it straight into the alien's face. As it exploded, the alien armour ruptured and Taylor was rewarded with the sight of red-blooded guts and gore. The Jinx warrior's head was blown clean off, and the blood splattered across the bridge, the remaining soldiers, and all the Jinx within a 20-foot radius. The warrior tumbled like the giant in *Jack and the Beanstalk*, falling headfirst over the bridge and into the water.

For a moment the battle raged on around Taylor. *We've got one of them!*, he thought. It would provide an excellent opportunity to examine one of them close up. However, suddenly the vortex stopped spinning and the warriors backed away from the fight. Taylor watched with surprise as one of the Jinx jumped down into the Thames after the body of his comrade.

Taylor's remaining men stopped fighting as the Jinx army backed away. An extraordinarily tall Jinx hurried forward and scooped up the head and helmet of the dead warrior. Taylor saw the other alien return. Wet from the river, the Jinx soldier had the body wrapped over his shoulders.

'No!' yelled Taylor. 'Stop them!'

Along with a few of the others left standing, Taylor ran forward screaming with battle rage as the anomaly closed and disappeared. A rush of air settled where the vortex had stood. It was as though the atmosphere had been held back by the sheer force of its power.

'Fuck!' Taylor said.

Then he turned to see the carnage. The city was wreathed in smoke and dust. The discharged weapons had left the air tainted with gunpowder. There was a strong sandy odour on the breeze. Climbing over the mountain of bodies and disintegrated buildings, Taylor gathered together his remaining men.

'Come on,' he said, as he pulled Lieutenant Donovan from the wreckage that had once been the public library. 'We have to find any survivors. Have you seen Major Handley?'

'No,' said Donovan.

Taylor trusted Donovan and was glad to have found him still alive. By evening they had rounded up a small number of men. Minor injuries were treated and the survivors gathered round a bonfire made up of the debris of books that had scattered in the street after the library exploded.

'We need to dig through the rubble,' said Taylor. 'There could still be men trapped down there.'

At the time, they didn't want to believe it, but London had fallen, as had Manchester and all the other large cities in the UK. Despite the fact that this was obviously the end of the world as they knew it, Taylor's men set about the task. The army conditioned its men to follow orders without question. Taylor was their Captain and they had to do something other than just sit around dying.

How naïve we were, thought Taylor, looking around at his men working so hard. They were exhausted yet still they managed to carry on. Taylor felt inordinately proud. *We never stood a chance,* he reflected. The Jinx wanted the women, and there was nothing the army could do to stop them. Despite all their weapons and science, it was clear that the Jinx had some other power on their side.

Gazing into the bonfire flames, Taylor recalled what he had seen as he looked down the maw of the vortex, seconds before it closed. There had been what looked like a man wearing robes and holding a stick in his hand. It reminded him of the biblical image of Moses parting the water in order to let the Israelites leave Egypt. Religion may have flown from his psyche soon after he had enlisted, but Taylor hadn't forgotten the teachings he had grown up with. He mulled over the image, wondering what it meant. Was the man the Jinx leader? Somehow he knew that wasn't the case, but still the figure was important. Maybe he was the key to the whole thing.

'Captain?' said Donovan, returning with two more soldiers. 'We've managed to rescue a few more men. Supplies are being loaded onto one of the remaining trucks and we also pulled some weapons from the wreckage.'

'How many trucks do we have?' asked Taylor.

'Three, sir.'

'Okay. That's enough to get us back to the barracks. Did you find the field radio?'

Donovan nodded, but his eyes skittered away from Taylor's.

'And?'

'It's not working, sir,' Donovan said.

'Bring it to me. Maybe we can find an engineer among the survivors.'

'Sir, it's ...' Donovan paused. 'It's melted, sir. I believe it's beyond repair.'

'Show me,' Taylor said.

They weaved through the wounded as they lay in a row by the trucks.

Donovan brought Taylor to a man who lay on his side facing them. The man was half dead.

'I couldn't describe it, sir.' Donovan said shaking his head. His eyes were haunted black pits.

'What is it? Who is this man?'

Donovan turned the unconscious soldier over, and then Taylor saw and understood. The field radio was in a pack on the operator's back. It had been burnt into the man's spine, the metal melted and seared into his skin. Blood and wires interwove with protruding bone and flesh. It was hard to see where the radio ended and the man began.

Taylor looked away. In Afghanistan he had taken part in more than a few undercover operations and had seen some disturbing things. Once he had seen the disastrous splicing of a human with a wolf. The army had kept that secret, and Taylor hadn't condoned the experiments, but he had later been made privy to the results. It had been all in the name of creating the ultimate power, but all it had achieved was ultimate evil. Taylor swallowed, remembering the deformed foetus's head, the warped spine. Even that didn't compare to the horror of the soldier accidentally fused with his radio.

'He was standing right next to the arc of the vortex as it arrived. We think this was some form of side-effect.'

'What did the medical officer say?' Taylor asked.

Donovan shook his head: the radio operator was dying.

'Make him comfortable,' he said then returned to the makeshift tent that represented their new headquarters.

Later that day they did a head count. There were around 50 men fit and well and another 30 or so wounded.

'We need to move out,' said Donovan. 'The Jinx could return anytime to finish us off, and we are in no condition to fight them.'

Taylor nodded. He looked round at the men. Hard decisions would have to be made. 'At least ten of the wounded have no chance of surviving,' the doctor informed him. 'It's just a matter of time.'

'Help them along and make it pain-free,' he ordered. 'Donovan, get the rest loaded onto one of the trucks, along with whatever supplies you can find. We need to get back to base and report in.'

6

A group of refugees arrived at the village at noon.

Some 30 men, women and children drove in on two buses, tired and exhausted. The inhabitants of Stow-on-the-Wold were used to tourists but hadn't seen anyone outside of their own community for quite some time. Barely any radio stations were still broadcasting and news reports of the outside world were scarce, which meant that the villagers had effectively been cut off from the rest of the country when the fuel vans had failed to arrive to fill up the petrol station's tanks.

The villagers came out of their homes, one by one, and stared at the new arrivals as they disembarked at the church hall.

Gerald Avery was the local doctor, and as such one of the people 'in authority' in the village. Even though he was only five foot four, his wife Mallory always said he looked like a young Tony Curtis. This was partly due to his thick, black wavy hair and fierce blue eyes. Gerald and Mallory ran a small practice and had managed to get by, once London fell, by trading his medical skills for food.

The first bus-driver looked around, and Gerald found himself thrust to the front of the crowd as the village representative. At first he didn't take in what the driver was saying.

'... David Keen. This is my family and friends. We've come from London and have been making our way across the country to find a safe haven. We can pay for our lodging.'

'Money means nothing around here,' Gerald said. 'We haven't got any spare food. We've barely enough to supply the village.'

'We have some supplies,' David Keen said. 'We just need a place to rest. We've gathered cans of fuel and know where there are stations still working. If we can stay here until this whole thing blows over, we can send out scouts to help feed everyone in the village as well as ourselves.'

A murmur went around the assembled villagers. David was well turned out, despite the obvious nomadic existence he and his people had been living. He spoke well, too, and reminded Gerald of his local councillor. Obviously he was organised, and so far he had managed to keep the women and children in his care safe.

'All we need is a doctor to look at our sick,' David said. 'A place to rest ...'

'Wait here while we discuss it,' Gerald replied.

The villagers gathered in the hall for a meeting as the tired visitors collapsed on the village green outside.

'Of course we should give them shelter,' said the vicar. 'What are we, animals? We can't possibly turn these people away. There are children out there.'

'If they can do what they say they can,' Gerald said, 'I can't see it being a bad thing. We've been isolated due to our lack of fuel. I don't mind going out on these scouting parties. We're going to need medical supplies before long, and no-one is going to be delivering them anytime soon.'

'But, what if the Jinx attack?' asked Mrs Carlyle from the flower shop.

'That could happen anyway,' said Mallory. 'If the Jinx attack, we're all in the same boat. It makes no difference if there are more of us or not. He's definitely from South London, I recognised the accent. Probably based in Epsom or somewhere originally.'

Mallory was taller than her husband and had pale blonde hair and grey eyes. She was also ten years younger than him, but the age gap didn't bother either of them. Before the invasion, Mallory had worked in London, commuting a few times a week into the city to work as a translator. She spoke five different languages and had an excellent ear for accents.

'I don't mind opening the guest house to give them somewhere to sleep,' Jenny Briggs chipped in, 'as long as they can provide their own food. There isn't an individual room for everyone, but sharing will still be a lot better than sleeping rough on a bus as they have been doing. Would be nice to have guests again. They can pay me with supplies.'

Jenny was a pretty woman in her early thirties. She wasn't a native of Stow, having moved there some years earlier when she had bought the guest house. But the villagers had taken to her and she had rapidly become part of the community in much the same way Gerald and Mallory had.

Gerald glanced over at Jenny and nodded. 'That's very generous of you. And very trusting.' His eyes skittered away from the tight-fitting T-shirt the woman wore. He never wanted Mallory to notice how attractive he found Jenny Briggs and always felt guilty about his interest in the woman.

'They are in trouble. I'd like to think someone would help me out one day if I needed it,' Jenny said.

'I think maybe things are improving,' said the vicar, ever the optimist, as the villagers unanimously nodded and agreed that the refugees could stay.

The sun was shining when the villagers went out onto the green to give the visitors the good news. Mallory noted how the children sat silently around their parents as each family gave out food. She felt a deep sadness slip into the pit of her stomach. *Children aren't meant to suffer, they should be loved and cherished*, she thought.

'They've been through such a lot,' she said to Gerald. 'If I'd been blessed with children, I would protect them with my life.'

'I know.'

Jenny Briggs led the way and, with the help of the vicar's young cousin, Beth Turner, it wasn't long before all the newcomers were settled in the guest house.

'You've got working electricity!' David said, surprised, as Jenny showed them around the house.

'Yes. We don't know why, but everything seems to be ticking over that way. We just don't have fuel to run the tractors and motors. It's made the work of farming a lot harder and slower,' Jenny said.

'Maybe we can help find some,' David said.

'You should have seen the faces of the children!' Jenny told Mallory and Gerald as she met them outside. 'I reckon it will be hot baths all round tonight.'

Gerald smiled and went inside the guest house, where he found David in the hallway. 'You said you had some sick that needed attending to?'

'My mother's not too well,' David replied. 'She has high blood pressure, but obviously we haven't been able to get a supply of the pills. The truth is, we didn't know what to give her.'

Audrey Keen was coherent, but even before the examination began, Gerald noticed that her skin was sallow. Gerald speculated that she was in her early seventies. There was a blue tinge around her mouth and nose. Her blood pressure was far too high and her heartbeat was erratic.

'What's the verdict, doc?' she smiled, her eyes lively.

'You'll live. But you are going to need to rest a while.'

'Thanks to you people I can now do that,' Audrey said.

Gerald left the room and went in search of David. He found the other man in the kitchen, supervising the stocking of the cupboards. True to their word, the refugees did have plenty of food to support themselves.

'I'm not terribly happy with your mother's breathing,' Gerald said. 'How long has she been like that?'

David shrugged. 'She's been breathless for months. I'd noticed how it was slowing her down but just thought it was, you know, old age.'

'I'd like to check her lungs. Can you bring her to the surgery tomorrow for an X-ray?'

David nodded. 'Thanks, doc. You guys really don't know how great you're being. We've been turned away at every house, village and town still standing for miles around.'

'Why?' asked Gerald, surprised.

David's eyes grew dull and sad.

'People have changed. The world has changed. They are all out for themselves. I'll tell you the truth, doc, we all expected the same here too. But we were desperate, and I was really worried about Mum.'

David handed Gerald a bag. It was filled with canned food: tuna, fruit salad and Carnation evaporated milk.

'What's this?' Gerald said.

'Your fee. You've got to eat too. I told you, we'll help the village.'

Gerald nodded.

When the local farmer, William Brewster, heard about David and his people, he came into the village. True to his word, David had plenty of fuel, so he traded some for fresh milk, yoghurt and cheese. The farmer and the villagers were pleased. This meant that work on the farm could begin to speed up again. Brewster and his wife went away feeling optimistic. After that, life settled into something that resembled sanity. Hope for the future made the villagers and the visitors light-hearted, and the people of Stow rapidly accepted the new arrivals as part of their world.

David Keen's scouts soon proved themselves invaluable. They went out every day, returning with more and more supplies. Sometimes these included luxury items that the villagers hadn't seen for months.

'Look what we found,' David said one day, opening his car boot.

Gerald, Mallory, Jenny and the innkeeper, Pete Beamish, looked down and discovered a stash of wine bottles, liqueurs, and a crate of beer.

A few weeks later, Gerald joined David with the scouting party. Using some more of their fuel, they planned to take the doctor's small ambulance and a car out of the village in search of extra supplies. David's men had been scouting every day since their arrival, always returning with more provisions, which they distributed fairly amongst the villagers.

'We could do with some advice though, doc,' explained David. 'We found an abandoned pharmacy. I thought you could make a list of things you might want, but then realised it would be far quicker to take you there and just let you choose what you need.'

Gerald was eager to go. He hadn't been out of the village for months, and it was a good plan. He had spent many a night in David's company since the visitors had arrived, and they had formed a strong friendship. David had even helped Pete Beamish restock his bar and the social element had returned to the village, with many nights spent at the inn setting the world to rights.

'Are you sure this is a good idea?' Mallory said as Gerald set off for the trip.

'We could do with supplies, Mal. And Dave's right, I'm the only one who knows what to get. I was thinking we could do with needles, tetanus vaccines and all manner of antibiotics. Now there are more people in the village, the supplies I had have rapidly depleted.'

Gerald got in the ambulance with David and they set off with the small party out and away to a location that the scouts already knew.

The small town of Ascott-under-Wychwood was ten miles away from Stow and, unlike other areas of the Cotswolds, wasn't known for its tourist attractions. It was a normal village, with a large supermarket nearby and a retail park that had a chain store pharmacy.

'Where is everyone?' Gerald asked as they passed through the village.

'Don't know,' David said. 'It was like this when we came through here weeks ago. We don't take resources from places still thriving; only those that apparently have no occupants.'

'It's deserted?'

'As far as we know. Occasionally we've come across the odd gang.'

'Refugees like yourselves?'

'No,' said David. 'Not like us at all. We're trying to survive. Those sorts are …'

'Hey, look over there!' said Chris, who was sat in the back of the ambulance with two other men.

'That's what I mean,' said David.

Gerald looked where Chris was pointing and saw a group of men gathered outside the supermarket. His heart lurched into his mouth.

'That was where we were headed?' Gerald asked.

'Yeah. But not now. We'll go on to the pharmacy and see if we can get the medical supplies first.'

Gerald heard a click. He turned to look at the men sat in the back of the ambulance. Each one of them was armed, and they were fishing out more weapons from a holdall that Gerald had assumed to contain equipment to help them break into the pharmacy.

'Did they see us?' asked Chris, loading thick cartridges into a double-barrelled shotgun.

'I think so,' said David. 'But so far no-one is following.'

'What's going on?' asked Gerald.

'If you want to survive and protect your women and kids, sometimes you have to do things you're not proud of,' Chris explained.

Gerald scrutinised the other man's face. Chris sounded old, and yet he was no more than early twenties.

'Dave?' Gerald said.

'They are scum,' David said. 'Just remember, whatever happens, keep your head down. We can't lose you, you're our only doctor.'

'But … surely we can come to an arrangement with …'

'No,' said Chris. 'We tried that. My brother got killed. Believe me, doc, these guys can't be trusted.'

David pulled the ambulance into the retail park and straight up to the pharmacy, mounting the small kerb so that the entrance door was covered by the side of the vehicle. Behind them the other car pulled in and two more scouts got out, positioning themselves behind the vehicle, guns at the ready.

'You're really expecting a fight?' Gerald asked. His heart was thumping in his chest and he rubbed his palms over his jeans to wipe away the dampness that had suddenly sprung up there. He hadn't expected this when he had agreed to come with them.

David shrugged. 'Maybe they didn't see us, but we aren't taking any chances. Chris? Get that door open. Let's get the doc in and out of here in one piece with everything we need to keep us going for a while.'

Gerald nervously watched as the men started to break into the pharmacy. His day had suddenly taken a turn for the worse.

7

They decided on the garden. Jas and Andrew took turns digging the grave, but it was hard work for the boy. He was emotionally wrung out and physically weakened by the enforced starvation.

'It's Dad's pride and joy,' Andrew said. 'He was always out there, making it look nice. I don't think he'll mind being here for now.'

'Your parents were good people,' Jas said. 'I don't want you to ever forget that.'

Andrew nodded. He held back the question that was always on his lips. *What has happened to Mum?*

Jas jumped out of the hole, and they dragged Mr Carpenter's body, now wrapped in a sheet, over and into the pit. They rolled him in as carefully as possible, but the body was heavy. Jas now understood what 'dead weight' really meant. She tried to support it, but momentum pulled the corpse from her hands and Mr Carpenter hit the bottom with a loud thump.

'Sorry,' said Jas.

Andrew shuddered as he thought he heard bone break. He looked around the garden, letting his eyes settle anywhere other than the grave.

'You carry on with the marker,' said Jas. 'I'll fill this in. Do you … want to say a few words?'

Andrew looked down at the bundle in the grave. As they had carried him downstairs, Andrew had tried not to think that this empty shell was his dad. He had thought he was all cried out, his emotions a dull throb, cut off by shock, but now the tears came again and his throat choked.

'Don't worry,' said Jas, hugging him awkwardly. 'When this is over, we'll make sure he gets a proper funeral.'

Jas picked up the shovel. In her normal routine she went to the gym regularly. Even so, she felt totally unfit for this type of work: her muscles were screaming. Despite this, she continued to push the shovel into the soil. She couldn't let Andrew down, no matter how much it hurt. It wasn't fair to the boy to expect him to cover his father's body.

Andrew turned away. He couldn't bring himself to watch, so he sat down and with a penknife carved his father's name into a makeshift cross; two pieces of wood that they had taken from the shed and hammered roughly together. When he had finished carving, Andrew stood up and went back to the shed. Inside he found an old pot of black paint hidden among the spare plastic plant pots and jars of nails. Having prised off the lid and stirred the contents, he used a small brush to paint in the words he'd carved, then he placed the cross down flat on the lawn to dry.

Jas patted the ground smooth, put down the shovel and went inside the house. From the fridge she took out two cans of Coke, then headed back outside. As she reached the door, she saw Andrew sitting by the grave. She stopped.

'I dunno what to think, never mind what to say, Dad,' Andrew said quietly. 'The world has gone to shit and I'm scared. Maybe Mum is still out there somewhere?'

Jas waited until the boy fell silent, then she sat beside him, holding out one of the cans. She had built a scenario around Mr Carpenter's death, one that she would never share with Andrew, but somehow thought he would figure out for himself one day. The Jinx had come. They had taken his mum, and his dad had been too afraid to resist. It was the only explanation she could find for his apparent suicide.

As the afternoon wore on, the two unlikely companions comforted each other as they sat in silence. When Jas finally stood, took up the marker and hammered it into the head of the grave, Andrew had reached a new level of calm. Jas wondered if it was just shock, but he appeared to be almost cheerful when they went inside to wash up and make dinner. Then she recalled how she had heard that children were amazingly adaptable. Some survival mechanism made them more resilient than adults. For the first time, she realised this was true.

She made them pizza, something she would never eat under normal circumstances, and they sat in front of the television eating and watching the news. It was total chaos in England, and new sightings of the Jinx had begun to occur in other countries too.

'Is this … an apocalypse, Miss?' asked Andrew. 'Only it's not what I expected to happen. I thought there'd be atom bombs or some meteor exploding in space.'

'Me too,' Jas said. 'These Jinx, whatever can they want?'

'Women,' said Andrew. 'It's obvious, isn't it? Maybe they don't have any of their own.'

Jas nodded. 'They are like marauding Vikings.'

Andrew laughed. 'Yeah. Sailing across oceans to kidnap our maidens.'

'Or sailing across time and space …' Jas said, smiling at the absurdity.

Jas knew as much about time travel as any science teacher might, and didn't believe it was possible, but she reflected on the appearance of the Jinx.

They did look as though they had come from another time: but another space, another dimension seemed more likely. Jas mulled over the possibilities, zoning out from the images and interviews being repeated in a loop on the channel. There hadn't been anything new for hours, and she was beginning to wonder what that meant.

Andrew flicked through the television channels as Jas nodded off in his mother's chair. He couldn't take any more of the same repeated information and he wanted some light relief. He eventually found *Sponge Bob Square Pants* on one of the children's channels, and even though Ray Steinberg always said it was 'gay', he lapsed into the mindlessness of the programme. It was a relief, and deep down he had always liked the show, but had been afraid to admit it, even to his closest friends, because it wasn't grown-up.

Andrew pushed aside the sadness he felt when he recalled his school friends. He had liked Ray Steinberg, for all his silliness and the fact that he didn't try hard at school. They had been friends, sort of, and Andrew felt a small pang in the pit of his stomach when he recalled leaving the others behind. He glanced at his sleeping teacher. *Let her sleep,* he thought. She was kind. She had saved him. She had never deserved the threats and nastiness that Ray had inflicted on her, and he was always glad when she had stood up to him.

When Jas woke a few hours later, Andrew was gone. She couldn't say exactly what had disturbed her, but she found herself jumping from the chair. Then she heard the downstairs toilet flush, and Andrew came back looking bleary-eyed. He had changed out of his school uniform and was wearing pyjamas.

'I thought I heard something,' she said.

The lounge was lit by one small lamp, the television was still on, but the volume was low. Jas noted that Andrew had made himself a bed on the sofa and there was a discarded blanket on the floor by her chair.

'You fell asleep, thought you would be cold, Miss,' Andrew said, noticing her confusion.

'Thank you,' Jas said. 'Perhaps for now you should just call me Jas?'

Andrew beamed. He had never been allowed to call a teacher by their first name before, and he liked the idea that it made him somehow equal and more grown up.

At that moment a loud noise, like shattering glass, came from the kitchen. Jas and Andrew froze. They looked at each other in confusion.

'Must be other survivors,' Andrew whispered, but neither of them was willing to bet their life on it.

'More likely looters,' Jas said.

Jas looked around the room for a weapon. She had to protect Andrew, and whoever was out there might not be friendly. They heard more breaking, and the opening and slamming of the back door.

'They're wrecking my mum's kitchen!' Andrew was outraged and ran to the door, but Jas caught his arm, pulling him back just as it swung inwards.

Two men entered, and Jas knew on sight that they weren't the kind of fellow survivors they would have hoped to meet. They looked mean and hard. There was a calculated coldness behind the eyes of the first one and a frightening smirk on the face of the second.

'Oh, look what we got here. A woman and a kid,' said the first man. 'We saw your light on.'

'Hi,' said Jas, hoping to find some decency lurking behind the cold eyes. The man was practically bald, his head shaved down to a number one. There was an unmentionable violence radiating from them both: a kind of odour of desperation. 'You're survivors too, huh? We've been watching the news. Do you know what's happening?'

The first man glanced at the second and smiled lecherously. 'Nice to find a female survivor. We thought those bastards had got all of you.'

'I'm Jas,' she said, but she didn't hold out her hand. She had no intention of touching either of them. 'Have you guys eaten? Can we get you some food?'

'Dean,' said the first man, taken aback by her calm and generous offer. 'This here is Shaun.'

'Well we're glad to see you,' Jas said.

The men looked her up and down, taking in the blazer and emblem.

'Teacher, eh?'

'Yes,' said Jas.

Jas *was* a teacher, and her calm demeanour was something she had worked long and hard to maintain. She never forgot the need to be in charge of the classroom, and her training helped her to assess when a situation could blow up out of control; especially if she didn't handle the kids right. She told herself that the men were just tall pupils, year elevens, ready to leave and go on to college. They were children who thought they were fully grown men.

She tucked her hair behind her ear, suddenly aware that she was dirty and untidy. She felt unprofessional. The hair in her tight bun had worked loose over the last few days of sleeping rough. She hadn't found a change of clothes, so her suit and shirt were covered in dirt. Even so, Jas rose above her dishevelled appearance and became authoritative. She applied the first rule of controlling a class of potentially dangerous pupils; she got them to sit down. That way, she towered over them and was more completely in charge.

'You must be tired. Please sit down,' she said.

The men took a seat as Jas fussed around them. Then she handed Dean the remote control, advising that he check out the news.

She took Andrew into the kitchen. It was a mess. Broken glass had scattered over the worktops where the men had smashed a window to get inside.

'Why are you being so nice?' Andrew demanded. 'Look what they've done to my house?'

'Sometimes,' Jas said, 'you have to keep calm and react later.'

'If they saw the light, why didn't they just knock on the door? We can't trust them,' Andrew said.

Jas agreed with Andrew. The men could have knocked, but they had arrived intending violence. To what purpose, Jas had no idea. But she wanted to keep things calm, at least until she formulated a plan for how to get Andrew safely away from there.

'Sometimes you have to pick your battles carefully.' Jas slipped a kitchen knife down into her boot and put another one in her blazer pocket.

Andrew's eyes widened but he said nothing. He was learning a lot of things about Jas that he had never even considered would be part of her nature. He knew she was tough, but could she handle herself in a fight? Then he remembered what she had said to Ray – was that only a week before? She had said, 'I pack a mean punch.'

Jas took the men a plate of cooked meat and salad and a glass of lemonade each.

'Don't you have anything stronger?' asked Dean.

'No. But we know where to get some,' Jas said. 'So, do you live around here?'

'No,' said Shaun. 'Salford.'

'It was hit hard a few days ago,' said Dean. 'The place looks like this does, only worse.'

'Worse? How can it be worse?' asked Andrew.

'Shops, houses, people. Everything was exploded,' said Shaun.

'By the Jinx?' asked Jas.

'No. The army. They turned up and blew the place to shit. Then they said it was 'cos their weapons weren't working properly. That the Jinx had done something to them.'

'Where is the army now?' asked Jas.

'Dead,' said Dean.

Jas and Andrew grew silent. When the men had finished eating, Jas stood and reached for the plates.

'The world's ended,' said Shaun. 'It's every man for 'imself. There's no-one out there. How about showing us a little more kindness?'

'What do you mean?' she said, but she recognised his meaning in the dark pits of greed that showed in his eyes. 'We're more than willing to share food with you.'

'It's not food I need right now,' Shaun said, and Dean laughed.

Jas weighed up the situation. She had recognised immediately that these were dangerous men. She had even suspected it might come to this. She believed what Shaun had said, that there was no-one out there, and therefore knew that no-one was going to come to her aid. She glanced over at Andrew. He was young and innocent, and he had been through so much already. She couldn't face his fear, or risk him getting hurt.

'Okay,' she said quietly. 'But not in front of the boy.'

Dean sat forward on the couch, his eyes holding the same madness as Shaun's. 'Get out of here, kid. Go to your room or something.'

'Miss … Jas?'

Jas nodded. 'It's okay.'

Andrew backed away toward the door. He knew something serious was going to happen but he didn't know what. Jas closed the door behind him, then turned around to face the men. She took a deep breath as they both stood and moved toward her. For the first time, her calm façade dropped. Her trembling hand slipped into her pocket. She would survive; she had to. Andrew was relying on her.

Shaun's hands ran over her breasts as Dean began to tug at her clothing. This close, Jas could smell their sweat and foul breath. She thought she would vomit with fear and disgust.

'Hey, hold on boys,' she said, trying to keep her voice steady. 'Let's make this last. You first …'

They backed away, both eagerly beginning to strip their dirty clothes, dropping them down on Mrs Carpenter's clean carpet.

'Nice,' Jas said with fake appreciation.

The pizza she and Andrew had consumed threatened to come up as she watched Shaun remove his top. It wasn't that he was unpleasant to look at. He had obviously spent some time in the gym; his body was toned, and under other circumstances Jas might have thought him at least attractive. He was covered in various tattoos: not a look Jas had ever found particularly appealing. But what sickened her was the threat of violence. She knew that if she didn't comply, they would rape her and probably kill both her and Andrew. Despite this, she wasn't sure that she could go through with it.

Shaun was the first to notice the doubt in her face; he stopped stripping and began to advance on her once more. Jas had the knife out of her pocket before he reached her.

'Well look at that. The little lady has claws,' laughed Dean. 'I'll let you handle this one, mate. Then we're going to have some real fun with you, sweetie.'

Jas lowered the knife, feigning acceptance, but as Shaun grabbed her, she reacted on instinct and stabbed up at him. The knife sliced through his arm. Shaun grunted, pulled back, and delivered a reactive backhand slap. Jas was knocked backwards off her feet and lay stunned as Shaun prised the knife from her fingers.

'That was a big mistake, you stupid cow,' he said. 'When I'm finished you won't ever turn a knife on anyone again.'

'Don't mess her up too much before my turn,' Dean said, chuckling. 'I like my meat pretty fresh.'

Shaun laughed, casting a glance back at Dean. At that moment new images came through on the television and Dean turned back to watch another reporter die as the Jinx arrived at the featured location.

'Hey, I haven't seen this,' he said. Then he sat down in Mrs Carpenter's chair, his back to Jas and Shaun, as the news channel began to show the update.

Shaun turned back to Jas, and the laughter died in his throat. In the few moments it had taken him to glance at Dean, Jas had got up on her knees and drawn the knife she had hidden in her boot. She buried it deep into the side of Shaun's neck.

It took Dean a moment to realise that the noise Shaun was making was not the usual sounds of lust. By then, Jas had retrieved the other knife and as Dean turned, she ran forward, swinging it at him. The blade bit into the soft flesh under his chin. Dean staggered from the chair, blood pumping down his chest and spilling onto Mrs Carpenter's carpet. This angered Jas even more, so she threw aside the chair and kicked out at Dean, knocking him off his feet. His head smashed against the fireplace. Blood oozed out over the marble. He lay still. Jas saw the life go out of his open eyes and stepped back, her rage rapidly dissipating. She had killed him already with the first blow, but had failed to realise it. She stared down at the gaping wound in his throat. Blood poured down and over his shirt.

Jas had always hated his sort. Dean and Shaun, the takers of this world. She was certain that before the Jinx had arrived, these two had been criminals. They had taken to looting, destruction and rape all too easily. She remembered witnessing a woman being attacked in the street once, just outside the hairdresser's. She had been powerless to help, as had all of the other people in the salon, but she had always wished she had been brave enough to go outside and punch the attacker in the face, just as he had done to the poor, unsuspecting female.

After that she had taken up boxercise at the gym. It wasn't real martial arts, but it had kept her toned and her reflexes sharp. Many times since then she had taken out her frustrations on the punch bag after a hard day at school.

She turned around. The house was quiet. She hoped that Andrew was safely tucked up in bed and didn't see what she had done. She stepped over the still form of Shaun, half expecting his hand to reach up and grab her leg, but that sort of thing only ever happened in the movies. Shaun was dead, just as his partner in crime was. It had been easy, and Jas felt no remorse, just a dull sense of despair that she and Andrew would now have to leave his home.

She opened the door to find Andrew stood outside, holding his mother's rolling pin. His scared eyes took in her blood-soaked clothing, but she blocked the doorway. She didn't want him to see what she was capable of.

'You okay?' she asked, closing the door behind her as she came out into the hallway.

'I should be asking you that,' he said.

'I'm fine. We have to get out of here though. It's just not safe. It's too … obvious.'

Andrew looked sad but nodded. 'My mum has clothes upstairs you can use. I know she wouldn't mind.'

Jas glanced down at the spoilt white shirt, already dirty, but now stained red.

'I'd rather borrow your dad's things,' she said. 'Might be more practical.'

In the bathroom, Jas showered and washed her hair. Then she stared at her reflection in the mirror. Her mid-length hair hung wet and loose over her shoulders. She opened the medicine cabinet and looked inside. Her eyes fell on a pair of nail scissors. Underneath the sink, Andrew's mother kept bleach and cleaning products. She pushed aside the containers, searched around but couldn't find what she was looking for.

'Andrew?' she called, opening the bathroom door. 'Did your parents ever have any hair scissors?'

Andrew appeared with a pile of clothing. A man's fleece, a pair of large and baggy jeans, and a black heavy metal T-shirt.

'Yeah, I think mum had some.'

Jas took the clothing and dressed while Andrew searched. When he returned, she took the scissors from his hand and re-closed the bathroom door. She studied her disguise in the mirror. She looked like a teenage boy; and in the current climate that was the safest look to have. She began to hack away at her hair, cutting it as short as she could, and the disguise evolved before her eyes. Jas had never worn her hair short before, and it did make her look and feel more male.

8

The trucks pulled up to the checkpoint barrier the next morning and the soldiers waited impatiently for someone to let them in. After ten minutes, when no-one came out of the guardhouse, Donovan jumped out of the first truck and walked up to the small window.

'There's no-one inside, Captain,' Donovan called as Taylor got out of the second truck.

Taylor knew the combination and quickly keyed in the code, opening the door. Donovan went inside and raised the barrier while Taylor waved the trucks through. They moved slowly forward, and Donovan left the booth and climbed back into the first one as it passed.

Taylor went back inside the guardhouse and looked around. On the shallow desk the visitor's log had been left open. Taylor studied the neat writing, noting that the last entry had been 24 hours earlier and that it had logged the return of Major Handley.

Taylor and Donovan had debated what had happened to the Major when a thorough search had failed to bring up his remains. This new revelation left no doubt that Handley had deserted them, long before the battle was lost. Taylor picked up the book as the second truck crossed under the barrier, then he left the booth, closing the door securely behind him. Ashby, the driver of the second truck, stopped and waited for Taylor. He glanced over at the Captain as he climbed into the cab beside him, noting the tension around his chin and mouth and taking in his white knuckles where he gripped the log book tightly. It was clear that the Captain was furious, but Ashby said nothing; he merely released the handbrake and followed the first truck into the complex.

Normally the journey to the barracks would have taken only a few hours from the centre of London, but the damaged roads and abandoned cars had made the motorway an impossible route. Instead they had travelled over farmland for most of the trip. Once or twice the truck carrying the wounded had had to pull over so that the doctor could check on them. Now at least the medical officer had the resources of the infirmary at his disposal, so the third truck headed down the long driveway and turned left into the camp, heading for the hospital building.

Taylor was furious. He would have to report in before he could return to his room and change. He had a lot to tell Handley, but he was angry that the Major had left without informing anyone. Already he was planning to send a complaint to his superiors about the Major's handling of the situation.

They arrived at the office building. Taylor climbed out of the cab and met Donovan, who was waiting by the first truck. The barracks was unusually quiet. Normally at this time of day the sergeant was drilling the new recruits on the forecourt.

'What's going on?' asked Donovan, glancing at the book under Taylor's arm.

'I don't know. Looks like there's been an evacuation.'

'That's not possible,' said Donovan. 'They wouldn't have left us without orders.'

Taylor didn't answer but turned and walked up the steps toward the main building. In the event of evacuation, procedures had to be followed. Taylor knew where he could find the answers and the orders for their future manoeuvres. As he reached the top step, Donovan caught up with him.

'What should I tell the men?' Donovan said.

'To go and get some down time. Might be their last chance for a while.'

Donovan yelled the instruction as Taylor pressed the code to enter the main building. The door buzzed open and, as he went inside, Donovan followed him in.

'At least the doors weren't on lockdown,' said Donovan as they entered the main building.

'Emergency protocol,' Taylor said. 'They have to give any battle strays time and opportunity to return to base.'

Donovan nodded; he knew the protocol, but deep down he was convinced that Handley had abandoned them because he believed that there would be no strays. So he was doubly surprised to find the building still accessible.

'How long have we got to gain access?' Donovan asked.

'If the codes aren't activated within 48 hours after e-vac the base shuts down. Permanently.

Donovan had never trusted the Major, but he took orders because he was a good soldier and because he trusted Taylor with his life.

'Let's find that code,' said Donovan.

In the Major's office they found filing cabinets left open, the drawers empty. The normally pristine wooden floor was covered in boot prints. The Major and his retinue had left in a hurry. Donovan checked the desk, but not a scrap of paper had been left. The Major's computer monitor was there, but the base unit had been taken.

'They wanted to travel light,' said Taylor.

'Where've they gone?'

'I'm clearly not privileged with that information,' Taylor said.

Donovan was surprised to hear a tinge of bitterness in the Captain's voice.

'They left us for dead,' Donovan stated.

'They were almost right on that score. We've only 50 fit men, and god knows what we'll do with the wounded if we don't find the code.'

They left the Major's office and went to Special Ops. Here Taylor found a generic working computer and he logged into his e-mail, checking his memos.

'Handley left me a message,' he said finally. '*The base will shut down (Stop). No protocol in place (Stop). Shut down commences 22.00 hours, Friday 17th. Disband and lie low until this is over.*'

'Disband? What kind of orders are those?'

'It means,' Taylor said, 'that we're on our own from now on. The powers-that-be are probably in some bunker somewhere, safely tucked away with their families. They don't give a shit about those of us left out here. I guess they expected us all to die.' He slammed his fist down on the desk. 'Those bastards deserted us.'

Donovan fell into a depressed silence. He looked to Taylor to tell them what to do. He had been in the army since he was 17 and hadn't contemplated doing anything else in the near future. He would face any unknown enemy if given orders, but this new ambiguity made him feel insecure and afraid.

'What we gonna do?' Donovan asked finally.

'We're on the clock. We have to get any medical supplies, food and fuel that might have been left behind. Plus any artillery, tanks and trucks we can find. These buildings have to be vacated before 10 pm,' Taylor said.

'Is there nothing we can do?' Donovan asked.

Taylor shook his head. 'Fuck it. I can't see any way of stopping it.'

They left the building and found the remaining men congregated in the mess. They looked confused. Some food had been left but the place was deserted. Donovan explained the situation as Taylor pulled a drink from one of the fridges.

'The thing is,' Taylor said, 'as of now, you're all free men.'

The soldiers erupted into mixed discussions. Some, like Donovan, clearly didn't want to be free. Taylor let them talk around the possibilities before pointing to the clock. It was noon.

'This place shuts down in ten hours. Whatever you decide, we have to be out of the main buildings by then.'

'Are the barracks closing down?' asked Sergeant Harvey. 'Only this seems like the army has totally fucked us over, Captain.'

Taylor looked him over. He hadn't always seen eye to eye with Bill Harvey but he couldn't deny him the outburst. It was true. They had been abandoned and they were left to their own devices as of now.

'Yes. All the buildings. Even the barrier won't budge, so we'll need trucks and equipment out of here before that happens,' Taylor said. 'I do have a proposal though.'

The men listened. They were willing to hear anything other than the word 'disband'.

'We could split up. Go our separate ways and try to stay alive as the Jinx take what's left of our world. We've already learnt we can't defend it. But that doesn't mean there isn't safety in numbers. I propose we stay together. Do the best we can to help any survivors we find. That's our job, after all; to protect and serve. The army's screwed us over. I can't deny it, and Handley is one dead Major if I ever get my hands on him. But the only chance I'll ever have of revenge is if I survive the next few months, the next few years. However long this goes on. Like I said. We *could* disband. We'd be following orders. Being the soldiers we've always been, blindly doing as we were told, even when we didn't agree. Even though they've fucked us in the ass big time.'

A murmur went up through the group. They had felt this many times, just as Taylor had.

'Call me insane,' Taylor went on, 'but the thing is, I think we could still win this war. The Jinx think they've defeated us. So we'll lie low and we'll watch. We won't waste our time and weapons getting into any new scrapes. Not until we're ready. We're going to do what the authorities should have done all along. We're going to study the Jinx. Find out what makes them tick. And when they least suspect it, we'll hit back, hard and strong.'

'How we going to do that?' asked Harvey 'We barely have any equipment.'

'Our technology isn't any good, we know that,' Taylor said.

'Then what is?' Donovan said.

Taylor shrugged. 'That's the point. We need a little patience, but we're going to find out.'

It seemed a bizarre request, but the soldiers had heard others in their time, and so the vote was unanimous. The best chance any of them had was if they stayed together.

They set about packing up everything they could that would help them survive and loading up the trucks with food and weapons, intending to leave the camp with only minutes to spare before the place shut down, locking them out forever.

'We can't move the wounded again, Captain,' protested the medical officer.

'We can't stay,' Taylor said. 'But we'll find a hospital for you *en route*.'

As they drove away, Taylor felt like the Artilleryman in *War of the Worlds*. He could almost hear the voice of David Essex singing 'Brave New World'. Was his vision an impossible pipe dream too? Taylor shook the thought away. He felt sick and worried. He was tired and overwrought. They had fought and survived a battle that many others of his men had lost. He understood better than most that the surviving troops needed hope, or, one by one, they would all die; and, although he pledged never to make false promises, he would do his damnedest to discover the flaw in the Jinx army and find a way to stop those bastards. Otherwise there was no future, and Earth would be destroyed by the barrenness enforced by the attacks and the lack of remaining women.

Driving through the wasteland that had once been England, Taylor thought about his parents and wondered if they were still alive. Was the world worth saving? He didn't know. But he would do his best to destroy those alien bastards, even if it killed him.

9

The scouting party were half way through filling the ambulance when two cars pulled up containing the type of survivors that David had described. They were armed, angry, bitter men, and they wanted all that David and his group had found – including the medical supplies that Stow urgently needed. Gerald couldn't help noticing the desperation on the men's faces. He pitied them, but he trusted David's instincts.

'We're not prepared to give you our stuff,' David shouted. 'So you have an opportunity to leave now.'

Then the shooting began.

Chris threw Gerald back inside the pharmacy, pushing him down behind the counter.

'Keep your head down, doc!'

Gerald didn't need to be told twice. He cowered down and waited until the interminable battle ended. It sounded like the gun fight at the OK Corral, and although he was scared, Gerald saw a strange humour in this similarity. He couldn't help feeling he had stepped back in time somehow, for the world he once knew had turned into a barren and hostile wilderness. An overwhelming sense of unreality descended on him. From a distance, he recognised his symptoms as shock and hysteria, but he didn't know what to do other than to go with the feelings. And so he found himself chuckling at the absurdity of the situation. Even at the idea that he might be killed.

When the guns stopped firing, Gerald heard the heavy acceleration of a car speeding away from the building. The smile fell from his lips. He hunkered down behind the counter, too afraid to move. Then he heard footsteps approaching. Gerald's heart hammered in his chest until eventually Chris popped his head over the counter.

'You okay there, doc? We saw those bastards off. They may have been mean but they weren't as determined as us.'

Chris had a bullet wound in his arm, but fortunately the bullet had passed through the fleshy part of his skin without causing major damage.

'You'll live,' Gerald said.

'Ouch,' complained Chris as the doctor poured disinfectant in and around the wound before applying a bandage with surprisingly steady hands.

'Hey doc,' said David coming into the pharmacy. 'Look what we've found.'

David held the arm of a thin, dark-haired girl, no more than 15 or 16. She was crying, shaken and scared, constantly casting her jet black eyes around as though she believed the men meant to hurt her.

'Where did you find her?' asked Gerald.

'Those bastards had her locked in the boot of their car,' David replied. 'Lucky for her we killed the driver. I think she's Spanish. She doesn't seem to understand that we aren't going to hurt her. God knows what she's been through. Don't suppose you speak the lingo?'

'No,' said Gerald. 'But Mallory can. She used to be a linguist.'

Gerald noted that he was now speaking of Mal's job in the past tense. It hadn't been that long ago that she had still been commuting to London once or twice a week. Her job had involved translating texts; books mostly. His clever wife knew five different languages, and could read and write in them all. In fact Mal had worked right up until the day of the first Jinx attack on London.

They took the girl into the ambulance and Gerald tried to calm her, offering her a bottle of Lucozade he had taken from the fridge in the pharmacy; it was warm, but she was thirsty and took it gratefully. He couldn't help noticing her pert breasts pressing against the stained T-shirt she was wearing, nor her bottom's curves emphasised by her tight jeans. He looked quickly away, afraid he would be caught leering at the girl. Part of him understood exactly why the other men had taken her and what they would have used her for. He quelled the dark thoughts that lurked in the back of his brain as he felt a familiar tightening in his trousers. He crossed his legs as he sat down in the back of the ambulance with the girl.

'There's a shelf of chocolate and snack bars in there as well,' Gerald pointed out to David. 'The kids will enjoy those.'

Once the ambulance was full of supplies they moved on to the petrol station, filling all the spare canisters they had brought with them and the tanks of the ambulance and car.

'Wonder how much is left in this place?' Chris asked as he stood at the end of the forecourt, looking around, his shotgun clasped in his hands.

David shrugged. 'I guess one day we'll find out. The well has to dry out eventually. Especially if anyone else has been using it.'

'Then what will we do?' asked Chris.

'Find another one,' David answered.

Gerald noted how calm the men were, even though they continued to hold their loaded weapons. It made him realise that the scrape they had been in was nothing new to them. While they had been safely hidden in Stow, the world had changed dramatically, and Gerald was only just beginning to realise that the old rules no longer meant anything.

On the way back they passed the supermarket again, but didn't stop for fear of meeting up with more of the 'wrong sort' of survivors.

'It's funny,' said Chris. 'I never liked those movies about the end of the world. It always seemed ridiculous to me to consider that the survivors wouldn't work together for the good of all.'

'Me too,' said Gerald. 'Strange how it worked out that way though, isn't it?'

David said nothing, but turned the car into the road leading back to Stow.

'Make sure we aren't followed,' Gerald said, looking back nervously.

'I always do,' said David.

Mallory was frantic when they returned. 'You've been gone hours. What happened?'

Gerald met David's gaze, and the older man blinked. 'Nothing,' said David. 'We just had to travel farther than usual.'

David opened the back of the ambulance and Chris helped the Spanish girl out. After a brief discussion, the girl was sobbing with relief in Mallory's arms.

'She was on holiday with her parents when the Jinx attacked. Her name's Rosa and she's from Mexico. Who are these men she's telling me about?'

Gerald took Mallory inside and explained what had happened. 'You aren't to go out again,' Mallory said when he had finished.

'I have to, Mal. It's not David's responsibility to look after the village.'

'I agree with Mal,' David said. 'We can't risk losing you. The lives of the villagers and our wives and kids could be in your hands. You're important, doc.'

Gerald enjoyed the feeling that he was 'important'. He had never felt needed before. It made him feel powerful.

'What happens if those men find their way here?' asked Mallory.

'We'll deal with them,' David said. 'We'd have to. They can't be welcomed, Mal, not like you welcomed us. They are like locusts; they aren't seeing the bigger picture. They'll eat and consume until there's nothing left. Then they'll turn on each other.'

Mal couldn't argue, but she was worried about the two farms nearby. They hadn't seen the farmer or his wife that day.

'Will and Sue Brewster usually call round every morning with fresh produce,' Mal pointed out.

'They've probably run out of fuel,' said David. 'I'll drive over there now and take some. Chris? You coming?'

Chris and David headed back to the car with two canisters of fuel.

'Wait,' said Gerald. 'I'm coming with you.'

Mallory sighed. 'I'll take care of Rosa then, shall I? While you go gallivanting …'

The men climbed into the car and Mallory watched them leave. She had a weird feeling that things were about to change; that their normal, idyllic life was to be threatened. Mallory took Rosa's hand.

'You're safe here,' she promised in Spanish, but deep down she began to doubt if it was indeed true.

The three men drove out of town again, this time heading toward the farm a few miles away. They joked on the way, laughing about the battle and the Jinx; they felt invulnerable and safe in their little village haven. But as they drew closer to the farm, Gerald spotted a large plume of smoke.

'What the fuck?' said David.

'No. Oh no. The farmer has two children,' said Gerald.

'Chill,' said David. 'They may just be burning some waste.'

Gerald hoped David was right, but his gut twisted and he felt scared; even more so than he had earlier with the gunfire raging outside the pharmacy. He was afraid of what they would find. Afraid that it would be something his mind couldn't erase, or dismiss as some bizarre occurrence. For the last few months, cosseted in village life, with barely anyone suffering – despite the Jinx invasion – Gerald had been living in a fantasy world where monsters didn't really exist and bad things happened only to other people. He had buried his head in the sand, believing it would all blow over. Now he wished he wasn't a man of science and believed in God as the vicar did. At least then, whatever they found, he would have faith to convince him that things would get better.

As the car turned into the driveway, they saw that the farmhouse was burning. It was a one-storey structure, and the flames were licking up and out of the windows, reaching as high as the small thatched roof.

David pulled the car over and jumped out. He ran to the building. Gerald had never seen the man look so afraid. His face was white and he clenched his fists by his sides as he yelled, in a voice that had raised in pitch, 'Is there anyone in there?'

His frantic cries went unanswered, and Chris and Gerald caught hold of him as he attempted to rush headlong into the flames. As they held onto David, Gerald noticed that the horses were no longer in the field. The men skirted the burning structure looking for any sign of life. The farm had been stripped bare. The cows were gone, as well as the chickens.

'Looters!' said Gerald. 'Maybe it was the ones we met at the pharmacy.'

'There's no marks,' said Chris. 'The cows would have been herded away. There's no fresh animal tracks!'

'Maybe they were taken in a truck?' Gerald suggested.

'No,' said David. 'This isn't the looters.'

'Then who?' said Chris.

'Look.'

David pointed across the field to where the barn had once stood. The structure was now a jumbled pile of wood and hay.

'I don't get it,' said Gerald.

'That's because you haven't seen this type of devastation before,' David said. 'The Jinx have been here. It's them that took the cattle, them that burned the farm.'

'But why?' Gerald said. 'What can they possibly want?'

'The women of the farm, of course,' Chris said.

They found the farmer and his young son lying on the field as though they were sunbathing. Gerald ran to them, but when he reached the bodies he halted. They were dead; throats cut so deep it was almost decapitation. Gerald turned away and vomited on the grass. He had never seen anything so horrible in his life.

'It's the Jinx all right,' said David.. 'Now the cities have fallen they are working their way through the countryside.' He turned to the other men. 'So. What are we going to do to protect the village?'

Gerald wiped his mouth with the back of his hand. He was shaking, but he still had the presence of mind to admire David, who had recovered remarkably well after the initial shock. Gerald wanted to be as strong as David and his men, but he knew he didn't have the capacity to protect his wife physically. David was morally strong too. It was another type of strength that Gerald knew he didn't possess. Deep down, he feared his dark side. He wondered if he could sacrifice his own safety for that of others. Gerald shook away the black thoughts that seeped into his head once more.

'I have a safe,' he said, suddenly realising he could help in some way. 'It's large enough to hide some of the women and children. A small, lead-lined room. It's where I keep the more potent drugs.'

'Sounds like you have a panic room,' Chris said.

'I guess you could call it that,' Gerald answered.

10

Two Years Later

Jas watched them: a pack of dogs – teenage boys. It was always boys. There were so few females left, and any that hadn't been taken hid themselves away from male eyes, fearing them more than the Jinx. These were wild kids, not quite sane, thinking they owned what was left of the world. But Jas felt no fear or intimidation: she had faced worse, and nothing human scared her. Hiding out in the dirt like a sewer rat gave you the same fearless determination that vermin have. Jas would kill to keep Andrew safe. These days killing came easy. And killing dogs came easier still.

She tracked them, marking all of them by their peculiarities. The leader had long matted dirty hair that could be ginger; he was carrying a thick baseball bat. A thin scrawny one ranged ahead carrying a hunting knife, which he swiped through the air in agitation. His mouth protruded and he looked like a rabid fox. At least two of the dogs stayed either side of the leader as he walked, cocksure, through the abandoned street. They looked like nightclub bouncers, but without the black suits. One had a thick steel pole in his hand, the other carried a crowbar. Two more dogs brought up the rear, both carrying pieces of wood with nails hammered through: brutal weapons that could do a lot of damage if you were on the receiving end.

'What d'you think of this shit-hole, boys?' said the leader.

'It needs burning down, boss,' answered the dog with the knife, kicking over a bin full of rubbish, which scattered on the street. He removed a lighter from his pocket, kneeled down and set light to a piece of paper. It was dry and soon caught. A rush of flames burst over the paper and long-rotten dried-out food. The air stank of burning putrefaction. The arsonist gave a high-pitched whine like a hyena.

The other dogs laughed. They moved like a pack and began to smash their weapons against an abandoned car. *They are spoiling for a fight, that's why they are being so obvious and loud,* Jas thought. She shrank back as one of the creatures, a short, thick-set kid, swung a metal bar, smashing out the glass of one of the few remaining shop windows. The shards sprayed the street, and the boys all howled with laughter again.

Jas crept along, skirting the street corners as the dogs moved on, each one loudly destroying anything left standing. It was mindless. They were clearly stupid, and Jas wondered if it was because they knew there were no gangs here. There was only Jas and Andrew left in this small town, and that was because they hid their presence so well. To anyone passing through, the place appeared deserted.

Jas followed on, but she knew where the dogs would end up. Still she wished they would turn left at the end of the road, find themselves over at the tip and think there was nothing worth stealing. But it was too much to hope for, and as the dogs turned right they spotted the supermarket on the next street.

'Biscuit!' yelled the dog leader to one of the others. 'Smash that door open. Let's see what goodies are inside.'

Jas studied them again. They were emaciated, dirty and bedraggled. Desperate. Dangerous. She had to act before the door became damaged. She had kept the supermarket as their storage place, rather than go to all the trouble of moving the heavy cans of food. She and Andrew had long since disposed of all the rotting vegetables, and when the freezers had stopped working, carted van-loads of spoiled meat out onto the wasteland. It had been the best way to avoid attracting vermin. If the dogs broke in, though, they would probably take all that was left, or worse still, destroy anything they couldn't carry. That was what their type did.

'Stop!' she shouted gruffly, standing up from her hiding place. 'This is my town; you dogs aren't welcome here.'

The leader turned. He saw the dirty fleece, the grubby, greasy cropped hair and the thin and gangly frame covered in overlarge clothes. He recognised a boy, not unlike himself, but there was no feeling of empathy in him. His gang came first, and the food was theirs. 'Hey, kid. Do yourself a favour and mind your own fucking business, or the boys and me will teach you a lesson you won't forget.'

Jas smiled. Her teeth were white under the grime that smeared her face, and it amused her that the disguise was always taken at face value. They never expected to come across a woman, and certainly didn't think they would ever be challenged by one.

'I'm not a kid. And don't think for one minute that I'm alone.'

Jas pulled out the gun and fired a sodium orange flare up into the sky. At this signal, an arrow hissed through the air, burying itself in the leg of the dog referred to as Biscuit. The boy yelled, dropping his knife. He pulled the arrow out and screamed loudly as blood poured down his leg, soaking his worn-out jeans.

Jas smiled again, but it appeared on her face as a grimace. Obviously no-one had ever told him you should never pull an arrow out.

'Help me!' said Biscuit, but the other dogs ignored him, looking instead in the direction the arrow had come from.

Another arrow whistled through the air, then another. Arrows rained down on the boys, pinning them to the spot. The leader, being the quickest and the smartest, threw himself behind a street bin as the other dogs fell under the bombardment. One of the boys dived aside to avoid one arrow, only to fall into the line of another. It pierced his side and he screeched like an owl being pinned to a tree.

'I'll kill you fuckers!' yelled the leader.

'We don't tolerate thieving scum in our town,' Jas called. 'Leave now, while you still can.'

'All right boys,' said the leader cautiously standing up.

Jas kept the flare gun pointed at the boys as they slowly stood, one by one. Gathering their wounded, they staggered back out and away from the high street.

From the rooftop, Andrew tracked their exit as they tottered back the way they had come. All of them were injured with the exception of the leader and the boy carrying the steel pole. Andrew saw these two turn back as soon as they thought they weren't being watched, but the other dogs carried on to the end of the street and turned back the way they had first entered.

The two uninjured boys took a detour, following the ruined streets round to the back of the high street. Andrew blew his whistle, alerting Jas that the dogs were heading back. Then he climbed down from his vantage point and followed.

The boys didn't speak as they rounded the next corner. They kept close to the walls like practiced thieves and came full circle into the street from the other end. By then Jas was in position behind a burnt out car: a present left by the last dogs who'd tried to steal their supplies. She could clearly see the dogs even though this time their progress was silent.

'They must have something to hide if they're defending it so much,' said the leader as they reached the supermarket. 'We ain't leaving here empty-handed, and if we do, then we burn this fucking town down.'

Jas had heard enough. The dogs were irredeemable. They deserved all they got. She knew their sort: they would sell their own mothers and sisters to the Jinx for the price of a meal, given half a chance. She felt a moment of regret that she and Andrew couldn't share food with the boys, but they had tried to play nice with others of this ilk before.

Jas fired the flare as the boys reached the doorway. The ball of hot sodium hit the leader full in the chest, knocking him clean off his feet and back into an abandoned car on the corner. Flames burst over his filth-caked clothes, set fire to his long, matted ginger hair. His face was a burning blur.

He opened his mouth to scream but the flames burrowed in and ate his tongue, and the only sound that came out of his burning throat was a guttural gargle. He rolled, beating at his face and body in a vain attempt to kill the flames.

The other kid dropped his metal pipe and backed away, eyes darting in every direction as though he expected a flare to hit him too. As he reached the corner, he turned and ran. Jas didn't waste another shot. Instead she waited to hear Andrew's signal, which confirmed that the remaining boys had finally left town.

Leaving her hiding place she moved closer to the body. The leader was a smouldering, blackened mess lying face down in the dirt. Wrapping a piece of cloth around her hand, she bent down and checked his vitals. If he wasn't dead, he was almost there. She turned him over and looked down into the burnt out and blackened eyes.

You don't leave a dog to suffer in pain.

Jas picked up the other boy's discarded weapon, the long piece of steel pipe. She lifted it, weighing it in her hand; it was indeed a harsh weapon. Then she raised the pole above her head and smashed it down on the burnt lump that had once been the leader's face. His legs spasmed outwards, then he lay still. A smell of excreted urine and faeces wafted through the air as his bladder and bowels vented. She was certain now that he was dead.

Andrew appeared a few minutes later.

'They've gone,' he confirmed. 'Badly wounded. They've left a blood trail. I give it a day at best and most of 'em will be dead anyway.'

'Good,' said Jas, wiping gore from the steel pipe. 'We don't want dogs in our town. Let's dump this garbage on the wasteland.'

They dragged the body by its feet through the streets. Two years earlier, when the aliens had arrived and everyone had disappeared from their town, Jas and Andrew had realised that the rotting waste left behind was going to attract vermin and disease, and they had designated a former playground to become a waste tip. It made sense, since there were no longer rubbish collections and this stretch was far enough away from the centre that the stench was bearable.

Andrew opened the gate and they dragged the body up onto the pile.

'It's gonna stink,' Andrew said.

'Yeah, just like the others.' Jas looked around at the carnage. Their waste disposal area had become an abattoir for the dead.

'Guess we should have buried them. But scum don't deserve decent treatment.'

'Waste of energy,' Andrew agreed.

Over the last few weeks there had been a frequent flow of dogs entering the town, foraging for food. Andrew and Jas had seen them off, or killed those who refused to leave. Defending their food had been difficult to start with, but after the first kills it had become easier.

They left the burnt body as a flock of birds landed on its chest. Jas looked away as a pigeon pecked at the dead dog's burnt face.

'Birds have to eat too,' said Andrew. 'At least we cooked it for them.'

Jas laughed, then shrugged. Other than canned fish, the pigeons had become their only source of protein. The birds were nourishing and they had soon lost any squeamishness about wringing their necks. It was surprising what you could do when you got hungry enough.

'I think it's time we moved our food supplies,' Jas said. 'Maybe the supermarket, locked and secure, is a bit obvious to the dogs.'

Andrew nodded. He had been saying that all along, but Jas wasn't easy to persuade sometimes. In this case, he could understand why. The locked building afforded a lot of protection, and it would be an arduous job to move every single can and bottle from there to the theatre, which they had now made effectively their home. They had a car, but only limited fuel, and it wasn't likely they would find more anytime soon.

'You never know if we might need it one day to outrun the Jinx, either,' Jas had said.

'Let's fill a few carts each day,' suggested Andrew. 'Take back as much as we can, then lock up and do some more the next day.'

'Okay,' Jas nodded. 'Race you.'

Still carrying the pipe, Jas ran off down the street and back to the supermarket, with Andrew whooping and laughing behind her.

'Cheat!' he yelled. 'You never give me fair warning!'

The door was locked with a heavy chain and padlock, and Andrew and Jas each had a key chain around their neck. Jas placed the pipe against the doorframe, then unlocked the door just as Andrew rounded the corner.

'Er … Jas,' he said.

'What?' Jas didn't look around.

'Jas!'

Taken by the urgency in his voice, she span around just as a fist hit her full in the face. She fell back against the door, and the glass shattered under the impact. But her thick coat buffered her. Jas was dazed, blood poured from her nose and her eyes stung, but instinct made her shake off the fugue as she pulled herself up against the door. The pipe had fallen under her; she could feel the pressure bruising her back as she looked around at the ragtag band of wounded dogs. She recognised the stocky one who had been hit by the first arrow. He had a belt tied tightly around his leg, but blood still oozed from the wound. He was holding Andrew with one of the other boys. Towering over her was the boy who had witnessed her murder of their leader.

'Bastards! You killed Rocket!'

'This is our town,' Jas said.

'Shut it!' the boy yelled, kicking out at her.

Jas ducked in time to avoid getting his shoe in her face. His foot hit the broken glass door, crashing through it, and he cursed as a jagged piece of glass ripped through his jeans and sliced a deep groove into his calf.

Jas used the opportunity to roll. Grabbing the pipe, she was up on her feet and swinging it at the boy's head before he managed to pull his leg free.

The pipe hit, but it was only a glancing blow and not enough to daze him.

Andrew used the distraction to kick the wounded leg of the boy holding him. His captor crumpled in pain, and Andrew ducked free and away from the other boy and set off down the street.

Jas was ready. She swung again at the boy nearest to her, smashing the pipe down on his arm. She heard bone break, the boy screamed, and she backed away into her only haven, the supermarket doorway. She saw tears of pain glide down the boy's grubby cheeks. He staggered against the side of the building. Then he pulled himself upright; a look of cold determination on his face.

From the rooftop Andrew saw Jas back into the doorway. He set all the arrows free on the boys, but this time they were ready and dodged away with barely a scratch.

'There's just the two of 'em,' yelled the new leader, who was clearly brighter than the red-haired one had been. 'We can take 'em!'

His wounded comrades didn't look so certain. The new leader glanced around him, nursing his broken arm, but the backup he wanted wasn't there. The stocky boy's leg was now bleeding profusely and he fell to his knees, face pasty with blood loss and pain. Two of the other boys had been injured by the previous onslaught of arrows. One had a filthy rag tied around his arm, while another was holding his side as blood seeped out over his fingers.

Jas knew they were a sorry bunch and could so easily be crushed. She felt a momentary pang of pity for them, but swallowed it and ran out of the supermarket swinging the pipe. An insane roar poured from her lips. She smashed the pipe into the leader's face before he could react. His nose burst, his lips exploded, and blood sprayed into Jas's face. She blinked. Then swung again. The boy stood there, raising his undamaged arm in an attempt to protect his face, but the pipe landed true and he fell hard onto his knees. The pipe landed again. This time it sent the boy sprawling backwards, his spine arched at an unnatural angle, and a sickening crack echoed through the high street. He was dead before he hit the concrete.

The others stared on, already defeated. They had never seen such brutality. They had witnessed the Jinx arriving, slaughtering the men and stealing female family members while they cowered in dark holes afraid for their lives. They thought they were tough, but Jas scared the hell out of them, and they crumpled to the floor and waited to die.

Jas turned to the remaining dogs. 'I gave you a chance,' she said. 'And you didn't take it. There's no going back from that.'

Screaming. Blood. Gore. Snapping bone. Crying. Pleading. Jas's world descended into a red mist of violence and survival. She had to do it. She had to protect Andrew.

Andrew gently prised the blood-slick pole from her hand.

'Enough,' he said, and she met his eyes while shuddering for breath.

It was getting harder to survive. There would be more dogs, and maybe next time they wouldn't be so easy to beat. It should have been a small battle. They could have let the others live. But Andrew knew they had to win, and the risk of the dogs returning later for revenge or out of sheer desperation made it imperative to end it there.

'Sorry,' said Jas. 'You shouldn't have to see this.'

'I'm not a kid anymore,' said Andrew. 'I grew up two years ago when the Jinx arrived.'

Jas nodded. Andrew had grown into a gangly lad of 14. He was tough and funny and she loved him as if he was her younger brother. She wiped a hand across her bloodstained face.

'I need to clean up,' she said.

'Yeah. But not too much. You look more male with the grime in place …'

11

After dragging the dead bodies over to the wasteland, Jas and Andrew returned to the theatre with two supermarket trolleys full of cans. They stacked them up behind the safety curtain on the stage. It was cool inside the theatre, making it almost a perfect larder – not that it mattered with canned food particularly, but it felt like the right place to store them.

In the star dressing room, which they had long ago adopted as their bedroom, they had sleeping bags, blankets, pillows and two couches. It had its own *en suite* toilet, sink and a shower that no longer worked.

Jas picked her way through the mess of clothing and went to the sink. They had running water, but it was cold. Washing hadn't been a high priority on their agenda since the shower packed up, but occasionally they braved the cold and took turns to wash using water they poured into the sink. Even so, Jas always insisted that Andrew brushed his teeth regularly, and she too kept to this regime diligently, because there was no hope that they would ever find a dentist, sane or otherwise, among the remnants of humanity.

Jas filled the sink and washed her face and hands in the cold water. The water turned pink as soon as she submerged her fingers. They had lots of bars of soap and body-wash taken from the supermarket but it had been over a week since she had washed properly and the grime was already creating grooves in the creases around her neck. As Andrew had said, she looked more male when she was dirty, so she rarely kept her face too clean. That day though, Jas felt the need to wash more than usual.

Her bruised nose stung as she swilled her face, washing away the blood that clogged up her nostrils. She pressed the skin lightly. Fortunately there was nothing broken, but her eyes felt puffy and she knew she would be sporting at least one black eye for the next few days.

'Sometimes a girl just has to feel clean,' she murmured, catching sight of her face in the dressing room mirror.

Her body ached from the fight and her muscles screamed as she massaged soap into her arms, rinsing them off with a small plastic cup. The water in the sink turned black and she ran it out. She refilled the sink, this time submerging her head. She scrubbed at her scalp. Bits of blood and gore were lodged there in a stubborn mass. She picked up the soap and lathered it over her head, swilling more water over her scalp with the cup. She washed her head several times before what little hair she had began to squeak, signifying it was clean. Then she rubbed her hair dry while examining her reflection.

The dark brown eyes helped somehow with her male disguise. Jas thought she would look more like a girl if she had been born with pale eyes. Somewhere in the back of her mind she remembered her eyes as being blue. She pushed the memory aside as false: eye colour couldn't change, any more than gender could. These days, she was leaner and stronger than she had ever been. Despite having plenty of cans, she and Andrew limited their food intake, eating only what they needed and never any more. Jas was always afraid that one day they would run out – which was why they supplemented their diet with the birds caught in the traps. The shortage of food had given her figure an androgynous shape. Her breasts were far smaller and easier to disguise than before, and her hips were so lean that there was barely a womanly curve; particularly when she was dressed.

Jas slipped on a set of clean clothes. Men's jeans, two sizes too large, belted in with a sloppy T-shirt bearing the wording 'The Dead Tolerate the Living'. She had found the T-shirt on one of her excursions into the remains of the city. It had been on sale at Affleck's Palace. Part of the building had still stood, but the whole front corner had been ripped away as though someone had sliced a giant knife across it. The front shops were exposed, the clothing and goods spoilt, but around the back, Jas and Andrew had found the racks of T-shirts.

Jas was shivering after the cold wash and so pulled on her thick fleece. She had taken to bandaging her chest to make it appear flatter, and it was far more comfortable than the threadbare bras she had worn in the past. With her short cropped hair and emaciated frame she appeared very much like a teenage boy. She could still see her former self reflected in the sharp cheek bones, but she knew she could fool anyone into thinking she was male. It was a form of self-belief. She thought of herself as male: her actions and words just followed suit.

Some of her disguise came from studying Andrew. The boy had a particular way of walking, he slouched as though his height embarrassed him, and his hands were always in his pockets. Jas deliberately mimicked him, especially on those rare occasions when they met a pack of dogs. Except that she avoided walking with her head down, unlike Andrew. She was always alert and on the lookout for trouble.

Andrew knocked on the door just as Jas finished dressing.

'I've unpacked the trolley. Stacked the cans in order of what they are.'

Jas opened the door and smiled. 'You're so OCD. Next you'll be cleaning this place up in order to make it more habitable for the rats.'

Andrew laughed. 'Nah. I don't wanna encourage them.'

They made dinner: cold baked beans and tuna.

'I'd go a bundle for a slice of bread,' Jas said.

Andrew nodded. 'Some fresh eggs would be nice.'

They craved foods that were hard to get. Cheese, yoghurt and all other dairy products were high on the list. Jas listened as Andrew listed his favourite foods. *In the old days it was 'What would we buy if we won the lottery?',* she thought. Now the most important thing to them was food. Money and wealth meant nothing. You were only as rich as your larder, because without food they had no chance of survival.

'Jas, don't you sometimes think we should, maybe, leave here and try to find other people?' Andrew said.

'You know what happened the last time we tried to make nice,' she answered. 'I'm not saying there aren't some decent folks left in the world, but how do we know who to trust?'

Andrew's mind slipped back as he recalled the early days. He hadn't thought about the Rivers family for a long time. But he remembered they had seemed genuine, and he and Jas had let them into their lives …

The Rivers family consisted of a mum, dad and two brothers, both older than Andrew. The eldest brother, Nathan, was 19, and at first Andrew looked up to him, followed him around.

The family were all for sharing the food in the supermarket, but then the mum and dad, Christine and Warren, became greedy. Jas had to talk to them, explain the need for rationing. Not that it did much good. Christine and Warren just hid from her the extra food they took. Jas had been keeping a really close eye on the rations, otherwise she might not have noticed.

When Jas eventually confronted them, Warren became threatening. The family, Nathan included, turned on Jas and Andrew as though they were the drain on the resources.

They had all been bunking in the supermarket at that time. Jas filled a trolley full of food and moved her and Andrew back into the theatre. The tensions relieved a bit, except that Warren decided he would only let Jas and Andrew have food as and when he pleased. It made Jas furious. The supermarket was their place, and they had let the Rivers family in out of kindness. Even so, she didn't want conflict. She and Andrew hadn't yet learnt how tough they needed to be in order to survive.

'We'll drive out and find another place to eat from,' Jas said.

But that was easier said than done. They didn't have much fuel, and most of the surviving stores in the area had already been picked clean, or made into territory by surviving, unfriendly dogs. Jas was forced to go back to Warren and beg for food.

Things became worse when Nathan started to notice that Jas wasn't quite like other boys. She tried to avoid him but it wasn't always possible, because they had to return to the store almost every day to get the rations Warren allowed them.

'This is ridiculous,' Jas said one night. 'This was our home. We found the place first and now we're at the mercy of that jerk. I'm not putting up with this any longer.'

The next day, Jas went out alone. When she came back she had a sack full of weapons.

'Where did you find those?' asked Andrew.

'Army and Navy store. I spotted it the day we went into Manchester to find new clothes.

Andrew emptied the bag. He found automatic crossbows and arrows, two flare guns, three boxes of flares and two hunting knives.

Andrew looked at the weapons but said nothing. He remembered the day the looters broke into his house. Jas didn't know that while she had showered he had opened the living room door and had seen what she had done to her potential rapists.

'We're going to defend ourselves,' she said. 'I have to make sure you survive, Andy. No matter what.'

Andrew kept his eyes on the weapons and wondered how she knew what to do with them.

'Tomorrow we're going to start practicing with these,' Jas said. 'We'll plan our attack on the supermarket and regain control of our supplies.'

'Maybe we should just move away?' he suggested.

Jas looked around the theatre, her eyes falling on the crumbling walls, the ruined curtains and the stained seats.

'Strangely I feel safe here. I don't know why. The Jinx never entered, did they? In fact it was their earthquake that made us go out to them for fear that the roof would fall on us.'

Andrew knew what she meant. He had been happier since they had returned to the theatre, even though the supermarket was more convenient for provisions. There was something about the atmosphere that made him feel invisible. The theatre was their home and the thought of leaving it made them both feel insecure.

The next day Jas and Andrew returned to the supermarket. Jas was calm when she asked for provisions, and for once Warren was being reasonable. She didn't reveal her weapons; in fact they'd left them back at the theatre in order to keep them hidden until they knew how to use them properly.

'I've put in a few extra things for you,' said Warren, smiling. 'Thought we might start to patch up this silly argument.'

'Really?' said Jas. She was suspicious of Warren's change of heart. It didn't seem genuine, but she pretended to go along with it.

Later, after they had returned to the theatre, Jas and Andrew entertained themselves by having a mock fight with wooden swords on the stage, like characters in a play.

'I'm too hot,' said Jas, pulling off her fleece. Underneath she was wearing a sloppy T-shirt, which she also removed. She had removed the bandages earlier and so was merely wearing a vest top. Stripped down like this it was obvious what she had been hiding.

Suddenly Nathan came out of the wings, applauding. 'Well that's the best performance I've ever seen.'

Andrew laughed. He still liked Nathan and didn't immediately grasp that really he meant Jas's daily performance as Andrew's older *brother*. Jas, though, was instantly wary, realising that Nathan must have followed them back to the theatre, probably on his dad's instruction.

'You kept that well hidden,' said Nathan, his eyes shining.

Jas's face fell at the realisation her secret was out. 'Obviously I have good reason to protect this secret,' she said. 'Are you going to tell your dad?'

'No.'

'Good on you, mate,' said Andrew, but he didn't like the smile that played on his friend's lips.

'Things are going to change around here though,' Nathan said. 'I think we need to talk about this, privately.'

As Jas glanced over him, Andrew suddenly realised Nathan's meaning.

'You bastard!' he said 'She isn't a piece of meat.'

'If you want food and drink and your secret kept, then I say she is,' retorted Nathan.

'No,' said Jas. 'You can fuck off, Nathan. And if you try this stunt again I'll tell Warren you're following me around because you're gay. I'm sure he'd love that.'

Nathan, though, was sure of himself, and the next day when Jas and Andrew went back the supermarket for their food rations, Warren refused to let them in.

'Nathan tells me you have a secret stash, so from now on this place is ours.'

Andrew and Jas walked for a day and half before they found another place with a few remaining cans of food and some dented cans of drink; but the area was full of dogs, and the dogs were more dangerous than the Rivers family.

As Jas and Andrew hid from the gangs, managing to take and carry only a few cans, Jas wished she had brought the crossbows. At least then they could have fought for a little more food.

After that they started to set traps for the pigeons. A cardboard box, supported by a stick attached to a rope, and some crumbs left underneath, soon attracted the starving birds. Unfortunately this meagre source of poultry wasn't enough to sustain Andrew and Jas.

'I'll speak to Christine,' Jas said. 'Throw ourselves on her mercy. Maybe I'll even tell her the truth about Nathan and his threat. We're both women; surely she won't like the thought that her son tried to blackmail me for sex.'

Travelling back, they found a small mini with fuel, and they climbed inside, driving back to the Army and Navy store where Jas had found the flare gun and crossbows. They filled bags with all the remaining flare packs and all the arrows. The store had a selection of walking boots and thick warm coats that they could use as bedding on the coldest nights in the theatre. They kitted themselves out with Timberland boots and hauled an armful of the coats into the back seat of the car. Then they drove back to the theatre in much better spirits than they had been. The car would help them travel farther for food, and Jas hoped they would find more fuel along the way too.

They parked at the front of the theatre, but as they were unloading, Nathan and Warren turned up.

'Nathan's been telling me something very interesting,' said Warren. 'I know what you women are like about these things; and as the elder here, I think I'm qualified to perform a marriage. If that makes it any easier.'

'*What*?' said Jas. 'Are you completely insane? What is it about "No" that you fuckers don't understand?'

'I think that is incredibly selfish of you, Jas,' said Warren. 'We're trying to rebuild a race here.'

'Don't you get it?' Andrew protested. 'There's no point in rebuilding anything. The Jinx will just turn up one day and take it all away again.'

'Keep out of this, kid,' said Nathan. 'This is grown-up talk now.'

The hurt was evident on Andrew's face. He had been let down the final time by someone he truly admired. Jas put her hand on his shoulder.

'Jas is not for sale,' Andrew said firmly, and he raised the flare gun, pointing it directly at Nathan. 'Get the fuck out of here before I kill you.'

Nathan dived forward in an attempt to take the weapon. Andrew's hand was on the trigger and the shock of the sudden attack from his former friend made his finger clench. The gun went off in the older boy's face. Andrew fell backwards, clear of his assailant, as Nathan screamed in shock and pain.

Nathan's hair caught alight, his face was scorched, but the worst thing of all was how the flames ate his eyes. Nathan ran screaming through the streets, beating at his face as the fire licked over his skin. Warren chased him, eventually throwing his coat over the boy.

'I'll kill you. You little bastard!' yelled Warren, 'You've injured him. What use is he to me blind?'

'Dad?' sobbed Nathan.

Soon after that the Rivers family packed up and left the supermarket in search of a hospital or doctor that could help Nathan. Jas and Andrew placed the chain on the door the very same day, and in the following days they set their traps in and around the store. Never again would they allow their food to be stolen.

The Rivers family never returned, but plenty of others came and were scared away or killed as Jas and Andrew defended their food …

'The Jinx got them, I guess,' said Andrew, coming out of his recollection.

Jas shrugged. She knew he was talking about the Rivers family, but she didn't really care what had happened to them. Maybe they had found a better supermarket to live in; maybe that dogs had got them. Whatever had happened, it was a long time ago, and this town, no matter how deserted, was all theirs, and had stayed that way ever since.

Andrew went up onto the stage and began to rummage through the costumes.

'Hey, what about we dress up and create our own play? We haven't done that in ages,' he said.

'Okay,' said Jas, pulling herself up from one of the front row chairs.

Andrew bent down and began to empty a tea chest that was full of props.

'Ouch!'

'What is it?'

'Cut meself,' said Andrew.

'What on?'

It was a nail. A rusty, poisonous nail.

Within 48 hours, Andrew was bedridden. His skin was sallow and the wound from the nail livid and infected, lines of red following the course of the veins under his skin. Blood poisoning. And Jas had nothing to combat it.

12

There was a row of white goddesses high above the arched entrance. After two years left to the elements, the statues on the top of the Trafford Centre had a fine coating of green moss, but otherwise still looked in good order and held their harps and trumpets up to the sky with no less homage than they had from the time they were placed there.

'Mine's the one in the middle,' Donovan said.

'Good, because the one on the far left winked at me,' said Harvey. 'I think I'm in.'

Private Ashby had been on look-out duty as they traversed the M60, and it was he who had spotted the vast complex of buildings that made up the huge shopping mall that had once drawn thousands of people through its doors daily.

As they pulled into the deserted road that ran around the empty car parks, they noted that the building was surprisingly well preserved, with little damage to the structure or ground. It was unlikely the Jinx had been there, and it was a good place to try to search for provisions. Even so, Taylor wanted only a small squad to enter the mall for the initial inspection, and so his platoon, which now consisted of 96 men and six heavy-duty army trucks, parked outside.

There was a fuel station attached to the entrance to the main car parks. Donovan sent two of the drivers with their trucks to check if there was still fuel accessible in the tanks.

'Okay guys, leave the ladies alone and concentrate on the task in hand,' Taylor said as they climbed out of the first truck. 'It's improbable that we'll be alone in there. It's a mall and will potentially have some good vantage points on the upper tiers, so watch each other's backs.'

'Damn, boss! I was hoping for some time off,' said Ashby, waving at the statues. 'Hey sweetheart, wanna go out to dinner?'

Taylor laughed, then nodded his head toward the door. 'Move it soldier. The rest of you, keep alert. We may need you in there.'

Ashby grew serious and followed Taylor, Lieutenant Donovan, Sergeant

Harvey and Private Kline as they left the trucks and moved toward the entrance. The remaining troops took up positions around the entrance and the trucks.

Assault rifle gripped firmly in his hand, Donovan was surprised to find the automatic door opening for him.

'That's something,' said Harvey. 'The electricity is still working in this place.'

Taylor wasn't too surprised at this news. Over the past two years they had randomly discovered malls, supermarkets, hotels and even some houses that still had working electricity and running water. There wasn't much logic to it, but often it would be a whole street that had the utilities. Even so, they hadn't found anything running for over six months.

'Do you think there's a power station being manned nearby?' asked Donovan.

'Maybe we should find out,' Taylor said.

They went inside the building and were greeted by beige marble floors, ornate pillars and a fully stocked bar attached to a former restaurant.

'Don't get excited,' said Taylor. 'Even though this place doesn't look as though it's been looted, let's sweep the area first.'

Taylor moved ahead into the expansive eating area.

'The Orient,' said Harvey, reading the sign above the interior door.

'Good to know you can still read,' said Kline.

The Orient was a former eating space and was filled with tables, chairs and fast food restaurants of all sorts. Taylor indicated to Harvey, Ashby and Kline. They streaked off to the right while he and Donovan took the left.

'Mine's a Big Mac,' said Donovan, his mouth watering. He hadn't had a burger in so long he had almost forgotten the taste of it, but he imagined the tang of cheese and ground beef, pickles, mayonnaise and ketchup. He glanced wistfully at the faded menus hung above the tills.

'Focus,' Taylor ordered.

There was very little cover should some enemy decide to bombard them from the tier above, and Taylor was concerned to ensure that they wouldn't be caught out. Behind them the stage loomed. It would be a good place for a potential enemy to hide, even though the Centre seemed to be totally deserted. Taylor pressed his fingers in his mouth and gave a short whistle. Harvey stopped, looked across the stage from the other side and nodded.

'You two, check out backstage,' Harvey ordered to Kline and Ashby, and the two men filed off.

Taylor and Donovan moved on, but kept under the ridge of the upper tier. As they reached the other side of the food hall, Taylor spotted an ornate Egyptian-themed wall. It housed the lifts, and there was a sign indicating toilets. Taylor paused at the corner, glanced round and spotted an ice-cream stand next to a cold drinks stand. Bottles of water and coke remained intact on the stand, and as he and Donovan rounded the corner, they noticed that the ice-cream machine was still working.

'Pretty amazing find,' said Donovan. 'Looks untouched.'

'Yeah, but this is a big place. I still don't want to take any chances,' Taylor said.

Harvey, Ashby and Kline rounded the other corner.

'We've checked out the toilets. All clear,' said Harvey.

Taylor unclipped his shortwave radio. 'Berry?'

The radio hissed and then a muffled voice answered: 'Captain?'

'Secure the vehicles and bring everyone in.'

Once inside, the men were gathered around the former information desk and given orders to make a clean sweep of the Centre.

'There's a stack of maps here, which should give you some indication of how big this place is,' Taylor said.

Ashby picked a pile up from the desk and began to distribute them to the men.

'Keep your radios on and we can start packing up any supplies when we have the all clear from each unit,' Donovan said.

Taylor opened his map and gave orders for each group to cover specific areas. 'Like I said, there are lots of places to hide here. Don't take chances. Check everywhere.'

The men filed away, and although there were almost a hundred of them, they were rapidly lost in the shops and stores that filled the centre. Taylor, Donovan and Kline took up the search in Selfridges, moving through the ground floor, diligently searching every corner. The store retained the appearance of having been undisturbed prior to their visit.

'Christ, have you seen the goodies here: pâté, champagne, caviar,' Donovan said.

'Anything in tins, bottles or freeze-dried, you know what to do,' said Taylor. 'Is it just me that's noticing how *clean* this place is?'

Donovan stopped and ran his hand over the work surface of the sushi bar. 'This place looks like it's ready to welcome customers.'

'Precisely.'

After their initial sweep Taylor received confirmation from different groups of men that their areas were clear. Food and medical supplies were the main priorities.

'Captain? It's Harvey here. We've found a drugstore. There's evidence that some things have being disturbed. Over.'

Taylor looked at the radio. 'Harvey, have you swept the area?'

'Yes sir,'

'Good. I'll be over there as soon as I can. Ashby?' Taylor said.

'Sir?'

'Get the trucks to the loading bay.'

'Loading bay?'

'Yes. There's got to be a back door to every one of these shops. Find the way in and let's start loading – food, clothes, bedding, and above all some champagne. This is the best find we've had in months.'

Taylor caught up with Harvey, Sonberg and Kline in a large Boots store, filling bags with packs of aspirin and antibiotics.

'Get everything you recognise,' Harvey instructed. 'We may not be this way again for a long time.'

Taylor walked around the back of the pharmacy counter and looked at the dispensing desk. Things were clearly disturbed there. Someone had rifled through the contents, looking for something specific. There was a medical reference book left on the work surface, open at a page on antibiotics.

'I see what you mean,' Taylor said as Harvey came up beside him. 'Looks like someone was here recently. No sign of them now?'

Harvey shrugged. Taylor glanced around. His men had pulled out drawers and opened cupboards, but one still remained undisturbed, and it was directly under the counter. It was the place where the pharmacist would usually store the large sharps bins, but Taylor noticed that the bins had been pulled out and left to one side. A grubby piece of fabric was trapped in the door. Taylor reached down and pulled at it.

A grunt and a loud hiss came from inside. Taylor stepped back, then glanced around to see that Harvey and the other two men were busy and hadn't noticed.

'Okay, that's enough,' said Taylor. 'Let's get out of here.'

Harvey was surprised, because they had barely filled one sack with meds. He looked up and saw Taylor watching the cupboard. Taylor nodded his head toward the door and, grasping his meaning, they made a show of leaving the store noisily.

As soon as he was sure he could get away with it, Taylor doubled back with Harvey. They were just in time to see a boy leaving the shop clutching a bag in his hands. The boy hadn't made any move to gather food, he had just taken medicine, and Taylor could see that he wasn't one of the destructive types they had come across. This kid had a motive. Taylor felt immediately sympathetic to him. He shouldn't be out alone, and they'd sworn to help survivors where they could. Not that they had come across that many worthy ones, if the truth be told, but even so, occasionally they found a jewel. This kid looked just like that kind of gem.

After all, the kid had shown good skills already. He had hidden silently and gone completely undetected by his men. If Taylor hadn't spotted the fabric sticking out from the cupboard, he might not have noticed him either.

Taylor and Harvey hunkered down behind a large tropical plant pot as the kid looked back over his shoulder. It was as though he knew he was being followed. From this vantage point, Taylor could observe him undetected. He had close-cropped dark hair, was wearing sloppy jeans and a huge fleece, all of which were several sizes too big for his skinny body. He was covered in grime. Even from this distance Taylor could see the dirt gathering around the creases of his neck.

The boy stopped and gazed into the window of a women's shop. The mannequins were dressed in skimpy dresses. Taylor thought he knew what the boy was thinking: it had been a long time since any of them had seen a woman, and like his colleagues he was drawn to the female shape revealed in the clothing.

'I can handle this,' Taylor said. 'Go back to the drug store and carry on loading up.'

Jas didn't notice Taylor following her as she sneaked past the clothing shop, narrowly avoiding three other men moving through the mall. They looked like soldiers, but Jas didn't trust their uniforms and certainly didn't like the look of the weapons they were carrying. The men were searching every corner of the place and clearing it of as many supplies as they could carry.

She was disappointed that she couldn't look around now, but it was probably just as well, since she really had to get back to Andrew. She had never left him alone for this long before. If he hadn't been so ill she would have brought him with her. She glanced down at the paper bag containing the antibiotics. She prayed they were the right thing and would cure the boy.

So far the excursion had taken a few hours. She had driven around looking for a likely place before she had remembered the Trafford Centre. She hadn't been holding out much hope of finding anything there, but had been pleasantly surprised when she entered and found the place empty and untouched.

After that she hadn't wasted much time. She had visited the Centre many times in the days before the Jinx and knew where the pharmacy was. When she had arrived and begun to wade through the mountains of medication, she had become unsure which she needed, but fortunately had found a medical book and a full directory of medication on the pharmacy counter. After comparing Andrew's symptoms with those described in the book, Jas had confirmed what she had first thought: Andrew had an infection in his wound. She had gathered up some clean dressings, antiseptic creams and lotions.

Before leaving him, Jas had asked Andrew several times if he was allergic to anything, and he had insisted he wasn't. However, he had been feverish and a little confused. So despite his protestations Jas was still worried about administering penicillin – which would have been easiest treatment, since there were packets of the medicine on the shelves. After reading about the options she had decided to look for another type of antibiotic called erythromycin. The book recommended it for people who were allergic to penicillin. She had had no idea if this would work, but couldn't see any other choice. At the last minute, she had put a couple of packets of penicillin in her bag also. Then she had heard the soldiers moving around in the store and decided to hide from them.

She had realised there was no way she could beat these guys alone and without her traps set up. She couldn't help Andrew if she was wounded, either. She was really worried about him. Letting him die, or at least lose a limb due to infection, just wasn't a failure she was willing to contemplate. After all they had been through, Jas couldn't live with the idea of losing Andrew now. All she had ever wanted to do was keep him safe, and she had done some terrible things to ensure that he remained unharmed.

Inside the cupboard under the counter she had stilled her breathing. She had hidden from multiple enemies before, always taking her own advice about picking her fights. Then someone had pulled her coat. Jas had let out and involuntary gasp, but when the cupboard hasn't been pulled open, had assumed she had still gone undetected.

She had waited for the soldiers to leave. They had been noisy and confident. Then Jas had crept out of the cupboard and back into the shop. From the doorway, she had watched the men move off in the opposite direction. Then she had hurried back toward Debenhams, as her car was parked near there. That was when she had seen the small band of soldiers heading her way.

The group were so confident that they were alone they never even searched the area. Even so, she kept her head down and waited until she heard their noisy chatter grow farther away.

Silence descended on the store. She waited. Then, when she was sure there was enough distance between her and the men, she stood up – and came face to face with one of them.

'Don't be scared,' Taylor said. 'No-one's going to harm you.'

He was American. Jas stared into cold grey eyes, wholesome features, but didn't believe for one minute anyone holding a gun would be a safe person to be around.

'I have to get out of here,' she said. 'I don't want anything. You can have it all. I need to go.'

'Hey, kid. There's enough here for all. Please, we aren't looking to hurt you,' Taylor said.

'Yeah? Then why are you searching the place? Why are you holding weapons ready to fire?'

Taylor lowered his gun. 'You're right. It must look like that to you. Only, normally these places are filled with …'

'Dogs,' Jas said. 'Wild kids who are more than a little bit crazed.'

'Dogs?' Taylor laughed. 'Good name for them. Yeah, they are crazy all right.'

Jas found herself smiling, then stopped herself. Some instinct made her trust the American soldier, she didn't know why, but even so she resisted it. Trusting anyone was foolish and a mistake she couldn't afford to make.

'I have to get this medicine to my brother,' Jas said. 'He's got a wound. An infection.'

'Maybe we can help?' Taylor said.

'No.'

'Kid, how long have you and your brother been alone?'

A rack of clothes toppled over behind Taylor and he swivelled round, gun ready.

'Don't shoot! Don't shoot!' a voice cried out.

There was a man behind them. He was short and lean from hunger, like everyone was these days. His dark, wavy hair was unkempt and he looked kind and unthreatening in a 'mad professor' way. Jas was initially relieved by his presence. It took the emphasis away from her, as all she wanted to do was slip quietly back home to Andrew.

'My name's Gerald Avery. I'm a doctor. I was listening to the boy say his brother was sick.'

Jas stared from one to the other of the men, ready to flee.

'Please. I'm telling the truth. Tell me his symptoms,' Gerald said. 'You need to make sure you've got the right thing or it won't work.'

There was something unsettling about his eyes – they had seen things that were none too pleasant, she was sure of it. But then, hadn't they all seen horrors they had to live with? Even so, Jas felt uncertain of Gerald. His appearance was benign but his eyes frightened her.

'He cut himself on a rusty nail,' she explained. 'We washed it but he got really sick. His face and arms feel funny.'

'What do you mean, funny?' asked Gerald.

'Stiff, crampy.'

'Tetanus,' said Gerald. 'I'm sure of it. He needs a tetanus and diphtheria shot and a dose of tetanus immune globulin as soon as possible. Let me see what you have for him there?'

Jas handed over the medicines reluctantly, explaining why she had chosen erythromycin.

'You did a good job there,' said Gerald.

'I have a degree in biology and chemistry,' Jas said without thinking.

Both Gerald and Taylor looked at her in surprise, as neither of them had thought she was old enough.

'Look,' said Taylor. 'I know neither of you know us, but we've been combing the country, looking for recruits. I think you're both resourceful, and we could use your sort in this fight against the Jinx.'

'You're fighting the Jinx? That's crazy, you can't possibly win,' Jas said.

'We've learnt some things in the last two years,' Taylor replied. 'I'd be willing to share them with you, if you and your brother join us. You too, doc. The more men the better.'

'I'm not much of a soldier,' Gerald said. 'But I could certainly help heal wounds.'

Gerald and Taylor shook hands.

'My … brother is only 14,' Jas said. 'I'm not sure about this. We don't know if we can …'

'Trust us? Of course you don't. Which is why we have to prove ourselves worthy of it first. Come on,' said Taylor. 'Come meet the other guys. Hey, what's your name, kid?'

'Jas,' she said without thinking.

Taylor weighed her up for a moment, and a slight frown furrowed his brow as he looked her up and down. 'Nice to meet you, Jas.'

He felt there was something not quite right about the boy, but couldn't put his finger on it. Clearly he was older than he looked, but the skinny frame in baggy clothes gave the impression of youth. He was, however, smarter and more mature than his appearance suggested. Taylor determined to take his own advice about trust as well, and to keep a close eye on this Jas.

13

'This is private property and you're trespassing. We prosecute thieves.'

The man was tall and thin with closely cropped hair that looked like the military haircuts the soldiers were wearing. He had appeared from the doorway of a jewellery shop just down from the chemist's in the mall, and his features were serious. He reminded Jas of a weasel, and her danger alarms were firing off on all cylinders. This man was a dog, but a very different kind of dog. She wasn't sure yet how far the damage went, but she understood he was nothing like the soldier he was talking to. He was wearing what appeared to be a kind of uniform. A bright red blazer and black trousers pressed with a perfect seam down the front. A white shirt and a black tie finishing off the ensemble. Such pristine clothing was a rarity in these times.

Another man appeared from the shop doorway. This one had a side parting and comb-over but wore the same uniform, and Jas again felt a strange prickle of anxiety at the sight of him. She expected more men to appear, and her eyes darted around the mall, looking for the flame-red jackets.

Taylor kept his weapon lowered and held out a hand in a placating manner. He was a soldier but hadn't forgotten the prime rule: talk first, fight only if you have to.

'We're not looking for trouble, just supplies. We'll only take as much as we can carry and then we're gone.'

'You'll put everything back and leave,' said Comb-Over.

'Look,' said Jas, 'I need this medication. My brother is sick.'

'Do you have a prescription for that?' asked the first man. His piercing green eyes were bloodshot, the whites a strange and unhealthy yellow.

'Are you crazy?' Jas said.

The answer was in the men's eyes. There was a strange, possessive determination in the gaze of the first man, and the second mimicked his expression with clone-like ease. They looked insane, and their movements were strangely robotic, like they were going through the motions, fulfilling duties for which they were once paid.

'I'm a doctor, if that helps,' said Gerald. 'I've advised this young man what he needs. We are just going back to the pharmacy now to get the shots, and I'll be the one to administer them.'

Taylor began to lead the way back to the pharmacy. For a moment the two men in the red blazers didn't react.

Then Comb-Over raised his arm. Instinctively Jas looked at his hand and saw that he was carrying something. It looked like a remote control.

The hairs stood up on the back of Taylor's neck. He felt, rather than saw, Comb-Over raise his arm, and knew without doubt that there was a weapon in it. He turned and kicked out his leg, and the black square thing was knocked from the man's grasp. It skittered across the marble floor and Comb-Over screamed, holding his arm outward. His wrist was bent at an unnatural angle and was clearly broken. He crumpled to his knees, his eyes glazing in shock. Spittle dripped down his chin and fell on his pristine blazer, leaving a dark stain on the vibrant red. The blot grew, and it was unnerving to see the imperfection there. Then the man began to laugh. It was a cold, manic chuckle.

Jas felt her nerves burning with adrenaline. The first man dived at Taylor, but Jas was ready for him. She swept her leg out, catching the man unawares as she kicked his feet from under him. He tripped over, falling head first into the large plant pot. There was a dull thud as his head collided with the side of the pot. Then he slid to the ground dazed, a red blotchy bruise appearing on his forehead. If it hadn't been for the blood trickling down into his left eye, the fall would have appeared comical.

'Check them over please, doc,' Taylor said. 'I think I broke that one's wrist. It's hard to estimate what reasonable force to use with these crazies.'

He retrieved the little black box and held it up. 'Taser,' he said. 'Now I know why this place is so empty. These guys have been keeping it looter-free.'

'Just the two of them?' asked Gerald, gazing round.

Taylor spoke into his radio: 'Donovan, we've got an issue with some crazies in red blazers. Put everyone on full alert. Sweep this place again. Look *everywhere*.'

'They are security for the centre,' Jas explained. 'I'd forgotten about them. I had a friend who worked in the book store. She told me once that the Red Coats were the Trafford Centre's private police force.'

Several of Taylor's men came running in their direction. They surrounded the two Red Coats while Gerald gave them first aid.

'Why are you helping us?' asked the first man. 'You're looters.'

'No,' said Taylor. 'We're what's left of the army, and these two are survivors.'

'How many more of you are there?' demanded Harvey, pulling Comb-

Over up into a seated position.

Neither of the men answered. Comb-Over sat back against the glass of a shop front, rocking back and forth like an agitated in-patient. The other man, though, was silent and sat calmly watching the soldiers as they darted in and out of the shops, this time searching more thoroughly for signs of life.

'Get those vans loaded up,' Taylor told his men, then turned back to the Red Coats. 'Listen, you two. We're taking what we need. There will still be plenty left for you. Or you can come with us and join up, since you're so keen on law-enforcement.'

'Join up?' said Comb-Over. Spittle dripped from his lips as he leered insanely up at the Captain. Jas noticed his rotten and pointed teeth. She was reminded of a character from some horror story featuring a demon dressed as a clown.

'We've a job to do, Yankee,' said the first Red Coat. 'We were left in charge here and we have to protect the stores.'

'Who's going to care whether or not you continue to do that job?' asked Taylor.

Comb-Over stopped rocking, and the soldiers looked at each other. Taylor glanced around, this time really seeing the mall for what it was. It was perfectly clean and preserved.

'Who's been cleaning this place? You guys?' he asked. 'Why hasn't anyone, not even you, taken things from the stores?'

The Red Coats said nothing.

'Where are you living?' asked Donovan, but again the men gave no answer. 'You won't tell us? Don't worry, we'll find it.'

Donovan went off with another search party. It didn't take Taylor's men long to discover a storage room in a frozen food store, with clear signs that two men had been living there for some time.

'We've found their living quarters, and you need to see this,' reported Donovan.

'What is it?' Taylor asked.

A bead of sweat lined Donovan's forehead and his face was pale. 'I'd rather show you.'

'Don't let them out of your sight,' Taylor ordered the men guarding the Red Coats.

The frozen food store was on the second level of the mall, and Taylor followed Donovan up there. Jas went too. She wanted to see what had freaked the lieutenant out so much. She suspected he had been sick, or was trying not to be ill in front of his men. As they entered the front of the store, Jas noticed that this one at least looked as though the men had been using the products. The fridges were empty of anything that would have been perishable, but the chest freezers still had things in them.

Donovan nodded to the back of the store and Taylor moved forward. He glanced down into one of the freezers, then took an involuntary step back.

'Jeezus.'

'What is it?' asked Jas.

'This isn't for your eyes, kid,' said Donovan.

'I'm not a kid, and I've survived this shit hole for two years without the bloody army telling me what to do,' Jas snapped.

'Knock yourself out,' said Donovan, but a sly smile appeared on his pale lips as Jas moved toward the freezers.

The glass sliding doors were steamed up, so she had to peer closely into the chest. At first she couldn't make sense of what she was seeing, then shapes began to form before her eyes. A hand, fingers outstretched, lay next to the lower part of a human leg, foot still attached. There was a male torso, cleaved into two pieces. The pieces had been positioned in such a way as to resemble cuts of meat from an animal, but they hadn't been skinned, and the hair on the torso left Jas no room to deceive herself as to what she was seeing. The head was the worst. It was half buried amongst the other body parts and facing upwards, its frozen eyes wide open. The expression of terror on the face was awful, as was the mouth, which seemed to be open in a silent scream.

'Oh God,' said Jas. 'You think they …? Are those men …?'

'Cannibals?' asked Taylor. 'Probably. We've seen a lot of that along the way.'

'But that's insane. All this food. This entire mall is crammed with things to eat. The two of them could live here forever and never starve.'

'It is insane,' Taylor said. 'That's the point. Look Jas, you and your brother aren't safe out there alone. As society deteriorates to the last man, this is only going to get worse.'

'What are you going to do with them?' Jas asked.

Taylor looked at Donovan and then shrugged. 'Leave them to it, I guess.'

'They are killing innocent people who come in here to get food,' Jas said.

'Yeah,' Donovan murmured. 'That's why this place hasn't been looted. Every time someone tries, they get zapped.'

A deep moan followed by a soft whimpering echoed through the empty store.

Donovan span around, hushing the soldiers, and they listened intently, trying to identify the sound. Jas thought she heard a rustling, like paper or cardboard scraping across a floor. She turned toward the sound and found Taylor by her side.

'There,' she murmured.

Taylor nodded and, with a wave of his hand, directed two of his men to move in toward what appeared to be a storage cupboard. The whimpering grew into a gentle sob. One of the soldiers reached for the handle and pulled the door open.

The cupboard was large and dark, and at first they could make no sense of the thing they saw inside. It was a mess of blood and sinew, a naked body that was only vaguely identifiable as female. Her legs and arms were skinned down to the bone. One breast was cut off in a clean sweep, and the wound was blackened as though it had been cauterised. The other looked perfect and unmarred. There was a plate with a knife and fork on a small table beside the body. The smeared remains looked like dried out Chinese food. Jas was reminded of Char Sui sauce with pork when she saw the shrivelled red stain marring the white porcelain.

Jas fought the urge to press her hand to her mouth. She was aware that her movements had to remain masculine at all times. She felt nauseous and turned away, unable to look.

'Harvey,' said Taylor into his radio. 'Get the doctor over here. Now.'

Jas found herself leaning against a fridge. Sweat poured from her, mingling with the grime on her face and hands, but the cold pouring out of the open unit didn't help her feel any better.

'That's the sickest thing I've ever seen,' Taylor said beside her.

'I'm glad Andrew wasn't here,' Jas answered. 'He's seen enough already. What kind of animal could do that?'

At that moment Gerald arrived and was shown in to the woman.

'Oh my God,' Gerald said.

He forced himself to kneel down beside her, then began an initial examination. But his hands shook as he pressed his fingers into the woman's neck, trying to find a pulse.

'She's dying,' he said quietly. 'And to be honest, it's a good thing. No-one could recover from that. Seems to me they were trying to keep her alive. They were eating her raw, piece by piece.'

Jas couldn't hold on any longer. She ran from the shop and vomited on the floor outside. Then she sank down by the doorway, back to the cold glass, legs splayed on the marble, looking out on what appeared to be a normal mall.

Gerald joined her a few minutes later. 'You okay?'

'That's the only woman I've seen in 18 months,' Jas said. 'And they did that to her.'

'Yeah. Guess we got lucky that they didn't find us before the soldiers did. Fuck, but I need a drink. There's whisky around here someplace, isn't there?'

Jas said nothing, but her ragged breathing began to steady and her racing heart slowly recovered its regular pace. She was strong, she could bounce back, but she wasn't sure she could ever forget what she had just seen. It outweighed the guilt she sometimes suffered for the crimes she had committed in the name of survival.

Taylor appeared next to them. He held out a flask to the doctor. 'Purely medicinal,' he smirked.

Gerald took the flask, unscrewed the top and took a huge swig. Then he held it out to Jas. She took the flask, sniffed the contents and sipped it, rapidly choking on the burning contents.

'Jack Daniels,' Taylor said. 'I'm not much of drinker, but at times like these, a dram of this stuff helps.'

Just as he pulled the flask to his lips, an explosion of gunfire echoed through the mall.

'What the fuck …?'

Taylor dropped the flask, sending its contents splashing out onto the marble floor, and Jas jumped to her feet and followed him as he ran full pelt back down the stairs to the shop where his men stood over the dead bodies of the two Red Coats.

'What the hell happened?'

'One of those bastards bit me,' said Ashby.

He held out his arm and showed Taylor the fierce bite. The skin was ripped; it was as though the Red Coat had tried to tear Ashby's skin off with his teeth.

'I hate to say it,' said Jas as she and Gerald caught up with Taylor, 'but that's probably the best result of the day.'

'What?' said Ashby, taken aback. His pale skin was blotchy, emphasising the red in his hair.

'Oh, not that you were bitten. I meant that these dogs were put out of their misery.'

Taylor looked at Jas as Gerald bent down to make sure the Red Coats really were dead. He had the feeling that the boy was tougher than he looked.

'I hate dogs,' she said, meeting his eyes coldly. 'You have to get them before they get you. Shoot them in the head too. Just to make sure.'

Taylor said nothing, but he suspected that Jas had seen and been through plenty in the last few years. He had a new respect for the kid. He knew instinctively that Jas had done everything to survive, but had still retained some sanity and common sense, which wasn't easy in these times.

'What about the woman?' Taylor said, turning to Gerald. 'Can you help her along?'

Gerald nodded. 'It's the only thing we can do.'

Gerald returned to the frozen food store and administered a lethal injection of morphine to the victim. He avoided looking at her one perfect breast, which reminded him that she might be the last woman left on Earth.

'Okay,' said Taylor. 'I'm going to go back to Jas's place with him and take the doc to see his little brother. Donovan, make sure the trucks are loaded and ready to move out. Also, make goddamn sure there are no more of these … dogs … hiding out here. This place is like a rabbit warren; there are so many nooks and crannies. And if you see one, shoot him. They will all be complicit in this shit.'

'That's okay. If the doc tells me how, I can give the medicine myself,' Jas said. 'Best you stay with your men.'

'No, it's best I take a look at him,' Gerald said, coming out of the freezer shop. 'It might be the wrong diagnosis.'

'That settles it kid, no arguments. We're coming with you, and you have my promise that you're safe with us.'

Jas felt the colour rising in her cheeks. She didn't want to fall out with the Captain, he was clearly a good man, but joining his group permanently was out of the question. Even so, she nodded. It would be good to get the doctor to check Andrew over and make sure he recovered. His life was all that mattered to her and she couldn't risk him, no matter how insecure she was about showing the two men their hide-out.

'Sir!' said Kline. 'We've found a huge transport freezer truck in the store's loading bay. It's got half a tank of fuel. Plus, the men have reported finding fuel at the petrol station. There's not much and the pumps aren't working, but they broke down into the tank.'

'That's going to come in very handy,' said Donovan. 'Fill up the freezer truck with food. And don't forget to put in some burgers. Tonight we're having a barbeque.'

14

Andrew was unconscious when they arrived back at the theatre. He was still wrapped up in his sleeping bag and his breathing was heavy and strained. Gerald kneeled beside him and began to examine the wound on his arm. The boy was feverish, and he only half woke during the check-up.

'It is tetanus,' said Gerald. 'Plus the wound is badly infected. These living conditions don't help.'

'Tell me about it, doc,' Jas said. 'But we've been safe here for two years.'

Gerald opened his small doctor's bag and retrieved a scalpel from an operating kit wrapped up in a velvet cloth.

'Captain, can I have that whisky again?' Gerald asked.

Taylor handed him the flask, which he had retrieved and refilled back at the mall, and Gerald poured some of the liquid over his scalpel, then immediately lanced the infected wound. Vile green pus poured from the cut and Gerald mopped it up on a clean bandage, squeezing at the wound until only blood came out. Jas watched on. Wounds didn't upset her – Andrew being ill did.

Gerald poured antiseptic into the cut, and fortunately Andrew had lapsed into a feverish sleep again and so didn't react to the stinging liquid. After he'd bandaged the wound, the doctor retrieved the tetanus and diphtheria vaccine from his bag and began to fill a new syringe with the liquid. He rapidly vaccinated Andrew, and gave him an injection of antibiotics at the same time.

'It'll be a few hours before we know if it's worked,' Gerald explained. 'Best to let him sleep now.'

'*If* it's worked? Is there a chance it won't?' Jas said.

'Yes. But the odds are stacked in his favour because we got to him quickly. He's fortunate in that respect. Tetanus is a killer.'

'Best vaccinate us all then, doc,' said Taylor. 'None of us is up to date. Our medical office got killed during an attack quite some time ago. One or two of us has first aid training, but it's not the same as having someone with you who really knows his stuff.'

They left Andrew sleeping and went out onto the stage. Taylor noted the cans of food, bottles of water and tins of Coke and lemonade stacked up high behind the curtain.

'You really have it going on here, kid,' he said.

'We've been careful,' Jas replied. 'We want to live. I *have* to protect Andrew.'

The troops arrived soon afterwards, and the men set up camp outside the theatre. At first Jas was nervous about their presence. She wasn't used to having so many people around. But despite her issues with trust, there was something about Taylor that made her feel safe.

'The Jinx attacked here,' Taylor said, looking around at the churned up pavements and road outside the building.

'Yes,' said Jas, 'and they've never been back.'

'I think that's their usual MO,' said Taylor. 'We've never known them to attack the same place twice. So hiding here was probably a good move.'

'What is your motivation, Captain?' Gerald asked.

'We're travelling the country, always taking different routes, and attempting to find survivors,' Taylor said.

That evening, true to his word, Donovan made a barbeque with the frozen burgers and sausages they'd taken and stored in the freezer truck. They sat around the camp fire, and despite herself Jas enjoyed the company of the Captain and his men. They were a lively bunch, always joking, particularly Ashby.

Occasionally Jas got up and went inside to feed water to Andrew. It was a warm night, and once he saw the boy was rallying, Gerald suggested they might bring him out to get some fresh air. Within a few hours he had revived a lot, his temperature had rapidly reduced and he was becoming more coherent. He also wanted to meet the visitors.

'It's not like you to trust anyone,' Andrew commented to Jas, as he propped himself up in his sleeping bag. 'They must be pretty special.'

Jas held the cup of water to his lips and helped him sip. 'They are … interesting,' she said. 'Proper soldiers, and their leader, their Captain – he's called Taylor – he's …'

Andrew was watching her carefully as she spoke. 'Interesting?' he smiled through cracked lips.

'I was going to say trustworthy. It's strange, but I just have this instinctual feeling that we should spend time with them. At least for a while. Plus they have food that we haven't eaten in years.'

Andrew looked around. 'They don't *know*, do they?'

Jas shook her head. 'I'm fooling them, just like I fool everyone. But I didn't think my disguise would live up to this much close scrutiny.'

'It's weird,' said Andrew. 'I can tell a mile off that you're … a girl. But when we're with others you do seem to almost …'

'What?'

'You seem to really turn into a boy, like it's some kind of magic.'

Jas fell silent. It was strange that Andrew had observed this side of her too. She had long believed that if she convinced herself she was a male then everyone else around her would just accept it too. Like role-play. Once she had put on the costume of Jas the man she forgot what being a woman was. The costume had become her, and in these dangerous times, she knew that this was a good thing, not a bad one.

'Come on then, if you really feel up to going out?'

'Yes I do. I'm really hungry too,' said Andrew.

Jas helped him up from his bed and draped a blanket around his shoulders. Tears sprang to her eyes at his words. He hadn't eaten for days, so this surge of interest in food was definitely a good sign. He was weak and needed a lot of support as she led him down the steps from the stage and out to the side exit, which took them closer to the soldiers' camp.

When they reached the camp fire, Jas placed a pile of coats and blankets down, creating a makeshift chair for Andrew. As he sat down at the fire, his eyes still fever-bright, she was relieved to see that the sickly tinge had already begun to diminish from his pale cheeks.

The smell of cooked meat made both of their mouths water.

'You're looking much better, young man,' said Gerald. 'Looks like we caught things in the nick of time.'

'Thanks,' said Andrew. 'Wow! Is that a beef burger?'

Donovan handed him a bowl with sausage and a burger in. 'You up to eating this?'

'You bet!' said Andrew, and he picked the hot meat up with his fingers and began to eat it greedily. 'Ow! Ow!' he said as the meat burnt his fingers.

'Slow down there!' said Jas.

'There's plenty more, so no need to panic,' Taylor laughed. 'Tonight we're saying rations be hanged. It was a good result. A good day.'

Ashby popped the cork of a bottle of champagne and handed Jas a plastic cup full.

'It's cold,' she said, surprised.

'Yeah,' Ashby said. 'Courtesy of this great freezer truck.'

A surge of happiness dared to push its way into Jas's chest, but she pressed it back, afraid to hope, afraid to have fun again. It was a peculiar sensation, and for a moment she couldn't recognise the swell of feeling. She thought it was excitement because of the food, but the company pleased her just as much, if not more.

She took the bowl offered by Donovan and then ate the sausage and burgers while glancing around at the men. Ashby and Sonberg were now doing a jig around a second camp fire. Ashby had a scarf around his head and the men laughed as he gave a very camp rendition of a coy female. Jas found herself laughing at his antics. She hadn't seen such sane behaviour in years, and it was a relief to find a reason to celebrate.

'So what's your story, doc?' asked Donovan, sitting down at the camp fire and handing him a cup of champagne.

Gerald took the plastic cup and stared into the flames for a while. The light cast shadows on his face. By then, all of the soldiers were gathered in clusters around various fires, food warming their bellies, alcohol colouring their cheeks. The small cluster around this fire included Taylor, Donovan, Kline and Harvey, as well as Jas, Andrew and Gerald.

'I was living in a village down south,' said Gerald. His voice was low, and the group fell quiet and listened. 'We were pretty self-contained and sat out the initial Jinx attacks without any problem for the first few months. Then, one day, they arrived in the village.'

No-one spoke as they waited for Gerald to finish.

'They took the women, including my wife, and killed the men. You know the story ...' Gerald said flatly.

'How did you survive?' asked Jas.

'I was out on a scouting trip, bringing back supplies,' Gerald said, and everyone nodded. This was what they all did on a daily basis. They combed the country like scavengers looking for food; all in the name of survival.

'After that,' Gerald said. 'There was nothing to stay there for. I've been looking for others, but you're the first normal ones I've found for a while. The rest have been ...'

'Dogs?' said Andrew.

'Yeah.'

Jas quashed the vague feeling of distrust that had made her dislike Gerald on their first meeting. She felt sad as he told his story, but not enough to shatter the new emotion that was building up inside her. She recognised it, but refused to admit it. The feeling was irrational and impossible, and no way could she allow it to cloud her better judgement.

The soldiers partied, but after eating, Jas and Andrew went back inside the theatre and slept in their little room for the night. Jas locked the door as she always did, but despite herself, for the first time in a long time, she wasn't feeling scared or vulnerable. Instead she was happy and hopeful. The soldiers might not really be able to defeat the Jinx, but being with them made her feel safe; and if it hadn't been for the doctor, Andrew would still be sick and would have probably died. Already the boy was looking more like his old self. He was flushed and happy. Full of good food, Jas was now sure that Andrew would recover and grow strong.

Jas gave Andrew another dose of his antibiotic medicine, then she curled up in her sleeping bag. Her stomach was fuller than it had been for a long time, and the wine had relaxed her enough for her to be able to feel the benefit of the company of the soldiers. For the first time since the Jinx had attacked, Jas allowed herself to feel there could be a future for them after all. A sigh escaped her lips as her body relaxed in the sleeping bag.

Taylor was genuine. He could be trusted. She knew it. And he was just what they had been waiting for. For once, the burden of their survival didn't weigh heavy on her heart. She fell asleep recalling the smile that had played on Taylor's lips as he watched Andrew eat his food, and it floated through her mind that what she had seen on his face was the same thing that hovered in the back of her own consciousness. The thing she was almost too afraid to admit. But still it was there, pushing into the corners of her mind, and it refused to be ignored. Hope.

15

The soldiers settled into a routine of living in and around the theatre.

'We've been constantly on the road for the past six months,' Taylor said. 'It's time we had a base again. Plus we can only sharpen our skills if we stay in one place. We were driven farther north because of the lack of gas and provisions where we were. Even so, to keep travelling just burns up valuable fuel.'

'Yeah. I understand.' Jas nodded.

Taylor enjoyed Jas's company but didn't quite know what it was he found so interesting or why he sought the kid out sometimes. When he wasn't training with his men, he relaxed in the theatre with Jas and Andrew, learning more about them. They were likely recruits, but he found Jas to be the most intelligent and charismatic.

'We want to train with you,' Jas said. 'It's like this: Andrew is young, but training could save his life. If anything happens to me I'd like to think he could handle himself.'

Taylor weighed this up. The kid had stamina – he had seen that already – and on making a sweep of the area his men had discovered the waste pile. At first he had wondered if Jas and Andrew were merely crazies that appeared to be sane, but the more he was around them, the more he realised that these ordinary kids had just done what was needed in order to survive. He had admired the strength he had seen in Jas's eyes the day they had killed the Red Coats. Taylor had known that to be the only solution after they had seen what the cannibals had been capable of. They couldn't have left them alive to attack any more poor, unsuspecting survivors. And what had impressed him the most about Jas was that she too had realised the need to end them. That was why he never mentioned the bodies they had found on the waste pile. He felt no need to question them. It was obvious that all they had done was protect themselves and their food.

Once a week the soldiers had a formal meeting. They gathered in the foyer of the theatre and discussed strategy for the forthcoming week. At these times Jas would hear Taylor give orders for reconnaissance missions, or food retrieval from the mall, or wider searches for fuel supplies. Sometimes they even discussed finding a permanent base.

'We should set up camp in the mall,' Donovan suggested. 'We have everything we need there and working electricity.'

Taylor thought it over. It was a huge landmark and one that should attract survivors in the area. That is, unless the Red Coats hadn't killed them all. But he felt uneasy every time he thought of the mall. He couldn't understand why it was still being fed electricity or how. He also didn't really get why the Red Coats had resorted to the things they had when there was food in abundance. It was as though in their crazy minds they had seen the food as off-limits to them. Even so, setting up base at the mall made a lot of sense, and he couldn't really justify not moving the camp there.

'How's your arm, Ashby?' Taylor said.

'Better. The doc gave me a shot and stitched it up,' Ashby replied.

'Good.'

'You worried he's going to turn into a crazy cannibal?' asked Gerald, overhearing the conversation and almost reading Taylor's mind.

Taylor smiled, but the curl of his lips was more cynical than pleasant. 'No. But I've seen some things that don't add up. I'm thinking maybe some kind of drug affected those guys. Perhaps they were some kind of experiment.'

'What do you mean?' asked Gerald.

'Well, you don't think the government are dead or *their* wives have been stolen by the Jinx, do you?' said Donovan.

Gerald frowned. He hadn't really thought about anything beyond surviving recently. 'You think there's some conspiracy?' he asked.

'Since this happened we don't trust anything,' said Donovan.

'The powers in charge are gone; this place is ours,' said Taylor. 'Even so, it's easy to be paranoid. Suspicion keeps us sharp. One thing that keeps bothering me though – I sure would love to know how the electricity still works in that place. There has to be a power station running. We need to do a recon of this entire area.'

As was the tradition of the soldiers when a dangerous and perhaps unnecessary mission presented itself, Donovan called for a vote. This time the soldiers were unanimous. They wanted to find out how the mall was being supplied, and whether or not their suspicion that their superiors were still alive somewhere was true.

Jas and Andrew sat on the counter in the theatre foyer as Donovan picked men to go out on the recon. She said nothing as she watched them, but she knew the area and thought she might even have an idea where the power station was.

'Jas?' said Andrew. 'What you thinking?'

'Heysham ...' she murmured. 'But I'm not sure.'

Andrew knew she was probably right – after all, she had been his science teacher and she had known about these things.

Taylor unfolded a worn map and placed it on the table that had once been the programme stall. He spread it open and the men gathered round.

This could take days, Jas thought. *And they'd still be no nearer.*

'This is how it's gonna work,' said Taylor. 'I'll go out with the first party. We'll search this area from here, to here ...'

From where she sat, Jas could just make out the red crosses Taylor was marking on the paper but not the scope of the area. She didn't like the idea that Taylor would be gone. She felt his influence kept the other soldiers calm and focused. She jumped off the counter and went up to the table, glancing down at the areas on the map that Taylor was recommending. They were all in the opposite direction from Lancashire.

'It's here,' she said, pressing her finger down. 'A nuclear power plant called Heysham. I'm sure that's the nearest.'

'You know your geography?' asked Donovan.

'I could show you,' said Jas. 'It's about two hours' drive.'

'You sure?' Taylor asked ,weighing her up.

Jas nodded.

'Okay. Show me.'

They packed up quickly, 20 men, all armed. Sergeant Harvey was driving. Jas climbed into the front seat of a truck between him and Taylor. In the back, the rest of the men sat quietly, armed and alert.

'Okay, kid, we're in your hands,' Taylor said as the truck pulled away from the theatre.

Jas glanced back. She saw Andrew talking to a couple of the soldiers, and a pang of guilt made her feel slightly nauseous. She didn't like leaving him, even now; but this could be important and she wanted to be part of it. She gave the first set of directions and Harvey turned left out of the theatre car park and out toward the motorway.

Since the arrival of the Jinx, Jas had rarely ventured out onto the roads and, other than for her brief trip out to the Trafford Centre, she hadn't been on the main motorways. She had noticed then that the roads were fairly bare. Some part of her mind had expected to find abandoned cars or dead bodies rotted down to the bone. It was a concept of the end of the world that had been firmly planted in her head from numerous movies. She recalled seeing one with Charlton Heston, *The Omega Man.* She remembered it well, because it had been based on a vampire novella she had read, called *I Am Legend.* The movie had shown images of dusty corpses still lying in the streets years after the apocalypse. This was after everyone had died of some obscure virus. And now she thought of it, in most catastrophe films everyone died from some germ warfare or flu virus or turned into zombies.

The reality of her dystopian world was far different from fiction.

Sometimes she thought about mankind's obsession with technology. She often wondered, in her wildest musings, if this was some kind of punishment for that obsession. Before the Jink had come, she had been addicted to her mobile phone, wouldn't have been without her laptop, or dishwasher – just like most people in the 21st Century. *Strange how things turned out*, she thought. Now they had nothing. The best tech was building a bonfire to cook food on and keep warm. Bows and arrows were the most effective weapons. But for all this, they hadn't learnt their lesson fully. Jas was aware how much they were still relying on their vehicles. Not her and Andrew, but Taylor and his army. She thought it might be a serious mistake. It was okay while they still had fuel, but what would happen when they ran out? They would all be restricted to whatever area they found themselves in.

'Look!' said Harvey.

Jas pulled herself out of her reverie. A huge fuel tanker lay abandoned on the motorway.

Jas's eyes widened. 'I was just thinking …'

'Pull over next to it,' said Taylor.

Harvey and a couple of the other soldiers got out of the truck. After assessing the tanker, they discovered it was almost full. There was no sign of the driver and no apparent reason why it had been left on the motorway.

'Is it out of fuel?' asked Jas.

Harvey climbed into the cab and bent down under the steering wheel. Within seconds he had hotwired the engine. It briefly sputtered into life, then died.

'Empty,' he said.

'How did you know?' asked Taylor. *There really is something unusual about this kid.*

Jas shook her head. She didn't know.

'You'd think the driver would have just used some from the back to fill his own tank, wouldn't you?' said Harvey.

'Get the empty fuel canisters from the back,' Taylor instructed, and two of his men hurried to the task and began to fill the canisters from the tanker. They always carried spares in case they came across a fuel resource, and this was an amazing find.

They refuelled the truck, then Harvey started the engine, but it had been standing for a while and fought to regain life.

'Goddamn battery,' Harvey said. 'Why is nothing ever easy?'

Just then the engine coughed into life and Harvey revved as hard as possible.

'You two,' Taylor said to the soldiers who had helped refuel. 'Take the tanker back to the theatre.'

'That will keep us mobile for a while,' Harvey said.

'Am I the only one who's starting to feel this is a little too convenient?'

Taylor said. 'Freezer truck waiting to be filled with a whole supermarket full of food we've not seen in two years, and now this tanker full of fuel just materialises.'

'Maybe the spell of the Jinx is wearing off,' said Jas. 'Our natural luck is recurring.'

'Spell?' repeated Taylor.

Jas shrugged. She didn't know why she had used those words exactly, or why she had been thinking and worrying about their fuel supplies moments before they had come upon the fuel tanker. It was all just coincidence, but it was a little strange. Jas wasn't naturally superstitious; she was a scientist by nature and didn't believe in magic. *Coincidence*, she thought as the soldiers climbed back into the truck and Harvey drove them on to their destination in Lancashire.

It was midday by the time they reached Heysham Power Station.

It was not far from what was once a suburban area, but the truck passed by piles of deteriorating buildings that were all that was left of previous civilisation. Driving on the motorways for most of the journey had spared Jas, Taylor and Harvey most of the sights of destruction left by the Jinx, but as they turned into the streets they could no longer avoid it.

A body had been pinned to the front door of one house. It was little more than skeletal remains, held in place by threads of fabric, but the corpse was grinning in the only way that a bare skull could, and it was macabre. After that, Jas kept her eyes on the power station as it loomed on the landscape like a gothic monstrosity. It was surrounded by a high fence and sat in the middle of a field just outside of the housing estate. Jas wondered how the occupants had felt about it, as most of them would have been able to see it from at least one window in their houses.

The power station appeared intact and unmolested.

As they drew closer, Jas saw a large sign hung on the gates. It was a warning: 'Electric Fence and Gates.'

'Strange,' said Taylor. 'But if this place is shut down it's unlikely that those gates are still electrified.'

Jas looked up at the windows. She saw lights on inside.

'It's not shut down,' she said. 'Look.'

'This is getting weirder by the minute,' Harvey said.

Taylor shrugged. It would answer a lot of questions if there were still people inside running the place.

'Stay here,' Taylor said to Jas as she made to leave the truck with him and Harvey. Jas wasn't used to taking orders and it annoyed her, but she obeyed him anyway.

Taylor climbed out of the cab and walked directly up to the gate. Harvey followed closely behind.

'Back away from the fence,' came a voice from nowhere. 'This is a military order.'

Taylor looked up to see a camera trained on him. 'I'm Captain Taylor Arch from the US attack force brought in to fight the Jinx,' he said. 'If there are any officials in there, I and my men would be more than happy to report for duty.'

'We don't care who you are, Captain,' answered the voice. 'You and your men need to leave this area or we will be forced to open fire.'

'Don't you understand?' Harvey said, running closer to the gate. 'We're soldiers!'

A warning shot pierced the atmosphere above the gates and flew over Taylor's head. He ducked down and away from the gates, pulled out his handgun, a semi-automatic Beretta, and pointed it in the direction of the cameras.

Taylor's men poured out of the back of the truck. One did a forward roll, then came up onto his knees facing the fence, his assault rifle in hand. Another ran in a crouched position round to the front, opened the cabin door and took up point behind it. Several others found places around and underneath the truck. But all were facing the fence.

More bullets hissed over their heads, but again they were warning shots and not aimed at any of the soldiers.

'Orders, Captain?' Harvey said.

'We're getting out of here,' Taylor answered. 'We know where we're not wanted.'

Taylor stood up, holstered his gun and turned his back on the gates.

'Stand down,' he ordered, and the men, surprised, backed away from their fighting positions and gathered around the back of the truck. Taylor followed them, and after a brief discussion the men climbed back into the truck.

Taylor opened the door and stepped up, sitting down beside Jas. He glanced at the kid, noted the wide, shocked eyes, but said nothing. Harvey climbed back into the driver's seat and started the engine.

'Captain? Am I driving this truck through those gates?'

'No,' Taylor said.

Harvey was surprised. 'I don't understand.'

'We have to pick our battles carefully. We don't know what kind of arsenal they have in there, or how many men. I won't risk everyone's lives unless we're already in a life or death situation. We'll do a little more recon of this place first. We've already learnt a lot today as it is.'

'Such as?' asked Jas.

'There is still someone in charge and they are hiding out. Just as we suspected.'

'How do you know? It may just be that some of the station staff are hiding out there. We've probably scared the hell out of them by coming here.'

Through the corner of his eye, Taylor noticed Jas scrutinising him. She was aware that he had said the same thing she frequently told Andrew: *We must choose our battles.*

'I think the Captain's right,' said Harvey, backing up the truck until he had room to turn around. 'We know how the military works, and all those conspiracy theories you've heard, well they were probably true.'

'What the hell is going on?' asked Jas. 'Aren't we supposed to be on the same side?'

'Not anymore,' said Taylor. 'The authorities cut us loose. They don't need more mouths to feed. I suspect that station is feeding power not only to the mall but to an underground bunker that's protecting the chosen few.'

'What?' said Jas. 'Aren't they glad some of us survived?'

'You don't get it, Jas. They really don't care what's going on out here anymore. We're surplus to requirements.'

Jas fell quiet, but one further thought nagged at her subconscious. *The power station was completely intact. Why had it been overlooked by the Jinx?*

Harvey turned the wheel of the truck sharply and they pulled away from the station, driving back through the estate. Through his rear view mirror he could see the cameras tracking his progress.

'What will we do Captain?' asked Harvey.

Taylor didn't answer. His lack of response told Jas that he, like the rest of them, really had no clue what to make of this strange turn of events. As they returned to the mostly empty motorway and headed back to Manchester, the three in the front cabin remained quiet.

Jas suspected this wasn't over yet: there were too many unanswered questions. She glanced at Taylor. His expression gave nothing away but she knew him enough to realise that already a plan would be forming in the back of his mind.

'I want to check that place out again,' Taylor said after an hour's complete silence.

As they reached the motorway slip road, the ground began to rumble. Jas hadn't felt another earthquake since the day the Jinx had attacked the theatre, and she had been lulled into a false sense of security. She had begun to feel it was unlikely she would ever see the Jinx again. But the truck shook violently with the underground ripple that rocked the slip road. They reached the roundabout, and the road to the left split open before their eyes.

'Jinx attack!' yelled Taylor.

Harvey swerved the truck right, and it skidded from one side of the road to the other. Jas was thrown into Taylor, and she braced herself against the dashboard as Harvey pulled to a sudden, sharp halt.

'Everyone, you know what to do,' Taylor yelled, but his command was unnecessary as the soldiers were already pouring out from the back of the truck and taking up defensive positions.

'Here,' yelled Harvey tossing a gun to Jas as she jumped out of the cabin behind him.

Instinct made her bob down beside the truck as they waited for the portal to open. It took some time, and Jas realised she had never seen the beginning of this process before, as when she had emerged from the theatre the portal had already been open and the Jinx pouring over their victims. Taylor on the other hand had been in close quarters with the Jinx before, and he was ready for this attack.

Wind swirled in a tornado, whipping at the truck and pulling at their clothing, and Jas was blinded by the grit thrown up from the dusty earth and into the atmosphere. She squinted at Taylor and noticed that he and his men had all put on goggles. She suspected they could now see perfectly without the risk of damaging their eyes.

'Fire!' Taylor shouted.

As the portal began to open, the soldiers bombarded it with bullets and grenades. The ground shook in angry protest. The wind lashed at the soldiers in retaliation, but they stood firm.

Jas fired her gun in response to everyone else's gunfire. She couldn't hear the orders Taylor shouted, but the men seemed to be able to understand his hand signals and responded accordingly. Two of them ran forward with grenades and threw them right into the small opening of the portal. Immediately the portal snapped shut, but not before the men had the satisfaction of hearing the explosion inside hitting several of their targets and sand blasted out into the air around them.

The atmosphere settled, the ground ceased shaking and the men cheered, high-fiving each other.

Jas remained by the truck, the gun still aimed at the spot where the Jinx had tried to appear. It took her a while to realise that they had scored a victory.

'How?' she said as Harvey took back his gun.

'We figured out they are at their weakest as they are just arriving. There hasn't been one successful entrance anywhere near us in the last year.'

'The problem is,' Taylor said, 'they'll now just open up somewhere else and some poor unsuspecting group may suffer at their hands.'

'The earthquake. You knew they were arriving because of the earthquake?' Jas said. 'It's the first sign that they are coming.'

Taylor laughed. 'I knew you were smart, kid. Once we figured that out, we beat the bastards every time.'

Jas began to laugh with hysteria. She laughed until her sides hurt and her eyes streamed. She could barely breathe as the soldiers climbed back into the truck. Taylor watched her struggle back into the cabin, weak with laughter. A slight frown covered his features. The laughter made Jas appear girly. He wondered if the kid was gay.

'It's a small victory, but at least it is one,' said Harvey. 'Laugh your guts up, Jas. It's not gonna be the last time you see the Jinx pussy-whipped.'

16

'Heysham may be well protected. They had surveillance and weapons, but we couldn't make out where the gunshots were coming from,' Taylor said that night around the camp fire. 'It was just too quick.'

'Yeah,' Harvey chipped in. 'And they've gone free of attack for two years. Wouldn't you think that the Jinx would have tried that spot by now?'

'We've been up and down this country. There are very few places that haven't been hit,' Donovan pointed out. 'But there are a few. You guys got lucky today, it seems.'

Gerald sat down beside Jas; she was feeding wood into the flames, building the fire higher.

'Have you … ever come across any surviving women on your travels?' Gerald asked.

'Once or twice in the early days,' Taylor replied. 'We helped a few families set up camps. When we left them they were trying to rebuild their lives. But we haven't come across any sane survivors, male or female, in the last six months. At least, not until we met you guys.'

'They can't have taken them all,' Jas commented. 'I reckon a few are being resourceful and are hiding.'

Taylor nodded. 'I'm sure there's some.'

'Jeez,' said Ashby. 'I've almost forgotten what sex is like.'

The men laughed.

'Yeah,' said Harvey. 'If I ever find a woman I think I'll go back to the caveman style of thinking. Knock her on the head, bend her over and just get me some of that honey.'

Harvey stood up and mimed the action by thrusting his hips into thin air. The laughter continued.

'What about you, Captain? Remember how it was with a woman?' asked Donovan. 'What would you do if you found one?'

Taylor smiled. 'These days I'm more likely to train her to fight than fuck her. We need all the soldiers we can get.'

The men sobered up. Jas avoided looking at Taylor, but she imagined she could feel his eyes on her. For the first time she began to wonder if her disguise was still intact. Had Taylor realised what she was, and if so was this his way of telling her she was safe? If she were found to be the only woman among all of these men, she didn't know how they would cope with her presence. Harvey's words worried her, but she had laughed along with the men as though she were one of them. It was the only way she could deal with it. She denied even to herself that she was anything other than Jas, young man, older brother of Andrew.

'The Captain said he'd begin our training tomorrow,' Andrew whispered. 'He maybe doesn't realise yet that you're already a bad-ass.'

Jas smiled. '*Bad-ass*? You've been around these Americans too long, Andy.'

Andrew winked at her and stood up. He went over to the water tank and poured himself a glass, then added some Vimto cordial to it. Jas shook her head but smirked at him. She felt such a surge of love and pride. Andrew was doing okay. He could have so easily become messed up by all that he had seen. But even with everything he had been though, he had somehow managed to remain stable and strangely well-adjusted.

'So what do you want to do about Heysham, boss?' asked Donovan.

'Tomorrow we'll send out a small recon team. I don't want anyone to get too close. No-one's to take unnecessary chances. But let's have some guys watching the place for a few days.'

Donovan nodded. Jas noted again how informal Taylor was with his men, although it was still clear that he was the leader. He was in charge and they deferred to him on every important decision. If they screwed up, though, Taylor never hauled them over the coals. She had heard him say things like, 'Think before you act next time' and 'Maybe you've learnt your lesson,' as well as, 'At least you came out of that in one piece'. It wasn't weakness, it was a positive attitude, and Jas felt that it had kept the soldiers safe for years. He cared about each of their lives. *Valued* them. His men knew it too, which was why they trusted him.

He could lead them into an erupting volcano and somehow he would manage to get them through it alive, Jas thought, and then she pulled herself back, withdrawing her emotions from the scene before her. She couldn't really put all her trust in a man she had only recently met. True, she and Andrew had never eaten so well since the Jinx came. Andrew had recovered from his illness and he loved the hot food that Taylor's crew provided. It was far better than the cold, canned offerings they had had to make do with these last two years. Even so, Jas had kept all of their own supplies hidden behind the curtain on the stage, and was pleased that although Taylor had seen them, he had never suggested that they should be added to the haul taken from the mall. She liked to keep them, just in case Taylor and his men decided to leave. For all that, the soldiers showed no sign of going; and Jas wondered if, when that day came, Andrew would want to go with them. She suspected he would, but she wasn't sure yet if she herself wanted to.

Andrew adored Taylor, and even when he followed him around in an annoying teenage way, the Captain never lost his temper or became impatient. The man was perfect. A brilliant and skilled soldier, a natural leader and a good provider for his men. Jas wondered what the catch was. There had to be one. No-one was really that good. Not these days. Taylor seemed to be too moral, too sane.

Jas stood and went back into the theatre. Lately she had been sleeping in their room alone as Andrew now preferred to hang out with the soldiers. She couldn't blame him, really. Things were changing and maybe it was for the best. She felt less worried about him now, but still no less responsible.

She unzipped her sleeping bag and stripped off her fleece jacket. She felt grubby. *What I wouldn't do for a nice hot bath?* But of course being clean would be a dead giveaway. Jas climbed into her bag. It smelt of her sweat and years of dirt and grime, but she didn't notice.

Outside, the soldiers were celebrating their victory, and planning their reconnaissance of the power station. Jas drifted off to sleep listening to the sounds of revelry, and glad for once that the dark no longer offered the cold, black silence that she and Andrew had experienced for the last two years.

It was a dark and barren landscape. Jas remembered catching a brief glimpse of it when she had gazed down the mouth of the vortex as the theatre had been attacked. She found herself stepping down, walking through a spinning tunnel, and she could see the light at the end. *This is corny*, she thought. *Tunnels, light … Maybe I've died and I'm finally going to heaven.*

There was no-one else inside the vortex. It was cool, but not cold, as though it insulated the outside and nothing could penetrate it. The tunnel narrowed, it felt like she had been walking forever, and a strange anxiety made her chest hurt as she was propelled forward. There was no way she wanted to reach the end, but somehow she couldn't stop herself from moving forward.

Sand swirled in the tunnel sides as though it were the source of some threatening intelligence. It smelt of something drier and older than the sea, like ancient caves containing images from the past. If she looked closely enough she could see shapes and shadows, hands reaching out to pull her into the spinning void. The odour of time seeped into the atmosphere, it smelt like old furniture, the musty scent of antique books and the faint aroma of old and rotting skin.

Once or twice she glanced back the way she had come. She could see her world. The theatre; the bonfire; soldiers drinking and dancing around; Andrew sipping at a beer that Harvey had given him; Donovan smoking a cigar and drinking directly from a bottle of whisky. Someone was singing an old Irish ditty. Taylor was nowhere to be seen.

She looked ahead once more. The tunnel, or vortex, or wormhole – whatever the hell this thing was – pulled her onward. She couldn't resist the call, and she knew why. She was a woman, not a man, and her disguise, no matter how clever, didn't fool the Jinx one little bit. She wrapped her arms around herself, kept away from the moving walls and allowed the tide of Jinx magic to show her the way.

There was another step and another. This time she found herself descending a long and winding staircase: but she knew it was only metaphorical. Somehow she was traversing time and space. Her scientific mind tried to analyse how, but failed to form any logical conclusion. This was no wormhole, no fold in space-time allowing her to stumble blindly through to another dimension – or was it? She forced herself to stop; it was like swimming up a waterfall. Gravity, or some such force, pulled and dragged her. She stared down the steps. *Only three more!* But then what?

The steps disappeared as though the vortex had grown too impatient for her to decide. She found herself staring at the opening to an elaborate tent. It looked like something she had seen on the National Geographic channel: Bedouin perhaps. She remembered they were a nomadic tribe with strange, ancient traditions and little or no technology. They rode camels, travelled on desert land and lived simply.

Her bare feet sank into soft, dry sand. She looked down. *So this is where it's been coming from?*

The desert made perfect sense, but Jas couldn't explain to herself why. It was just something she knew and understood. The world of the Jinx was strangely familiar. A feeling of *déjà vu* made her stop once more. *I know this place. But how? I've been here before.* She shook her head. That wasn't true. She had never been in the desert in her life.

The tent flaps pulled back and Jas moved forward, compelled into the gloom. She could see enough to avoid the furniture. A chest was to her left, a table full of strange jars and bottles to her right, and just ahead was a large and ornate bed. *Not merely a mattress with a pile of cushions as you might imagine.* The tent, no matter how bizarre, appeared to be a grand and permanent structure, and it was full of ornate and expensive antique-looking items.

Someone was asleep in the bed. She could hear breathing, a slow and steady lift and rise that indicated full and deep sleep. To the right of the bed was another table. This one was huge, and spread out on it was a large piece of parchment bearing markings that made it look like a map. Jas pored over the markings and images. It looked like an atlas of the Earth, only this was roughly drawn, and incomplete. There were empty spaces, like black holes on the page. But she didn't understand what it meant.

Deeper in the tent was a small pool of liquid. Jas stood beside it and, as with the sand-covered walls of the vortex, saw movement in the water. The more she looked, the more defined the pictures became. It was like watching a digital 3D television. The images had depth and detail, colour and light.

A sigh came from the bed, and she glanced over her shoulder to see the body within the shadows move and turn over, but not wake. He – she assumed it was a male – began to breathe noisily, almost snoring, but not quite.

She backed away from the pool and turned back toward the door. As she did so, her eyes fell on a suit of armour. A helmet, encrusted with expensive looking jewels, stared back at her with blank-slitted eyes. It was the armour of a Jinx warrior.

What the hell am I doing here?

She hurried back to the opening of the tent, panic making her heart beat so loudly she was sure the Jinx would hear it.

Outside, the camp was quiet. It was night and all slept. The air was heavy and humid. It felt like she *was* in the desert. She stared around, blinked, looked for the vortex but found nothing in the space she had stepped down from.

'*Am currin dei zah?*' said a voice behind her.

Jas span around and came face to face with a man. He was dressed in long robes. His black hair hung clean around his shoulders and the moon reflected on his pale features. He had a moustache, which was long and thin in the way Chinese Emperors were depicted, but the man's features weren't oriental. He had a look of his own; human, but not. His height dwarfed her, and she knew he was alien, other than human, despite the average appearance. Perhaps it was the eyes? They were more oval than regular eyes, and the irises, in the dull light, shone in a strangely supernatural way. They were cat-like if anything, reflecting what little light there was. She blinked again. His pupils swirled as he looked down at her.

'*Am currin dei zah?*' he said again. Only this time Jas knew what he meant. She understood his words. He was asking 'Who are you?'

She stepped back from him, and he didn't pursue her, but his smile was terrible. Despite her clothing she knew he recognised she was female.

'*Ha mien zah ...*' he said, nodding. *I see you ...*

Jas shuddered awake and found Andrew snoring beside her in his sleeping bag. It was one of those rare nights when he must have felt a need to be near her. The air smelt of beer, and she wondered how much of it Harvey had allowed the boy to drink. She would have to talk to the soldiers about it. Andrew was still so young and drinking wouldn't be good for him.

The theatre back room was pitch-dark, and all was quiet outside, but Jas stood up and went over to the door. She listened for a while, breathing deeply until the pounding of her heart steadied. Then she checked the lock. Andrew hadn't run the bolt across; he was feeling safe and confident about their new friends. Jas pulled the bolt into place. Then, as an extra precaution, she pressed a chair under the handle. Once the chair was braced against the door, she returned to her bed. This time, however, sleep was slow to come.

17

Jas and Andrew began training as planned. They had their own beginner's class, which Taylor took the trouble to teach. Each morning they warmed up and fought on crash mats taken from the theatre's storage room.

After the usual warm-up, Jas and Andrew had weapons training. They had become adept at loading and handling the semi-automatic weapons that made up their new kits, and Andrew, despite Jas's initial fears for him, behaved sensibly with his gun.

'This is for you,' said Donovan one lunch time, throwing a rucksack at Jas's feet.

'What is it?'

'Standard issue army kit,' Donovan said.

'It doesn't look like it,' Andrew commented as he stared at the black rucksack. It looked like something he would have kept his schoolbooks in back in the old days.

'Well,' said Donovan, 'I have improvised a bit on the sacks, but not what's inside.

Jas opened her bag and pulled out a semi, bullets, three grenades and a pair of clear plastic goggles.

'To protect your eyes when the Jinx hit,' Donovan said.

'Yeah,' Jas said. 'I saw you guys wearing them last time.'

'What you have to do is practice pulling out the goggles and grenades in record time.'

For the first time, Jas and Andrew joined the rest of the drilling soldiers. But this was no ordinary drill. Donovan put them through their paces, but it was all about reaction time, not smart marching.

'The faster you are, the better the result. We've always got to be one step ahead of those bastards. Especially now they've reared their goddamn ugly heads again.'

Donovan was tough, and once he had finished his drill, Harvey took over and ordered the soldiers through the arming process. This time they had to load and prepare their weapons within a short time. Taylor had worked Jas and Andrew hard already in this area and they kept up with the others well.

'Not bad,' said Harvey. *'Now do it again! Faster.'*

The soldiers practiced and practiced.

'If you can't get a bullet in the hole you'll have no chance with a skirt,' said Ashby, nudging Kline so that he dropped a handful of bullets. They scattered on the tiled ground, and Kline had to rush about trying to retrieve them.

Harvey was not impressed: he had no tolerance for fooling around during drill. 'Drop and give me 20,' he told Ashby. 'Sloppiness costs lives. Loading has to be automatic, so that no matter what stress you are under, you can load and fire quickly, taking down the enemy before they can get you.'

Ashby hit the deck without argument and rapidly did 20 press-ups.

'Get your sorry asses up and ready to march, soldiers,' yelled Harvey, and the men fell in line.

Jas and Andrew tagged onto the end of the line and the march began, away from the theatre camp and out toward the high street.

'Being a soldier and surviving this war requires fitness,' Taylor had told Jas and Andrew when their training began. Fortunately their fitness was good, and thanks to the new influx of food, as well as the new training regime, their body strength was much improved. Jas felt better and stronger than she had in a long time, and she enjoyed the exercise. It was just too easy to sit around and do nothing when you had no motivation, and the drilling and training gave her and Andrew the kind of incentive they needed.

The troop marched for half an hour and reached the outskirts of the small town, doubled back and began to weave in and out of the streets.

It was a hot day and sweat was pouring from the faces of the men, but in a matter of minutes the sky clouded over and a chill breeze rose from nowhere. Jas realised something was wrong seconds before tremors shook the street, and she pulled her rucksack from her back and reached in the pocket for the goggles, slipping them across her eyes as quickly as she could. As the first shudder struck the street, the troop fell out of their neat lines, took up defensive positions and slipped on their eye wear. The goggles gave Jas tunnel vision, but she turned her head, rapidly noting their location and where each of the soldiers crouched as they waited for the fight. She noticed they weren't far from the supermarket. The thought crossed her mind that Andrew regularly came this way alone to check that their traps were still in place.

Where was Andrew?

She saw him crouching beside Ashby and her heart began to pound in fear for him. *I shouldn't have let him take part*, she thought. *This is just too dangerous: he's still only a child.* But her thoughts were irrational. Andrew had grown up, and he was taking responsibility for himself these days. There wasn't much she could say or do to stop him from doing anything he wanted to do. He saw himself as a man, and being around Taylor's soldiers made him want to be a part of the group and be one of them.

Jas felt a surge of anger and fear gnawing at her insides. She hated it that Andrew was anywhere near potential danger, so when she saw the vortex open she acted on instinct, running headlong toward it and firing her weapon as she recalled the soldiers doing the last time. Harvey also ran brazenly in with a grenade, followed by Ashby. Still firing, Jas gazed down the mouth of the vortex. She thought she saw a shape: a man in robes with a long moustache. Then she heard the words that struck terror in her heart:

'Ha mien zah' – I see you – and then 'Ick venin azah.'

The vortex closed, leaving Jas staring at the spot while the men excitedly cheered and thanked whatever god they believed in. Harvey slapped her on the back.

'Well done kid. You're a brave one, I'll give you that.'

'Is it me, or was that just too easy?' said Andrew behind her.

'We've got them on the run now,' Harvey said, smiling.

Jas said nothing. Her mind was on the figure. She could see his face clearly. In a daze she followed the excited men back to camp. This time they marched and chanted with the taste of victory warming their lips, and she and Andrew joined in, but Jas was not feeling confident or victorious. She had the overwhelming feeling that the Jinx were playing with them, and she could still hear those strange and foreign words: 'Ick venin azah'. I've come for you. She couldn't explain how she knew what the Jinx warrior had said, but she was certain she was right.

Jas shook away the insanity of her thoughts. The Jinx didn't know who she was, why would they? And why would they come for her and her alone?

They returned to camp, singing all the way. Nothing could dampen the spirits of the soldiers and Jas didn't give her true feelings away, not even to Andrew.

'Perhaps the mall would be a better place to hide out,' Taylor said.

''Bout time you decided on that, Captain,' said Donovan amiably. 'Me and the boys wouldn't mind asking those moss-covered chicks out on a date.'

Taylor laughed, but underneath the humour he knew they had to change location as soon as possible. It was strange that the Jinx had started to appear before them so frequently after months of absence, and deep down Taylor was concerned. The only thing different was that they now had three new members and more food.

'It's like they have some sort of tracking beam and it's focusing in on us,' he said.

'Yeah. Normally we only come across them when there's a woman in the vicinity,' Harvey agreed.

'Well there's no chance of that or we would have seen her,' Taylor said.

Andrew looked sharply at Jas, then hung his head. Taylor glanced over at him. He had seen his sudden movement in the corner of his eye, but didn't know what had caught the kid's attention. He glanced over to the group of men packing up bedding and supplies. There didn't seem to be anything untoward about the group. He looked away as the men passed him, and barely noticed that Jas was among them.

Without being told, the soldiers packed up their personal effects. They were used to movement, to closing one camp and opening another. This was just another day to them. But to Jas and Andrew it was a big deal to leave the safe haven they had lived in for over two years.

'I'm not sure we should go with them,' Jas said to Andrew.

'What are you talking about? We're safe with them …'

Jas knew it was true, but she was reluctant to give up all of her independence. The way things were, she and Andrew could come and go as they pleased, but if they joined the soldiers permanently they would be subject to their laws, punishments and regimes. She looked into Andrew's eyes and saw the answer to her unasked question. He loved her like a sister, but he really wanted to go with Taylor and his men. He was happy, and it was true they were safer with the soldiers than they had ever been.

'Okay,' she said. 'Looks like we've been enlisted.'

Andrew gave her a beaming smile and ran inside the theatre to start packing his personal things.

18

They moved into the Trafford Centre mall without any real incident. It was a big step for Jas and Andrew, so they had only taken their clothing, sleeping bags and a few toiletries. Jas reasoned that their own cans of food should remain hidden in the theatre just in case they ever had cause to return there. In those early days, part of her reasoning was insecurity: she still wasn't sure how much she could trust the soldiers. However as the summer rapidly moved into autumn, she and Andrew found themselves settled and happy, living safely in the Trafford Centre with Taylor and his men, and all thought of leaving the platoon fled completely from her mind.

Their life had changed dramatically from the feral, scavenging existence they had when they lived in the theatre. Food was rationed among the soldiers, but the rations were generous, and because Jas and Andrew had begun training with the men, they were treated as part of the team. They settled into a strict regime of exercise. Following a run around the top shopping floor of the mall, four or five laps every morning, the two of them would take turns to have private training sessions with Taylor. He taught them to fight in an empty storage unit that had been converted into a training space. The soldiers had taken blue padded crash-mats from the old children's play area, and there were also hand weights of various sizes for the soldiers to work out with and maintain their strength.

Taylor taught Jas a variety of fighting moves using techniques taken from judo and tai chi as well as karate. She enjoyed the physical contact more than Andrew did.

'You're a natural at this,' Taylor told her one morning. 'You may be skinny kid but you sure are strong.'

'Is this what the army teaches people these days?' said Jas, narrowly avoiding a kick aimed at her head.

'All methods. The idea is to use any move at any time,' Taylor said. 'That way you keep your opponent on their toes. You'll notice there is a rhythm to each of the disciplines. A worthy opponent would know the pattern of the moves. That's why mixing them up works the best. It breaks the pattern.'

Jas knew that if she were to face a real opponent using these techniques then she would need more strings to her bow than just physical strength. The philosophy behind Taylor's teaching wasn't what she had expected. It was not about defence but about attack, which went against the philosophies behind most martial arts disciplines.

'Fight hard and don't give an inch,' he said.

'Well that's nothing like the *Karate Kid*,' laughed Jas, ducking as he swung his arm.

'Stay focused,' warned Taylor.

But Jas was having too much fun. She was alone with Taylor and enjoying the fight, even though she knew she would be a mass of bruises and aches and pains later for her troubles. She ducked, narrowly avoiding another kick aimed toward her head. His fist went out and she blocked him with her arm, but at that moment Taylor swept his foot under her, knocking her over, and then landed with his full weight on her stomach and chest. He knocked the wind out of her chest, and her lungs heaved in the air in painful gasps.

So much for over-confidence, she thought.

'Sorry about that, kid,' Taylor said. Reaching out his hand, he helped her up. He banged her on the back as she continued to gasp. Then he turned away and began to walk from the mat. At that point Jas made her move. She dived on Taylor, knocking him to the ground, and had him in a headlock before he could react.

'Gotcha,' she said, but her victory was short-lived as Taylor bucked underneath her, spinning her over onto her back. He lay across her, his whole body pressing hers into the mat.

Jas struggled and Taylor pressed her down harder. She was good, but Taylor didn't want the kid to get too confident too soon. His chest was on Jas's, his legs held hers down. Something felt wrong to him. His eyes saw the boy, his body felt something else entirely. He looked into her eyes, and in that moment knew what it was he had recognised but had denied to himself all these months.

'You're a girl,' he said.

'Don't be stup–'

'You are. You're a girl. I can feel your … breasts.'

'Get *off* me,' she said.

Taylor jumped away. 'Sorry.'

He stared at her as she stumbled to her feet. Now that he knew, it was obvious really. She fitted the oversized clothing a little better than when they had first met, and that was partly to do with the food the soldiers ate. To be strong they needed energy. Jas was wiry, though, and strong for her build, although not as strong as Taylor. But he had accepted that, because he had thought of her as a boy of no more than 19.

'Why didn't I notice sooner? I mean, I knew there was something off about you.'

Jas didn't like the way Taylor's eyes ran over her.

'Don't,' she said, folding her arms across her chest.

'Sorry,' he said again. 'I'm just looking at you, trying to understand why I didn't see it sooner. I didn't mean …'

Taylor was confused. His eyes still saw the boy, but the mask had slipped in some way. He had fought with Jas many times before and had never noticed the obvious differences. He wondered why that was. It seemed to be by some sheer miracle that he had discovered her true nature.

'You weren't meant to notice. And I'd appreciate it if you forgot this and still treated me the same.'

'I … don't know if I can,' Taylor answered.

Jas sighed. 'Then Andrew and I will have to leave.'

Taylor turned away. He took a swig of water from a bottle he had placed by the mat, but really he wanted something stronger.

'Look Jas. This is a helluva secret to keep from my men.'

'Taylor, Andrew and I have been friends with everyone. I fought alongside you when the Jinx attacked. I'm every bit as good a soldier, or at least I will be, as the rest of you.'

'True. But …'

Jas picked up her fleece and threw it over her head. 'I won't be whored out to your men.'

'Oh my god! Do you think I'd allow that?' Taylor said.

'I don't know. We've had some issues like this before,' she said, but the fight had gone out of her. Jas knew she was in Taylor's hands, and she couldn't fight off an entire army.

'I won't say anything – for now,' he said after a moment of silence. 'I just don't know if …'

'If … you could control them?'

Taylor didn't reply. The question hung in the air between them like a poisonous miasma.

'That's the point though, isn't it?' Jas said. 'I think there are other women out there. But they are hiding, like me. The men we've come across have been …'

'I can imagine. And I'm sorry, but we're not all like that, Jas. I'd like to think my men wouldn't act like savages. We've been trained to be soldiers first, men second.'

'Well, I'm not willing to take the risk of finding out. Are you?'

Taylor shook his head. 'I need to think.'

Jas left the training room and went in search of Andrew. She had to prepare him with the knowledge that they might have to leave suddenly. She thought back to the theatre. It wasn't that far away and she still had the car; it was parked outside with a half-full tank of fuel. They could get back easily anytime they wanted, but it made her feel sad to think of leaving the army. They had, in their strange way, become a family. The mall had become a village in which they worked, trained, ate and socialised. The only missing element in their little town was women, and other than the occasional joke, they were rarely mentioned.

There was a bed shop in the mall and each of them had been allocated a mattress to take to their designated home. Jas and Andrew had chosen a single mattress each and pulled them through the mall until they found a shop to live in. They had eventually picked a women's dress shop. Jas had liked the way the racks zigzagged across the shop floor. It meant there was no direct line of attack to the back room, which is where they had set up camp among the mannequins and spare stock. Jas had considered the small stockroom an ideal place to lock up at night, and felt more secure with an extra door between them and the wide open spaces of the mall. For a time she had felt safe again. She had even managed to push away the memory of the cannibal Red Coats and the poor victim they had been consuming.

Jas found Andrew in the main food hall, which the soldiers had nicknamed 'the mess'. He was hanging out with Ashby and Kline, as he often did these days. The three of them were fooling around in the shallow pool in front of the stage. Watching their antics made Jas realise how hard it would be to ask Andrew to leave. He was happy, and even more importantly he was safer with the soldiers than with her. Over the last few months spent in the mall, he had developed muscle, and Jas was sure he had grown a couple of inches too. The boy was tall for his age, around five foot ten, and she felt he was rapidly losing that baby-faced look he had worn when this all began.

The three men ran in and out of the water, wearing nothing but shorts. They splashed and yelled and laughed. *I can't even join in*, she thought. *Imagine me taking my top off and running around in boxers!* A smile curved her lips at the insanity of the thought. She would have loved to have been in the water, felt the coolness wash away the grime she deliberately sustained. Instead, she walked away without interrupting, went into the book shop and browsed the books to take her mind off everything.

'Hey,' said Donovan when he tracked her down there, sat on a sofa and reading. 'Thought I'd find you here. You're a regular bookworm, kid.'

Jas closed the book and put it face down on the small table beside her. 'What's up?' she asked, and fear clenched in the pit of her stomach.

'The boss wants us all in the mess. He's called a meeting.'

Jas stood and followed Donovan, worry colouring her cheeks. They found the entire platoon gathered in the mess. Jas joined Andrew in the food queue, took her ration of food and sat down on a table near the stage.

Jas remembered this stage often appearing on television in the old days.

When she had been female she had quite enjoyed watching the re-runs of an old Gok Wan programme called *How to Look Good Naked*. The show had been very much about teaching women to accept how they looked. It was ironic that this place had once hosted the show. Jas felt a pang of anxiety as Taylor stood up before the men. She wondered if this new update was about her, and what would happen if it was. Her shoulders were tense as she waited for the axe to fall.

'What's up?' asked Andrew, noticing her body language.

But Jas shook her head and forced her shoulders down, presenting a veneer of calm that wouldn't rouse suspicion.

The mess was full of noisy, chattering men, but as Taylor climbed up onto the stage and raised his hands, silence descended.

'We've had some news from the latest recon team over at Heysham,' Taylor began. 'As you know, we've been watching the place for some time and there has been no movement at all. We've been drawing in around the place for closer scrutiny at intervals. It seems the fence is sensitive to a radius of two hundred feet. The latest team drew in and was bombarded by fire. I have to tell you that there were a few wounded, but fortunately nothing fatal, and thanks to Dr Avery everyone will recover.'

A murmur rippled through the crowd. Jas picked out the occasional 'Go, doc' and 'Goddamn military'.

'The fact of the matter is this,' Taylor said. 'I don't think their external surveillance is that good. It seems to be limited to bog standard security cameras, and nothing state of the art or military as you might expect. If this place is servicing some bunker that the military, Prime Minister and all of the favoured few are in, then it was probably set up last minute. Whoever is manning the place will know what's going on and where the bigwigs are hiding. I want a team to volunteer to move in with me. We're going to hit hard and fast. It's about time we got some answers.'

There was a cheer from the men. They were feeling the lack of combat, and fighting helped to allay other frustrations.

'It's going to be a very dangerous mission,' Taylor continued. 'Which is why I'm leading it. Harvey and Donovan, you guys are staying here.'

'What?' said Harvey.

'Captain, we want to fight beside you,' said Donovan.

'No. I need you both here to keep to the mission if anything happens to me.'

Jas knew, just as the soldiers did, that Taylor was too valuable to lose, even with Harvey and Donovan left in charge. But, as he said, this was a dangerous mission and they didn't know what they would find inside the power station. Either way, Taylor wasn't going to ask his men to do something he wasn't prepared to face himself.

'What's the plan, Captain?' asked Jas.

Taylor's eyes fell on her and gave nothing away of his knowledge. The men had erupted into discussion again, so the Captain raised his arm once more. Next to Andrew, Kline punched Ashby in the arm to silence him and the soldiers turned back to their leader to hear what he had to say.

'We assume the Government are hiding out somewhere below ground,' said Taylor. 'We've always known they just abandoned us. They left us to suffer. And that angers me. Does it anger you?' The men jeered in agreement. 'What we don't know is where they are or how they are being supported. This station could give us that information. So the plan is this. We leave at dawn. I want 20 volunteers. We're going straight through that barrier and we're going to find out what the hell is going on.'

The room erupted as the men rushed forward, all of them volunteering for the fight.

'I won't take you all,' cautioned Taylor. 'We have to leave a line of defence, just in case we don't make it back.'

'We'll draw for it,' Donovan said.

And that was how Jas ended up in the final 20.

19

'You,' Taylor said to Jas. 'Ride up front with me.'

Jas climbed into the cabin alongside him.

'You shouldn't have volunteered,' Taylor said once they had started the engine and were heading out toward the power station.

'Would you be saying that if you still thought I was male?'

'Yes,' he said. 'This has nothing to do with your gender, although that is still a major issue for me. But this does have everything to do with you being a new recruit.'

'Your arrogance never fails to amaze me,' Jas said.

Taylor glanced at her. Under the grime he could see a pretty girl. He had never noticed how blue and clear her eyes were; strangely they had always appeared a muddy brown. She kept her hair cropped, not much longer than his soldiers wore theirs. It was almost as if she hid under some kind of spell. The others all took her for a boy, and when she was among them, she appeared male. But he knew now that it was an illusion of some sort.

'You're a chameleon, I'll give you that,' Taylor muttered. 'Why is it when I'm alone with you I see what you are and when you're with the other men … you're just one of them?'

Jas shrugged. 'I believe I am one. I'm no different from them. I'm a soldier at heart. Don't kid yourself that I didn't do some terrible things in order to survive before you and your men came along.'

Taylor said nothing; survival was something he understood.

'Let's focus on the mission, or mistakes with be made,' Jas said.

'I always focus on the mission. Just, don't take any unnecessary chances.'

'Don't worry about me. I can look after myself.'

Taylor glanced at her again. Her jaw was set and she was determined. He was certain that she could take care of herself, but he was struggling to come to terms with his newfound knowledge. Of course, he had fought alongside female soldiers before. Women that had the same hard edge to them that Jas had. But she was different in a way he couldn't quite understand. This disguise of hers went beyond role-play. It was almost as if she actually became male at times.

Jas kept her eyes on the road and looked ahead, stubbornly refusing to look at Taylor. She felt his eyes on her from time to time during the journey, but she never looked at him. She didn't know how he had seen through her disguise, and it was somewhat disconcerting after all this time living as a man. The problem was, around him she wanted to be female, and she felt it weakened her. Even so, there was nothing she could do. He had learnt the truth and she could no longer hide it from him when they were alone.

She glanced at Taylor as he focused on the road. Even in this strained situation she found him incredibly attractive. Jas shook away the thought of Taylor's looks and kept her eyes on the road as they travelled the rest of the way in awkward silence. It was a relief when they finally drove into the housing estate that led to the power station.

Once on the streets, Taylor pulled the truck into the kerb. He turned and opened the hatch that separated the front cab from the rear of the truck.

'We're there,' he said.

The 20 soldiers were armed and ready, and without a moment's hesitation, Taylor drove the truck headlong into the electric gates. The steel bowed out and the gates were yanked almost off their hinges with the impact. Jas jerked forward painfully against her seatbelt, even though she had braced herself. Bullets hit the truck as the vehicle careered to a halt before the main reception doors. The windscreen cracked in one place, but didn't disintegrate, as the bullets bombarded them. Jas suspected it was made of armoured glass, as the bullets pocked and whined off it.

Jas and Taylor jumped out of the truck and headed toward the main building in a crouched run. The courtyard was barraged with gunfire, but even so, men poured from the back of the moving vehicle, taking cover by pressing themselves against the walls of the main building and the truck.

'Back away from the door! Back away from the door!' screamed a voice over the speakers, as Taylor jammed plastic explosives into the hinges. He backed away far enough to blow them, then he and Ashby raced through the smoke to be the first inside, closely followed by Jas.

They ran headlong down a long, grey-painted breeze-block corridor. Machine guns fired down at the men from somewhere in the walls above. Kline was hit in the left shoulder as he entered the doorway on their heels. His body jerked with the impact as he was knocked off his feet. But he dragged himself back up immediately. He raised his gun arm and shot out a surveillance camera mounted on the wall above him. Two other soldiers joined him, and together they took out all the other cameras dotted along the corridor. As soon as they had done so, the machine guns stopped firing.

'They're automatic,' Kline said. 'Take away their sight and they can't fire.'

'Lucky guess,' said Ashby. 'They might have just continued with random shots.'

There was a red-painted door at the end of the corridor, and Taylor and his men regrouped beside it.

Kline shook his head as Ashby raised his gun to shoot open the lock. 'It's rigged.'

They pressed plastic into the hinges and around the lock, then all of the men backed off down the corridor as Kline blew the door. Just as he had expected, the lock was booby-trapped, and a second, more powerful explosion blew the door back into the corridor. Anyone standing nearer would have been crushed by the impact. But fortunately the soldiers knew what they were doing, and they were all far enough away to avoid being hit.

'Primitive, but effective,' Kline said.

Jas, Taylor, Kline and Ashby ran back toward the doorway. Taylor entered first, weapon pointed inwards.

'Don't come any closer,' ordered a voice. Ashby shot out the cameras and the speaker mounted directly across the room.

'Bastards,' Ashby said.

The soldiers filed into the room, cautiously looking around. This was a large reception area. But it looked dusty and unused. There was a desk that had presumably once been manned by a receptionist. Now it was empty and a thick layer of dust covered the computer keyboard. Kline leaned over the desk and looked down at the visitors' book and the switchboard. Thick grime and cobwebs covered the buttons, and the book lay closed.

Jas looked around. She noted a plush sofa positioned against the wall opposite the reception, with a coffee table set out in front of it on a red rug. There were two machines, one for hot drinks and the other for refrigerated snacks. She slid over to the machines and discovered that both were fully functional.

The reception floor was made of wood. Taylor crossed silently to the other side of the room, where yet another door led off. This one was painted blue, and Jas wondered briefly if the colours had any significance. She tagged onto the group, keeping her semi-automatic Beranger ready.

'Intruders will be met with force,' said a voice as they reached the inner door.

'Bullshit,' said Taylor. He blasted a hole in the door with a grenade. The explosion shook the building, but no armed forces responded to the attack.

Inside this room was a small office with working computers.

'As I suspected,' said Ashby. 'Recorded messages to ward off any intruders. This place is all automated.

Ashby and Kline examined the computers, switching off the automated responses.

'That'll shut them up,' said Kline.

Beyond this basic office they found the control room.

Jas had toured a nuclear plant once before, and this room was just like the one she had seen then, except that there were no employees operating the equipment. It was like something you would see in a NASA control room. Large, free-standing machines lined all four walls, and in the centre was a square of tables, computers and more machines that were monitoring the reactors. Jas knew that usually this control room would be manned 24 hours a day by a qualified engineer. Today, however, it was empty. All of the machines were active, though, and seemed to be fully functional.

'It's a bit hard to believe that this lot is working on its own,' she said. 'A safety feature of nuclear plants is that they are *always* manned and the machines constantly monitored.'

'Yeah,' said Ashby. 'My old man was a nuclear engineer.'

'Plus,' said Taylor, 'their response wasn't automated the first time we arrived ...'

Jas nodded. 'That's right. They responded to you directly.'

Taylor looked at her; a brief frown furrowed his brow. She was in her male guise now, and the knowledge she showed didn't quite fit with the teenage image. Even so, his men took her words at face value, displaying no signs of suspicion. None of them appeared to be aware of her gender at all; and, as he looked closely at her, he realised he couldn't make out any of those female features he had previously noticed in the truck. Her eyes looked darker again too.

I'm going nuts. Maybe I'm imagining it all, he thought.

Jas ran a finger over the work surface of a console, leaving a clean smear in the thick layer of dust. She passed machines that were marked 'Cooling Ponds' and 'Reactor' and searched her memory for any information she could find.

'Ashby, check out the computers. See what you can find out,' Taylor said.

On the other side of the control room was a door marked 'Gas Circulation Hall'. Taylor left two more men behind with Ashby, and the rest of them went through the door and into a huge room. The soldiers entered the room cautiously, but there were no more attacks and no more verbal warnings.

The room reminded Jas of one she had seen in a film called *Resident Evil*. The film had been a classic apocalypse story, and Jas recalled watching it sometime or other during her teens. Although it was an old film, the memory of it had a profound effect on her, and she began to feel a strange sense of paranoia as they moved through the plant.

Above her head, large pipes led in and out of the two main reactors, pumping gas through and around the reactor core. Somewhere in this process the gas was heated and then cooled, only to be returned and recycled through the core again. The reactor was clearly operating at full pelt, providing power for some unknown purpose.

'Don't fire unless you absolutely have to,' Taylor ordered. 'One stray bullet and this place could blow.'

The thought of being unable to use their weapons made the soldiers extra cautious. Jas felt sure something was lurking around every corner, or hiding behind the massive pipes, but they searched the room and found nothing of note, and so proceeded to move on to other areas of the plant.

They passed briefly through the 'Reactor Hall', which was just like a huge, empty warehouse with two main reactors housed at one end. There was nowhere there that anyone could hide, other than being inside the reactors, so they continued exploring and went into the next area, which was marked 'Cooling Ponds'. Here Jas noted the large ponds of gently steaming water, the tall towers, and the intricate weavings of pipes. The soldiers searched every nook and cranny that might have conceivably hidden someone, but without success.

They met back in the control room an hour later, having confirmed that the whole power plant was deserted.

'How is everything working?' asked Jas as she returned with Kline.

'Automated,' Ashby said. 'It's all being run by the computers. I checked the system. Everything is well maintained, but I couldn't gain any real access. This place is being operated by remote, and I suspect it is also being monitored and accessed elsewhere.'

'Isn't it dangerous to leave this place unmanned?' Jas asked, shaking her head. She had fully expected them to find someone throughout the search.

'Oh yeah,' said Ashby. 'Very. But I guess maybe because they have remote access it wouldn't be so bad. If a pipe burst, though, or there was a leak … I dunno what remote control could do for that. The place would probably just go up in smoke.'

'Unless they do have a repair team that could be here in time,' said Jas.

Ashby nodded.

'How's your shoulder, Kline?' asked Taylor as he returned with the rest of the men.

'Just a scratch, Captain.'

'Good. Is everyone accounted for?'

Ashby nodded. 'We're ready to leave.'

They piled back into the truck and set off back to Manchester. It had been a wasted journey. All they had learnt was that the plant was working, and Kline had been injured into the bargain. It seemed such a pointless operation.

Who is operating this thing? Taylor wondered. *Why are they hiding? Why did they abandon us?*

He couldn't dismiss the thought that the powers-that-be had been watching him and his men through some monitoring device, laughing at their wasted efforts. And if, like Ashby said, a leak could destroy the place,

Taylor wondered if there was someone on hand near enough to take care of any such problem. It seemed likely under the circumstances. Other contingencies had been put in place, like the remote monitoring, so why not have a crew nearby to fix potential problems?

'Sometimes I feel like I'm an experimental rat in a cage,' Taylor murmured on the drive back.

Jas glanced at him but said nothing. She thought maybe Taylor was talking to himself anyway. Strange how she didn't think that was too odd, and how she accepted his conspiracy theories. He could be considered paranoid, but she rationalised that he had good reasons to be. He and his men had, after all, been abandoned by their Commanding Officer, and Jas was sure that in the years he had served, Taylor had seen plenty to feed his suspicions.

The truck made rapid progress down the M60. Jas glanced at the speedometer and saw that Taylor was doing over 80, but it didn't matter. The roads were clear and there were no police to stop them speeding. Even if there was any film left in the many speed cameras they passed, who was going to act upon it?

'Hello? Hello? Is there anyone out there?' a muffled voice broke the silence.

'What the ...?' Jas said.

The voice was clearly female, and it was somehow tapping into Taylor's two-way radio, which lay on the seat between him and Jas. Taylor picked up the radio and put it to his mouth. He pressed the button and began to speak.

'Hello? This is Captain Taylor Arch of the US Army. Where are you?'

'Oh thank god! Prestwich! We're in Prestwich. We're trapped ...' the radio signal broke.

'Take the next exit. I know Prestwich,' Jas said. 'That was a woman's voice.'

'Yes, and she said "We're",' Taylor said. 'Here.' He held out the radio, and Jas took it. 'Answer if she breaks through again. Try to get an exact location from her.'

As Taylor steered the truck off the motorway at the next exit, the radio burst into life again.

'Are you there?' said the voice. 'We're trapped.'

'Where are you?' Jas replied. 'We're nearby.'

'Riley's ...'

'We're on our way.' Jas turned to Taylor. 'Take the next left. Riley's was a snooker club just in the centre.'

They passed a large supermarket and two petrol stations on the right. Jas looked all around, surveying the streets for signs of life. They came rapidly up to the junction leading into the small town, and Taylor swung the truck across the street onto the right-hand side of the road, bringing it to a halt before the snooker hall. Jas noticed that the town appeared undamaged even though it was deserted. It made answering the SOS call all the more imperative.

Maybe this surviving group are being attacked by dogs, Jas thought.

'Hello?' said Jas again into the radio, but this time there was no response.

'You stay here,' Taylor ordered Jas, Ashby and Kline. 'Radio in if you see anything.'

Taylor left them and led a small group of the men inside the building while the rest searched the immediate vicinity.

There had been no earthquake, no early warning at all. A Jinx had just appeared from nowhere. He jumped high into the air, as though he could completely disregard the laws of gravity, swinging his sword. As he sliced down, Ashby ducked and turned, bringing up his semi-automatic. He shot the Jinx full in the face, and for once the weapon didn't freeze up. The Jinx crumpled. At this close range his armour was useless against such a powerful weapon.

'Take that, you Jinx bastard,' Ashby laughed. An agonising pain ripped a scream from his lips as a Jinx sword penetrated him from behind.

The sword swung again, sweeping through the air, and cut his torso in two. From the waist down his legs froze, then crumpled. His top half then fell forward, completely separated from his bottom half. The Jinx sword was so sharp that it took a moment for him to feel the pain. He tried to move his hands to stop his fall, but his limbs wouldn't obey, and so his face hit the ground. He felt pain then. His cheek ruptured up into his left eye socket, exploding bone into his eyeball. He screamed again, but the sound was swallowed by the concrete beneath his lips.

He found himself staring at the other half of his body, not comprehending what had happened, while around him the battle raged. A tear slipped from his remaining eye. The pain was so excruciating that he found it hard to focus on anything else. His torso felt as though it was on fire. He didn't realise that this was because the nerves had been sliced through. The fire raged inside him until he thought his head would explode with the pain. Then, just as suddenly, it cooled. The nerves died. The pain slipped away, became a dull ache, and Ashby was able to think again.

He saw his comrades fighting around him, and he knew they would be beaten down. The Jinx were too strong hand-to-hand. The Captain had always told his men they were to avoid combat at close range, because physically they just couldn't compete.

His eye found Jas, who had somehow got hold of one of the Jinx swords and was using it to kill one of the attackers. Jas jumped, swung and sliced, severing the head from the alien's body. *The kid was just like one of them.*

'That's for Ashby, you bastard,' Jas cried. 'I liked him.'

Ashby heard the voice, but it sounded different somehow. It wasn't the gruff sound of a teenage boy; it was higher-pitched than that. More feminine. But then hysteria and battle could do that. Today the kid was different in other ways though. Ashby knew, in those last moments before his brain closed down, that Jas had something like these alien invaders, some power to call on or tap into. They were strong, but in some markedly different way the kid was so much stronger.

Around him, Ashby felt the bodies of more of his friends fall as they returned with the Captain to join the fight. Sonberg, Harris, Clifton. All good, clean American boys. All dedicated and god-fearing soldiers. Another tear slipped from his eye. Jas came into focus again. This time Ashby noticed something else. A shimmer that surrounded the kid; a blurred light that reminded him of the haze you sometimes saw rising off a lake on a hot summer's day. He felt dizzy when he tried to look at it too long. Instead he looked through it, and then he saw, he really saw Jas for the first time.

A girl! he thought suddenly. But no! Surely Jas was a boy. An unusual boy, but nevertheless still male. *I'm dying, losing it.* Fear surged into his heart, and he knew the truth of his thoughts. He was dying; might as well say already dead. *The doc can't patch this scratch up.*

Jas twirled around like a whirling dervish. Ashby's confused, dying brain wouldn't give up. His good eye wouldn't close. He felt no pain at all now, but was aware of the blood flooding from his torso. It felt like someone had turned the tap on and was letting all his energy just flow away down the sink. He felt so cold. Colder than the grave. Even so, he held on. The tears that flowed freely from his eye had nothing to do with fear now: instead he felt happiness and a strange kind of hope as he watched Jas.

Taylor came running into his line of vision. He shot a Jinx in the head from behind. It was the coldest execution Ashby had ever seen. His mouth moved, he wanted to cheer, but no sound would come from his dying lips, and his tongue lolled, useless.

The battle sounds began to diminish. His vision blurred once more, but another flush of tears cleared his eye of the smoke and dust, of even that fine layer of sand that floated in the air around the Jinx.

Jas and Taylor fought back to back. Circling instinctively as the remaining Jinx attacked. There was some sort of kinship between them, something similar in their make-up. Both survivors, both soldiers. Ashby felt a surge of pride as he saw Taylor take down another Jinx. It seemed that the Captain and Jas were the last of their troop left standing. He felt like he was watching a movie, or playing one of those action games he had enjoyed so much in his youth. The enemy was being defeated by just two warriors.

The ground shuddered beneath them.

'There's more coming!' yelled Jas.

Ashby tried to open his mouth again to cry out a warning. He saw the vortex opening. He saw Taylor reach out and grab Jas by the arm as she cut into the belly of the last Jinx. Ashby grimaced as the alien's stomach poured out onto the pavement. His blood was the same colour as human blood and his guts looked like those of any man. The Jinx fell to his knees and Jas raised the sword again, bringing it down on his neck. The enemy's head fell and rolled toward Ashby, briefly blocking his view of the whole scene. And then he saw Jas and Taylor running across the carnage, away from the earthquake, Jas still gripping the Jinx sword, while Taylor held her hand.

Ashby's eye blurred with more tears. Then it finally closed. *Run little lady, run. Don't let them catch you. You're our only hope.*

20

'In here,' Taylor said, smashing the lock on the door of an old sweet shop. He raised the grille, pulled Jas inside, and ran it back down again behind them.

'Christ. Do you think they saw which way we went?' Jas said.

There was a glass door between them and the shop. Taylor hammered his penknife into the Yale lock and twisted it. The door opened. Inside the shop they hauled the counter across the door and barricaded themselves in, then hunkered down behind it, weapons ready.

The ground shook and Jas looked nervously up at the ceiling, but the building seemed to be holding fast despite the earthquake.

They heard feet running toward them. By this time the vortex was fully open and the ground was steady.

'They are getting really good at opening and settling quicker,' Taylor whispered.

Jas imagined the vortex; saw it in her mind's eye poised at the top of the high street. She could *feel* the Jinx as they stepped down, onto the foreignness of Earth's landscape. She could almost visualise the world through their eyes. A rush of heat ran up her arms and met the coolness of armour. Jas looked down at her herself. She was still holding the sword, but now it felt as though the weight of chainmail had been added also. She put the sword down on the floor, and the strange vision dissolved as rapidly as it had appeared.

'*Al makim ain zevnen,*' said a voice near the shop.

Taylor and Jas both tensed, expecting the grille covering the front to suddenly fly upwards. Through the slats, they could see the jerky movements of a group of three or four Jinx outside the door, talking in their guttural and alien tongue.

'They are looking for us, but I don't think they know for sure if there are any humans alive in the area,' Jas said.

Taylor said nothing but continued to watch.

The sweet shop was in a small precinct. Jas and Taylor had run across the road from the snooker hall, down between a pub and a bank. As they had reached the small group of shops they had heard the vortex swirling open on the main street behind them. Hiding had seemed the only option at that point. They knew they couldn't outrun the Jinx and were certain that there were too many of them to fight. Jas wondered if hiding had been a mistake. Now, trapped in the shop, she doubted their reasoning. Perhaps it would have been better to have fought to the death after all? Better than being trapped like vermin waiting for the rat poison to drop into your food.

The Jinx scouts moved on and their jabbering speech receded.

Jas sighed, turned away from the door and rested her back against the counter. Her eyes fell on the clear plastic containers lining the walls. They were full of sweets and candies, things she hadn't tasted for years.

'They'll have to give up soon,' Taylor said. 'Then we'll make our way back to the truck – that is if it's still in one piece.'

'What about the survivors?'

'The snooker hall was empty,' Taylor explained. 'Then we heard the battle and came running out to find you in the thick of it with Kline. What happened? Only we didn't feel the vortex arrive.'

'There wasn't one. One minute we were looking around, the next this group of Jinx were on us. It all happened so fast, and then Ashby …' Jas's voice broke.

'Yeah, I saw,' Taylor said. 'I also saw how you fought, Jas.'

'I was pissed off that they'd caught us out like that and killed my friends.'

'What happened to Kline?' Taylor asked.

Jas shook her head. She couldn't speak, but she recalled seeing Kline drop as two Jinx fell upon him, their swords singing through the air. She remembered thinking that they looked like avenging angels. But if that was so, what did it make humans?

'There's something so different about them,' Jas said. 'I notice it more and more each time we come in contact.'

'They're aliens.'

'Definitely. But they also have something we humans don't have.'

Taylor waited for Jas to elaborate, but a movement outside caught her eye and she was sure she saw a pair of combat-trousered legs run past the grille.

'What was that?' she said.

Taylor looked, but all was still.

'I think maybe one of our guys survived,' Jas said hopefully.

Taylor looked into her excited, now female, blue eyes. In the last few minutes the male façade had slipped away completely and Jas was back to being a strong and pretty woman. Her hair looked less cropped and more urchin-cut in style. Taylor rubbed his eyes and looked away from her and back through the front of the shop.

'Even so,' he said. 'We need to stay hidden. It could be a trap.'

Jas nodded.

'The Jinx are capable of that,' she said. 'I feel … I *know* they have the ability to use some form of magic.'

Taylor said nothing but frowned. A few years earlier he would have dismissed magic as something impossible. But since the Jinx had arrived he couldn't explain the anomalies in any other way. For all the speeches the scientist Manet had given, he didn't believe the vortices were wormholes, or that the Jinx arrived by any means connected to science. At least, not science as he knew it.

'Magic,' said Jas firmly. 'And it's something we humans don't have. Which is why it was naïve to think our science could defeat it. Science versus magic – I never thought the end of the world would happen that way. It's somewhat ironic, especially since we believed ourselves so powerful.'

Taylor watched Jas out of the corner of his eye.

His mind flicked back to the moment when he had run out of the snooker club and onto the street. Jas and Kline had been surrounded. Jas's gun had been knocked from her hand, and a Jinx had grabbed at her shoulder. She had bent double, ducked under his arm, drawn his sword and pierced him with it. Taylor had been momentarily frozen by the sight of her, twirling and hefting the sword up and around her head, taking down every Jinx she encountered. He hadn't known she could fight like that. It had been like watching some fantasy movie where the heroine had superpowers. Only Taylor knew that Jas wasn't that strong. He had fought her, and he had always won. So, what was it that had given her the strength that day, to overcome so many of their enemy?

Taylor had heard stories before of supernatural happenings in moments of adversity. He had heard of mothers rescuing their children from burning houses, getting out without so much as a singed eyebrow. He had heard of someone once who lifted a car off the trapped body of a loved one. He had never been sure whether these stories were fully accurate or exaggerated for media titillation, but the fact remained that the people involved had saved lives, and had drawn on some inner strength to do it.

Taylor looked down at the sword resting on the ground beside Jas. Maybe if the Jinx had magic then it was in their weapons.

He reached for it.

'Don't,' said Jas. 'They may be able to track us through the sword.'

'How do you know?'

Jas shrugged. 'I felt something when I held it. I had a sort of …'

She couldn't finish her sentence. She was afraid to admit to a vision. It sounded so insane.

Taylor knelt above the sword, examining it. The jewel-encrusted and totally impractical hilt was completed with a gold pommel. The blade was thick and wide. It looked heavy, yet Jas had wielded it effortlessly.

'It looks like a relic,' he commented.

'Passed down through generations of Jinx, probably.'

Taylor kept his eyes on the sword, but Jas's apparent insight into the Jinx worried him. He recalled seeing her leap into the air, seconds before she had brought the sword down onto the neck of a Jinx. He had heard her furious cry of revenge and seen nothing female in her, only warrior. *Just like the enemy.* There was also the question of her disguise. Jas's mask slipped whenever they were alone now, and it was like a physical transformation that couldn't be explained. Taylor wondered what other secrets she was hiding.

'It's getting dark,' Jas said. 'I don't think we should leave here until we're sure the area is clear.'

'Agreed. We'll take it in shifts to sleep.'

Taylor took the first shift. It would give him an opportunity to observe Jas while she slept. As she closed her eyes reluctantly, Taylor divided his attention between her and the grille. She tossed and turned a little, trying to get comfortable on the hard, cold floor, and eventually settled down with her head resting on her rucksack.

The street lights outside were still working, and as Jas's breath levelled out, Taylor turned to look at her in the half light that seeped into the shop. She looked younger in her sleep, but Taylor knew that she really must be in her early twenties. He watched the grime fade from her cheeks, her eyelashes lengthen. Her lips grow slightly fuller. Her cheekbones were defined, and her frame, as she slept, was definitely female.

Jas jumped awake as a crashing noise came from outside the shop. Taylor saw a bin tumble to the ground and heard the screech of a startled cat and the sound of an urban fox crying for a long lost mate.

'It's nothing,' he said. 'Go back to sleep.'

Jas drifted back off, exhaustion taking away her natural paranoia. She felt strangely safe with Taylor and expected him to keep watch until it was time for her shift. In her sleep she pulled the sword closer. It was her weapon now and she knew how to wield it. Touching the pommel gave her a strange comfort.

Later Jas woke to find Taylor asleep beside her. It was still dark, but outside was silent. The Jinx were nowhere to be seen or heard. Without realising it, she mimicked Taylor and watched him sleep, admiring his features. There was a faint scar above his eyebrow. She had never noticed it before, even when they were in close proximity during training, but the thin shafts of light emphasised the mark. He was breathing softly; a slight hiss escaped from his lips and he turned, rolling over onto his back. Jas found her eyes focusing on his lips. An urge to touch him almost overwhelmed her, so she pulled herself up and turned her attention back to the front of the shop.

A mangy dog – of the canine variety – sniffed around the doorway, then cocked his leg and peed against it. But fortunately Jas was spared the smell of urine as the glass-fronted door still lay between them and the protective steel grille.

'I thought it safe to let you sleep,' said Taylor.

Jas nodded. 'Nothing out there but animals now, I think.'

Taylor sat up, then stood and stretched. 'Let's go and check it out.'

They pulled back the counter as quietly as they could. Then, silencing the shop bell, Taylor opened the door and peered out through the grille. All was silent, and daylight was beginning to break onto the small precinct. Taylor lifted the grille, but it creaked and protested, so he raised it only halfway up.

Jas picked up her rucksack, slid it onto her back and then lifted the Jinx sword. It felt heavier than when she had first hefted it, but there was that feeling of possession again. It was now hers somehow. She had earned it through battle.

As Taylor pulled his own backpack on, Jas bent and looked out into the precinct. All was quiet, so she passed under the metal grille. Taylor pulled the door shut behind them, but left the grille up. Creating more noise for the sake of securing an abandoned building didn't seem worth the risk.

They crept through the precinct, sliding in and out of doorways as they made their way back to the snooker club. As they rounded the corner, they could see the truck, the mass of dead bodies. A fox was gnawing at the bloody arm of one of the soldiers. It scurried away as Jas and Taylor approached.

'Jesus,' Taylor said, looking down at the remains of the 20 men he had brought with him.

'We can't bury them,' said Jas. 'The Jinx could return at any time. We need to get away from here.'

'I know,' said Taylor.

He checked each body for signs of life, then closed his eyes, hands clasped down in front of him. He looked as though he were offering a silent prayer.

Jas walked around the back of the truck, leaving him to his private moment. She wasn't religious, didn't believe in a god, and wasn't sure how to react to this ritual, but Taylor was entitled to his beliefs.

She found Kline at the back of the truck. He was badly injured but still alive.

'Taylor!' she called in a whisper.

Taylor came running, his semi-automatic in one hand, a grenade in the other.

He stopped when he saw Jas bent over Kline's body.

'Alive?'

'Yes.'

Taylor helped her lift Kline into the back of the truck, and she climbed in with him. She pulled off her rucksack, removed the hard weapons from inside and rested Kline's head on it.

'Hang on in there, buddy,' she told him. 'We're going to get you back to the doc.'

Taylor backed the truck out of the carnage, then climbed out of the driver's cabin and came round to the back.

'What's up?' asked Jas.

'I can't leave them like that. Just give me a moment. My men can't become dog food.'

Jas nodded and watched silently as he took the fuel canister from the back. It was some time before she heard the whoosh of flames flare up. Even though the truck was some distance away, she could feel the intense heat coming from the bonfire of bodies. The air was thick with the smell of cooked meat, and she turned her mind away from any thought of her former friends burning. Already she missed Ashby's fooling around, and she couldn't imagine how she was going to tell Andrew, as she knew he had been close to him.

There was a first aid kit in the back of the truck – standard issue for every mission – so Jas opened it to see if there was anything she could use to help Kline. She found disinfectant and dressings, but as she attempted to examine Kline she realised the blood on his clothing had dried. It would take water and scissors to remove his vest, and she didn't really want to know what she would find there. Instead she used the dressings to try to staunch the flow of blood from his shoulder and stomach while she waited for Taylor to return.

21

Kline's clothing was stuck to his flesh in congealed lumps of blood, and Gerald had to cut the uniform from the soldier before he could examine him properly. Not only had a Jinx sword pierced his side, but the bullet wound in his shoulder from the power station assault was infected and festering. Fortunately Kline was unconscious and couldn't feel Gerald digging inside the hole as he searched for the bullet. By some miracle the sword wound had missed the soldier's major organs, but he had suffered massive blood loss. On top of this, Gerald could retrieve only part of the bullet on the first attempt. Somehow it had fractured inside his shoulder, and it took the doctor over an hour to pull out all the shards of metal, as well as pieces of shattered bone.

'I'm not a surgeon, I'm a GP,' Gerald murmured.

'Just do your best, doc. That's all I ask,' Taylor said.

They were in the first aid medical centre at the mall. Gerald had established early on that it had a modicum of equipment, and had spent some time creating a surgery there in case any of the soldiers got wounded.

Kline lay on an ambulance trolley that the soldiers had salvaged on one of their many excursions.

'He's lost a lot of blood,' Gerald said. 'Maybe as much as four pints.'

'How the devil did he keep going?' asked Taylor.

'Probably adrenaline. But it's finally caught up with him, and we need to give him a transfusion as soon as possible.'

The doctor ran some tests, and once Kline's blood group had been established he asked for volunteers to give some blood.

'O Positive. The common variety. Which is good news for us,' Gerald said.

'I'm O Pos, doc,' Harvey said.

'You sure?' asked Taylor.

'Definitely.'

'Good. Because we don't have time to do any more tests,' Gerald said. 'Sit down. We're doing this the old fashioned way, vein to vein.'

Harvey sat beside Kline and turned his head away as the doctor pressed a needle shunt into his arm.

'I need to go and brief the others on what happened,' said Taylor. 'Don't lose him, doc. Enough good men have died already.'

Jas walked to the door with Taylor, and it was only then that she noticed the dog tags clutched firmly in his fist. She met his eyes and knew that in the time he had stayed to burn the bodies he had also removed the tags.

'I'll stay and help the doc,' Jas said, and for a moment the male façade slipped from her features, only to be restored as she turned to talk to Gerald.

Taylor stared after her for a while before slipping silently from the room.

Kline groaned on the table. Gerald leaned over him and injected him.

'Morphine,' he explained to Jas and Harvey. 'He's coming round and it will keep him woozy and pain free.

Once the transfusion was complete, Gerald began to stitch up Kline's stomach wound. Jas watched him sewing the man's body together layer by layer, and she was impressed with his skill, despite his protestations that he wasn't a surgeon. She took away the bloody dressings and used instruments, placing the latter in the makeshift steriliser that Gerald had devised. It was an infant bottle steriliser and would have been no good if the electricity hadn't still been working in the mall.

Then she watched as Gerald took the shunt from Harvey's arm.

'That's enough for now. Go get some rest,' said Gerald. 'There's nothing more we can do for Kline now. Time will tell.'

Harvey stood up, then swayed on his feet. Jas caught hold of his arm and held him up until his equilibrium restored.

'Whoa. Head rush.'

'I'll get him to his quarters,' Jas said.

'Lie down for an hour or two,' Gerald recommended.

Harvey nodded, then allowed Jas to lead him from the clinic.

Taylor was leaving the stage as Jas arrived back at the mess. The soldiers were unusually quiet, and Jas noticed how thin on the ground they seemed. Losing almost a quarter of their number had a real impact. She now understood why Taylor had refused to take chances with them before.

Andrew was on the stage, helping to hammer nails into the back wall.

'They are using that as a tribute area. Gonna hang the tags there,' said Donovan as Jas approached him.

'Good idea,' she said.

Donovan nodded. Jas couldn't help noticing that this normally strong man had tears in his eyes. He dashed them away in an attempt to hide them from her, and Jas knew this was because he, like Taylor, instinctively realised she was not one of them. It made her feel sad, though, that he wouldn't show his emotions in front of her. He would let his men see the tears, but not her, though he might never realise why it seemed so bad, or a sign of weakness, if he let a 'boy' see him cry.

'You okay, Andy?' Jas asked.

Andrew met her gaze and nodded, but his face was more serious than she had seen it in the months since they had joined Taylor's army. She was glad, though, that he was strong.

'I'll miss him,' he said. 'He was my friend.'

'I know,' she said, resisting the urge to hug him.

'I need to talk to you,' Taylor said, appearing beside her.

Jas followed him off the stage and into the mall, away from the mess and the monument being erected to commemorate the deaths of their friends.

Taylor had created a private space for himself in a small shop near Debenhams. Jas had never been inside his sanctum, but she remembered that the shop had once sold leather coats and handbags. Years before, its owner, an Italian man in his forties, had tried his best to sell her a coat for £400. At the time she had been a student teacher and there was no way she could afford the extravagance. Now, walking into the shop, she found it furnished with a sofa, a small table and four chairs, and at the back a double mattress with four pillows and a blue duvet. Any remaining leather goods were pushed back into one corner.

'You've really made this homey,' Jas smiled.

Taylor shrugged. 'It's important that we all develop a home wherever we are. That's kind of what I wanted to talk to you about.'

Jas felt a strange prickle of nerves as she sat down at the table opposite Taylor.

'Don't look so worried,' Taylor smiled. 'It's just … you're the only person I can really talk to about this.'

'What is it?'

'My men have suffered a terrible blow today, and yet the only thing I can think of is that our food supplies may now last a little longer with fewer mouths to feed.'

'That's a reasonable consideration,' Jas said. 'You've got a huge responsibility. The supplies won't last forever; we've always known that.'

'No. They won't. And we're not doing anything that will make that situation any better, either. We need to be out planting seeds and trying to rebuild the world. But how can we do that with no hope for the future?'

'What do you mean?' asked Jas. 'It's about survival, isn't it? And striking a blow against the Jinx whenever we can?'

'Yes. Partly. But what have the men got to survive *for*? They need wives, families. Something worthy of the fight. Only then do I believe that we can really bring the Jinx down.'

Jas sat back on the chair. She had lost the boyish aspect again. Instead of sitting with her legs apart as the other men did, she had crossed them, and her arms were folded in a defensive and feminine way.

'What are you suggesting?' Jas said.

'Don't worry,' he said, noticing her expression. 'I promised I wouldn't reveal your secret. But the truth is, we heard another woman's voice on the radio yesterday. What if we could find her, and more? We could offer them protection, and maybe relationships would be forged with my men. Maybe families would be rebuilt.'

'You think that would give them a future? Because I don't.' Jas' voice was flat and cold. 'I think it would give them something else to lose to the Jinx. Don't you realise it's better this way?'

Taylor stood up and began to pace the room. 'No, Jas, I don't think that at all. I'm a man, after all. I've been a soldier since I was 17. I've always put the army before my personal life, and look what the army did to me – it screwed me over. I know how the men feel right now. They've tried to cut themselves off from their natural urges because they can't do anything to satisfy them. Sure there are a few guys in the mix that aren't that unhappy. Marcus and Peters for example – everyone knows they're together, and we have no problem with it. It's not for me though. It's not for most of my soldiers. They need life. Real life. And only love and friendships can give them that in the end. I'm amazed at myself for saying this, but the army and the fight aren't everything.'

Jas said nothing, and Taylor stopped pacing and turned to her.

'Ever since I realised what you are ,I can't help but appreciate that this is what we're lacking.'

'Don't start this.'

'I'm not starting anything. I'm merely stating a fact.'

'I can't help you. I don't know what it is you want from me. All I want is to be one of the guys.'

'You could help us,' Taylor said, 'if you dropped this masquerade – and for the life of me I don't know how you're managing it. If you stopped hiding, maybe other women would too. Maybe we could find them. Help them.'

'Use them as brood mares?' Jas said.

She stood, arms still folded, and began to walk toward the front door of the shop.

'Wait,' Taylor said. 'I didn't mean ...'

'It sounded like that to me. We're not a commodity, Taylor,' Jas said. 'Maybe society should have learnt that sooner. I can't say I'm not surprised that any surviving females are hiding from you. On one side they have the Jinx, coming along and taking them against their will to god only knows what fate. On the other they have survivors, and that seems to come down to dogs and soldiers. The dogs steal, rape and kill. It doesn't matter what order.

The soldiers are warriors, but they are also men. If you were me, who would you trust? What would you do?'

The boy disguise was back before she reached the door.

'How are you *doing* that?' he asked.

'What?'

Taylor took her arm and pulled her back into the shop. 'Look,' he said, holding her before a full length mirror attached to the wall. 'Right now, you're a boy.'

Jas stared at her reflection and saw the boy. It was what she expected to see.

Taylor turned her to face him, then pressed his lips against hers before she could object or even register his intent. The kiss was over as quickly as it had started, but almost immediately Taylor span Jas back to face the mirror.

Jas gasped as she came face to face with her old self, Jasmine, and she realised for the first time that her disguise had nothing to do with grime and clothing.

'See.'

'I don't ...'

'But you see what you can do?' Taylor insisted.

'Yes, but I really don't know how.'

'Neither do I,' Taylor said. 'I hate to use the word, but it's magic.'

Jas suddenly remembered something; had a kind of flashback of her old life. The life when she had been Jasmine Regis, newly qualified science teacher. She recalled lots of times when luck had seemed to favour her – like when she had interviewed for her first job, and had won it against stiff competition from other outstanding candidates. More recently, she had also been aware of how lucky she was. When the Jinx had first attacked, for example, she and Andrew had hidden, and she had wished that the Jinx wouldn't enter and come looking for them. Luckily they hadn't. Even the other night, in the sweet shop, the question had floated in the back of her mind, *Why don't the Jinx lift the grille and come in, when they've searched every other shop?* That wasn't simply luck or coincidence or fate, was it?

'Glamour,' she said suddenly. 'I think it is called glamour. I don't know much about Wicca but ... my mother always said my grandmother was a witch. I used to think she was just referring to her personality – Mum and Gran never got along.'

'I don't believe in magic or witches,' Taylor said. 'But you do have some gift that I can't explain, Jas. Will you help me?'

Jas had almost forgotten what Taylor had called her in for, and she blinked at her reflection as she recalled his words.

'We need to find other women?' she asked.

Taylor nodded.

'I don't know how I do this; it's automatic. I'm around the men, I become one. I'm around you, I …'

'You're a woman. A beautiful, strong woman.'

Jas felt a strange sensation in the pit of her stomach as she looked back at Taylor. She recognised it, but didn't believe it. It was a feeling she had been denying to herself ever since she had met him. *It isn't love,* she thought firmly. But it was attraction. She turned to face him. There was no moment of instant obsession, no feeling of absolute need. What she felt was an acute curiosity.

The male façade was long since gone. Taylor wasn't sure what this meant. Was she agreeing to show her true self in order to help them? The answer came when she reached up, pulled him firmly toward her and kissed him.

22

Their affair would have to be kept secret, even from Andrew. Jas wasn't sure how he would react to the news that Taylor knew her real gender and that she and Taylor had feelings for each other.

It's not love, Jas thought constantly. *But we do need each other. I can see that.*

They stumbled around in the dark of Taylor's home, lights off so that none of the soldiers merely passing by on patrol, or wandering about because they were bored, would glance in and accidentally see them in Taylor's bed.

She let him strip away the grubby fleece and unwrap the bandages that kept her breasts flattened, but and then when it came to removing the bottom half of her clothing a sudden shyness came over her.

'Wait. I'm ...'

'Nervous?' he said. He felt her nod against his chest. 'Me too.'

They stood awkwardly, half undressed and both ready to flee the situation at any moment.

'Hold me,' she said, and he pulled her into his arms. By then his chest was bare and they both felt the press of skin against skin.

Her breasts were small, her figure slender. She seemed smaller and less strong than she had appeared to him previously. Taylor was around six feet two. Jas was tall, around five eight, but felt so much shorter stood in her stockinged feet, semi-naked in his arms.

'We don't have to do this,' Taylor said.

'Yes. We do,' Jas said. 'I want to.'

'Then we'll take it slow.' But that was easier said than done.

The kissing began again. This time it became more intense, more passionate. Jas felt a surge of lust in the pit of her stomach. Her loins ached, reminding her again that she was female; and as his hand stroked her breast, she groaned against him, partly with pleasure but partly because she wasn't sure she could go through with it after all.

Taylor tugged at the belt on her baggy jeans, but his fingers were awkward. He could load a gun in the dark, but somehow couldn't undress a woman. It was an art that required practice, and he hadn't done this for longer than he could remember. Jas's hands reached down and she unbuckled the belt with ease. The jeans fell to the floor and she pushed them aside with her foot.

I hope I can find them again in the dark, she thought.

Her hands found the waistband of his combat trousers. She felt around, then down, and her fingers brushed the hardness of him, sending a thrill through her. Jas had almost forgotten the sexual urge; the need to feel another person pressed against her, inside her. Part of the thrill was the realisation that Taylor wanted her. She pushed aside the doubts she had. Of course he wanted her; she might be the only living female left in England.

Before the Jinx had arrived she had been planning to move in with her boyfriend, Mark. They had met at university, both gone on to teach in high schools. But Jas hadn't thought of him since the first few days after the world ended. It occurred to her, as she released Taylor from his boxers, that she had barely given Mark a thought at all in the last two years. She didn't even know, or care, if he was alive or dead.

Taylor gasped as she stroked him. A drop of liquid slipped out of the tip of his cock in his excitement. He could barely hold on. He wasn't the type to spend time with porn magazines, unlike some of his men, who he knew browsed them in the newsagent's in the mall. Taylor had cut himself off from his sexuality, just as much as Jas had. He had held it in check, used the aggression to fuel his strength in a fight. He had become a soldier and forgotten to be a man.

Please don't say no, his mind cried as he felt Jas back away from him. *Oh my god, I need you.*

She took his hand and backed toward his mattress. Light from the mall poured in through the glass in the shop door and Taylor could just make out her shape. He wanted to throw her down and plunge into her as hard as he could, but he held back, enjoying the sway of her hips. She sank down on the mattress. *God she's beautiful.* In the gloom he could see her outstretched arms, the welcoming smile. *I'm dreaming. Or I've died and gone to heaven.* But even as he thought this he knew it was both corny and untrue. This wasn't a dream. Jas was more real than anyone he had ever met.

Her arms surrounded him and she lay back, pulling him close. Her skin was hot but dry and his hand ran over her, even as his head lay down on her breast. He turned his head, licking and searching until he found her nipple. She sighed as he sucked her as gently as he could. The moves were coming back to him and his confidence grew. His hand slid down her flat stomach and found the soft place between her legs. She opened up to him, let his fingers explore her, and her breathing became shallow as he probed and touched, felt the inviting wetness dampen his fingertips.

She rocked her hips against him, urging his fingers to move quicker, and he couldn't help it, he had to slip one of them inside her, feel how tight she was.

'Oh,' Jas gasped, then her body jerked and spasmed as she came against him.

He slid over her as she was recovering. His cock ached so much he thought he would go insane if he didn't enter her soon. She opened her legs and he positioned himself above her, then paused. This moment would change everything between them. After this, he could no longer just forget what she was.

Her hand reached down between them. She stroked him, rubbed the tip of his penis against herself and wrapped her legs around him. Then she positioned him in her opening and pressed upwards.

'How much more of an invitation do you need?' she whispered.

He pushed in, body shuddering as he felt her tightness tense and then open slightly. She was wet from her orgasm but so tight, so small. He eased in, and she groaned and arched against him, grasping him harder with her legs.

'God,' he murmured. He pressed harder, found himself all the way in and stayed there, feeling her excitement washing over him.

She instigated the movement once more. A groan escaped his lips as he felt her gripping his shaft with every thrust. His hips jerked inwards with a will of their own and he found his rhythm, taking her slowly at first and then harder as she opened up more.

'Yes,' she urged. 'Oh fuck yes.'

Taylor's cock throbbed, but he took her hard, loving the feel of her lust gushing over him as she came again, gasping against his lips. His tongue plunged inside her mouth as his hips ground against her. He thought he would split her in two, but just couldn't help himself, and he pounded her so hard he could almost feel the ground against his knees through the mattress.

He came, and it went on forever. His brain exploded as his semen gushed into her, and still he couldn't stop fucking, couldn't stop moving, forcing every last drop he had right up inside her.

'I'm sorry,' he said later.

'What for?'

She was pressed against him, head resting on his shoulder.

'I was a bit rough with you. I'm sorry if it hurt.'

'In case you didn't notice, I was having a great time,' Jas laughed.

He pulled her into his arms and Jas felt like she was being enveloped. She felt loved. She lay on his mattress feeling the remnants of his lust seeping out of her, and she loved the sensation of having his semen in her. She felt like a woman again.

There was no regret, but briefly the thought crossed her mind that she might not be able to hide who she was anymore.

They made love a few times more, waking up, reaching for each other. Each time was less urgent and more loving. But as the morning broke, Jas slipped on her clothes and returned to her quarters, leaving Taylor sleeping and exhausted.

Later, Jas found Andrew asleep as she entered their quarters. The bandages were back over her breasts, as was the sloppy T-shirt and the old and dirty fleece. Jas the boy once more, she slipped into her duvet, drifting off to sleep almost as soon as her head touched the pillow.

23

'Girl …' murmured Kline.

'Kline, can you hear me?' said Gerald. Raising one of his patient's eyelids, he focused his penlight into the man's eyes but gained no reaction.

Gerald had slept in the clinic all night on the sofa because he didn't want to leave Kline

'Ashby …' murmured Kline.

'You're safe, Kline. You're back at the mall.'

Kline blinked. Then his eyes closed again. His head turned in panic as though he saw some hidden terror lurking behind his eyelids. He dreamt of Ashby, saw him cut in two, and then he saw Jas. Beautiful and powerful. Like a goddess or an Amazonian warrior. She had fought the Jinx off. His dream stalled, then restarted. Jinx. Attack. Ashby. Jas. Girl. It was caught a loop in his fevered mind. A haze that was both memory and dream surrounded the repeated images that floated over his mind again and again.

Gerald turned away and began to fill a syringe with a strong antibiotic to fight the infection developing in the wound in Kline's shoulder. The fever was a sign that the infection was bad, and he was afraid for the soldier. He was worried that gangrene might have set in somewhere deep inside the wound. He cursed the fact that he didn't have the right equipment there. His little makeshift clinic had even less than a regular surgery might have, and yet he was forced to operate in these less than hygienic surroundings.

'Girl …' Kline murmured again. 'Jas is a girl …'

Gerald looked at the delirious man sharply. 'That fever's really going to your head, isn't it? Imagining girls now, are we? Well, we're all wishing we could find one of those.'

Kline fell silent as Gerald injected the antibiotic into the drip. 'A few hours of this and you'll be feeling much better.' *I hope*, the doctor added silently to himself.

Kline drifted back to sleep, but his delirious brain was tormented by images of Jas. There was a white haze around her as she turned and fought, swinging the huge Jinx sword around as though it were nothing.

'She's special ...' Kline murmured.

'All women are.'

Harvey put his head around the door. 'How is he?' he asked.

Gerald shrugged. 'Feverish. He's imagining men turning into women.'

Harvey came in and stood looking down on the unconscious soldier. 'Kline's a good man,' he said. 'How's the injuries looking, doc?'

'The shoulder's not good,' said Gerald. 'It became badly infected. As you know, with a bullet wound, the sooner you get the foreign body out the better. Unfortunately that didn't happen for almost 20 hours after he received the wound. He fought with it, giving those bullet shards time to do more damage inside. I think it's unlikely he'll have the same amount of movement even if he does survive. As for the stomach wound, it's going to take some time to recover from. The Jinx aimed to gut him and then left him for dead. Luckily for him the Jinx missed. The weapon pierced his side and somehow managed to avoid hitting any internal organs. Fortunately the wound was clean. Let's hope a little more luck is on his side.'

'I'll go and report to the Captain,' Harvey said as he left. Then as an afterthought he turned back to the doctor. 'You haven't seen him this morning?'

'No,' said Gerald. 'You're the first one in. I haven't seen Captain Taylor since he brought Kline in yesterday with Jas.'

'They were lucky to come out of it without a scratch,' Harvey said. 'The boss looked exhausted last night. I noticed he turned his lights off early. Think he just crashed.'

'I'm sure he needed the rest.'

Harvey left and Gerald looked once more at Kline. The man was sleeping now, and his face had become calm.

'It's okay,' said Kline. 'She's the one ...'

Gerald sighed, but Kline's words set off a chain reaction in his gut, and a feeling of anxiety made his hands tremble as he looped a blood pressure monitor around his patient's forearm. The words 'girl' and 'Jas' felt like an oxymoron; they didn't go together. And yet somehow the idea fitted.

I'm going mad, Gerald thought. *Or it's just wishful thinking.*

But the thought seeped into his subconscious and he couldn't shake the suspicion, no matter how absurd it felt.

Gerald took a seat on a chair beside Kline. The soldier was breathing softly. The morphine had kicked in and he was sleeping soundly. No more rambling, no more delirium. But Gerald waited and listened anyway. He wanted to hear more of what Kline had seen.

Harvey passed through the mess and noticed that Donovan had begun breakfast food distribution. He was hungry, but he wanted to talk to Taylor, so his ration would have to wait for his return. He passed the old information desk, turned left and headed toward Debenhams. It was 6 am but the mall was lit up like a Christmas tree as it always was: the lights permanently on. It occurred to Harvey that none of them had ever really tried to figure out how to turn the main hall lights off at night. It wasn't as though they were worried about a fuel bill, but it was a waste of energy.

Harvey passed the clothing shop where the two boys, Jas and Andrew, lived. He glanced in and noticed Jas passing through to the back room. The kid looked weary and he suspected the Jinx attack had taken a lot out of him too.

He reached the leather shop and saw that Taylor's door was closed. He looked in through the glass, but the lights were off, and despite the light that poured in from the mall, he could barely make out the back of the room.

He thought for a moment, then rapped lightly on the door. Taylor jerked awake and glanced over to the door to see Harvey peering into the shop. He stretched his hand out to the other side of his bed. It was still warm. Jas hadn't left that long before, but he had been so soundly asleep that he hadn't heard her leave. He briefly wondered if Harvey had seen her go, but then shrugged. What was the worst thing he could possibly think? That his Captain was having an early meeting, or that he was gay? Neither scenario worried Taylor much. But what if Harvey realised Jas was female?

Taylor got out of the bed and pulled on his combats, walking to the door as Harvey knocked again. He opened the door and stood back. Harvey entered and Taylor reached around him to switch on the lights. The shop lit up and both Taylor and Harvey blinked until their vision adjusted to the light.

'Sorry to bother you, Captain. I was just checking in on Kline, and the doc is still very concerned about him. His fever's bad and he's hallucinating.' Harvey glanced around, and his eyes fell on the bed. 'Looks like you had a rough night.'

'I didn't sleep much,' Taylor agreed. 'Tell the doc I'll be over there when I freshen up. What I wouldn't do for a shower this morning.'

Harvey left and Taylor looked around at the disarray of his home. The bed was the worst; it looked like an orgy had taken place in it. Taylor smiled tiredly to himself as he bent down and straightened the sheets and duvet. Jas was something else. A soldier, a woman, sometimes a boy, but god was she sexy in bed.

He felt sore as he washed in the small bathroom at the back. *Lack of use,* he thought. The room had only a toilet and a sink, but it sufficed for him to wash, shave and brush his teeth before leaving and heading over to see the surgery.

He passed Jas's shop but saw no movement inside. He assumed she and Andrew would be sleeping like babies still, even though under normal circumstances she would be meeting him in the gym for their training session at this time.

Taylor reached the clinic as Kline woke and burst into another feverish babble of chatter.

'He's been like this for most of the night,' said Gerald. 'I've just given him some more morphine for the pain, but I can't give him too much as it will slow the healing process. He needs all his natural defences.'

Taylor looked down at Kline. The man was moving from side to side, and Taylor noticed that Gerald had strapped him down to the bed.

'Girl … she's a girl.'

Taylor felt a flush of guilt colour his cheeks as Gerald leaned over Kline again.

'He keeps saying that. He says Jas is a girl. Stuff is all muddled up in his brain. Tell me, Captain, have you seen any females on your travels that can account for this sudden obsession?'

Taylor had recovered his composure while Gerald was looking the other way.

'We heard a woman's voice on the radio,' Taylor shrugged. 'That's why we were in the area. We thought there were survivors.'

'And were there?' Gerald asked.

Taylor became aware of a strange intensity in Gerald's posture and expression. 'If there were any survivors we never saw them. But there was definitely someone calling us via a shortwave radio. I guess the Jinx got to them before we did though.'

'What a pity,' Gerald said, dropping his eyes away from the curiosity he sensed in Taylor's.

Taylor left the clinic with a strange, uncomfortable feeling prickling along his scalp. He realised Gerald was the last person he would want to know about Jas, but he didn't understand why he felt that way. There was something about the way Gerald had asked him about women. *Maybe Jas is right*, Taylor thought. *Even the doc seems dangerous when it comes to it. How will my men react if they find out about her?*

He headed back to her shop, deciding to check in on her, but came across Donovan as he passed by the mess.

'This is for you, Captain,' Donovan said, handing him a bowl full of food. It was powdered eggs and English hash browns. Taylor observed that they were the type of hash browns served for breakfast in burger restaurants or sold in packets as frozen potato. He didn't care for them, but he knew he needed his strength, so he took the food gratefully and headed off toward the mess, passing Jas's and Andrew's shop without glancing in.

There was excited chatter in the mess at the possibility of female survivors. Taylor listened but said nothing. A party of men was scheduled to return to the Prestwich area to search again. Taylor was concerned that the

Jinx might return, but he knew he couldn't insist his men stay away. It was only natural for them to want to check the scene, and try to find others.

'You've got to be careful out there,' the Captain said as Donovan placed a mug of coffee down on the table before him.

'We will,' Donovan replied. 'It's not usual for the Jinx to return to the same place though.'

'They'd left a scouting party,' Taylor said. 'I'm certain that's what the first group was, and the vortex came back for them. We just happened to be in the way. I'm not sure they've ever done that before, so anything is possible.'

'You didn't see survivors though? They weren't captured?'

'No. Which is the only reason I can agree to you guys going back there. We definitely heard a female voice. And she said "We" – meaning there must be more survivors. Although I can't say what gender they might be.'

'We're leaving as soon as the men are kitted up and armed,' Donovan said.

Taylor nodded, rubbing his hand over his forehead. His men were beginning to feel less and less under his command as the days wore on. They were turning into the survivors they had sworn to help. He didn't want to risk losing more of them, but couldn't refuse the opportunity for them to return and search.

Donovan slugged his black coffee, then stood and saluted Taylor. It was the first time anyone had done that for a while, and it made Taylor feel strange, as though they wouldn't be seeing each other again.

'Be careful, Sergeant. No unnecessary risks,' Taylor warned returning the salute.

He felt old as he watched Donovan leave with 15 of his men. If they didn't return, they would be down to two-thirds of their starting number.

At that moment Jas and Andrew came into the mess. Andrew ran across the room and sat with Harvey, while Jas fetched coffee for them. She was bleary-eyed but she smiled at Taylor as she passed his table. She didn't stop though. She was afraid to be around him in case she gave herself away to the others. Any change of routine might reveal their new relationship.

Taylor downed his coffee and stood. He picked up a bowl of food and another coffee and headed back toward the clinic to give Gerald his ration.

24

'We have to be careful,' Jas said as she began to strip in the dark.

She had slipped away from Andrew as soon as she had heard his breathing grow shallow. Fortunately she knew not much woke the boy once he was asleep. She had pulled on her old fleece, but underneath all she had worn was a vest top. She was enjoying the feeling of freedom, the press of the fabric against her bare breasts. She was in love with her re-found sexuality, and hiding it on a daily basis had become more of an effort than it had been.

'Donovan came back with news,' Taylor said. 'They found an abandoned camp. Definite evidence of women and children having been there.'

'I'm glad they returned safely,' Jas said, slipping naked under the duvet.

She ran her hands over him, loving the feel of his body. They kissed and Taylor reached to the side of the bed and began to fish out a condom from the packet he had taken from the pharmacy that day.

'What's that?'

'Like you said, we need to be careful. At least until there are more women; then I don't care who knows about us.'

Jas was surprised. She hadn't thought of the possibility of pregnancy, partly because she hadn't had a period in over two years. She knew something wasn't working right with her body and wondered if indeed she could have children, but it made sense to take precautions. It would be inconvenient and a dead giveaway if she did become pregnant. In fact, that was an understatement. It was the last thing in the world she would want to happen.

Once Taylor spread the condom down over himself, Jas climbed on top of him, swallowing him inside herself almost immediately.

'I've wanted to fuck you all day,' she said.

Gerald hadn't seen a woman for a long time. He was almost afraid to find one again. He knew what would happen among the men, knew that just having a woman among them endangered them all. But worst of all he didn't trust himself.

He had watched Jas that day. He had always thought there was something odd about the older of the two brothers. But every time he had tried to stare at him for two long, his eyes had begun to hurt and his head ache. Even so, he couldn't get Kline's words out of his head.

He left his patient with Harvey, saying he needed a night's rest, which was quite true. He planned to return to his small home in the jewellery store and get some serious sleep. But instead of going directly home, he found himself walking around the mall for a while.

In Debenhams, he wandered around the clothing department, picking out a new shirt and trousers as his own were becoming threadbare. Then he wandered into the women's department. He wondered why he tortured himself like this. Everywhere he looked the clothing reminded him of Mallory, or Jenny Briggs, or Beth Turner. In the teenage section he thought of Rosa, the little Mexican girl they had rescued and brought back to the village. But what he remembered most was how he had treated the women.

Eighteen months or more had passed since David Keen and two coaches of survivors had arrived at the village. They had been safe until then, it seemed, living in their tiny isolation. Life had improved a lot for the villagers at first. David had been a good provider, his men tough but sane. Gerald had had medical supplies whenever he needed them. Times had been good. Briefly.

Gerald flashed back to the farmhouse. The discovery of the bloody bodies of the farmer and his son was burned into his memory as the moment when it had all changed. It had been the beginning of the end. He had known it then and he knew it now. It wasn't long after that that the Jinx had attacked and taken most of the women away. But not all of them ...

Gerald managed to keep some of the women safe, hidden away in the basement of the surgery. There was a huge walk-in safe there. Lead lined. A place where he kept dangerous drugs under lock and key. He hid Mallory, Rosa, Jenny and a few others in there until the attack was over.

Afterwards, he let them out and they found the village ransacked. The Jinx weren't just taking women and children anymore, they were taking other things too, mostly food. It left the few remaining survivors even more desperate than they had been.

Gerald found David Keen dead on the village green with most of his men. The slaughter was a terrible sight. Their beautiful village had become a killing field. Inside the church he found the vicar decapitated and his wife speared through the throat with a long lance. She hung from the door, palms facing outwards like some diabolical parody of the crucifixion. He found old man Sage, the vicar's curate, dead behind the altar, although physically unharmed. Gerald figured he had died of a heart attack when he saw the carnage occurring around him.

Later he burnt the bodies. There were too many for the small handful of women and children survivors to bury, and somehow none of them had the heart or the physical strength to take on the task.

The village was all but destroyed. They searched the buildings that were still standing for anyone else that might be hiding, but the Jinx had got them all. At that point they pooled all of the food resources and brought them all into the surgery.

The Jinx never touched vehicles; they never bothered about machines at all. So the ambulance was still there in front of the surgery. Gerald filled it up with fuel and once again went out alone looking for food for them all. He believed they would be safe. Everyone said the Jinx never attacked the same place twice.

'Any sign of an earthquake,' Gerald told Mallory, 'you guys get downstairs and lock yourselves in again.'

'We will. Please be careful out there,' Mallory said. 'I don't want to lose you.'

After his scouting trip, Gerald returned with a few provisions, but knew it wasn't going to be enough to keep them alive for long. He would have to go farther afield if he wanted more, and that would require fuel.

The women were jittery and scared. Naturally so, Gerald thought, and he issued a few of them with sleeping pills as they were too afraid to rest. They all slept in the house attached to Gerald's surgery, setting up makeshift beds on the floor. Each of them seemed afraid to risk being too far away from the drug safe. Gerald felt the responsibility of their lives weigh heavily on his shoulders and – he *liked* it.

They limped on like that for months. All sleeping together in cramped accommodation, Gerald the only man among them.

'I want to come with you, on the scouting trips,' Mallory said. 'It's not fair you should do this alone.'

'No,' Gerald said. 'You need to be here. Other than me, you're the only one who can open the drug safe. But you're right, I should have some help.'

Jenny Briggs and Rosa went with him on the next trip, and they took a journey spanning 50 miles before they found a decent supply of food. They filled up the ambulance and took it back to the village, and everyone ate well for a few weeks. But during the trip Gerald had noticed some things about Jenny that hadn't occurred to him before. He had always thought her attractive, and had enjoyed the variety of tight-fitting tops she wore over her large breasts. She kept thanking him, as did Rosa, for taking care of them so well, and he enjoyed the gratitude. Thought he deserved it.

156

Gerald felt like a king. He knew he could provide for the women in a way that they were unable to do for themselves. He loved to feel their appreciation. They turned to him for advice, hung on his every word – especially Jenny, who constantly pointed out how he had saved them all so fearlessly.

Gerald had always liked Jenny. Especially when she praised him so much to everyone else. She made him feel really good about himself in a way that Mallory never did. After that, he found himself watching her a lot around the village. She was a *very* attractive woman.

The night before they went on the next scouting trip, Gerald had a dream about Jenny. He saw her wearing a slave costume, serving him wine and grapes. He woken feeling strangely aroused at the thought of Jenny belonging to him, doing everything that he wanted her to do, and he began to have fantasies about her. Even on those rare occasions when he made love to Mallory, it was Jenny he imagined squirming beneath him.

When the time came for the next trip, Rosa was ill; she had developed a flu virus, which had quickly spread to almost all of the others. Gerald realised he needed medication to cope with the new illness, as well as new food and fuel supplies. Being two of the few remaining able-bodied, he and Jenny went alone.

In the ambulance he tried to keep the conversation light, but out of the corner of his eye he couldn't help looking at the shape of Jenny's breasts pressing against the tight T-shirt she was wearing. They were larger than Mal's. He had always liked big tits and, if he was honest, had often got a little thrill from examining women like Jenny.

'Well, the world has gone to shit,' he murmured. 'I guess we should live every moment we can.'

'What do you mean?' asked Jenny.

'Seems to me there's no-one left out there. I haven't seen another person for ages.'

'I don't believe the whole world has ended,' Jenny said. 'We have to have hope.'

'But if it has, what then?' asked Gerald. 'Old rules don't matter anymore. You have to take care of those that take care of you.'

He glanced at her chest, and this time Jenny saw. She flushed and turned away, looking out of the window.

'I like you, Jen,' Gerald said, placing his hand on her knee. 'You've always been so appreciative of me.'

Jenny said nothing, but she stiffened.

'Like I said, you have to look after those people who look after you.'

'Where are we going?' she asked, changing the subject. 'Do you think the last place will be any good?'

Gerald stroked her thigh, his hand slid up and slipped between her legs.

'What are you doing, Gerald? What about Mal?'

'Mal will understand if she has to share me. I'm the only man around. I've been thinking about you a lot lately, Jen.'

Jenny crossed her legs, folded her arms across her chest and leaned away from him, sliding as far over to the other side as she could get.

'That's a little ungrateful of you,' he pointed out. 'Especially since I did save your life.'

Jenny was quiet. They travelled for a few miles in silence before they saw the petrol station and Spar shop. It was off the beaten track in a country lane, and it looked deserted. Gerald pulled the ambulance into the petrol station and got out of. He went inside to check the fuel pumps.

'Fill her up, Jen!' he had called. 'Then come in here and help me pack up. There's chocolate and snack food we could use.'

Jenny got out of the car and Gerald had watched her pull off the fuel cap and begin to fill up the ambulance. Then she removed the canisters from the back and filled them too. She had a gorgeous figure; curvy and sexy. Gerald admired her bottom as she bent over and secured the caps back onto the fuel cans. Then he watched her stow them in the back again.

Gerald took a stack of plastic bags from behind the counter and was rapidly filling them with everything edible when Jenny came inside. She helped him complete the task, then took the filled bags out to the back of the ambulance. When she returned, Gerald was so aroused that he knew he had to have her.

'There are some other things in the back that might be useful,' Gerald said, and he followed Jenny into the back room. There was a small staff cloakroom with a tiny sofa and a few large bottles of water stacked beside a cold water machine.

'Yes, I see what you mean,' said Jenny. 'Can we carry those between us?'

'Eventually.' Gerald caught hold of her and pulled her into his arms. She was stiff and frightened but didn't resist.

'Gerald,' she said, 'I don't want ...'

'Come on, Jen. Let's have a little fun. I mean ... who's going to know? Aren't you a little lonely? Let's face it, you haven't been getting any from elsewhere, now have you?'

Jenny let him kiss her, though he could feel her heart pounding with fear. She had never seen this side of Gerald before and he knew she was too afraid to fight or argue with him. They were alone. How could she refuse?

His hands were all over her breasts, squeezing painfully, and he yanked up her T-shirt and bra, then kneeled down and began to suckle on her.

'You're gorgeous, Jenny. These are magnificent, just like I thought they would be.'

He tugged at her tracksuit bottoms, pulling them down.

'Sexy girl,' he gasped when he saw the thong she was wearing. 'I want you so much.'

'No Gerald. We shouldn't. I don't want ...'

He stood up, turned her around. His hands were cupping her breasts and he was gasping excitedly as he pressed against her.

'Gerald, please,' she said.

Then he bent her down, over the back of the sofa, and she felt him fumbling with his clothes, freeing himself.

'Stop it!' she said, struggling to stand back up, but he was too strong for her and he forced her back down and over the couch. 'I don't want to, Gerald. I said stop it.'

His cock prodded her from behind but couldn't find the right spot. Gerald was amused that Jenny tried to keep her legs closed. He knew how to deal with that. His knee hit the back of her leg, her knee gave and he was able to force her legs open.

'Please stop it, Gerald,' she sobbed. 'This isn't right, surely you know that?'

He pushed inside her and she screamed. She was dry and tight, clearly not ready, but he continued to force his way in until she collapsed over the sofa sobbing. Her cries had excited him and he pulled back, plunging in and out of her until he felt her natural lubrication kick in.

'Fuck. You're so tight,' he gasped, coming hard inside her.

Jenny stopped crying as he pulled away. She stood up, pulled up her jogging pants and turned to face him.

'I can't believe you just did that to me. You raped me, Gerald.'

Gerald's face hardened. He still wanted her. Wanted to throw her on her back and fuck her until she was insensible. Some part of his brain felt a momentary pang of guilt but another part, a more primal instinct in him, said that he owned her. He owned all the women because he cared for them and there was no other man to challenge him.

'Take your clothes off, Jenny,' he ordered. 'All of them. I want to see you naked.'

'No,' she said.

He struck her then. A tiny stinging slap across the cheek. It wasn't hard enough to mark her, but was enough to show her he meant business. Jenny put her hand to her face, shocked, and stared into Gerald's eyes. He could see she thought him insane, and she was afraid, so afraid that he would do more to her than the rape. She began to undress. Gerald felt triumphant. 'Good girl,' he said as she dropped her clothing over the sofa. 'Now kneel down.'

He forced her to suck him until he came in her mouth, then after she had spat and heaved his semen out of her throat he made her suck him hard again. This time he fucked her on her back. He loved watching her big breasts bounce with every thrust, and as he shot into her again, he knew he would be able to make her do whatever he wanted from then on.

Afterwards Jenny went into the service station bathroom to clean up. Gerald made her leave the door open. He watched emotionlessly as she washed. Then he turned away to continue packing the bits of food they had found.

She came out of the bathroom looking composed, 'Ready?' she asked Gerald, and he was surprised by her reaction.

Gerald had been considering the possibilities while Jenny was in the bathroom. Part of him had begun to think that maybe he couldn't now take Jenny back to the village. A sliver of guilt went up his spine as he thought of Mal's reaction to what he had done. It wasn't merely betrayal. He had raped Jenny. Even though he had thought she was asking for it, he had got off on the power it gave him. He had never felt so strong before.

After they loaded the bottles of water into the ambulance, Gerald opened the passenger door for Jenny, and as she climbed into the front, his hand slid over her bottom, between her cheeks. She was always wearing these tight-fitting clothes. She was just asking to be fucked. He was a man, so how could he help it? Clearly this was what she had wanted all along.

Gerald got into the ambulance and started the engine, 'You're mine now, Jen. I'm going to fuck you whenever I like. How does that make you feel?'

Jenny forced a smile to her lips. She knew the score.

'Excited,' she said.

If Gerald had known what she was really thinking, he would have killed her long before things got out of hand, but he was blind to anything other than his sense of invincibility. He felt he owned the women of the village, and as he drove back, he began to fantasise about all of them. Rosa and Jen both in the bed with him. Doing everything he wanted them to do to him and each other.

They would be his personal harem. His dick hardened at the thought of them all serving him. Somewhere in his crazed brain, Gerald imagined them all having children by him. They would rebuild the world like Adam and Eve in the Garden of Eden. He didn't consider this beyond his reach.

They headed back to the village, but first made a detour to a small pharmaceutical company that Gerald remembered had a warehouse in the area. And even though they found the place had been raided, there were still enough supplies left to help top up what he had back home.

His girls would recover from their flu and then he would start to sample them all.

About an hour from the village he pulled the ambulance over.

'Get out,' he ordered Jenny.

She looked over to him afraid.

'Over there. In the grass.'

She got out of the ambulance and stood in the field at the side of the road. Gerald's cock was sticking out so hard that his trousers could barely contain him..

'I want to see if your arse is as tight as your cunt,' he said.

Jenny may have thought it had been as bad as it could get, but she was wrong. Gerald was only just getting started. She screamed in real pain as well as degradation, and Gerald loved it.

She was quiet and shocked by the time they returned to the village. Gerald knew he had cowed her good and proper, and she wouldn't put up a fight any time in the near future. He didn't even feel he had to give her a warning not to tell.

Once inside the surgery Jenny went to the bathroom and showered, washing away all physical signs and traces of what Gerald had done. Gerald knew she was scared now, really scared. She had realised his madman's vision was far worse than she had first suspected. 'You were gone a long time,' Mallory said.

'It's getting harder to find things,' Gerald said quickly. 'It may take longer still next time.'

Jenny kept her eyes averted. Under the table, Gerald had grown hard again as he began to plan which one he would have next and where and how it would happen.

25

Jas left Taylor and slipped away. As she headed confidently back to her shop she didn't see Gerald on the tier above, looking down at the Captain's shop front, and wasn't aware of him following her progress as he walked silently in his bare feet along the balcony.

As she slipped inside the clothing store, Gerald looked at his watch. It was 4 am. Why would the kid be spending so much time with the Captain, in the dark of his shop, unless there was something between them? Gerald hadn't put Taylor down as gay, but he now wondered if this was all that Kline had seen. So the kid was young and fresh faced. Maybe the Captain could imagine he was female. Maybe Kline had seen there was a relationship blooming. Kline wouldn't be the first soldier to be homophobic. Gerald could imagine that in the soldier's delusional brain it might be better to imagine that Jas was a woman disguised.

But he felt there had been something different about Jas's walk that night. Or had there? Gerald wondered what he should do. He didn't want women around him. He didn't want the little world he had developed here with the soldiers to end. But he knew if there was one or more, he would have a problem being with them. It was so much easier to stay away, than resist temptation …

Gerald's mind flew back to Jenny and then to Rosa, screaming and crying while he fucked her at the side of the road. Jen sat in the car saying nothing, like a good accomplice. Rosa had been a virgin and he loved that he had broken her in. She was a clean canvas, he could teach her what he wanted her to learn.

Sticking his cock in her inexperienced mouth was a bad move though. He knew he should have taken it slow, but he just had to fuck her mouth. She had such pert, pouty lips. He didn't like it when she was sick over him, so after that he made her swallow him until she learnt to do it without puking. It was either that or he hurt her more.

Gerald hardened as he recalled Rosa. She became so good at it. And so enthusiastic, in a way that Jen never managed. She would suck him over and swallow as much as he liked. She even went for the girl on girl thing. Rosa got into helping him far easier than Jen had. And when they both fucked Jen, Gerald loved watching Rosa use a bottle on the older woman. He would make Jen strip so he could see her breasts moving. When she was all sore and begging them to stop, Gerald would get on top of her, and she would be so tender and wet inside that he would come in seconds. Then Rosa would lick Jen out while Gerald watched. Her little bottom would tip up in the air invitingly and Gerald would be behind her, fucking her too.

Although he knew deep down that Jenny hated everything he did to her, it never occurred to him that Rosa did as he told her only because she was scared he would kill her. Of course Gerald had threatened them both at the beginning.

'I'm a doctor; all I have to do is inject you with something and you'll be paralysed for life,' he had warned them both.

Jenny and Rosa knew he drugged Mallory. He had the pair of them in the same room while Mal was unconscious, and he had even fucked his wife while they watched. Mal never knew, of course. Gerald made sure she never woke during these times.

'I feel a bit sore,' she would say the next day.

'Let me look,' Gerald would say, and he would lie her down on the bed and examine her. 'Everything looks fine to me.'

Fortunately for him, his wife never realised it was bruising from the assault her body had experienced in her drugged sleep. Before long he was drugging all the women, putting it in a medicinal tonic that he made them drink at night. Except for Jenny and Rosa, of course. He liked them to be alert when he played with them.

Of course this all added fuel to their fear of him. It demonstrated the power he had over them all. Gerald could put them all to sleep and do whatever he liked, and none of them would know at all. But for Gerald the best fun came from the power he had over Jenny and Rosa. He got off so much on the fear he induced in them that he really wasn't interested in trying out any of the others for a while. He had no need, after all; the two women fulfilled everything for him, both so different in looks and attitude. And he had trained them to know their place completely.

It had all gone so well, hadn't it? Until the day the Jinx came back.

Gerald went back to the jewellery shop where he lived. He had all the home comforts he could want or need there. He even had a little fridge where he kept bottles of water and chilled wine. This was luxury compared with how he had lived before he met up with Taylor and his personal army.

He stripped and lay on his mattress, then let his mind wander back to Rosa. Skinny, boyish Rosa with her sexy coffee skin and her small pouty mouth. He remembered being in her mouth, fucking her throat so hard she gagged. He remembered looking down at the fear-filled eyes. She had worked so hard to get him off, so that he would be satisfied sooner.

His hand took his cock and he began to work himself as he thought of flipping Rosa over and taking her from behind. She was so tight, every time, and so small inside that this position was painful to her. Especially when he got really excited and started to bang her hard. She would cry sometimes, and hold herself afterwards. Then he would make Jenny kiss her better.

In his memory he saw the two of them, naked on his bed, writhing in each other's arms, while Mal's body was dragged aside and tossed carelessly on the floor. He would sit in his chair by the window, facing them, and they would slip fingers into each other, kiss and lick and suck, and Rosa would gasp and spasm when Jenny sucked her between the legs. It was her reward for doing what Gerald told her to do, and Gerald had loved watching her face frown as she came. It almost looked like the expression she had as he hurt her, except for the relief that softened her features afterwards. These moments were tender between the women, but all Gerald saw was the sexual act that he wanted.

Then he had learnt that the bitches did each other sometimes when he wasn't there.

Sometimes Gerald sent Jenny and Rosa out alone to find fuel and food. They never came across any other survivors, and they were all starting to believe that even the scavengers were dead. It was easy to get complacent, to begin to feel you were the last alive and therefore safe from others.

It had started when Mal got sick one day. Jenny had suggested she and Rosa do the scouting trip while Gerald looked after his wife. It would have looked odd if he had refused, but Gerald had been more than a little nervous when the two of them had driven away. *What if they don't come back?* he had worried. *What if this is all some kind of trick?* But at the end of the day the girls had returned, bringing better provisions than they had found in a while.

That serves me right, Gerald had thought. *Whenever I go out with them, I'm more interested in fucking than finding food.*

'You did good,' he had praised, and he had felt truly excited by their return. *They came back!* It meant he did have ultimate power over them and they were his slaves, just as he had fantasised.

He had plans to bring another into their group, so one night he gave Beth Turner a minor draught of the sleeping drug and paid her a visit, leaving Rosa and Jenny in bed alone.

After he fucked Beth – and the stupid bitch was still too drugged to make it fun – he came back to find his girls playing together. At first he thought it must be for his benefit. *They are jealous that I just did Beth instead of them.* But then he overheard them talking.

'Do you like that, Rosa,' asked Jenny. 'Or do you want Gerald's rancid dick in you?'

'No, I want you. I want your tongue,' gasped Rosa.

Gerald stayed unseen in the shadows, stunned as Jenny slipped her fingers gently into Rosa as she sucked her. 'Who'd want that stupid old man with his tiny cock when I can have a beautiful woman like you, Jenny?'

His anger bubbled up inside him. He felt betrayed. They weren't supposed to get off on each other, they were his slaves! But Gerald stayed silent and watched the girls until they fell asleep.

Gerald stopped playing with himself and cursed the turn his memories had taken. It pained him to think of the tenderness the women had shown each other. His cock deflated, he turned over in his bed and tried to push the recollections aside. But he couldn't get the bitter taste of jealousy from his mouth. He climbed out of bed, switched on the light and went to the small fridge. He opened it, took out the water jug and poured himself a drink.

He stood in the open doorway of his fridge, feeling the chill air on his hot skin. The echo of his wife's voice pierced the hollow room, and he felt like a world war veteran recovering from shell-shock.

'Earthquake!' shouted Mal, running into the house. 'The Jinx, Gerald!'

He quickly gathered the women and children, sent them down to the safe.

'Not you,' he said to Jenny.

'But the Jinx,' Rosa cried.

'She's staying here.'

'Then I'm staying too,' Rosa said.

'You'll do as I tell you,' Gerald said. 'Get downstairs with the others.'

'Not without Jenny!'

Gerald couldn't believe she was standing up to him, but he could hear the frightened calling of his wife downstairs. Jenny and Rosa clung to each other, and he knew he wouldn't win this argument. They had to go, so he would let the Jinx do his dirty work for him.

'Fine. Rot, you treacherous bitches,' said Gerald.

He ran downstairs, pushed Mal into the safe and slammed the door behind them.

Later they found the surgery ransacked and the women gone, but the Jinx hadn't even attempted to open the safe, so they knew for certain they could always take refuge in there.

'What about Jenny and Rosa?' Mal asked. 'Why didn't they come down with you?'

'I couldn't find them,' Gerald lied. 'I think the Jinx had already got them.'

'Oh no! That's terrible,' Mallory said, her eyes filling with tears. 'Those poor girls!'

'I don't think the Jinx'll be back for a while,' said Gerald, ignoring her tears. 'We're short of provisions. Beth, you come scouting with me. I need to show someone else the ropes. I think maybe we relied too much on Jenny and Rosa.'

Mallory said nothing, but Gerald had seen the frown that crossed her brow, and he wondered if she was suspicious of him after all. For this reason, the first time he took Beth out, they did nothing other than search for food and water. He wasn't stupid; he had to allow more time this time.

Gerald closed the fridge and pushed aside the thoughts of Mallory, Beth and his two favourite slaves. He didn't want to think about them or any women anymore. He didn't want another one around him under any circumstances. They attracted the Jinx and drove him to distraction. They made him do things he wasn't proud of. He never wanted that temptation again.

PART TWO

Jinx Town

1

'I see her,' said Kale.

'Where?' asked Arven.

'Glimpses here and there, and then suddenly invisible once more.'

Emperor Arven walked around the pool. He was tall, like all his kind, but far more imposing than most of his predecessors, with his broad shoulders and muscular build. They were a warrior race and their Emperor was the fiercest of them all. His long black hair was pulled back into a tight knot on the top of his head, but sometimes, when he wore it down, it floated thick and heavy over his shoulders and halfway down his back. His eyes were a swirl of greens and blues. He was a handsome man by Arrak Nah Tiaman standards. He appeared human, despite his height, but his eyes gave him away. They moved and pulsed rapidly as he stepped toward the pool, reflecting his curiosity. His face was shaved smooth, but for a small tuft of beard on his chin.

Images swirled in the centre of the water, but Arven couldn't read them like Kale could. Magic was for the Al Kuzemen alone, and Kale was the strongest of the mages, the leader that the others looked up to.

'Show me,' he said.

Kale raised his staff and shook it quickly over the pool. The water solidified and an image came into view. Arven saw the woman for the first time. She was disguised, dressed as a man, but it was clear to the Emperor that she was indeed female. Powerful. A strong essence radiated from her aura. It was a vibration that he had only ever seen in the likes of his magicians.

'Tell me about her.'

'A warrior,' Kale said.

'A warrior woman. Good enough to be an Empress?'

'Yes. But a dangerous woman, my Lord,' Kale warned. 'You must be wary of her at all times. She has a talent for artifice and feels no remorse when she kills.'

Then Kale showed Arven the atrocities Jas had committed. The pool froze over the image of bodies. Dead. Burnt. Decapitated. All deaths at her hands. A mountain of carcases left out in the sun for the animals to pick at.

The frozen pool showed Jas once more. The clothing she wore was ugly and dirty, but Arven saw through it. He imagined her in the Imperial robes, or a silk chemise. She looked fragile and harmless in his mind's eye.

'How can a mere woman do all this?' Arven wondered aloud, but Kale did not voice his suspicions, because he knew how absurd they would sound. He shook his head, and his long moustache swayed then came to rest over his deep purple robes.

'Where is she now?' asked Arven.

'In one of the uncharted regions.'

The Emperor was furious that Kale couldn't show him the woman as she was right then. The pool rippled and Arven leaned forward, looking deep into the watery realms.

'Here!' said Kale. 'She has left cover.'

Jas and Andrew ran from the mall, their arms full of supplies of food and drink and a small medical kit.

'Where is that?' asked Arven. 'We must open a gateway now.'

'No,' said Kale. 'We can't open there. Or anywhere within a five mile radius.'

'You disappoint me, Al Kuzemen,' Arven said. 'You are supposed to be the best of your kind. Is your magic waning?'

Kale bowed his head, and his long moustache drooped down and almost touched the water. 'Somehow, these peasants are able to block us. It is only a matter of time before she returns to the place she truly calls home …'

Arven gazed down into the pool once more.

'This is home to her,' Kale said. 'It's where she will run when the men she hides with learn the truth about her.'

This time Kale showed the Emperor a building. It was the site of their first attack, and Arven remembered it well as he had led the onslaught. A huge building full of people and an initial influx of the women they needed.

'This is her real home. The place she feels safest,' Kale said, watching his Emperor's stern face soften as he lapsed into memories of their attack. 'We must get to her before she enters.'

'Show me more,' Arven ordered, and Kale swept his hand above the water, changing the small tide, turning ripples into images.

A picture evolved from the clear liquid, water shaping into the features of a woman.

'She's hidden well …' Kale murmured.

'Leave me,' said Arven, bending over the pool's edge to look closer at the girl.

Kale backed away from the pool and out of the tent. He bowed to Arven as he reached the opening, but the Emperor wasn't paying attention. He was gazing into the pool, looking at the image of the woman who might one day be his.

Kale made his way through the town to his own tent close by. It was the equal of the Emperor's, and in the eyes of the people Kale had just as much power in their community. He was the Al Kuzemen – the magician to rival all others – and he had a string of apprentices working in the other towns, raising their portals and helping them rebuild their population.

At his tent Kale hesitated. This was where he had first seen her. Somehow, in a dream she had infiltrated his world and visited them. This one was special – very different from the others – and she had the ability to dream-walk, projecting her spirit from one dimension to another. It was how Kale had found her, but it scared him. The woman was powerful, fit for a King, but would Arven be able to tame her? Yet, Kale could not deny to himself that she had sought them, found them, all of her own free will. It was a sign. A sign that she belonged here.

At that moment Kale's tent opened and his servant girl, Ailsa, came out.

'*Do ... hak ... im memzah, Al Kuzemen,*' she said, but her use of their language was clumsy and halting. Ailsa was new to the camp, taken on their last successful raid some six months before. Since then, the raids had failed to find any more women.

'You can speak in your own tongue to me,' Kale said.

'Good evening, Al Kuzemen. May I serve you now?' Ailsa said.

Kale followed the girl into his tent. She had set out a light supper of fruit and cooked meat for him. In the corner, his bath, a curved ceramic bowl, big enough to fit two people, had been filled with hot water ready for him to cleanse the desert filth from his skin.

'Good,' said Kale. 'I'll bathe now.'

Ailsa attempted to help Kale remove his mage robe, but his height impeded her. Kale shrugged the robe from his shoulders and let it fall into her waiting hands. Ailsa was small, even for the Earth women; less than five feet tall. Kale was almost seven feet tall, slightly shorter than the Emperor, but still among the tallest of his people.

Ailsa kept her eyes downcast as she tidied away Kale's clothes. As his servant, she knew he could use her in any way he pleased, but so far he had kept his distance and showed no sexual interest in her at all. She felt herself fortunate to be assigned to him, but never made eye contact as she was afraid to appear anything more interesting than a servant. She didn't understand that Kale would never take advantage of her that way. It was against the charter. And the Arrak Nah Tiaman never went against their own rules.

Kale stepped into the water, and Ailsa's eyes skipped away from the firm, defined body that sank into the bath. He was attractive, but Ailsa avoided contact with him. He was alien and she was afraid of him. The glimpses she had had of his hairless chest had already shown her how different from human men were the Al Kuzemen and the Arrak Nah Tiaman – those whom the humans called Jinx. She busied herself around the tent, laying out the nightshirt that Kale would slip over his body to sleep in.

Ailsa didn't understand the language or the alien nature of the Jinx very well, but she had been told when she arrived how things would go. She would be assigned a male to care for at first – given a servant's role – and then eventually she would become wife to one of them. She didn't like the idea at all, but had quickly learnt she had no choice in either matter.

When she had first arrived from Connemara, Ailsa had been terrified and in shock. She had seen her brother and father slaughtered before the aliens took her. She didn't know what had happened to her fiancé, Shane. She had been wearing her wedding dress, on her way to the church, when the Jinx had arrived. They had taken her bridesmaids – even the children – and she had witnessed the brutal slaying of her nephew, a mere boy of six. A child who had never hurt anyone! At the time, Ailsa hadn't known why the Jinx had come, but she had soon learnt that they had no need of males, and sought only females. It seemed they had none of their own, but nobody had been able to explain why. The other women had rarely spoken, and Ailsa had realised that most of them were in shock too. Shock at the sudden change to their lives. Shock at the marriages that were being forced on them. But that was all in the early days, and now things were better for new arrivals. Mallory had seen to that.

Jinx Town, as the human women had dubbed it, was nothing like the world they had left. It was basic for the most part. Water was pulled from a river, clothing washed in natural streams. Food was cooked over camp fires. Ailsa felt she had been ripped from the 21st Century and thrown back into the dark ages. Here the women were servants and brood mares. They cared for the men, cooked and cleaned, gave birth to their alien babies.

Ailsa shuddered as she poured wine from a leather pouch into a bejewelled chalice. At least in the home of the Al Kuzemen she had some finery. A bed of her own to sleep on in the corner, and food and drink as long as she did all she was ordered to do.

Ailsa heard the water move and turned to see if Kale was ready to get out of the bath.

'Ailsa, wash me,' was all the Al Kuzemen said, and she hurried back to lather the homemade soap up over his nipple-less chest.

Then she rubbed his arms, swilling water over his opaque, hairless skin. She washed his long hair, rubbing in the soap and swilling his bowed head with the warm, fresh water waiting in a bowl at the side of the bath. Then she washed away the dirt and grime from the top half of his back and prayed that that night he wouldn't ask for more.

'Go to bed now,' he ordered.

Ailsa went. Silent and scared as she was every night. She was a good Catholic girl. She hadn't been with Shane; good girls only did that on their wedding night with the man they loved. On her small bed, Ailsa pulled the covers around her, cold despite the desert heat. She didn't want to give herself to an alien, let alone have an alien bastard growing in her belly. She heard Kale get out of the bath and listened acutely as he rubbed his skin dry. Then she heard him dress, and relief flooded her cheeks. She hoped she would continue to be uninteresting to the Al Kuzemen.

Ailsa said her prayers as she partly hid her face under the covers. *God help me! God help me! I just want to go home.* But she didn't know that her own home had become a wasteland. Ireland, like many parts of the world, had been devastated by the greed of the Arrak Nah Tiaman. They had taken the women, taken food and plant life, but most of all they had taken away anything that resembled humanity.

2

'What happened? Why are we leaving?' asked Andrew.

'Get in the car,' Jas said. 'We've outstayed our welcome.'

'I don't understand.'

'The doctor found out that I'm a woman.'

'How?'

Gerald had found Jas browsing the aisles of the pharmacy. She had already placed the contraceptives in her pocket and was pretending to look for something for a headache.

'Jas?' said Gerald. 'Can I help you?'

'Nah. Just got a few aches and pains and a little headache, doc. Mostly from the training. I overdid it a bit yesterday.'

'Yes. I was watching you train with the Captain. You're helping Kline too, I noticed.'

'You did a good job of patching him up,' Jas said.

'I'm not sure if he will ever get the strength back in his arm, but I note how hard he is trying.'

Jas nodded, but she knew Kline was determined to aid his recovery with exercise, and building the strength back in that arm had become the focus of his training sessions with her.

Jas had chosen some Ibuprofen pills and turned to leave the pharmacy.

'You know, Kline said some very strange things when he was feverish,' Gerald said.

'Yeah?'

Gerald noticed that Jas didn't look concerned by this. He glanced at the boy, trying to read his body language. Then he saw the corner of a white box poking out of his pocket. He reached out on instinct and snatched the medication.

'What are you doing?' Jas demanded.

'Don't you know it's dangerous to take pills without a doctor's advice?

Microgynon. This is a contraceptive pill, Jas. Why on Earth would a *boy* want that?'

'Is it? Must have picked up the wrong thing.'

Gerald folded his arms across his chest and looked closely at the impish face, the dirty grooves that showed up the fine lines on Jas's neck. The lack of an Adam's apple was obvious when you looked hard enough. Gerald forced aside the feeling of nausea he felt when he tried to look at Jas directly. The blurring effect gave way to focus. The façade had slipped. Gerald could see the female behind the masquerade.

'You mustn't think much of my doctoring skills if you imagine I can't even notice a girl when there's one stood before me.'

'Look, doc, you've got this wrong.'

'I don't think so. The contraceptives are because you're shagging the Captain, right? He knows. No-one else does. How did he find out?'

Jas shook her head. 'You've got to understand it's a dangerous time to be a woman. You can't tell anyone about this, doc. I've a right to chose to live my life how I want, and I don't want the guys to see me in any other way than as a soldier like them. They'd treat me different.'

'I understand that. And of course I'll keep your secret. The men would go crazy knowing there was a woman here.'

'Thank you,' Jas said, relief making her cheeks flush in an all-too-feminine way.

'So. You'll come to my shop tonight and give me some of what the Captain has been enjoying all this time. Okay?'

'*What?*'

'Well, I see it this way. You can give it willingly to me, or you'll be forced to give it to all of the soldiers when they learn the truth. You want your secret kept? Then you look after me. I'm sure it's the same deal you have with the Captain anyway, so what's the difference?'

'You bastard!'

'My shop. After dinner. And you won't go to the Captain until I've had all the fun I want … If you don't turn up, I'll be making an announcement to the men, and it will be all about you and your affair with the good Captain.'

Gerald walked away, sure of his power. Jas would be under his control and he would enjoy every minute of it; but his heart pounded with guilt as well as excitement. The cycle was beginning again, and he had been unable to stop himself. That dark, vicious side of him wanted to see Jas squirm, cry and beg as he took all the pleasure he wanted from her.

Jas stared at his back, her fist was clenched, and she had to force herself not to follow. She wanted to kill Gerald. She had killed men for less, but this placed her in a quandary, as she knew the soldiers needed the doctor. Leaving was the obvious solution to the problem: she and Andrew could go back to their old lives any time. The only trouble was that Andrew was happy here; and when Jas thought of leaving Taylor she felt a black sickness in the pit of her stomach.

She left the pharmacy and watched the doctor as he walked away through the mall. He was whistling. There wasn't even a trace of anxiety in his posture. He looked confident, relaxed and happy. Jas knew that she would have to try to persuade him somehow that what he proposed was wrong.

That's naïve of me, she thought. *He knows already it's wrong. He just doesn't care. Look at him. He and men like him are the reason I hide myself.*

Gerald turned the corner, heading toward the mess, and Jas used the opportunity to walk on toward Taylor's place. She didn't know if he was there, but she had to talk to him, tell him what had happened. Maybe he could make Gerald see reason.

The Captain was not in his quarters, and as dinner time rapidly approached, Jas began to panic. She loaded her car, which was parked in the delivery bay of the shop she and Andrew lived in, and left Andrew waiting for her as she went back inside for their sleeping bags. To her delight, she found Taylor waiting in the front of her shop.

'You alone?' he asked.

'Yes. We've got a problem. The doctor knows, and ...'

'How?'

Jas told him what had happened.

'That son of a bitch. I'll kill him.'

'No, Taylor. You need him. He's the only doctor we have. I'm going to leave. This whole mess has become too complicated.'

'No-one's leaving. I'm going to visit the doc and sort this out.'

'You can't sort this out. Don't you understand, he's going to tell everyone if I don't do what he says.'

'That's not an option. You're mine.'

Jas had never seen him like this before. His whole body trembled with rage. His eyes were fierce and murderous. *He really cares about me,* she thought, and the revelation shocked her more than it would have before the world ended.

'Come on,' Taylor said, his lips set in a thin line.

'Where?'

'We're going to see Gerald, and I'm going to persuade him to keep his mouth shut.'

Jas followed him down to the jewellery shop. He rapped firmly on the door twice, but didn't wait for Gerald to open up. Instead he pushed open the unlocked door and walked straight in.

'I believe you think you know something,' Taylor said.

Gerald was sat on his sofa in a robe. He smiled, and it was the most horrible sneer that Jas had ever seen. He reminded her of a crocodile that was sure of its next meal.

'Come to watch, Captain?' Gerald said.

'I've come to talk some sense into you. You can't betray this girl. Do you know what my men would do to her?'

Gerald stood. 'My dear Captain. You've been a very greedy boy, haven't you? You want to keep this quiet and keep a tasty morsel all to yourself. Then there will be a small price to pay. You'll share a little with me, or you'll share with everyone else.'

Taylor noted the cold arrogance and confident stance the doctor had taken beside the jewellery counter.

'She's not a piece of meat.'

'No,' said Gerald. 'But there wouldn't be much left after 70 other men, would there?'

The image of his men hurting Jas floated behind Taylor's eyes, and red rage came down over his brain, washing away all sense of reason. His arm came up and he swung, levelling a hard punch right onto the doctor's chin. Gerald fell. There was a hard crack as his head connected with the jewellery counter. Smashed glass exploded over the shop and Gerald fell heavily onto the shards, his face a mass of small cuts and beads of blood blossoming on his skin.

The rage left Taylor then and he stared down at the body.

'Shit. I think he's dead,' Jas said.

Taylor bent down and searched for a pulse. 'No, but probably concussed.'

'What are we going to do? I never realised he was so … so …'

'Vicious?'

'Yes.'

'I'm sorry,' said Taylor. 'I totally lost it. I can't help myself at all when it comes to you.'

Jas was quiet. She wasn't used to the kind of words that came from his lips. His passion was all she had seen and enjoyed. She'd had no idea at all that this strong soldier was capable of such deep feelings. No-one had ever really loved her, and she wasn't sure how to respond. She wasn't sure she felt the same for him, and it was this thought that frightened her the most.

'You need to get out of here, baby,' Taylor said. 'Go back to the theatre so I can find you later. I have to talk to the men. Tell them the truth.'

Taylor stood up and Jas ran into his arms. 'I don't want to leave,' she said. 'I've been happier here than I've ever been.'

'Hush,' said Taylor, kissing her lips gently. 'I couldn't and won't let you be treated like …'

Jas held him tight. In all their moments of sexual intimacy she had never felt closer to him, but there was still a nagging doubt in the back of her mind.

'I love you,' he said. 'You know that, right?'

'Yes.'

'I'm going to take care of this.'

'I'm not some weak and fragile female. I could have knocked that jerk out myself,' Jas pointed out, and Taylor smiled at the thought.

'You can't fight them all, Jas, and as much as I'd be by your side, we'd never win against all of my men.'

He kissed her again, pulling her close and holding her as though he felt he wouldn't see her again.

'Get out of here. Take Andrew,' Taylor said again.

'I am going to see you again?'

'Nothing would stop me ...'

Gerald groaned on the floor. Taylor pushed Jas away and held her at arm's length. He looked at her, and she was all girl: no sign of the boy at all.

'Go.'

She turned and ran from the shop and didn't look back. Outside she found Andrew waiting. He looked anxious and scared as she climbed into the car beside him.

'Time to go home,' Jas said, and started the engine.

3

Jas parked the car some distance away from the theatre, around the back: she felt it was less conspicuous that way. But as she and Andrew rounded the corner, they came face to face with the enemy.

There was no earthquake warning; the vortex was just there waiting, in almost the exact same spot as it had opened the first time, right before the theatre foyer. Jas felt the vertiginous sensation of *déjà vu* and stared in paralysed shock at the Jinx warriors stood in two ordered lines near the vortex.

It was as though somehow they had known she was would be there, that she was in fact female, and had homed in on her as soon as she had left the safety of the mall. She saw the magician from her dreams, recognising him from his long droopy moustache and the fine black hair that tumbled over his shoulders, framing a face that reminded her of classical paintings of mythological gods. He was quite beautiful.

'Come with me if you want the boy to live,' he said in perfect English, and then he held out his hand to her.

'Run Andrew!' Jas yelled.

Her eyes darted everywhere. The car seemed too far away for her to reach, and her arms were full of supplies.

Jas glanced over her shoulder and was relieved to see Andrew running into the theatre. He would hide out in one of their many specially-prepared boltholes. He was safe. She dropped the supplies and ran back toward the car. The sword was in there. She would fight them with their own weapon, even if they eventually killed her. She would never willingly go through that vortex.

Lightning cracked the floor before her, splitting the ground open. Jas tumbled and almost fell headlong into an opening crevice.

'Foolish woman!' cried the magician. 'We'll kill the boy, then, if you won't surrender.'

Jas turned back as she saw the lightning hit the side of the building. The walls had already been compromised by the first attack, and Jas screamed as she saw the foyer cave in.

'No!'

'Come,' said the man again. The lightning dropped from the air as she screamed.

She turned and looked into black and silver eyes, writhing with magic and power. The Jinx surrounded her, babbling in their alien tongue.

'*Mek zien*,' said one soldier.

'We'll bring the building down on him. Make sure he's dead. If you come now, there's still a chance he lives,' said the man, and she knew he meant it as he raised his staff again and turned to face the theatre.

The soldiers drew closer in.

'All right!' she yelled. 'Don't kill him!'

The magician turned to face her once more, and then Jas saw her opportunity. The Jinx were so close she could almost touch them. She reached out, grabbing for one of the warriors' swords. But then she felt, rather than saw, his armoured fist crash down on her, sending her into complete blackness after a burst of skull-cracking pain.

Jas woke up in the middle of a bizarre dream. She had felt as though she had travelled through time and space. Her body ached, and as she opened her eyes she saw a myriad of lights and colours reflecting on the bow of curtains swathed above her. She blinked. Purple fabrics were intermingled with deep reds. She closed her eyes again, trying to push aside the notion that she was in a whore's boudoir; but the feeling that she was in a brothel just wouldn't leave her.

Sounds rushed in. The soft chatter of female voices. *Impossible. There are no women. I'm dreaming for certain.*

She tested her limbs, stretching each leg and arm, and arched her back. Her head hurt and she could feel the remnants of a bruise on her temple, but at least it lay on a comfortable pillow. She opened her eyes, slowly this time, and without moving her head she looked around, trying to establish her location. She was in a bed: a four-poster, with drapes around her, isolating her from whatever was outside. She could hear the sounds of laughter, the chatter of female voices. Definitely. Fragments of her broken dream burst into her memory. The voices were real – they had fed into her subconscious – and she felt that she knew what lay beyond the silken drapes even before she sat up.

'You're awake. Good,' said a female voice beside her.

'Where are you from?' asked another.

The drapes parted and Jas stared up into eyes only: the face was heavily veiled. Pale grey eyes smiled warmly down at her. The expression was meant to be reassuring, but Jas was uncertain how to react. Was this some

Jinx female?

Her head hurt and she pressed her fingers against a tender spot at the side of her temple.

'You were knocked out cold,' said the veiled woman. Then she reached up and pulled away the thick white fabric from her face. Jas looked into the soft features of a woman in her early thirties. She looked human and was of average height – unlike the Jinx soldiers she had come across, who were all exceptionally tall.

'*Parlez-vous Anglais?*'

'Yes,' said Jas. 'I'm English.'

'Good. I wasn't sure if I was speaking to you in the right language. There are women from all over, here.'

'Where is *here*?' Jas asked.

'You're in Sharik, but everyone calls it Jinx Town. I'm Mallory. I'm kind of the Royal translator.'

'Jinx Town?'

'Yes. You were captured. Like the rest of us. Except we've been told you're to be given special treatment.'

'Shit! We have to get out of here!' Jas said, leaping off the bed; but as her feet touched the floor, a wave of nausea and dizziness overcame her and she swayed, then sank back down onto the edge of the bed.

'You have to take it easy,' warned Mallory. 'The Al Kuzemen looked at you and said you'd be fine, but that could have been a concussion you had. They aren't very good when it comes to medical matters.'

Mallory pushed aside the heavy drapes to reveal that the room was in fact a huge tent and was full of women, dressed like something out of a Sheik's harem.

'Where am I?'

'You can't get out of here,' Mallory said. 'This place is impenetrable. But you'll figure that out as you go along.'

'Tell me now. Why is it so hard to escape from here?'

'We're in another world. The Jinx dragged us through a vortex. We're on a different planet or in a different dimension. It doesn't matter which, but it's best you realise right away that there's no escape. Because, frankly, there's no going back home; and out there,' Mallory pointed toward the drapes that represented the opening of the tent, 'beyond the town, there's nothing but harsh desert. You'd never survive if you managed to get out of the camp. Besides, there's nowhere to go.'

Jas ignored the curious eyes of the other women.

'Come,' said Mallory. 'We better get you cleaned up in the pool.'

Jas let Mallory lead her away from the bed and through the tent. She took in the scene around her. Two women sat at a low table preparing food, another was grooming the hair of a beautiful girl of 17 or 18, who looked as though she was Spanish. Although the carpet was covered in rugs, Jas could feel the slight movement of sand or earth beneath her bare feet.

The large tent was luxuriously furnished with silk cushions and rugs, a chaise and several beds, and it was as huge as a palace. There were several areas within it that were cordoned off with more curtains, and Jas caught a glimpse into one of these as a beautiful woman, in pale green robes, lifted the curtain to enter. It looked like some giant walk-in wardrobe.

Mallory pushed aside a curtain to reveal another room. Inside was a pool the size of a small swimming pool. It was sunk into the ground and the floor was covered not with carpet but with tiles.

'Let's get these filthy clothes off you. You're going to feel so much better when we dress you in some clean things.'

'I like my clothes.'

'Why? You look like a boy in them.'

Jas felt too tired to explain that that was the point of her disguise. A warm glow of steam was coming off the pool, and the thought of submerging herself, scrubbing her cropped hair, getting rid of the dirt she had worn like a cloak for the last two years, finally overcame any inhibitions she had. She let Mallory strip her. Then, when she stood naked, she felt so exposed that her instinct was to get into the warm water immediately.

The pool was shallow enough to stand in and deep enough to swim in. Jas felt the water ripple over her skin, soothing all of her aches and pains. She accepted the soap offered by Mallory and began to clean her body automatically. Her mind was numb, so she focused on the mundane job of cleaning, and the sensation felt good on her skin.

The water stayed hot and golden, barely muddied by the filth and grime she washed away. Then she swam, enjoying the feel of the liquid.

'Feels good, doesn't it?' asked Mallory, but Jas knew it was a rhetorical question. 'The water is magic. It never gets dirty and never cools down. It always stays at this perfect temperature.'

'Built from some natural hot spring, I presume?' Jas said.

'No. Like I said, it is magic. You've a lot to learn about this place, Jasmine. There is a powerful force at work here.'

Jas stopped swimming and turned to look at Mallory, who sat on the steps leading into the pool, her feet gently patting the water.

'How do you know my name?'

'Kale, the Al Kuzemen, told me.'

'How did he know it?'

'He's the magician here, Jasmine. He's the person who opens the vortex, and he made it his personal mission to fetch you from Earth.'

'Why?'

Mallory shrugged. 'I'm not privy to that information, but maybe it was because they haven't had one successful raid in months. They haven't found any women at all for a very long time, and there are still many of their race without companions.'

'You'd better tell me everything,' Jas said.

'Do you like stories?' asked Mallory.

'What?'

'This tale is best told as a story, I think.'

Jas shrugged. 'I'm all ears.'

'The Arrak Nah Tiaman were a powerful and beautiful race of people,' Mallory began. 'They lived in their perfect world. They were warriors, with some potent magicians among them. But the days of war had long since passed, and it left the people merely living their lives with their families. The Emperor, Arven, was happy. He had a lovely wife, a beautiful daughter and another baby, which he hoped would be a son, on the way.

'Then the magic began to fail them. Some thought it was because the warriors had turned their backs on the old ways. No longer were they out conquering the universe; the warriors had become farmers and husbands instead. Their race was multiplying and expanding. Soon it became necessary for them to spread to farther towns, build new encampments. Arven was their leader, their Emperor, and so he gave each encampment a gift. Each one would have their own Al Kuzemen, leaving Kale free to send out his apprentices into their new roles among the people.

'Magic was power and all that they knew. Medicine and science – the magic of men – were seen as heresy. The sick could be cured only with a spell, or with herbs given by an Al Kuzemen.

'It could be said that contentment filled the land. The barren landscapes, once abandoned, began to bloom with the care the people gave them. Arven was a benevolent ruler. He liked the feeling that emanated from his subjects, and all thoughts of war left his mind. His ancestors were warriors, but times had changed. The Arrak Nah Tiaman did not want to conquer anymore. They wanted love and peace. It was a natural evolution. It was also why they chose to make this world their permanent home. You see, before then, they were the nomads of time and space, travelling through their vortices to conquer worlds, taking the food and possessions they needed along the way.

'For a short time, all was well. They prospered, their race grew. And then, disaster. Sickness and plague fell upon the women and girls, striking them dead within weeks. The Empress was one of the first to die, taking with her the unborn child, and her daughter soon followed. Arven was struck with the most terrible grief. He felt the pain of his own suffering, as well as that of his people, who also had to endure the loss of their female family members.

'The plague spread to all of the cities and encampments, and despite the efforts of the Al Kuzemen, all of the women died.

'A year passed. A year of more death. You see, without their women and children, the men were predisposed to die too. Arven's warriors had nothing to live for. Suicide after suicide was brought to the Emperor's attention.

'Then Kale, the chief Al Kuzemen, came up with a solution. They would resume their travels through time and space and search the universe for a suitable race, one that would provide them with the women they needed.

'The Arrak Nah Tiaman had little sophistication. They didn't think beyond their need to save their race. Instead they opened portals on many worlds, and the search went on for years. But with each new doorway, each new world, the men held onto their hope.

'Many worlds failed them. The creatures who inhabited were too different, too alien, to become part of their community. The Arrak Nah Tiaman lost the art of love and seduction and once more became warriors.

'Then, one day, Al Kuzemen Kale found Earth. He saw in his pool of images a world brimming with life, where the people were growing, expanding, building, and rapidly destroying their own planet; poisoning their atmosphere with the science they held in such esteem. Kale saw a message in this. If they were to take the women, the men must be destroyed. The men of Earth were the corruptors, and science had all but ruined the soil and air. It would be only a matter of time before this world failed altogether and its people became extinct.

'Kale knew that the women were strong and would survive the leap through time. But could they survive the harshness that had become the Arrak Nah Tiaman landscape? And, more importantly, were they immune to the illness that had destroyed their own females?

'When Arven saw the images he ordered Kale to open a portal to this world. They would take some women and see if the disease that had killed their own females could infect the humans.

'In the first batch, many died. But it was not the plague, but the shock of their new environment that killed them. It was the enforced marriages, the hard and challenging living conditions. The women of Earth were used to freedom and to using technologies that the Arrak Nah Tiaman did not need or comprehend. The Arrak Nah Tiaman were forced to raid the planet over and over, looking for those with the strength and will to survive their world.

'Kale advised his ruler that the women needed to be treated better, integrated slowly; and rape, which they had previously considered justified by the label of marriage, was soon forbidden. Even so, by then new children had been born, and they had the immunity to the disease. The mix of human and Arrak Nah Tiaman blood proved to be good.

'And so the new batches of women were cared for when they arrived, given time to adjust and learn the ways of their new owners. Given time to accept that God had given them the unique opportunity of an unsullied planet on which to live and to birth new children.'

Mallory fell silent, and Jas didn't wait to hear more.

'That's a fairytale all right,' said Jas, her smile cynical.

'A sad tale,' Mallory said. 'And I tell it so that you won't judge the Emperor and his people too harshly. They've suffered a great deal and lost so much.'

'Sounds like you've been brainwashed to me.'

'When you've lived here for a while, Jasmine, you'll understand that these aren't bad people. They have merely been driven to extreme measures in order to keep their race alive.' Mallory's voice was soft and calm.

'I see why you might think that,' Jas said. 'But I've seen what's left of our world. It's completely destroyed by these bastards. Why is their need greater than ours?'

'Earth is damaged and yet she limps on. To be free of humanity may save her yet.'

'I've heard all that stuff before from the Green Party. Maybe you should stand for Parliament next time?'

Mallory smiled. 'I understand your hostility completely. Everyone feels this way when they first arrive. Let me show you around. You need to see your new home and meet some of the other women. I'm sure that will help you immensely.'

Mallory held out a towel as Jas climbed from the pool. Then, when Jas was dried, she helped her into a long straight dress that slipped on over her head. It reminded Jas of a kaftan. It fell to her ankles and felt as though it had been made to fit her perfectly. Then Mallory draped Jas's head with a headdress that covered her short hair and most of her face.

'The Arrak Nah Tiaman faith says that all unmarried woman are to be covered until they are taken by a husband. You'll have to wear this any time you leave the tent, but only until you're chosen, and then you'll be able to have your face and head uncovered in public. No Arrak Nah Tiaman would ever touch the wife of another. It is a crime punishable by death.'

'Nice place,' Jas said. 'But what if I refuse to marry?'

Mallory smiled. 'When the time comes you'll be ready.'

4

Taylor, Kline, Harvey and Donovan arrived at the theatre as the portal closed and the Jinx disappeared from Earth with their usual flash of earthquake drama.

'Jesus. Look at this place,' Donovan said, his face white.

Donovan had never seen real fear affect his Captain before. Taylor was always the one to run headlong into battle. Right then he appeared to be on the brink of collapse, and Donavan knew it had nothing to do with a near-miss battle with the Jinx. He was clearly worried about Jas and Andrew.

They had left the rest of the men back at the mall. Naturally the Captain had told them the truth, omitting his affair with Jas but revealing how the doctor had attempted to blackmail her. The men had been appalled.

'That bastard should be burnt at the stake,' Marks had said.

'She's a soldier, just like us,' Donovan had chipped in. 'I don't know any man that could've fought the Jinx off like she did. Why the hell should it make any difference that she's a girl? Besides, we swore to protect survivors, didn't we?'

His short speech had elicited a cheer from the soldiers as they sat around the mess, facing the stage.

'Why should she be afraid of us?' Harvey had asked. 'Jas has been a friend to most of us here. So what if she's female and not male? It doesn't make her any less tough.'

'Is there anyone here that would disagree?' Taylor had demanded to know.

A ripple of 'No' had swept through the crowd.

Taylor had been relieved. He had expected recriminations, perhaps even a mutiny, but his men had showed him, as always, how very professional they all were. And it was this professional attitude that had helped them survive all this time. True enough, they had promised to protect survivors, but when it came down to it, they were men as well as soldiers. Taylor had always hoped they would all be made of sterner stuff, and their attitude had proved that his confidence in them was well-placed. His heart had felt as though it would burst with pride. His men had impressed him more than he could ever articulate.

'I'm going to find her and Andrew,' Taylor had told them. 'She needs to know that she'll always be safe with us.'

'No,' Donovan had corrected. 'She needs to know she's one of us.'

Taylor had nodded, and the men had all cheered again.

'Keep that bastard under surveillance,' Harvey had instructed Gerald's guards. 'Doc or no doc, he makes one wrong move and you shoot him.'

The theatre entrance was a mess of rubble. Taylor and the other three men began to dig with their bare hands. They pulled lumps of concrete, plaster and glass out of the foyer in an attempt to make their way further into the building. Taylor was hoping he would find both Jas and Andrew still alive. His biggest fear was that the Jinx had taken Jas and killed Andrew.

They found Andrew unconscious but breathing. He had almost made it to the stairs before the roof had tumbled down and the foyer collapsed.

'Jas?' Andrew murmured, opening his eyes.

'Where is she?' asked Taylor.

'The Jinx ...'

Taylor's colour became even more ashen. Donovan said nothing, but he lifted Andrew over his shoulder and took him out of the wreckage. Although the boy was injured, it didn't seem to be too serious, but they needed to get him back to the safety of the mall as soon as possible.

'Let's get the doc to look him over,' Donovan said.

'After his behaviour?' Harvey replied.

'We'll keep him under close supervision,' Taylor said. 'He's still the only doctor we have, and we mustn't forget he's patched all of us up at one time or other. That doesn't mean I'd trust him much in the future though.'

Donovan nodded. 'I'll make sure he looks after the kid, or I'll slit his treacherous throat for him.'

They placed Andrew in the back of the truck and drove back to the mall.

Inside, Gerald was in the sick-bay under guard, but he stood up and got to work as soon as he saw Andrew's injuries.

'Minor head wound, some scrapes and bruises, but no bones broken,' he concluded. 'He'll be fine with a little rest.'

'Good,' said Donovan.

'What's happened to the girl?' asked Gerald.

'She was taken by the Jinx. Thanks to you, doc.'

Gerald turned away and smiled. He was pleased that Jas was gone. At least now he could put all thought of her behind him. The temptation had been removed from his sight, and he could lapse back into the congenial family doctor he had always been.

'Why the fuck are you smiling?' asked Donovan.

'She's gone. That's good,' said Gerald 'Now no-one can have her. Not even the Captain.'

'She could be dead, you bastard!' said Kline.

'Women are nothing but an evil and corrupt temptation to men. Don't you see the world is a much better place without them?'

'You're crazy,' Donovan said.

'No,' replied Gerald. 'But their corruption made me so once. Now I don't have to be tempted again.'

Donovan left the surgery. His mind was buzzing with the insanity he saw in the doctor's eyes. Maybe that knock on the head had done more damage than they had first thought? Donovan didn't think so though. It occurred to him that what he was seeing was Gerald's true self. It was like a mask had dropped, just as Jas's disguise had been discovered. The doctor was insane. How could they trust him to care for any of them anymore?

'Can you help us? Are you there?'

Donovan looked down at his radio. He had forgotten it was still attached to his side since their return from the theatre.

'Is there anybody there? We need help. We're a group of survivors hiding out in a place called Prestwich ...'

5

'This is Rosa and Jenny,' Mallory said.

Jas held out her hand to the young Mexican girl first, but the gesture felt awkward. She was plunged into a form of politeness she hadn't felt the need to use for a long time. Jenny put down the brush she had been using on the younger woman's hair and looked into Jas's eyes. She smiled.

'They arrived here a little before me,' explained Mallory. 'But we came from the same village.'

'Hi,' Rosa said, taking Jas's hand and shaking it.

Jenny was older, maybe late twenties, but Jas sensed closeness between the two women, which she assumed had much to do with the things they had been through. She had heard that hostage victims often built relationships with both their captors and with each other.

'You'll be okay here,' said Jenny. 'It's a hell of a lot better than back on Earth right now.'

Jas said nothing. It was like she had stepped onto the film set of *The Stepford Wives* mixed with *The Sheik*. She felt confused and unsettled by the women, and since she had had only male company for the last two and a half years, she didn't know how to react or behave around females.

'I'm not one of you,' she said, backing away from Jenny, Rosa and Mallory. 'I can't behave like this.'

'Like what?' asked Mallory.

'Like a girl.'

Mallory shook her head. Like Jenny and Rosa, she suspected that Jas had been truly traumatised back on Earth. She would have to put a case forward for keeping her longer in the arrivals tent. She couldn't let any of the girls go to the auction until they were fully equipped to deal with it.

'You've nothing to fear,' Mallory said. 'I look after the girls and the Emperor listens to my advice. You won't be married until you're ready.'

'Then I'm never going to be ready,' Jas said. 'I won't marry a Jinx, and I damn well won't breed with them. What's the matter with you all? Don't you remember freedom? Don't you remember being your own person? How can you let someone put a veil over your face? It's like they have even refused you the right to be yourselves.'

'I remember Earth men,' said Rosa in her thick Mexican accent. She looked down at her hands. 'And how quickly they turn to savages.'

Jas backed away to the four poster bed on which she had woken. 'Is this where I sleep?' she asked Mallory.

Mallory nodded.

'I'm tired. I need to be alone.'

Mallory nodded. Jas retired to the bed, pulling the curtains down around her, shutting her off from the rest of the room.

Jenny picked up the brush and began brushing Rosa's thick black hair once more. Occasionally her hand strayed to the girl's shoulder. She stroked and patted her as though gaining as much comfort from the contact as she gave.

An overwhelming sense of vulnerability assaulted Jas as she shut herself away. She couldn't see the others, but she could hear them talking. The women appeared to be happy, but Jas couldn't believe that everything was as simple as it appeared. Maybe there was something in the water or food that pacified them? She thought it suspicious that they were taking this change of circumstances so lightly. But then she didn't know what each of them had been through on Earth. Maybe belonging to just one man was better than the alternative? At least there seemed to be fresh food and water here.

As if she had been listening to her thoughts, Mallory appeared beside the bed and lifted the curtain.

'Are you hungry? Do you need a drink?' she asked.

Jas shook her head and turned her back rudely, despite the obvious kindness the other woman was attempting to show her.

'Leave me alone.'

The curtain fell back into place. She heard Mallory sigh and walk away. Then the real panic set in, and Jas began to experience the first overwhelming feelings of claustrophobia. Jas knew that what Rosa had said about Earth men was mostly true; but she had been fortunate enough to experience camaraderie with Taylor and his men. Even so, she would never know how they would have treated her had they known her secret earlier. Plus she had no way of knowing if Taylor had really come looking for her as he had promised.

Listening to the women chatter while she lay behind the curtains, Jas recalled a time when she had been in hospital for an appendicitis operation. The illness had struck her suddenly when she was 17 and she had been rushed into hospital and onto the surgical ward. The ward had consisted of one long corridor with several smaller wards off it. There had been no doors closing off the wards, and Jas had learnt that the ward next door had contained men. She had felt strangely uncomfortable with the idea. Plus, she had been so near the nurses' station that she had been able to hear their inane chatter all through the night. The nurses hadn't seemed to care that the sick needed to sleep, and had made no effort to be quiet at all.

Immediately following the operation Jas had cried and begged to be allowed to go home. She had hated the hospital. She had felt exposed. She had been unable to sleep. It had been much like stepping into a completely different and unknown world.

At the time, the nurses had treated her as though she was being silly and oversensitive. But she had had an awful feeling that if she slept then one of the men would find his way into the women's ward, and this had fed her paranoia. Eventually they had given her a sleeping pill to calm her, and after a few days she had been allowed to go home. But Jas had never forgotten that feeling of not being in charge of her own circumstances, and she hadn't liked it at all.

Being in the Jinx tent with other captured women felt the same. She didn't feel she had any control at all over what would happen to her, and all she wanted to do was go home.

An image of the theatre, of the foyer collapsing and of Andrew in the middle of the debris floated behind her eyes with startling clarity. She could smell the brick dust as the walls fell. She could hear the explosive noise, and she could feel the burning heat of the lightning wielded by the Jinx mage.

Oh no! Andrew! He could be dead or dying. How can I get help for him from here?

Jas curled up on the bed thinking about Andrew. In some ways she thought of him as a son, even though she treated him like a brother and fellow soldier. Andrew had relied on her and now she couldn't save him, and it was all the fault of that magician – or Al Kuzemen – Kale.

Jas remembered Kale well from her dream of walking through the vortex. And as she lay in the bed, feeling small and helpless for the first time in years, she cursed Kale and vowed to avenge Andrew's death on the Jinx and especially the magician. She felt her eyes fill but refused to shed the tears. Crying was weak and female. She was neither. She would find a way out of there and get home. She had to help Andrew, and water leaking from her eyes wouldn't make that any easier.

A plan was forming already in her tired and overwrought brain. She lay silently, waiting for the women to settle down in their own beds. Then, when all was quiet, without a sound, Jas slipped from the bed and made her way through the empty tent to what she thought would be the exit that led out into the camp.

Mallory was summoned soon after she had settled Jas into the arrivals tent. She went with beating heart to the pavilion that housed the Emperor and waited outside to be called in to her audience with him. As she stood, veiled and trembling, Kale came out of the tent and nodded to her.

Because of her talent as a linguist, Mallory was in the valued position of interpreter for the Earth women. On arrival at the encampment, she had quickly proved useful to Kale. The Al Kuzemen had learnt English, but struggled with the grammar of other Earth languages. Mallory had spent a few months talking with him, and had very soon learnt the Arrak Nah Tiaman language from him. Kale had found her aptitude for languages impressive. It was on his recommendation that Mallory had been given the task of helping the women adjust. She had quickly chosen her team of helpers, including Jenny and Rosa, and the 'arrivals women' had become off-limits to the male marriage auctions. At least for the time being.

Despite her words of reassurance to Jas, Mallory considered the practice barbaric, but despite her best efforts, she couldn't save most of the women from this fate. All were given a week or two to settle in, learn a little of the language and the ways of the aliens, and then they were auctioned off in a bizarre bonding ceremony that represented an Arrak Nah Tiaman marriage.

Some were spared the auctions, though, and it was these women that worked in the camp as servants to the aristocracy. They were always the youngest ones, and were often kept back for later marriages. It was the way here for the mature women to be married first, which Mallory thought was a good thing, as they were more able to cope than the young girls might have been.

Fortunately this meant Rosa was safe for quite some time, but Mallory found herself wondering if she would be forced to part with Jenny soon. So far she had managed to keep the two of them together. She knew of their relationship, of course, and sympathised with them, but it would be only a matter of time before Jenny would have to be sent into a permanent relationship with a Jinx male.

'*Kin veria zah,*' said the guard, and he bowed his head to Mallory in respect of her position. She knew and understood the alien, and her mind translated the words even as she stepped forward in response. 'In go you' was the literal meaning, but Mallory understood the phrase as 'Go in now'.

The guard lifted the curtain and Mallory walked into the Emperor's tent. Her head bowed, her hands folded in front of her.

Despite her respected and trusted position, Mallory was nervous in Arven's company. He had the power of life and death over them all, but aside from this he was indeed an attractive man. She found herself drawn to his looks and strength, as she always was, and the feeling dismayed her, because the Emperor showed no interest at all in making her, or any of the women, his Empress.

Arven stood by the seeing pool, watching images that he couldn't read but nevertheless held a significant fascination for him.

'Lord,' Mallory said in the alien tongue, bowing her head lower. 'You sent for me.'

Arven didn't respond immediately. Mallory raised her eyes and studied his face while she waited for him to notice her presence. His eyes were still on the pool, and his features, classically beautiful like a Greek marble statue of some obscure god, bore a softer expression than usual. She loved to see this look. She saw if often when he thought himself unobserved, and he reminded her of all the classical heroes she had read about in Homer as a teenager.

'You have a new arrival,' Arven said suddenly, and Mallory found he was abruptly meeting her gaze.

She averted her gaze, not because the Emperor had a problem with her looking directly into her eyes, but more because she felt as though she had been caught out.

'Yes. Her name is Jasmine.'

'How is she?'

'She's a wild thing. She will be hard to tame,' Mallory said. 'I'm certain I will need more time with her than the usual allotted weeks. The poor thing has been living feral and has almost convinced herself that she isn't even female.'

'You like her?' asked Arven.

Mallory was taken aback by the question. 'Like? Why, yes. She's very likeable.'

'Already she has inspired emotion in you. Like the other two?'

'You mean Jenny and Rosa? No. My feelings for them are very different. As I explained ... They have been through some terrible things and I wanted to help them recover before they were auctioned.'

'Then what is this feeling you have for the new one?'

Mallory shook her head. 'I can't explain it really. I've never felt more certain about a new arrival that she just doesn't belong and will never fit in.'

Arven grew silent. His eyes returned to the pool and a slight smile played on his lips. Mallory wanted to move closer to the Emperor and see what he was looking at, but she was afraid to stir.

'She is wild,' Arven said suddenly. 'She is a warrior, and you are right that she does not belong with the other women.'

Mallory felt a tense fear grip her chest as Arven reached toward the pool and stroked the surface.

'What will you do with her?' she asked, then instantly regretted being so forward.

'Kale believes her dangerous,' Arven said. 'I think she may be tamed by the right husband.'

'The auction, then?' Mallory murmured, dropping her head. She was disappointed that he hadn't given her more time with Jas. In two weeks the girl would go to marriage whether she was ready or not. Mallory believed Jas wouldn't be ready, and she felt an overwhelming certainty that the

Emperor would regret this decision.

'I'll do my best in the next few weeks,' she said softly. 'But I fear that this one may not survive.'

'Tomorrow,' Arven said.

'My Lord?'

'Tomorrow's auction. Have her ready for then.'

'But … the charter, my Lord. All the women are granted some time to …'

'I insist on it,' Arven answered, and then he turned away, effectively dismissing her.

Mallory backed away bowing until she reached the exit. The guard raised the curtain and she turned and left, walking rapidly back to the arrivals tent. She wasn't sure how she would prepare Jas for the auction with so little time. The girl was pale and thin. Her body, more muscular than softly curved, was still so boyish and unwomanly. Robes would have to be made to show her off to her best advantage, but there was no time for such extravagance.

The other women were close to retiring when Mallory returned to the tent; most of them would be part of the next day's auction and so were as prepared for the event as they could possibly be.

'I'm not sure how to tell her,' Mallory said to Jenny. 'She is so alien to the rest of us. I'd hoped that the next few weeks would soften her and help her build relationships with the other women. Now that won't be possible. Becoming part of the community overnight, taking on the duties of a wife. It's all too much.'

Jenny patted Mallory's arm. 'You did your best. You know when they brought her here they said she was different. Maybe the Al Kuzemen thinks this is the best solution. A shock integration.'

'But Kale has always been against that,' Rosa pointed out. 'He was the one who helped Arven see reason in the first place.'

'I'm going to see Al Kuzemen Kale,' Mallory said. 'Maybe he can cast a spell that will help her settle in quickly. Or at least give her a potion that will keep her calm during the auction.'

Jenny watched Mallory go, then pulled Rosa into the corner where they slept together. She curled up with her young lover and, like all the other women in the tent, they pulled the curtains down around their bed and settled down for the night.

6

It was as though they had been rewarded. One minute they had lost the only woman they had seen for almost two years and suddenly a whole group of them had been found. Taylor couldn't help noticing the irony. His men had been righteous and giving, even though Jas had been taken so cruelly from them.

Then there was Dawn and her band of tough females. Twenty of them in all, and three small children: two little boys under eight and a baby girl of only two, born to one of the women after the world fell apart. It was a wonder they had survived so long alone out there, living in the small village of Prestwich …

At first Taylor had been afraid to let his men go back there again. The last time had felt like a trap; but naturally it hadn't been the women's fault at all. And he knew that if there was even the remotest chance that there were survivors, particularly women, then they had to investigate it.

This time Taylor stayed at the mall and Donovan led a small recon team and two trucks to the location the woman gave him on his radio. The men were armed to the teeth and ready to fight at the drop of the hat, but as soon as the trucks pulled up on the high street the survivors ran out to greet them.

The soldiers watched the women and three children running out of hiding places scattered up and down the street, and Donovan's cigarette dropped from his lips as his mouth fell open in surprise.

'I'm Dawn,' said the leader.

She was a tall brunette, pretty but with slightly hardened features. Donovan found it hard to judge her age. She could have been anything from early twenties to mid-thirties. It didn't matter, of course; all he wanted to do was throw his arms around her in glee as she rapidly introduced the others to him.

He couldn't remember all of their names, but one of them, Caroline, struck him as really pretty, and her smile almost blew him away.

They prepared to take the survivors back to the mall.

'I don't want you to worry,' Donovan said to Dawn. 'We're soldiers, ma'am, and we're sworn to protect survivors. You ladies are going to be very safe with us. We don't condone no shenanigans.'

'Well that's fine, soldier,' Dawn laughed. 'But maybe a few of us would kind of like some … *shenanigans*. We've missed being around men. If you get my meaning.'

Donovan was left speechless for the first time in his life.

The soldiers were polite and respectful as they loaded the survivors and their possessions into the trucks.

'How have you stayed hidden all this time?' asked Harvey, climbing into the back of one of the trucks to sit with Dawn and Caroline.

'Long story. But basically we move around a lot. The Jinx don't seem to be able to find you if you're underground or if a building is lined with lead. It seems to make them blind.'

'Lead? They can't see through lead? Like Superman?'

Dawn laughed. She had an easy humour and she, like the other women, was pleased to have found some other people, especially soldiers, to sit the war out with.

'I guess,' said Caroline. 'Are you all American?'

'Yeah. Except for the doc and for Andrew. There was Jas, but he … *she* was captured by the Jinx recently.'

'Fucking Jinx,' said another woman, and Harvey glanced at her. She winked at him. ''Scuse my language. We swear a lot in Salford.'

'That's Kim,' Caroline said.

Harvey had already been hooked at the wink, but he liked her name too. *Kim*. She was beautiful and quirky and her broad Northern accent was endearing. Harvey had always liked British women. They had a certain edge to them that the girls back home didn't have. They were bolder, more confident, and very often they liked him too. He smiled at Kim. She winked again and then gave him a salacious smile. Harvey sat up a little straighter and looked away. He felt his cheeks redden. He knew Kim was flirting with him, but he was trying to remain professional. Plus, he had almost forgotten how to respond in a situation like this.

As the women entered the mess they were greeted by shocked silence from the soldiers eating there.

'Sit down, ladies,' said Donovan. 'We have plenty for everyone.'

The mess erupted into sound and the men burst from their seats to surround the group. Introductions were made and the soldiers found themselves fetching food and drink and offering words of reassurance.

Taylor watched the commotion from the surgery door.

'See,' said Gerald. 'They are nothing but trouble. Just wait and see. The Jinx are going to be down on us like a ton of bricks now that you've brought that lot here.'

'Shut up,' Taylor said. 'If you step out of line with any of them, I'll put a bullet in your balls and watch you bleed to death. Is that clear?'

'It isn't me you need to worry about,' Gerald said. 'It's your men. Clearly it's now on offer, but there still isn't enough to go around.'

Taylor left the surgery and joined the group. As he approached, the men parted and let him through.

'Ladies,' said Donovan. 'This is our Captain. He's the guy in charge around here.'

'Oh?' Caroline said, looking up at Donovan over her bowl of chilli. 'I thought you were in charge?'

'This is Caroline … and Dawn, Captain,' said Donovan, quickly hiding the confusion he felt just from looking into Caroline's eyes.

Dawn pushed her empty bowl aside and stood up, holding out her hand to Taylor. He took it, shook and let go almost immediately, but in those moments Dawn recognised that he was just the type of man she was looking for. His strength emanated from him, and the men obviously held him in very high regard.

'Thanks for rescuing us,' Dawn said. 'Our supplies had run out and every time we tried to move anywhere the Jinx arrived.'

Donovan explained what the women had told him about their hiding places.

'Lead lining?' Taylor asked for clarity.

'Strangely it's much simpler than that. A piece of lead pipe in a small place is enough. Most old buildings are riddled with old lead pipes, even though they aren't used anymore because of the health risks. We've brought some with us. We've found that placing it over doors and windows repels the Jinx. We've never seen them cross a leaded door.'

'How did you find out?'

'It was completely by accident,' said Caroline. 'But Dawn here is a nuclear engineer. She was working at Sellafield before this happened. She's the one who realised it was the lead that repelled them.'

'Most of the old plants have lead lining built into the walls,' Dawn explained. 'It was believed in the early days that it might provide insulation from fall out. Naturally since then we've devised much more efficient methods of insulation, but the lead can't be removed without completely taking the plants apart. Plus its dangerous stuff to handle, so there's all the health risks involved. The energy companies wouldn't foot the bill, and the disruption would have had a phenomenal impact on the service. Hence why you'll that find most of the stations are still running and have totally avoided violation by the Jinx. Though we've noticed that they generally don't even touch our tech. It's like some kind of taboo to them.'

'It's our magic,' said Kim. 'They are afraid of it.'

'Look at this place,' said Dawn, 'completely untouched by the Jinx. I suspect it has something to do with lead in the ceiling. Though I don't know for sure why a relatively modern building would have it.'

'If that's the case,' said Taylor, 'then why have the Jinx been able to attack people directly in their homes? Maybe I'm wrong, but I thought a lot of British houses had lead on their roofs?'

Dawn shrugged. 'Only the older ones, I think. And even then, maybe not enough to do the trick. It's mostly just in the corners of the roofs, I think.'

Taylor fell silent.

'Thanks for the heads up,' Donovan said. 'It might explain some of the things we've noticed lately.'

Taylor exited the mess, leaving Donovan with his survivors, and returned to his home in the leather shop. Jas had been missing for less than 24 hours and already he was going crazy with worry. He felt like he was losing his edge. All he could think about was what might be happening to her. Was she lying open-eyed, her throat slit by an alien as he feasted on her skin? For all any of them knew about the Jinx, they could fancy the taste of humans and consider women to be luxury food.

He shook the thought away as his stomach began to churn. Jas deserved better than ending up like that. Anyone did.

He switched off his lights and removed his clothes, then lay naked in his bed. The duvet smelt of Jas. Not Jas the grubby boy, but Jas the beautiful, sensuous woman who had trusted him when he had promised he would see her again. Taylor had never broken a promise in his life. He doubted he would be able to keep this one, and through no real fault of his own. Even so, the thought tortured him.

Taylor turned and pressed his face into the pillow, breathing in her scent. He had never met anyone like Jas. He loved her and knew he would have loved her on sight had they met before this madness started. He pulled the duvet up over his face and fought the rage and anger that surged through his body as the realisation finally dawned on him that he had lost her for good.

The tears came in his sleep. It was the only way he could give into them and not feel like a total failure. And when the morning came, he washed away the devastation from his face, dressed and stepped out into the mall, once more the Captain, once more in charge and once more with his feelings locked up inside him. They had to live and move forward, especially now his men had a reason to.

7

Jas slipped from the tent unnoticed. She was surprised to find that there was no guard lurking outside. All the Jinx and the Earth women had settled down for the night and the town was so silent she could hear the whistle of a soft wind through the rows of tents. She glanced back at the arrivals tent. *It's a marquee, really,* she thought as she took in the size of the structure.

She walked through the camp unhindered, and the memories of her dream of the place came flooding back in a rush of the same familiar *déjà vu*. So this was the city of the Jinx. Miles and miles of tents flowed out across the desert in an extreme parody of a Bedouin camp. Except that there was such order to it. They weren't randomly set up, but rather appeared to follow the lines that a city might. They were in rows according to size, and the rows gave way to pathways that apparently led to different areas and ghettos. Jas could clearly see the hierarchy of the Jinx men. The size of the tent dictated the wealth, but what did the Jinx judge wealth or status by? Was it gold and jewels as it might be on Earth? Or was it livestock?

There were several pens containing animals of all nature. Some looked vaguely like camels, but Jas had the strong sense that they were something quite different. She looked at the double-humps, the puppy faces, the razor-sharp teeth that grinned in grotesque mockery as she stood beside one of the pens. The animals weren't camels, but they were a breed of something designed to survive in this barren landscape. One of them pawed at the sand beneath its feet and then bent, opening its mouth impossibly wide, and scooped up the sand and chewed as though it were moist grass.

As she walked on she found a herd of cows too, and she knew they were the real deal: probably stolen along with the women. Perhaps even on the advice of the likes of Mallory, who was so clearly aiding the Jinx. The cows were in an impossible field of grass that sat on top of the sand like a fake garden, but the animals were eating it slowly and showed no signs of distress. Jas knew the terrain wouldn't have created this oasis. It had to have been done by the Jinx, but she couldn't understand how. She shook her head, pushing away the concern that formed in her mind. She might never understand how this place worked, but she had to watch and learn.

Jas walked on, following a path, trying to make sense of her environment. She was determined to find a way back to her own world. She wondered if there might be just randomly open portals, but knew it was more likely that Kale was the person who created them.

Jas stopped beside a campfire that was slowly burning down to ashes. It was very dark, but there were some stars to light the way, and as she looked up she saw not one moon, but two, each a fiery red, casting a scarlet glow over the camp. In the dark it was difficult to see more than the tops of the tents when she looked ahead. The flamboyant colours she imagined were nothing more than varying shades of grey in the gloom, or crimson when the light from the moons fell on them.

Red sky at night, shepherd's delight ...

The sky turned a deep burgundy and Jas found herself mesmerised by the two moons. But what of a sun? Was there even daylight here, or was this it?

She turned in circles at a crossroads, unsure which way to go. There was a pen with chickens and a coop. The birds huffed and clucked as one red glowing moon appeared to rest on the rooftop of the wooden structure, and the small building looked more alien to Jas than the whole of the rest of the town. This was Jinx Town: an alien planet of alien people who lost their women to some mysterious plague. It was a world of encampments, from what Mallory had said, and Jas began to wonder why the people would chose to live this way instead of building permanent structures. *This* is *permanent to them,* she thought.

Two tents stood head and shoulders above the others, and these, Jas knew, must be the ones that housed the Emperor and the Al Kuzemen. They were in the centre of the town, and Jas realised as she drew nearer to them that all of the sandy paths between the tents led ultimately to these two. They stood alone, but side by side, like detached stately homes, and they were just as sprawling in comparison with the other tents, though similar in size to the one housing the women she was with.

She walked toward the tents. One she recognised, and although it seemed insane, she knew without entering that the Emperor was inside. She was certain it was the tent she had first entered when she had visited Jinx Town in her dream. In her mind's eye she could see clearly the war table with its maps, the pool of strange and swirling water that had images and pictures reflected in it, the large bed with the mysterious figure sleeping inside. And that peculiar table with jars, containing god only knew what, but Jas's imagination filled them with body parts – trophies from the Jinx attacks, maybe?

A giant guard slept in the doorway of the tent, his impossibly long legs stretched out across the entrance as if daring trespassers to cross. Jas had no intention of coming face to face with the monstrosity that was the Emperor, though. She wanted to see Kale, so she turned away from the Emperor's home and followed the side of the fabric to the marquee next door.

Another guard manned the curtained door. This one was awake and alert. Tall and overpowering, he looked like the Addams Family butler, Lurch. Jas hesitated. She had no idea what she would do or say to get past the guard, so she decided the best policy was to brazen it out. To pretend that she was some servant who had come to please the Al Kuzemen perhaps.

'I've come to see Kale,' she said.

The guard didn't answer her, nor did he turn his elongated face in her direction. It was as though he could neither see nor hear her. Jas walked on toward the doorway, expecting the guard at any moment to try to stop her, but he made no movement at all. A soft breeze whipped at the cloth and it lifted, opening for her as she entered. It was another weird anomaly of this place.

Inside was much like the Emperor's tent had been in her dream and was filled with luxurious cushions and chairs. The furnishings had many influences; some of them seemed to be taken from different periods in Earth's history. For example there was an ornate writing desk, with quill pen and ink sitting on the lowered writing flap. She was strangely reminded of Penrhyn Castle in North Wales, which she had visited many years earlier on a holiday with her parents. The castle had contained a mish-mash of styles – renaissance furniture along with Chinese and Russian pieces – and Kale's opulent tent was much the same. There were jars painted with colourful flowers that reminded her of Ming Dynasty china; furniture from Edwardian England; art deco bureaus; high-backed chairs from the Regency period.

It occurred to Jas that the raids of the last few years might not have been the first the Jinx had made on her planet. They had the means to travel through time and space. Maybe they hadn't made these any of these furnishings. Maybe they were all stolen. It would explain why the Jinx never built houses or permanent structures – aside from sinking pools into the sand, that is. They didn't seem to have the skills to do anything beyond fighting.

In the left corner of the sitting area, Jas saw a young woman sleeping on a small bed. She felt a sudden flush of fury. This poor kid had been ripped from her home and was now the slave of the magician. God only knew what he did to her against her will.

Her eyes flew around the tent, seeking out the huge four poster occupied by Kale. She heard him move and sit up behind the thick curtains. The drapes opened and she found herself once more face to face with the magician.

Jas reached for one of the jars. If she didn't have a proper weapon then she would make something into one. She wanted to kill Kale, but her hand met with thin air. She swiped at the jar again and saw her fingers pass through it. Her hand was a blurred mist; the jar was solid and real, but she wasn't.

'Dream-walker,' said the Al Kuzemen from his bed. 'But why have you come *here*?'

Jas turned and ran from the tent, this time passing through the fabric in a whoosh of air. Instead of running through the town and heading out over the desert as she wanted to, she found herself swept along. It was the same feeling as passing through the vortex, and a sense of unreality accompanied the sensation, making her realise that what had seemed so real to her was little more than a dream. *Or death*, she thought. *The tunnel, air, and so much light!*

Jas gasped and jerked awake. She felt as though she had just fallen back into her body with a huge thump. She gasped at the air. Had she been holding her breath while her spirit left her body?

'Are you all right?'

Jas opened her eyes to find a figure beside the bed.

'I'm sorry. I didn't mean to startle you,' said Mallory.

Mallory was holding an old oil lamp, which she turned up. She was wearing long, flowing robes, her mousy hair was loose and over her shoulders. She was like a phantom, an echo of another era, another world.

'It's okay,' said Jas. 'I was having a nightmare.'

'I've been unable to sleep,' Mallory said. 'Do you mind if I sit on the bed? I need to explain something to you.'

'Take a seat,' Jas said, but she was wary and confused. She rubbed the sleep from her eyes, but felt that everything she had seen and experienced that night had been absolutely real. She had been in Kale's tent, she had examined the camp, and she was beginning to understand where things were in Jinx Town. She had heard of these experiences before, but couldn't recall the name of them. Even so, Kale's exclamation of 'dream-walker' somehow seemed wrong. It wasn't that she had walked in her sleep at all; it felt more like she had actually left her body behind.

'There's no easy way to say this. Tomorrow you're going to the marriage auction,' Mallory said, pulling her out of her reverie.

'I'm *what*?'

'The Emperor has ruled that you must be married immediately. Both he and Al Kuzemen Kale feel this is the best thing in your case.'

Jas was stunned. She had thought she would have more time to plan her escape.

'I feel like I've failed you. I went to see Kale, told him what the Emperor had said, pointed out to him that in the charter this wasn't …'

'Slow down,' Jas said, rubbing her forehead with a cold hand. 'What charter?'

'It was an agreement I made with Kale and Arven that all women should be cared for and integrated slowly. This goes against everything that has been working so well. You see, when the women were married sooner, so many more of them gave up and just … died.'

'Not surprising really,' said Jas. 'We like to chose our own lovers these days, don't we?'

'It's not how things work in Jinx Town, Jasmine. The man bearing the greatest offerings wins the prize.'

'Wealth then? The richest buy the women? Doesn't seem very fair on the rest though, does it? So all the poorer guys are just left horny I suppose?'

'No. It has nothing to do with wealth. The auction is … It's very hard to explain. It's more about energy … or auras, if you know anything about that type of thing.'

'Let's say I don't,' Jas said. 'I think I need a proper explanation and nothing obscure.'

'You've heard of yin and yang?'

Jas nodded, 'The theory that two opposites exist because of each other?'

'You're a smart girl, Jasmine. Most people think it is two halves making a whole …'

'Opposites attract is another one,' Jas said.

'Yes. That is where this relates to the philosophies of the Arrak Nah Tiaman. They believe that opposites are meant to be together.'

'I don't understand how this works in your auction.'

'The men don't bid with their wealth. They bid with their souls. Once an Arrak Nah Tiaman mates, it's for life, and neither partner is free to be with anyone else. When the people of this world lost their life partners, they had to rethink their whole philosophy to save their race. You see, this is every bit as difficult for them as it is for us. They have to try to match up with a new opposite that fits their aura. They have to recreate something they thought they would have to do only once.'

Jas lay back on the pillows. 'My heart bleeds for them.'

Mallory sighed.

'By virtue of what we are, then we are bound to be opposite to all of them,' Jas commented.

'No. Surprisingly. We aren't that different at all. Oh, the men may be taller on average than our human males, but they are still men in every way.'

'They are aliens,' Jas said. 'Not men.'

'In Jinx Town *we* are the aliens. And yet they have pushed aside any natural prejudice to save their future. Don't you think we should do the same?'

Jas turned away. 'So I'm to be auctioned. I have no choice?'

'No, you don't. And I'm sorry, because I know this is too soon for you.'

Mallory stood up and began to move away. 'Try and get some sleep. We'll talk through the auction in the morning. That way you will at least be prepared for what happens.'

'Mallory?'

'Yes?'

'What if I'm not opposite to any of them? What happens then?'

'All the women hope for that. But it has never happened. Of course you'll be opposite to many of them. But the strongest aura will win you.'

8

The auction was scheduled for the early evening, and Jas soon learnt that the day was an important one of the month. An auction occurred every two weeks if there were women available, and it was limited to only ten women at a time.

The aliens feasted and drank in celebration of the forthcoming marriages. Mallory explained that it meant prosperity to them, as well as the release of the frustrations of being a single male. There was a strong odour of hormones in the air. The married men would come to witness the auction, then they would slake their lusts with their human wives, hoping that on this day they would father a child.

Jenny, Rosa and Mallory helped the ten women dress. As they were prepared, Mallory led each outside, and the woman was placed on a sedan chair, which was then lifted by several of the married warriors. The woman would be carried to the auction tent, and there she would face her future husband among the crowd of hopeful men. Behind the litter, the men and women already paired would follow and cheer on the future bride.

'I'm scared,' said a pale blonde as she waited for her turn. She was groomed and ready but the chair and procession taking the first of them hadn't yet returned. 'I don't feel ready to be a mother. It was never something I thought about. Never what I wanted.'

'The pregnancies take a long time to occur in the marriages,' Jenny explained. 'It took more than a year and a half before the first births happened, and only seven children were produced out of thousands of marriages. We suspect that this is something to do with the Jinx women having had a different ovarian cycle from ours.'

'Are the babies ... normal?' asked another women, this one a redhead, as Rosa placed an ornate headdress over her hair and then draped a veil over her face.

'Of course. They look as human as you or I.'

'But they aren't human, are they?' said Jas. 'They are alien and human combined. Half breeds.'

'Full breeds,' said Mallory. 'The Arrak Nah Tiaman have accepted us without prejudice; we should give them the same respect.'

'This is nothing to do with respect, Mallory,' Jas replied. 'This is to do with rape under the name of marriage.'

The blonde girl squealed at Jas's words. 'I'm not ready, Mallory. I'm not!' she said.

'You are, Daisy,' Mallory replied. 'Please Jas! You're not making this any easier on anyone.'

'I'll keep my thoughts to myself then,' Jas sneered. 'But everyone here is still thinking the same thing as me.'

The litter returned.

'There's a lot of excitement today,' said Rosa. 'Mallory, you won't believe it. Arven has put himself forward as a potential husband!'

Mallory paled. Her mousy hair looked thin and willowy, and Jas saw a noticeable withdrawal as the woman fell so quiet and still she appeared to be a statue.

Jenny led the blonde woman to the sedan, but the terror in her face was obvious. No amount of preparation was going to make this easy.

'I heard that some more pregnancies have been announced,' said the redhead suddenly. 'A lot more.'

'True,' said Rosa. 'Over a hundred now. Everyone is very pleased. The Arrak Nah Tiaman race will begin to grow again.'

Jas remained quiet as she watched each of the remaining women go in their turn out to the fate of the auction. It was a long process, one that reminded her of some historical novel she read years before as a teen. She had enjoyed some of those romantic stories of pirates and Arab sheiks, but it was somewhat ironic that she now found herself in the position of being sold as a sex slave, even though it was dressed up as a legitimate marriage. It meant only one thing to Jas. Ownership. And that was still slavery, however good you made it sound.

I was a modern woman, she thought. *I always thought I'd make these decisions myself.* Her mind slipped back to Taylor and their affair. Sex with him had been wonderful, even though it had been clandestine, or perhaps because of that. She hadn't thought about marriage. All of those old tropes didn't apply to what remained of the world, and it was something that had never occurred to her. But pregnancy had, and they had tried to avoid that happening. It would have been the thing to expose her for what she was.

'It's time, Jasmine,' Mallory said.

Jas looked across the room at Mallory and found herself pulled back to the reality of the moment. She gazed around the tent. All of the other women had gone and she was the last remaining.

'What if I refuse?'

'Then the guards will make you go anyway,' Mallory said. 'This isn't going to be as bad as you might think. Being with one man protects you from all others. You'll be safer as a Jinx-wife than you've ever been on Earth.'

Jas stood.

'You need to wear the headdress,' Rosa pointed out. 'Your face can't be seen on the way to the auction.'

Jas snatched the headdress from Jenny's hands and placed it on her own head. Her body was stiff, and fury rippled down her arms. She had refused to eat or drink anything since she had arrived, but now Mallory offered her the draft that Kale had made. It was in a golden chalice. Mallory knew it would calm the girl, make her more pliant.

'Please drink something,' she begged. 'The auction tent is hot and humid. I'd hate for you to get sick in there.'

Jas took the drink, gazed down into its contents, then tipped it onto the floor. She threw the chalice across the tent.

Mallory straightened up. 'So be it. We're trying to help you, Jasmine. You aren't making this easier on yourself at all.'

'Be in my shoes and see how easy it feels,' Jas said through gritted teeth. 'I'm not making it easy for you or those murdering bastards. I don't want to be here. I refuse to marry and be a whore to these monsters, and you will have to drag me kicking and screaming to this fucking auction.'

Kale loomed in the doorway as Jas pulled herself free of Mallory's grip. Jas started and stood straight as she saw the mage. She made the mistake of looking into his eyes, wherein magic writhed, and immediately she sank into a strange and placid state. She let Mallory lead her calmly to the litter and sat on it. The veil and headdress were straightened, along with the hem of the flowing red robes she had been dressed in. All that the people in the parade could see was the shadowed glare of her eyes.

Jas sat up straight and forced her mind to clear. The Al Kuzemen had done something to her. He had stopped her from running and making a fuss in the streets, and her body now seemed to have a will of its own, even though her mind was steaming with rage. She forced herself to frown, then to flex her fingers as they rested neatly on the arms of the chair.

The litter was lifted and she began her journey through the sandy streets and out into the desert.

It was daylight, but Jas couldn't see a sun anywhere in the sky. The two moons hung in the air. In the light they appeared more orange than red. *There must be a sun!* But it was the moons, somehow, they gave light to this world, then muted like a light bulb on a dimmer switch for night. This world was impossible and mysterious: so very different from Earth, and yet not as alien as it should be.

Jinx Town was just like in her dream. She saw once again the two large tents, the sandy streets that converged to form a centre in which they stood.

She saw the animals. How was it possible for a dream to have revealed so much?

Jas twitched her fingers again. It was by sheer force of will, but slowly she felt the press of Kale's magic releasing its hold on her, and as they reached the huge gazebo on the outskirts of town, she was ready to fight her way through the men. She was willing to die rather than give in to this degrading auction.

She stepped down from the litter, taking hold of the hands of two women who waited there for her.

'You're so fortunate,' whispered one. 'So honoured.'

Jas forced the sarcastic retort back into her throat and let them lead her into the tent.

A long blue carpet was laid down in the middle of the auction room, and the men were divided either side of it. It was an aisle and she was the bride, but Jas would never have the right to choose her husband. She paused and looked down. Ahead of her she saw the other nine women from the arrivals tent. They stood silently beside nine beaming Jinx men. But the women looked dazed and shocked. And it crossed Jas's mind that there may indeed have been some ceremony that included the consummation of the marriage. She shook the horrible fear away. No. There hadn't been time. The thought was ridiculous, and her vivid imagination was only causing her more panic.

She looked around, saw the anticipation on the faces of the men in the crowd, and knew she had to pass through them to reach the stage ahead. She looked at the women again. They were terrified, clearly, but seemingly unhurt. *Even so, that's not going to be me!* she thought. *I won't marry one of these bastards.*

Behind her the women urged her forward. Jas glanced behind and saw Kale entering the tent. If she didn't go willingly he would move her like a puppet on strings using the power of his mind. Jas took one step and then another.

Around her there was cheering and clapping as she walked forward, but the sound was dulled in her ears. Panic rose in her throat and she felt sickness swirling in the pit of her stomach. She looked up at the stage again and saw the other women staring at her. Their dull eyes, their bowed shoulders, all confirmed that they had been cowed long before the ceremony. Jas straightened her back again. She would go out with dignity. She wouldn't be cowed. She wasn't afraid. She would die fighting.

The crowd hushed as she walked by them. Her bearing was arrogant and regal, and the Arrak Nah Tiaman hadn't seen a human female walk with such strength and pride before.

Jas looked toward the stage and noticed there were several Jinx males waiting there. These were the possible grooms, then? She glared at them, her hatred burning over the veil. A ripple of energy surged through the waiting grooms. They couldn't see her face, but each one of them wanted her.

As she reached the stage, she saw her opportunity. Two guards stood like Beefeaters either side of the steps. Their swords were drawn in a salute, but she saw that each of them had a long dagger protruding from his belt. She lifted her head again and made to walk between them, but as she passed, she reached out both hands and snatched the daggers from the guards with one liquid movement.

She felt the power of the weapons pour through her fingers and up her arms with the same shock she had experienced when she had first taken up the Jinx sword. The fight in Prestwich felt like a lifetime ago now, but still Jas spun, turning and kicking, and she plunged the daggers into the throat of each guard before they had a chance to react.

The guards fell at her feet. The assembly plunged into total silence. Then erupted into guttural yells as Jas ran up onto the stage and turned to face the horde of men, holding the daggers aloft.

It was as if time stood still. Jas threw off the heavy robe and veil. Underneath she wore a plainer red dress. It was still long, but she felt freer to fight.

'Which one of you Jinx bastards is next?' she said.

'*Ael mye zool mek!*' shouted Kale from the back of the room.

Jas knew he had given the order to attack her, as several Jinx warriors came from the back and poured forward towards the stage. She threw back her head and laughed with vicious and hysterical humour. Today was the day she would die, and it was preferable to the alternative any day. She bent her knees slightly, head down, her martial arts training kicking in instinctively as she waited for the warriors to reach her. And the familiar red rage came down over her eyes again.

A stinging blow landed on the back of her neck and she fell in a heap long before the warriors reached her. The daggers were snatched roughly from her blood-soaked fingers.

'*Zah mien ack ma!*' Arven said.

The soldiers fell back.

Jas looked up and saw Arven for the first time; he had appeared from nowhere and now towered over her. He was at least seven foot tall, a powerful and strong entity, and she realised with a shock that he was utterly beautiful. His black hair was long like Kale's but pulled back from his face in a loose pony-tail. His features were defined with high cheek bones, and his eyes were slightly slanted and danced hypnotically as he looked down at her.

She was on her knees before him, and she felt no urge at all to rise: the fight had gone out of her. Arven raised his sword, and Jas knew he had been the one to bring her down. He would kill her now, she was sure of it, and she felt ready to die. She tilted back her neck, exposing it to his blade.

'Go on,' she said. 'I'm ready.'

Arven shook his head, then sheathed his sword. The warriors surrounded them and Jas became aware of the cries and cheers that had taken up in the crowd. She stared uncomprehendingly at his long fingers, his big paw, outstretched to her. He was a giant compared with normal men, and yet she no longer felt afraid.

Mallory ran up to the stage. 'Take it, Jas! For god's sake take his hand.'

Jas's hand lifted and she felt it gripped in strong, sensual fingers. Arven pulled her to her feet.

'*Al fethern mine zuok,*' said Kale as he joined Mallory at the stage.

'A match has been made,' Mallory said.

Jas looked down at her and saw a fleeting sadness float across the translator's eyes.

'You've done well. You're going to be an Empress, Jasmine,' Mallory said.

Jas said nothing. Her confused gaze went from Arven to Mallory until Mallory stepped forward and placed her arms around her shoulders. She let Mallory lead her away from the tent and sit her back down in the sedan chair, never once glancing back at Arven. Yet she felt his gaze burning after her. She didn't know it, but the Emperor was as shocked and surprised as she was.

9

The coronation was to take place after the nine wedding ceremonies were performed. Jas and Arven would be married the next day in a ceremony that involved the crowning of a new Empress. Jinx Town went into celebratory mode. The Emperor had found a new Empress and she was a warrior queen.

'The prophecy has been fulfilled,' Arven said. 'Just as you promised. She was the one.'

'Lord,' said Kale, 'I know it seems as though she is the one, but I'm afraid that she cannot be trusted. She's dangerous. You saw what she did today. She left two women widowed with barely a thought.'

Arven nodded. 'She is very dangerous and very *beautiful*. I'm going to enjoy taming her. Besides, the spilling of blood was a sign; you said so yourself. '

'Please don't be lulled by her obvious charms,' Kale said. 'Let me consult the stars. Let me test her more. Is there any need to hurry into this?'

Arven turned and stared at his Al Kuzemen. 'Why the sudden change of heart?'

'She ... I can't explain yet, Lord.'

Kale didn't want to reveal that Jas was one of those rare females with a latent magical ability. Women of that nature hadn't been among the Arrak Nah Tiaman since the beginning of the race's travels though time. Magic was the work of men alone, and Kale didn't relish the thought that Jas was possibly one of many Earth women with aptitude.

Arven was right when he said that the blood spilt was a sign, but Kale wasn't sure he had read the sign correctly. It didn't matter that she had killed two of the royal guards. Their deaths had been completely overshadowed by the matching of Arven and Jasmine; a match so strong that Kale had never seen the like. Jas would be an excellent consort if those indications were anything to go by, but Kale couldn't easily dismiss her strength and determination. Even so, he still couldn't deny that she had been a perfect match with Arven. When the Emperor had taken her hand, his aura had glowed so brightly that even the magically blind could see it. And for the first time, Kale had witnessed a human female aura glowing too. Jas may not be happy about the match, but she was made for Arven nonetheless.

It was Mallory who, unwittingly, had first alerted Kale to a possible threat from the women. Her manipulation of language, a skill she thought of as nothing more than a small talent, was basic magic. It was impossible, in Kale's eyes, really to be able to learn to think, translate and speak in so many different languages without mixing them up. Magic was the true translator, and Mallory was using it subconsciously with an instinctual flair. Mallory had no clue of her ability, though, Kale had realised, and that was why he had never seen her as a threat. Even so, he had kept her close, made sure she used her skills for the good of the community. It had been worth keeping Mallory unmarried in order to have access to her talents.

Jas was different, of course. From afar he had observed her ability to change her appearance, and then there had been the new revelation of her natural aptitude for astral projection. And of course when she had taken the knives from the guards, Kale had seen the ripple of power that surged through her aura. She had connected with the weapons, and they had recognised her as a warrior in a way that normally only Arrak Nah Tiaman males could be recognised. It had struck terror in his heart.

Kale watched as Arven pulled off his armour and threw his breastplate onto the table.

'I had not dared to hope to find another Empress,' he said. 'Look in the pool and tell me the future, Kale. Will I have a son?'

Kale stared down into the water, and the images swirled around, erratic and confused. They reflected his inner turmoil.

'I'm seeing nothing, my Lord. The future has yet to be decided.'

Arven sat down in his chair as a servant girl entered with a platter of fruit and a jug of wine.

'Keep looking,' he ordered.

Kale let his mind find calm, and centred his heart as he looked once more. The images fought against each other but finally settled. Kale saw Jas in the arms of Arven, and an overwhelming jealously plunged pain into his chest. The picture altered, Jas turned from the Emperor and Kale found his own image wrapped in her arms as she brought him to pleasure.

'Yes, my Lord,' Kale said, his voice devoid of emotion. 'You will definitely have a son, and this woman will be Empress.'

Kale backed away from the pool and the images dissolved, becoming simply water once more. He would never reveal what he had really seen, but he would do his best from then on to have little or no contact with Jas. She was his temptation. All Al Kuzemen had them at some point, but he would not fail his beliefs and give in to a base lust for women.

Arven ate the fruit thoughtfully. 'You see, my friend, there really was nothing to worry about. And if she fights on the wedding night, it will only add to the excitement of conquering her.'

Mallory peeled away Jas's auction dress. It was covered in the blood of the guards, although their killing was something that everyone had rapidly forgotten about as soon Jas had bonded with Arven. She couldn't deny there was a powerful connection between the couple. If she had been of a romantic nature she might even have thought of it as love at first sight. But she wasn't romantic; her own marriage to Gerald Avery had long destroyed any of those feelings.

'Do you even know how lucky you are?' Mallory said.

Jas said nothing. She had been quiet and thoughtful since they had brought her back, and Mallory wondered where the girl's mind was. Jas's eyes were far away, seemingly lost in some memory, or perhaps she really was shocked by her contact with the Emperor.

'Come, we'll get you cleaned up. It's finery for you from now on. You're a Princess today and an Empress from tomorrow.'

Jas let Mallory lead her back to the pool, but she barely noticed the warm, crystal water this time, and she allowed the other woman to soap away the blood without comment or objection. Her thoughts were of the time she had spent with Taylor. In her mind her association with him hadn't been love, but there had been a connection: a powerful emotion that had drawn her to him. She was aware that even before her façade had crumbled, she had wanted to reveal her true nature to Taylor. But still, it hadn't been *love*. It had been infatuation and need, a desire to be the woman she really was. It had also been safe. Jas had never had to lose herself in order to be with Taylor. He had always accepted her in whatever guise she wore.

She couldn't deny the attraction she had felt for Taylor though. It was much the same as she now felt for Arven, except that in Arven's case it had been instantaneous. She found herself looking at her hand. Had the Al Kuzemen cast some kind of spell that had made the Emperor appear so attractive?

'I don't understand,' she murmured.

'You're in love with him,' said Mallory. 'Is that so difficult to comprehend?'

'Yes it is. I don't love.'

'You've never met Arven before. He inspires love and loyalty in all his subjects.'

'It's some kind of spell …' Jas said.

'Love is a spell, Jasmine. We've just been too blinded by our technology to be really susceptible to it. When was the last time you felt any real emotion?'

Andrew, thought Jas. *Twelve years old*. He was such a cute, smart little boy. She had always favoured him. Then he had gripped her hand as they ran together, hiding from the Jinx. That was the closest she had come to love, wasn't it? And that had been born of guilt in the first place: her guilt for allowing all the other children to die. But her love for Andrew was different. It wasn't a passionate love. It was more the kind of love one feels for one's own flesh and blood. How a mother feels for her child.

Jas got out of the water and wrapped a huge towel around her body. An indescribable fear paralysed her limbs, and she stood hugging herself as a new thought occurred to her.

'Where are the children?' Jas said suddenly, remembering how the Jinx stole girls as well as women. 'Where are the little girls they took? What did these bastards do to them?'

'You're hysterical!'

'Where are the *old* women? What happened to them? There aren't any of them left on Earth that I saw.' Jas grabbed Mallory and dug her fingers into the soft flesh of her arms. 'What happened to them?'

'They are fit and well, Jasmine. What do you think the Arrak Nah Tiaman are? Animals? They wouldn't hurt little girls. That's what *human* men do. Children are protected here.'

'It didn't stop them killing the boys,' Jas said.

'You're hurting me.'

'I say again, where are the old women?'

'I don't know. I've never seen any here. But I'm sure they wouldn't have been killed.'

Jas let go of Mallory.

'I saw the Jinx kill an elderly woman. Now I understand why. She was no use to them, was she? Maybe they brought some back here and realised they couldn't breed them. Why would you tell me the truth? You're a sympathiser, Mallory. You'll do whatever they tell you to. Even betray your own kind.'

'You want to know why I prefer the Arrak Nah Tiaman to human men? Speak to Jenny and Rosa. They'll tell you all about men. They'll tell you how my husband betrayed me. Drugging and raping all of us for his own sick and perverse pleasure. They'll tell you how, when he couldn't control us, he fed us all one by one to the Jinx. Then ask me again why I prefer Jinx Town to Earth. At least here we are treated with dignity. At least here the men need, want and revere us.'

Mallory lifted the curtain and walked out of the tent, leaving Jas behind to think about her words. She wasn't really shocked by Mallory's story. She had seen what the end of the world had done to the remaining men. Hadn't that been the main reason she had hid her identity for so long? Jas felt a little guilty that her anger had caused her to accuse Mallory of conspiracy. What choice did Mallory have, anyway? If things had really been that bad for her on Earth then it was no wonder that she found the Jinx lifestyle less hazardous.

Her mind shifted to Arven. She was marrying him – whatever that meant in the Jinx culture. She was going to be an Empress. If the truth be known, she was curious about the emotions Arven stirred in her. She certainly found the man attractive, and despite their obvious height difference to the men on Earth, the Jinx looked quite human. She wanted to think of Arven as alien, but despite herself she had seen something in him that was more human than she had seen in the men on her planet for a long time. The light in his pulsing eyes was warm and compelling. He was a mystery that she found infinitely curious.

Jas couldn't deny that Mallory was right about the human race on the whole. After all, look at how the doctor had behaved when he had learnt she was female. Taylor and his group had appeared to be good men overall, but perhaps things would have changed if she had hung around long enough to find out how they reacted to the knowledge she was a woman.

After the Jinx had arrived Jas had noticed an immediate deterioration in attitudes on Earth, especially from the men. Maybe she had been unlucky in those first years, but she didn't think so. She believed instead that the men she had come across, the dogs of humanity, were in fact representative of the dregs of their society. It was as though this human scum had been waiting silently in the wings to inherit what was left of the Earth once it was destroyed. *The meek shall inherit the Earth ... Not bloody likely!*

Society had taken a dip long before the Jinx had arrived. Jas had seen it happen. Unemployment had been rife, mostly amongst people who didn't want to work; crime rates had been up; and the kids in school had been becoming more difficult to handle. If Jas had been religious by nature, she might have seen signs of impending doom looming long before it happened. But she had been wilfully blind, like everyone else. Although she had known the world wasn't right, she had simply done her best to cope with it and live the best life she could.

She thought of Mallory again, reflecting on the hurt she had seen in the other woman's expression. Being betrayed so badly by someone you trusted was enough to turn you against humanity, but maybe it hadn't turned her completely away from men? Mallory had looked disappointed when Jas had somehow 'bonded' with the Emperor, and yet she had still been kind to Jas when she had returned her to the arrivals tent. It had been only a fleeting expression, but Jas wondered if Mallory had feelings for the Jinx leader.

Jenny came into the pool area holding a nightdress of fine red silk and a thick robe.

'You need your sleep,' Jenny said, holding out the clothes. 'Big day tomorrow, Princess.'

'Please don't call me that,' Jas said. 'I prefer Jas. Not Jasmine, Princess or any other label you care to put on me.'

Jenny smiled. 'Yeah. Labels are boring. Here you go, Jas.'

Jas took the nightgown and slipped it over her head, then Jenny helped her on with the robe. Tiredness overwhelmed her suddenly and she realised that she was hungry. She had neither eaten nor drunk since she had arrived, for fear of being drugged. Right then, Jas would have welcomed a sleeping draft or some potion that would make her forget everything.

'I'm hungry, Jenny. Can I have something to eat and drink?'

Jenny smiled again, then patted her arm in a casual and friendly manner. 'Thought you'd never ask, love. We were starting to get worried that you'd become ill.'

10

It felt as though she had become lost in a story or a dream, but this was no fairytale that Jas wished to be part of. It was more like a nightmare. She was being married – completely against her will – and on top of that, crazy as it seemed, she would be made Empress.

'You'll be revered and respected. You'll be in a great position to help any of the women who aren't coping,' Mallory said. 'You could use your power to benefit those you worry so much about.'

Mallory knew that if Jas made this her mission then not only would the women feel supported but Jas would also learn more about the Arrak Nah Tiaman. Jas would grow to understand that things weren't as bad as they seemed. It would keep her busy in the next few months too. Help her settle into a new routine, a new life and ultimately forget all about Earth.

'I don't want to do this,' Jas said. 'I'm beginning to get annoyed that no-one is actually listening to me. Watch my lips. I. Don't. Want. To. Get. Married.'

Mallory shrugged. 'Maybe not. But you'll survive it, and Arven, I'm sure, will be a wonderful lover.'

Jas felt sick. The breakfast of bread and cheese lay heavy on her stomach at the thought of the coming night and of being alone with Arven.

Of course the food was clearly one of the good points about Jinx Town. There was fresh produce daily; things that Jas hadn't eaten for years. Bread and cheese, once such simple food, felt like luxury items. The fruit was excellent, too, even though it was weird and didn't taste quite the same as Earth fruit. There was one sort that resembled oranges, but once peeled they tasted like a cross-mix of apricots and apples, only much sweeter and with far more messy juice to contend with. These were in bowls scattered around the tent and presumably grew in abundance somewhere that so far Jas hadn't seen. There was a grape-like fruit too, only it was savoury and not sweet, with the stringiness of celery. Jas liked the taste of these but not the texture, and her brain couldn't accept the flavour if she looked at them first, because her taste-buds expected the sweetness and juice of a grape. There were nuts too. But these had more of a dry, woody taste. The 'camel' cheese was the strangest. It had the sharp tang of goat's cheese, but a nicer aftertaste that was creamy and more like Cheddar. Of course the creatures that Jas thought of as camels weren't called that by the Jinx.

'You mean the El Lien Mecks?' said Jenny when Jas asked her what they are. 'They do look a little like camels – but you have to stay clear of them. Those razor-sharp teeth give me the heebie-jeebies.'

At lunchtime Rosa gave Jas some soup. It tasted like vegetable and she decided not to ask this time what was in it. Instead she wolfed down the fresh food, mopping up the remnants with some more of the fresh bread.

'We have butter here too,' said Jenny. 'Made from cows taken from Earth. I think the early women requested them. There's a baker in the town, and a farmer, all from our planet. The women make the things you're eating. It gives us a combination of our own foods and the more exotic things that this world has. Some of which I'm sure you'll really like every bit as much as we do.'

The day was to be spent in meditation and relaxation. The wedding ceremony wouldn't take place until later that afternoon.

'The leaders of the other towns are travelling in especially for the wedding.' Mallory said.

'What's this place really called?' Jas asked. 'What does that name you call the Jinx actually mean?'

'I thought you'd never ask,' Mallory said, smiling. 'Arrak Nah Tiaman. The literal and closest meaning is "Warriors of Space". They don't mind our name for them though. When I explained it to Arven, and where it came from, he thought the name Jinx was hilarious. He has a very good sense of humour.'

Jas studied Mallory as she continued to talk about Arven and his virtues. Part of her knew that Mallory was singing the Emperor's praises to make her feel better about the situation, but she also believed that Mallory was slightly in love with the Jinx ruler. There was something about the animated use of her hands, the happy expression on her face that made it obvious to Jas that Mallory enjoyed talking about Arven.

It irritated her, but she listened. She wanted to learn all about the man before she killed him. Plus, concentrating on the details of the ceremonies that would take place was the only thing she could do. She took notes in the hope that there would be some way she could escape from what seemed to be her obvious fate.

I wonder if all brides feel like this? she thought, and then her mind flashed back to the wedding of Prince William to Katherine Middleton some years before the first Jinx attack. Jas had been a child at the time and had thought that the future Princess looked almost too calm all day. But then, that was supposed to be a love match, and in Jas's case it wasn't love at all. At least she wasn't feeling any positive emotion about Arven that day; only a whole lot of hate and a great deal of fear. Jas knew she was strong; she had fought off a whole platoon of Jinx, hadn't she? But she was afraid of Arven, and the thought of having to sleep with him later was more than a minor concern. The Jinx were alien, for a start. At the end of the day it was only sex, but sex with a Jinx – that was a whole different ball game. Or was it? The intense attraction she had felt the previous day had rapidly worn off with the reality of the marriage.

'Then of course there's the coronation,' Mallory was saying, 'followed by a wedding feast. Much the same as an Earth wedding really. There'll be lots of drinking, eating, dancing. They aren't big on speech-making though.'

'Thank god for small mercies,' Jas sneered, pulling her mind back to the present.

Mallory fell silent. Her animated hands fell down in front of her and she took on the stance of a stern matron.

'Really Jas, you'll be thanking me later for keeping you so informed. The whole thing will be in their language, so it will be very hard for you to follow until you begin to learn it.'

'How am I supposed to agree to the terms without understanding?'

'I'll be translating for you, naturally.'

'I won't say yes,' Jas said firmly. 'I plan to make this as difficult as possible. So you might as well go and tell your Emperor how I feel now, before I make a fool of him.'

'Your agreement isn't required in law. In fact if they have to render you unconscious to perform the ceremonies in peace, then they will.'

Jas swallowed a mouthful of soup and pushed the bowl aside. 'And I guess you think that's acceptable behaviour? They are savages, and yet you continue to help them.'

Mallory sighed. 'I'm not your enemy, Jas. I'm trying to help you, and you can't see it at all.'

'You want to help me? Then go and tell Arven, thanks but no thanks.'

'I can't. You've *bonded* with him. Even if he feels the same about you, he has to go through with this.'

Jas blinked. It hadn't occurred to her that Arven also might not want to get married. It had seemed to her that this whole woman-stealing thing was exactly because a bunch of horny aliens weren't getting any.

'Arven has been celibate since his wife died. I'm sure he's feeling some nerves too,' Mallory pointed out. 'Like I said, the Arrak Nah Tiaman only ever sleep with their wives.'

Arven looked into the pool. Kale had given him the gift of seeing *her* again. Images of his beautiful wife Celin, playing with their daughter, her swollen belly, filled with the man-child Arven desired as his heir. Celin looked up and into his eyes as though she could see him. Water sprung into his gaze as she smiled. They had bonded, and Arven had thought it was for life. He had never wanted another Empress, even though Kale had said there would be one.

Arven put his hand in the pool and swirled away the vision of his wife, then Jas came into view. She had the same strength he had seen in Celin, but something else, something untamed.

He saw Jas in the arrivals tent, being prepared for the ceremony. She appeared calm, and there was no denying that she was beautiful, despite the close-cropped hair. Her eyes were large and wild, a stunning shade of blue that somehow changed and became darker when she was angry, and now he found himself wondering what her expression would be like when she was aroused. Arven had denied the sexual part of himself for so long that he wasn't sure how to deal with this new emotion. He had allowed his men the choice of wives and never taken any of the women himself. Other than the servant girl who brought his food and tidied his tent, he rarely came in contact with them. There was no denying that Jasmine had appealed to the man in him on first sight. As he had seen her attack his guards, taking them out with the clean precision of an assassin, excitement had coursed through him, and he had known he had to possess her.

He had been the one to put her down, striking a blow to her shoulders. Then, as he had stood above her, sword raised and ready to strike, she had looked up at him and he had seen such shocking strength and vulnerability in her expression.

She was taller than most of the human women but still shorter than their own females, who had all stood above six feet. Jasmine was around five feet eight or nine, and that extra height had had aided her in hiding so effectively as a male among her own people.

All the women had a tale to tell; at least that was what Mallory had said. The Earth men were beasts, and Arven truly believed that he and his men had saved the women from their awful existence on the dying planet called Earth. They had offered them a new life, a new chance and a new culture. From what he had learnt, the women of Earth had been victims of their own success. Earth science – the religion of man – had had a lot to do with the dimming of their female auras. Arven and Kale had seen the change in them all since the first group had been brought in. Those that had survived were thriving here.

Despite their initial feelings and sexual needs, Arven was proud of his men. They hadn't resorted to random rape – it would have been against the charter and the beliefs by which they had always lived. Kale had been most instrumental in ensuring the good treatment of the females too. They had made a few mistakes at first, but had quickly learnt from them. They weren't savages, after all. Once the women had found their needs starting to be understood and met, they had rapidly become the mothers of their new race, and as such deserved respect.

Arven stared down into the pool and studied the small and pert breasts poking through the sheer fabric of the chemise Jas was wearing. It was all she would have on under the ceremonial robes, and Arven imagined opening the robes and touching her for the first time.

'Are Earth women like our own?' he had asked Kale.

The Al Kuzemen had smiled. 'Much easier to pleasure, from what I've been told, Lord.' And then Kale had told him of the sensitivity the women had in their breasts; something that their own women had lacked.

Arven imagined his tongue sliding over Jas's breasts: the thought interested him, although it wasn't something he had tried with Celin.

'Explore her, Lord,' Kale had said. 'I have been told this is immensely exciting.'

It would be a new experience. Arven's curiosity leant itself to a new feeling of excitement. Sex and love were things you gave to your lifelong mate. For the Arrak Nah Tiaman, sex was normally a ritual; it was about reproduction more than pleasure, even though both parties gained from the familiarity. Arven hoped he wouldn't fail as a ruler or as a man. He wanted an heir, and now by some miracle he had bonded again. He was going to do everything he could to make Jasmine happy and to impregnate her as soon as possible. He wanted a child with her, and he didn't mind if it was male or female. Or that Jasmine was a human. In times like these, petty prejudices belonged to the narrow-minded.

11

Arven was totally at home in the ostentatious surroundings and appeared comfortable on the red velvet-covered throne. Jas wasn't relaxed at all. Her hands rested on the arms of the throne as Arven relaxed back into his seat beside her. Under her fingers the carved wood was painted gold, or maybe it was real gold melted over it. Jas didn't know, but she focused her attention on it as the proceedings began.

She watched Kale as he stood before them and began to chant that incessant and guttural sound they called language. It was like a cross between German, Arabic and Japanese. It was all clicks and slurps and sounds that made her think the speaker's throat was full of phlegm. Jas thought she would never get used to hearing it and just wished that they could all speak English. At least this place would feel less alien then, and so would the people.

'*Ack zuik, meine ibber zuol fayim,*' said Kale.

'All hail the Emperor and his wife,' said Mallory behind her, where she stood slightly to the left of her throne. Mallory spoke loudly and clearly as she translated the Jinx tongue. She made the words sound as important and reverent as Kale did, but she didn't raise her hands and arms in the same gestures.

'*Alim marven. Ze hakim duz felin.*'

'One woman. One king. Joined in flesh and spirit.'

'*Il arkhem doon ...*'

'Promise to keep ...'

'*Zee swarven ...*'

'Eternally bound ...'

Out of the corner of her eye, Jas saw Arven bow his head, as though he were gesturing acceptance of the strange terms being imposed on him. Trembling, Jas felt an irresistible compulsion to rise, with her head bowed as though by some will of its own. Arven stood also, reached for her hand, and turned her to face him.

'*Zah zayin far zuol. Il varim mah zey. Zee swarven mi zah.*'

'You are now my wife. I'm eternally bound to care for you.'

Arven's touch was like electricity running through her fingers. Jas tried to pull back her hand, but her fingers wouldn't move. The words of refusal that she had rehearsed now declined to come from her lips. Jas's hand and arm went numb, and then a strange tingling sensation rippled all through her body like goose bumps. It made her hair stand on end and her breasts grow firm. Her nipples pressed sensitively against the silk chemise. A growing excitement began to warm the pit of her stomach. She found she could raise her head again, and she looked up into Arven's strange, swirling eyes. For now they were still. He appeared to be feeling this strangely erotic sensation too. It was like an artificially-induced orgasm, and Jas's knees gave under the pressure that wanted to burst from her loins.

The crowd gasped, then cheered.

'Oh my god,' gasped Mallory. 'The strength of this union ...'

Arven caught Jas before she tumbled to the floor. He had to appear calm and in control when really all he wanted to do was take her back to their tent and begin his exploration of her human body.

The ceremony was supposed to initiate the urge to reproduce, consolidate the sexual need between those joined; but even with Celin, Arven had never experienced such a sensual reaction. His fears of not finding Jas desirable enough were suddenly pushed aside. He wanted her, and he wasn't sure he could wait until after the coronation as was customary.

Kale's hand rested on the Emperor's shoulder and Arven felt the urge recede. He met the Al Kuzemen's eyes and realised that with Kale's help he was able to regain control over his senses. Jasmine was swaying in his arms, and he saw the fire and lust in her eyes as Mallory took charge of her. Reluctantly Arven released his new bride. Duty first, passion later, that was always their way, and he would never go against the rules of his society.

Arven turned and faced his people and gave the one speech his position required.

'This day I feel honoured,' he said. 'This day I am fulfilled once more and can give my people the future I promised. There will be more Earth women and continued happiness and fertility on the joined among you. May my people also pray that my union brings forth offspring and a new heir to the throne.'

Jas heard the translation as her heartbeat began to settle down and the sensation of desire fell back. She was once again able to think and function. Arven's speech was that of a benevolent ruler, and his words sank into her mind as she gradually realised this was it. She was married and somehow she had been unable to avoid it.

'The mage used magic on me,' she gasped.

'No,' Mallory whispered, tears in her eyes. 'You and Arven did that on your own. You're meant to be joined, Jasmine. You really do belong to him now.'

The rest of the day was a blur. Jas went through the motions as she was changed and dressed into the coronation robes. These were made of cream silk and trimmed with gold piping. Covering her hair was a cream veil, but her face was left exposed.

She was taken back into the ceremonial tent and then she knelt before Kale with Arven once more at her side. Arven had changed also, and his robes matched hers. As she felt the weight of the crown placed on her head, Jas began to wonder how she would ever get out of this mess. *That's another nice mess you've got yourself into, Stanley,* she thought, and a bubble of hysterical laughter poured from her lips.

Arven took her hand, helped her to stand. He too was laughing, and a strange happiness swept over the crowd.

I've been drugged or zapped with some supernatural juju, Jas thought. *This is just the most bizarre experience I've ever had.*

But even as she analysed the effect the ceremony was having on her, she felt an inner calm, and as she was led from the tent for the final time, she allowed herself to enjoy the pomp and extravagance of the bizarre occasion she had been part of. It was very like playing dress-up, and the truth was that she really couldn't take any of it seriously. Her marriage was alien to her own law and her own beliefs, and although she was resigned to playing her part, she told herself that when the opportunity arose she would slit Arven's throat with his own dagger. But even as this thought floated into her mind, it felt like an obscure daydream.

Outside the tent, food was laid out as if for some Jacobean feast. Hunks of meat, jugs of wine, fruit, sweetmeats and colourful delicacies that Jas couldn't identify. She sat in the central position of the main banquet table, with Arven and then Kale on her right and Mallory on her left. Jas couldn't help observing how like a human celebration the whole thing was. *Maybe eating and drinking is social for all beings, no matter how alien,* she thought.

A chalice was filled and placed before her.

'It's just wine,' Mallory said. 'But it is potent stuff, so try to pace yourself. Unless you like the idea of Arven carrying you back to the tent later.'

Jas was horrified by the thought, and she looked at Mallory, only to find the other woman smiling.

Mallory winked at her. 'I'm joking. It's actually very mild compared to Earth wine,' she laughed. 'I'm rather partial to the stronger stuff myself. Maybe you can persuade your new beloved to steal some next time they raid the place?'

Jas smiled back at Mallory. The expression 'new beloved' amused her in a way she couldn't quite understand. She felt a slight thrill on hearing the words, but quickly quashed the feeling, replacing it with cynical amusement.

'I feel like I'm already on something,' Jas said. 'God, this whole thing is like something out of a twisted nightmare. It's thrilling and shocking me, and I feel like I can't do anything other than go along with it.'

Mallory nodded. 'Bonding ceremonies are like that. It's very, very potent magic when two people are joined. Look around you. It's having the same effect on everyone else.'

Jas looked over the table at the other couples banqueting. She recognised some of the women who had been auctioned with her. The blonde girl, Caroline, who had been the most afraid, was smiling and flirting with her new husband, and he could barely take his eyes from her.

'It's a love spell then. That goddamn mage,' Jas said again.

Mallory laughed. 'It really isn't Kale's doing. Love spells don't work. I told you, you and Arven did this. You'll just have to learn to believe it's real.'

'Jassmin,' Arven said beside her.

Jas jumped in surprise. It was the first time the Emperor had spoken directly to her, and it felt strange and intimate. She turned to face him and found herself staring into his eyes. This close to him she could see how very different his eyes were. On first appearance they appeared human. But the pupils were dilated and the fine circle of the iris was not one colour, but several shades of blue and green. His eyes held shards of lights inside them. They swirled and swelled, throbbing in a hypnotic pulse. She remembered noticing the magic dancing in Kale's eyes, but had thought it exclusive to the Al Kuzemen. Arven's eyes moved and swirled, and it was hard to focus on them without feeling a tiny bit nauseous. She looked down, and then felt Arven's hand on her face as he stroked her cheek.

'Jassmin,' he said again in English. 'I fine you bioutifal.'

She wondered how long it had taken him to learn the words, and she lifted her gaze to find Kale watching her closely.

Her eyes shifted back to Arven, but she kept her gaze on his mouth, afraid to meet his confusing and alien gaze.

I'm in this now, she thought. *Escape seems impossible, but maybe it will present itself if I play along.*

She was drawn to his lips.

'Do Jinx kiss?' she murmured.

Arven made no move toward her. Jas thought this meant he hadn't understood her words, so she leaned forward and pressed her mouth against his. For a moment the Emperor didn't react. His lips remained against hers as she moved her mouth, encouraging him into the kiss. She felt his lips part and slipped her tongue inside his mouth, swirling around his lips and tongue until he gasped against her.

'I guess not,' she said, pulling back when he failed to respond.

Arven's fingers traced his mouth. He could still feel her lips and tongue and the strange ritual of pressing them together ... *That must be a human fetish*, he thought. It reminded him of eating, but it was so sensual he wanted to feel it again. He moved toward her, but Kale's hand pressed on his shoulder, pulling him back to his senses.

'Experiment with her in private,' Kale whispered. 'Learn what she likes and maybe you'll learn new things about yourself too, Lord.'

Arven sat back in his chair and looked out over his subjects. The banquet was in full swing, the people were happy and there was a sense of wellbeing in the air. Out of the corner of his eye, he watched Jas pick at a piece of meat suspiciously, and a tiny smile curved his lips. She was surprisingly adaptable. He had thought this day would be harder on her, but she was swept along with the excitement as well as he and everyone else. He watched her talk with Mallory, picking out the occasional word he had learnt but not really following the conversation. Jas was smiling and appeared to be relaxed. The worry frown that had been on her brow before the ceremony was now gone. He thought about the press of her lips again and knew that somehow it was important. She had been showing him something. Or maybe she had been testing him? How was he to react to her? A female so different, so alien, from those of his own race? He reminded himself that he and his people had no choice if they were to survive, but it was strange for them too. They had to learn so much about these humans.

Arven thought about the words he had said to Jasmine. He had meant them. He did find her beautiful, even though he didn't care for the close-cropped hair. It didn't concern him though, as he knew it would grow, just as the other women with short hair had grown theirs out. Arven liked Jas's eyes, though. She had only briefly let him look into them, and the still blue, so different from those of his people, was so pure and striking.

Arven looked up at the sky. Night was falling and the Ah Min Zins were rising to offer their fragile red light over the camp. Servants ran around quickly lighting torches. On this world, Emin, night came quickly, and within minutes it was full dark. But the torches were lit and the celebrations continued.

Arven glanced at Jas again. He wanted to be alone with her, but those moments were still so far away, and he had his Imperial duties to perform first. His throne came before anything else; even his passion and desire for his new human wife.

12

Jas shivered as Arven stripped the robes from her, even though she didn't realise that this simple task was fulfilling his first fantasy. She was scared, not like earlier when the bonding ecstasy had taken hold of them both. This was personal. This was one on one, and the trembling of her body had nothing to do with the temperature in the tent.

It's only sex, Jas told herself. *I have to use it, gain his trust.*

She was afraid though of how different the alien would be, compared with human men. As she stood in her chemise, his fingers traced the curve of her breasts, running over her nipples gently. She shivered again. This time a rush of excitement sent a flush of colour over her skin, and her nipples stood up in response to his touch.

Jas was unaware that Arven was monitoring her reactions. He wanted to know more about her and her body, and understand how the female human worked. Touching her gave him a thrill of excitement. It felt perverse but right. He began to remove the chemise, but she placed her hands on his and held them. Her shivering continued. He wondered if she was cold after all, but when her trembling hands began to remove his robes, it occurred to him that his new bride was very nervous but trying to be brave. The thought intrigued him.

Arven stroked her forearms as she unfastened his clothing, then let her push back the robe, allowing it to fall on the carpet. Underneath the heavy garment he wore a silk shirt and loose, Arabic-style trousers. Jas unfastened the trousers, kneeling down before him as the soft fabric slipped to the ground. He wore nothing underneath the trousers, and she could see he was aroused, and that he was made like other men – just the same, on first glance. At least it certainly appeared to be a penis and testicles, but she couldn't be sure they had the same function. Maybe his tongue was his sex organ? She had asked these questions of Mallory, but the only answer she had got was 'I'm sure you'll figure it out.'

Jas ran her hands over Arven, the shirt came off, and she found that the Jinx Emperor didn't have nipples, just a smooth, hairless chest. But still he gasped and writhed at her touch as she moved her hands over the muscles on his torso. She soon realised that her touch was electric to him; he had clearly never experienced anything like it. She didn't know that the coupling of the Jinx was not as much about touching as joining. They joined, and it was pleasurable, particularly for the woman as the recipient.

As the chemise fell to the ground, Arven wondered how Jas would react to his seed, and if he would draw the same response he had from Celin whenever he implanted her. He stared at her nakedness, and she squirmed a little under his gaze. She was leaner than he was used to, her breasts were small, the curve of her hips narrow. She was wiry and slightly boyish, but Arven felt a surge of lust as he gazed upon her nakedness.

Jas's hands reached down and she took Arven between her fingers, stroking him. He was hard and so big she was afraid it would hurt. The size of him was in keeping with his height, but it was still something of a shock.

'You're well hung, I'll give you that,' she said. 'I'm already thinking, "Ouch".'

Arven didn't understand her, but he realised she had said something about pain. Was she afraid he would hurt her? He began to stroke her gently again. As his fingers explored her, he felt her lust rushing to the top of her skin as her whole body seemed to flush with her excitement.

'That's never happened before,' she pointed out, and now she was so curious about him and his intentions that she took his hand, led him to the bed and lay down, waiting for him to lie beside her.

Oh my God, I hope that goes in the usual place! she thought, as he stood above her. His penis was protruding and she didn't want to even think about how long or how thick it was. It was just big. Bigger than she had ever experienced before. Not that she had been around, particularly.

She noticed the peculiarity in the testicles as he climbed onto the bed. They were larger, and more swollen, as though they really did contain a giant seed inside each of them. Jas tried not to think about it. He lay down beside her, resting his head on his arm as his hand began to caress her again. Jas wondered how different her body appeared to him. Had the Jinx women had three nipples, or two vaginas? The thought was absurd, as Arven was clearly enjoying her as she was. And, she reminded herself, other than size he was really not that much different from a human man. She felt insecure about her looks and shape in a way that hadn't occurred to her when she had undressed with Taylor. To distract herself, she put her arm around Arven's neck and pulled his face towards hers. Then planted little kisses on his lips. His mouth was so much bigger than hers; it was hard to find the position that would create the sensual French kiss she was trying to give him. But he opened his lips willingly this time and let her tongue enter him, and his body shuddered and he sighed against her. Then he pushed his tongue into her mouth. Quickly he got into the rhythm of the kiss, and Jas marvelled at how rapidly he learnt.

The kiss pulled at his loins. A corporeal experience he had never had before. He wanted her so much, wanted to lay on her and give her his seed; but he held back, afraid to rush things. She was clearly enjoying his touch, and his lips and tongue held a fascination for her. She pulled away and began planting small kisses on his throat and chest, and then moved lower down. She was above him. Her pale skin glowing in the weak light that spilled over the bed from one of the lanterns. Her pupils had dilated, the pleasure and excitement on her face was evident. Arven rolled her over onto her back and positioned himself between her legs.

He saw the relief on her face as he pressed himself against her, but didn't understand that she had been so afraid the ritual would be done in some other bizarre way. He reached his hand down between them, his fingers brushed against her, and she gasped and writhed beneath him. Curiosity made him explore her female organs more, and the reaction it drew pleased him. Her pleasure excited him. He positioned himself against her small opening.

'Oh God,' she muttered. 'I hope this isn't going to hurt too much.'

He pushed inside her and she arched and tensed with fear. She was wet and ready to receive him, but her fear paralysed her. He stopped and waited, felt the tension slip away as his hands stroked her face and lips. He kissed her, showing her he liked what she liked, and Jas opened her mouth, allowing his tongue to examine her. He pushed inside her in rhythm with his pulsing tongue, and excitement poured through her body as she opened up to him, letting him all the way in.

He was huge compared with what she was used to, but her excitement flooded over him, making the entry smoother. Jas felt such intense pleasure. His size as well as how he moved made it more exciting. He moved in the usual way, and she found herself pushing back onto him, wrapping her legs around his hips to allow him deeper access. It wasn't long before her body tensed against him as her orgasm rushed through her.

Arven had never experienced this. It was peculiar and different, but not as alien to him as it should have been. He loved her pleasure and lust. Her excitement spurred him on and he moved in her harder, feeling her slight gasp of pain as he went in deeper. He needed to be all the way in, as deep as he could go, in order to plant his seed inside her womb.

She opened to him, screaming and crying in pain and in ecstasy, and he took her harder; loving the grip she had on his member. It was as though she wanted to drag the seed from him. He wasn't so much giving it as she was taking it. Arven felt the pod burst from his scrotum and channel up his penis as his orgasm took hold and he poured into Jas. The pod exploded inside her, burrowing its way into her womb.

Jas felt the shock of stinging pain as something erupted inside her cervix, and then a series of electric charges powered through her loins. She cried against him, coming so hard that she almost felt her mind was exploding. Her body rocked and shook until the series of aftershocks gripping Arven's cock brought forth another pod.

She pushed him away after the second time. Her body was doubled up in sexual agony, jerking and pulsing until the second pod had evaporated into her womb.

'What. The fuck. Was that?' she gasped as soon as she had breath to speak.

Arven lay on his back, his arms folded underneath his head, a smile on his full lips. He loved how her body had reacted to him. Was this how it had been for all of his men? He was pleased and relaxed.

'Shit!' said Jas. 'What did you do to me?'

Arven looked at her. She was trembling, but her body smelt of ecstasy. He wanted her again, felt a new seed building for her and knew this kind of thing was generally unheard of.

'Jassmin. You pleze me,' he said. 'You raily pleze me.'

Jas looked at him from the other side of the bed and saw, with growing shock, that yes indeed she really did please him. She wondered if she could survive another round of this ecstasy. Already she was utterly exhausted, and even more scared than before their sexual union had begun. What was Arven's alien seed doing to her body right now? Jas wasn't sure she really wanted to know.

13

'I need to speak to you,' Jas said to Mallory.

'Of course, Empress,' Mallory said, bowing as Jas entered the arrivals tent.

Jas looked around and found the other women standing up and bowing toward her.

'Please don't do that,' she snapped. 'I'm just the same as you.'

She took Mallory's arm and pulled her away and into the pool room. 'He did something to me. There was this whole *thing* that happened when he came.'

Mallory nodded. 'It's nothing to worry about. It's perfectly normal.'

'Normal? For whom? What happened?'

'A pod,' Mallory explained. 'It's the Arrak Nah Tiaman version of semen, only it's one pod, and it tries it's damndest to hit the mark.'

'Fuck! It's not bad enough I have alien come in me, it has to be some exploding baby-maker instead.'

Mallory shrugged. 'I've heard the process is quite exciting.'

Jas blushed and turned away. Then she left the pool area and went straight out through the tent. She was in turmoil. Her vagina stung and she was afraid that Arven's pods were burning their way through her insides. Panic sent her running through the camp, rapidly followed by Mallory and the two guards that had accompanied her to the women's area in the first place.

Her mind was twisting in fear of some imagined terror. She had visions of an alien baby worming its way out of her womb to devour the world.

'Jasmine,' Mallory said, catching her up. 'Please believe me when I tell you this hasn't harmed you. I know you're scared, and perhaps I should have explained sooner, but I thought once you'd experienced it, you wouldn't be as afraid as the thought of it could have made you.'

Jas stopped running and stood beside the panting translator.

'Arven loves you. The Arrak Nah Tiaman need us. We aren't compatible in the same way as with human men, but in some ways we're more so. They gain from the contact, but the women gain so much more. Think of it as different breeds. Two similar animals – one more evolved than the other. The new breed isn't necessarily a bad thing, Jas. Come. Let me show you.'

Mallory led her away, back toward the arrivals tent, but turned left at one of the sandy roads.

'Do Pinky and Perky have to tag along everywhere I go?' Jas asked, nodding at the guards.

'I'm afraid so. But they'll get used to your wild ways, Jas. Eventually you'll have free reign. You just have to prove to them you aren't going to do anything silly.'

'Silly? Like kill myself, you mean?'

'It's been known. But no, I think in your case they are concerned you will kill them.'

'Where are we going?' asked Jas.

'I'm taking you to the nursery.'

The nursery was a large tent filled with babies and toddlers. There were over a hundred hybrid children being cared for by their mothers within the tent.

As Jas entered, she saw a little girl of, she guessed, around a year old, walking around holding a stuffed toy. The child looked perfectly normal until Jas looked into her eyes. One eye moved with the swirling mix of colours that the Jinx had, the other looked human. The child was pretty and already had a mop of long dark hair.

'Aneline,' said Mallory, bending down to pick up the little girl. 'She's six months old.'

'Six months? But she looks …'

'Yes. They are born normally, not excessive in size at all; and as I explained, the gestation period is only a little shorter than in standard human pregnancies. But once they hit the atmosphere, the children grow and develop twice as fast as our babies normally do. This is a good thing though. It means they will reach puberty much quicker, and the population here can be rebuilt sooner.'

'So they age quicker than us too?'

'Not really. From what I can gather, their life spans are similar. It's just that they become adults sooner than we do.'

Jas looked around at the children. They appeared to be like any she had seen, except that mostly they were quiet. There wasn't any crying in the tent.

'Come,' said Mallory. 'You need to speak to some of the mothers in order to put your mind at rest.'

Mallory introduced Jas to a group of nursing mothers and another woman, who was heavily pregnant.

'This is Marie,' said Mallory, 'and she was the first to have a baby here. Marie is the mentor for all first-time mothers. She's now expecting her second child. Needless to say, her husband is extremely happy and proud.'

'Empress,' Marie said, bowing her head. 'We're very pleased to have you here.'

'The Empress has some natural concerns,' Mallory explained. 'I'll leave her in your capable hands, Marie, as I'm sure you'll be able to allay her fears about the future better than I can.'

Marie nodded and excused herself from the group of women, promising to return shortly.

'Please let me show you around the tent properly,' Marie said.

The tent was made up of various sections. The entrance and largest space was occupied by the toddlers and their mothers. It had become something of a toddler playgroup, and Jas recognised that the women drew a great deal of social interaction from their meetings. It was something that had once been common on Earth before most women decided they would rather work than bring up their children. Through a partition Jas found a ward of cots containing 30 newborns. The babies all slept in eerie silence, and while she was in this room, Jas experienced an overwhelming sense of calm. She couldn't even shape the words to ask questions as she was afraid to make any noise.

'As you can see the babies are very contented,' Marie said. 'They sleep well, eat well and grow quickly here.'

Marie pushed aside another curtain, and Jas followed her into another room in the tent. This one contained older female children, ranging from around five to ten years old.

'These are human girls, taken in the first attacks,' Marie explained. 'They are taught how to live in the new culture. When they are old enough, they will go out and work in the camp, and when they reach the appropriate age, they will join Mallory and go to the marriage auction.'

Next door housed older girls. They slept in single beds, lined up like a dormitory in a girls' school.

The girls were aged between 12 and 15 and were by all accounts perfectly normal teenagers. A group of the girls were sitting together on one bed when Marie and Jas entered, but they quickly stood up and waited for them to approach. Jas noted they were all around 15.

'Susie, Romy, Elise and Talia,' Marie said. 'These young ladies have recently taken up duties in the camp. Talia is working in the bakery, Romy at the patisserie, and Susie and Elise help in the nursery. They'll keep these jobs until they marry in three years' time.'

'How do you feel about marrying?' asked Jas.

Susie blushed. 'Can't wait. It's so romantic.'

Jas fought back the temptation to explain that being auctioned wasn't romantic, but she felt as though she would be telling the girls that there was no Santa Claus or Tooth Fairy. She let Marie lead her away, and they returned to the central room of the nursery.

'We'll have tea,' Marie suggested, and quickly two older girls came forward and produced a tray with a pot of tea and two cups.

Marie led Jas through yet another alcove, where she found a table and chairs, and they sat down with the tray of tea between them. Immediately another girl entered with a plate of cakes and placed it before Jas, then bowed.

'They are pleased you came to visit, Empress,' Marie said. 'Now, please don't be shy, ask me anything you want to know.'

'First, why are all the babies here? Shouldn't they be living with their mothers?'

'Good question. Of course they do live with their mothers. Think of this place as the equivalent of a day care centre. All the women have household duties to perform. You must realise there are no modern conveniences here. We have no dishwashers or washing machines. It all has to be done the old fashioned way. So the children are cared for here, then they go home to their parents every evening.'

Jas's eyes fell on Marie's swollen belly then skittered away.

'You're afraid of the pregnancy and that's natural,' Marie observed. 'Although you probably won't have anything really to worry about for a year or more. It seems to take a long time for a seed to become imbedded in the first instance.'

'Was the pregnancy normal in most respects?'

'Yes. Quicker, but generally it felt the same. I was worried I was going to give birth to a reptile or a worm or something,' Marie laughed. 'Then my lovely baby boy arrived and everything was fine.'

'Can the … the sperm *hurt* us?'

Marie smiled kindly. 'You're experiencing a little soreness, a slight burning? Am I right?'

Jas blushed and nodded. She wasn't used to dealing with personal female issues anymore, and she was still finding it difficult to be around other women after so long away from them.

'It's perfectly normal under the circumstances,' Marie said. 'After all, these men are, shall we say, better endowed than human males? It's bound to be a little uncomfortable at first. Naturally that will improve with time, and with frequent sex with your husband you'll begin to cope with it better.'

Marie held out the cup and Jas sipped at the tea, finding it pleasant but not like the English tea she was used to.'

'It's herbal,' Marie explained. 'I'm rather addicted to it.'

Jas left the tent and found the guards waiting patiently for her outside. They escorted her back to Arven's tent and she did her best to ignore them all the way there. She took careful stock of the city. Marking it out in her mind so that she remembered where things were. She stopped and gazed down one of the streets to the left of the nursery. It appeared that this was some form of high street. She could see tents with painted signs that showed what they were. One had loaves of bread, another fruit and vegetables, the third – a much bigger tent – had a sign depicting animals, and Jas assumed it was the butcher's.

Once back inside Arven's tent and alone, Jas went to explore the crevices and hidden areas. Beyond one of the curtains she found a pool. Behind another, a wardrobe of clothing for her and Arven. She hadn't seen this earlier, as she had merely thrown on the clothing she had worn the previous day. One part of the room had silk shirts and trousers, with some robes and armour. Another was filled with fine satin chemises, long flowing skirts and pantaloons, with cropped tops that would cover her breasts but hardly reach her waist. The clothing was in a mixture of styles, but looked predominately Indian or Arabic. The fabric was light and most suitable for the desert world of the Jinx.

At lunchtime a servant girl brought her food, which consisted of a platter of fruit, some cheese and some cooked meats. Jas wolfed down the lunch and drank a huge draught from the jug of fruit juice and wine she was given with the meal.

She went into the pool room and stripped off. Washing away the aches and pains of the last few days suddenly felt like a good idea. She enjoyed the luxury of washing again, and so lost time in the pool. Staying in the perpetually warm water was easy, and she swam a little, loosening up her arms and legs again.

I'm going to be bored to death in this place, she thought, recalling the busy schedule of training that she had experienced in her days spent with Taylor's men at the mall. She was struck by how distant the memory of her previous life felt, and a pain stabbed at her heart at the thought of not seeing her friends and particularly Andrew ever again. What were they doing right now? Was Andrew even by some miracle still alive? She hoped so.

Her emotions were torn. The Jinx world was lulling her, just as it had all the women, but she couldn't believe in what she felt. It was probably some trick, some magic spun by the magician.

Kale was a mystery to her, one she would find a way to solve. He was responsible for all of this. He was the instrument they had used to destroy her world, making slaves of them all. She still wanted to kill the Al Kuzemen, but her initial cold rage had faded. Now it was replaced by the intense feeling that she would be wiser to observe him. Learn his weaknesses and then somehow use them against him.

I want to go home! The thought was petulant. The truth was that Jinx Town was not the hell she had thought it would be. True, she had been married against her will, but here there was food, water, shelter – and Arven, who, despite her fears and misgivings, was the most sexy man she had ever come across. Her heart hurt again. No. The feelings weren't real. This wasn't real. It was some illusion to brainwash her and turn her into one of the Stepfords. She would never become like that, never accept this as her home. And above all, she never wanted to give birth to a child here. The thought stressed her more than it should; after all, a hybrid human-Jinx would probably belong better here than on Earth. But then, she didn't want a child at all. She really didn't.

She turned in the pool and swam back, only to find Arven watching her. He had entered silently and she hadn't heard or felt his presence at all. *I'm already losing my edge. No Jinx could catch me out like that normally.* It was hard to imagine she had been there only a few days. She stopped swimming, but felt vulnerable in her naked state in the water.

She hadn't seen Arven since that morning, when he had dressed and gone out to attend to whatever duties the Emperor attended to. He wasn't in armour but still he wore his dagger belt, and his hand was resting on it as he watched her.

'Helloo, Jassmin,' he said, and smiled. 'I wented to zee you.'

Jasmine met his swirling eyes and saw love and passion for her in them. The feeling thrilled and horrified her all at the same time. She was his possession, his toy, and it was obvious he had come home to play with her.

'You're wearing too many clothes,' she said, then smiled.

Arven frowned. He wasn't certain what she had said, but the gesture of her hands showed him she was inviting him to join her in the pool.

He stripped quickly, casually throwing the dagger and belt aside with the bundle of clothes. Then, naked, he walked down the steps to join her in the water.

14

They made love again; something Jas refused to think of as *real* love. But she did lust after Arven, there was no denying that the sex was totally satisfying and exciting, and she felt ready as soon as he touched her in the water.

She spent time washing him, stroking him, bringing him to full excitement; and she tried to encourage him to come as she played with him. She wanted to see the pod, examine it. Her scientist curiosity was intrigued by the disparity in their bodies, and she wanted to know more about the thing that was trying to create life inside her. But Arven didn't seem capable of letting go that way, no matter how she encouraged him. He pinned her against the side of the pool, lifting her legs around him as he plunged into her, exploding almost as soon as he reached his mark. Jas squirmed around him, feeling the pod do its work. She was sure the feeling was more intense this time, but now it was less scary. It was almost as though her body was beginning to accept him and the alien quality of his seed.

Afterwards she tried to wash herself down, but Arven pulled her from the water before she could complete the task and led her, dripping wet, back to the bed, where the process started all over again.

Later he dressed again and went out. Jas returned to the pool and cleaned herself with neurotic obsession. The water soothed the sting of Arven's alien sperm and she felt better than she had earlier in the day.

From the pool Jas noticed Arven's pile of discarded clothing and realised he had just pulled on another set before he went out. She walked up the steps, reached for a robe and wrapped it around her body to soak up the damp.

The hilt of the dagger glittered with red and clear jewels. She picked it up, slipped it from its sheath and felt the Jinx magic leak into her arm. Her hand glowed and the weapon felt like it belonged to her, just like the Jinx sword she had fought with a few weeks earlier. She slipped it back into the sheath and then went out into the main tent again. She looked around, wondering where she could hide the weapon. She wanted to keep it, even if Arven noticed it was missing, and eventually she decided to place it under her pillow.

Her obsession with the idea of returning home came back fully as the day wore on. This wasn't her, and this housewife life was already beginning to irritate her more than she could have imagined it would. She prowled the tent like a caged lion.

When Arven returned, a servant brought in a hot broth that reminded her of her favourite type of vegetable soup, and it appeared to have pieces of meat and strange herbs in it too. They sat together eating in silence. The food was delicious. They had a variety of meats. One tasted like beef and she chose to believe it was that. The other could have come from a type of pig. It resembled and tasted a little like ham, but Jas knew that it wasn't ham. She suspected it had been taken from one of the huge boar-like animals she had seen in one of the pens as she had walked back to the tent that day.

For dessert there was more of the exotic fruit and some small cakes. Jas couldn't eat any more though; she was so unused to large quantities of food, having lived for so long on meagre rations. Her appetite slowly dwindled when she thought back to the times when she and Andrew had been so hungry that she had felt faint and sick. She knew that the food in the mall would run out eventually, and yet here she was enjoying food that came in abundance and wasn't rationed at all.

'Jasmine,' Arven said, observing the sadness that had slipped over her expression. 'You will grow happy here. I promise.'

Jas barely noticed that Arven was beginning to speak her language fluently, but as she listened to him talk, occasionally halting for words, she realised that the first days of silence between them were rapidly coming to an end. The Emperor was making an effort to understand her. Maybe he had asked for help from Kale? Jas was sure that no human could have learnt a language that quickly.

'I want you to make happy,' he said, then frowned. 'I want to make you happy.'

'I'm not a possession, Arven,' she said. 'I don't belong to anyone other than myself.'

Arven shook his head. 'You belong with me Jasmine. And I belong with you. From now on, whenever we are apart, it will cause us *both* great pain.'

Jas turned away and glanced down at her half-eaten plate of food. Arven poured wine into a chalice and lifted it, holding it against her lips. She drank to please him, but her mind slipped back to the memory of the dagger. She could so easily use it on him while he slept. That would put an end to this insanity and maybe even throw the Jinx into chaos, but she couldn't see how it would enable her to return to Earth.

He took her hand and led her back to their bed, pulled the drapes around them. Then he stripped her of her clothes, lay her down and, after removing his own outfit, lay down beside her. He held her this time, making no move to seed her again. It was as though he sensed how homesick and scared she really was, and wanted only to comfort her.

She slept in his arms feeling strangely safe, and the thought of using the dagger lulled from her mind as she felt the beating of his heart pressed against her cheek.

15

Over the next few months, Taylor noticed an increase in morale following the influx of women into the camp, and he enjoyed watching the natural order of the men pairing off with them as they began their small and unique families. He knew that this would give them all something to live on for.

'We need to search out undamaged farm land,' he said to Donovan.

It was six months after the girls had arrived, and now that Donovan was in a relationship with Caroline, and their first child was on the way, he, like Taylor, felt a need to plan for some sort of future.

'I'm from a farming family,' Donovan commented. 'I grew up helping out. There's not much I don't know about it.'

'Hell, most of the boys out there know how to work the land,' said Taylor. 'Me included. All of us were small town hicks at one time or other. We're a long way from our homeland, but it doesn't mean we can't bring some of the past to this place. Use our skills to improve things for us all.'

'The Jinx haven't attacked for so long, I wonder if they think we're done and there's no-one left here,' Harvey suggested. 'There's never been a better time to start thinking about moving on from all this.'

Taylor had called a few of the men to his home to discuss the future. Rations were rapidly dwindling. At the current rate they had enough canned, frozen and freeze-dried food to last a few years, but if they didn't start to think of growing food soon, then there was no real future for any of them. Especially as their numbers were increasing.

'So we have the skills,' Harvey said. 'Perhaps if we get out of here we can begin to rebuild some small piece of the world.'

Taylor noticed and enjoyed the positive attitude that both of his closest friends were displaying. He knew it was to do with the way their lives were now. Harvey too had begun a relationship with one of the women, Kim, and she and her young daughter had moved into Harvey's small shop, rapidly making it a home. They too had become a family.

Taylor nodded. 'I think we need an opportunity to test Dawn's theory of lead being a deflective shield, too.'

They sent out a scouting party to look for suitable wasteland nearby. The move from the mall wouldn't be immediate, but a farm and production of fresh produce had become essential.

After a few days of scouring they found a small plot of land; a field not too far from the mall that the new farmers could tend every day.

Several weeks passed. The soldiers, now turned farmers, worked shifts to prepare the land, and soon it began to look like a possible base for their fresh food sources. It was hard work, tilling the soil with basic tools, removing hard clumps of rocks, stacking them into wheelbarrows and emptying them into the lane beside the land. Further scouting parties brought back seeds taken from a garden store. By then the women had already begun to grow tomato plants, keeping them in the foyer at the mall, because this place, near the mess, received sun all day long and was as warm as a greenhouse. The plants thrived in there, and the small city in the Trafford Centre became the source of life once more.

Once it was cleaned and the soil roughly ploughed, the field was divided up, wheat on one side, salad and vegetable produce in one corner. The crops they planned to grow included lettuce, green beans, carrots, turnips, cauliflower and potatoes. The final corner was going to be dedicated to any livestock the scouts might find.

The women had taken to using the resources of flour they found in the shops at the Trafford Centre, and the smell of fresh bread permeated the mess every day. But the flour wasn't going to last forever; therefore, as bread was still a staple food, it seemed imperative that they experiment with growing their own wheat.

True to his word, Donovan was a good farmer, and he knew how to prepare the field to the best potential. Taylor thought Donovan was rapidly becoming their greatest asset, and it was all because Caroline was in his life. It made Taylor feel glad and sad at the same time. He missed Jas, but he pushed aside his natural jealousy and watched as Donovan led the new farmers.

'Fortunately we have a patch of land here that's been resting for the last three years,' Donovan explained. 'The soil is healthy and ready for use.'

Maybe we are getting a second chance, Taylor thought.

Dawn proved to be knowledgeable with plants, and she taught the other women how to tend their own herbs, which they also kept in the makeshift greenhouse.

'This is great,' Taylor said when he saw the women working in there.

'I've always had "the green thumb",' Dawn answered, and she smiled at him. 'Bit of a family trait.'

Taylor said nothing more, but Dawn was pleased to receive his praise. She really liked the Captain and felt they could get along if only he would loosen up a little. His men were champing at the bit to get a piece of her, but unlike her friends, Dawn had kept herself away from them, avoiding any involvement. The Captain was the one man she was interested in, and it seemed he barely knew she existed.

Of course she had heard the rumours about the woman who had disguised herself as a man among them and the slight sniggers that the Captain had been sleeping with her from the minute he found out, but Dawn wasn't sure she believed it. Taylor showed no interest at all in her as the only available female, and Dawn knew she looked good, especially since they had moved into the mall. It was easier to keep clean here, and there was an abundance of clothes in the stores to choose from. But whatever she did, Taylor appeared not to notice, and didn't react.

As the summer months slipped by, Dawn became restless. She and the other women had fallen into roles they weren't necessarily used to. They had become housewives instead of warriors. The end of the world had changed their perspective. The others seemed happy to be protected, and Dawn felt somewhat left out. Often she was alone for days, and she wandered around the stores, looking at clothes, trying different outfits on just for something to do.

One afternoon she tried on a low-cut summer dress in pale pink. Before the end of the world she would never have considered wearing anything so girly. She had always been in trouser suits, or if she had to get her hands dirty, combat pants and a T-shirt.. She couldn't even remember having owned a dress, let alone having worn one. This one was nice though. It showed off her figure well, and an idea formed as she looked at herself in the shop mirror.

I'm going to have to be blatant, she thought. *Especially since this nice-girl routine isn't getting me anywhere.* She pulled a long cardigan over the dress and left the shop, heading for Taylor's home.

She paused at the door, removing the cardigan, and then knocked loudly.

'Dawn,' Taylor said. 'Is something wrong?'

'No, I just wanted to talk about tomorrow's scouting mission. I've a suggestion about where we might find some livestock. I know that having chickens would be a really good start, and I've heard they are quite easy to care for. Not to mention how great it would be to actually have eggs again.'

Taylor invited her in and politely listened to her contrived reason for visiting.

It's a bit much having your cleavage out and the guy doesn't even have the decency to have a sneaky peek, Dawn thought as Taylor barely glanced at her, always keeping his eyes firmly on her face. Dawn was peeved, as she knew that once she walked outside and through the mall there would be lots of attention from the available soldiers, none of whom she was the slightest bit interested in.

'Anyway,' she said, 'is there *anything* I can do for you, Captain?'

'No, that's fine, the team are all set for tomorrow. Your suggestion is a good one though, and I'll put it to Kline in the morning.'

'Well, if there's *nothing* else, I'll say goodnight.'

Dawn left feeling more frustrated than ever. She wasn't sure what to do about Taylor. Maybe he was gay, or maybe the rumours were true and he was still in love with the stolen boy-girl, Jas. Either way, Dawn began to feel she was fighting a losing battle.

Outside she pulled on her cardigan again. As she walked away, she ran through the faces of the other single soldiers, none of whom really did it for her.

'Hello Dawn,' Gerald said. 'Feeling lonely tonight?'

Dawn looked into Gerald's eyes and saw nothing human in them. She took an involuntary step back. It was strange how she and the other women felt nervous around the doctor. Caroline had told her the story of his behaviour with Jas. But now there was a group of women living there, he had shown no sign at all of making any moves on any of them.

'No,' she answered, and folded her arms across her chest. 'I'm fine thanks.'

She made a move to pass, but the doctor blocked her way.

'I noticed you were looking a little peaky,' he said. 'So I brought you a tonic.'

Dawn looked at the brown glass bottle held out by the doctor.

'I appreciate the caring, doc, but I'm good thanks.'

'We wouldn't want you to get sick,' Gerald said, holding out the bottle and a measuring cup. 'Just 10mls a night. It might help you sleep too.'

Dawn felt a little prickle of concern ripple up her spine. She had always found the doctor a little strange, but this new offer seemed genuine.

'I'm going to give the tonic to all the ladies and children,' Gerald said. 'We can't afford to lose you.'

Dawn took the bottle and the measuring cup and thanked the doctor again. Then she walked around him. She didn't see the smile on his face as she walked away. Dawn headed upstairs to her private space in one of the high street chain shops.

Gerald watched her go, admiring the sway of her hips as she hurried up the steps. He was pleased that at least one of the women hadn't made any effort to pair up with a soldier. It made her vulnerable, and none of the yanks was going to take advantage of that, so Gerald thought he might just be in with a chance. He wondered if he had said enough to encourage her to take the tonic. It was always a close call between saying enough and saying too much. He had tried to appear benign, but perhaps it had been a mistake to block her, even temporarily, as she had tried to pass him?

As soon as Dawn was out of sight, Gerald followed. He knew where she slept, just as he knew where everyone else in the camp was, but he had deliberately stayed away from the women. So much so, that the soldiers had relaxed with him again, as though his minor craziness about Jas was excused because she had been the only girl they had seen for years. Now there were more of them, Taylor and his men treated Gerald like an equal again. It was so easy to get people to fall into your deceit – if you knew how to appear harmless.

Dawn reached her shop and turned to glance back. No-one was around. Most of the soldiers would be in the mess, or the ones who had found female companions would be settling down for the night. Strangely, though, she had felt sure she was being watched all the way back to her place. Part of her wanted to go down to the mess and just randomly pick one of the guys to bring back. She missed sex, missed the closeness and intimacy of spending time with someone who found her attractive. She knew there was an abundance of guys who felt like that about her, too, but she didn't want to screw someone just for the sake of it. It had never been her style.

Dawn went inside her shop. For the first time, the rows of clothes made her feel nervous. She saw shadows in every corner of the place, so she switched the shop lights on full and walked through to the back room, where she had placed a mattress and sleeping bag. She locked the door behind her, little realising that she was suddenly mimicking the behaviour of her predecessor, Jas. She had slept in this very shop once.

Dawn had made the place as homey as possible. She even had a bedside table and lamp, and on the table she placed the tonic bottle and cup.

She took off the dress, put back on some leggings and a T-shirt, then climbed into her bed to sleep. It was a warm night but she didn't feel as though it was safe to sleep naked as she often did, and she couldn't understand why. She tossed and turned, thought about Taylor and the other men, and sleep wouldn't come no matter how much she tried to make it.

She glanced at the tonic bottle. The doctor had said it would help her sleep. Maybe she could try it? If he was giving it to the other women too, then there was no harm in trying some, was there? Dawn remembered Gerald's eyes and how they had held such a deadpan expression. The doctor had always been fine with her, if a little distant. She didn't know where this sudden unease and mistrust came from. But something about him, especially his behaviour that night, made her feel uncomfortable.

Hours passed. She turned over in the bed, and when she knew she just couldn't sleep, she climbed out of the bag and got up. Her throat was dry, so she went to the small fridge by the door and opened it, reaching inside for the jug of water she kept there. That was when she heard someone trying her door. She froze, glanced at the handle and saw it turn.

Dawn knew she had locked the door, but still she suddenly felt paranoid that she hadn't and that the door would spring open.

Maybe the Jinx have found the mall? Panic surged into her body, and she trembled, her heart pounding against her chest.

'Dawn?' said a voice, and the volume was too low for her to recognise whose it was.

She was too scared to reply, and just stared at the door in shock. Who the hell was out there, and why now?

She glanced down at the summer dress. Okay, maybe she had been inviting trouble. One of the soldiers had suddenly got the idea that she needed company. She moved toward the door, ready to send whoever it was packing, but the handle was no longer being tried, and as she listened, her ear pressed against the wood, she was sure she could hear the rapid exit of the intruder from the shop.

I'll have to report this, she thought. *But I guess it's all my own fault.*

She thought again about the soldiers and considered which of them she found attractive enough. Maybe it *was* becoming unsafe to be single now. *If Taylor isn't interested, then I'll just have to settle for second best.*

16

'I need your help,' Mallory said.

'What's wrong?'

Jas and Mallory sat together in the arrivals tent. It was all but empty these days and the auctions were no longer taking place every fortnight. Six months had passed since Jas had arrived on Emin and she had settled into a routine as wife to Arven and Empress to the Jinx.

'There's a lot of unrest in the other towns. The unmarried Arrak Nah Tiaman are very unhappy that the raids on Earth have ceased.'

'I know about the problems,' Jas said. 'But it seems a reasonable thing that the raids have ended. They were pointless.'

'Yes. I agree. But the problem is that girls of any marriageable age are now scarce. There's a movement towards marrying them younger.'

'How young?' Jas asked.

'Sixteen.'

'No. I won't allow it.'

Mallory sighed. 'I was hoping you would say that. Last week I had to split Jenny and Rosa up. They are both to be married at the next auction. I'm keeping them apart until then – enforced meditation. Did you know that there has never been a case of adultery here?'

'Is that true? I didn't know,' said Jas.

'I was afraid that Jenny and Rosa would break their marriage vows. You see they *love* each other. It's genuine, and it seems grossly unfair to me that they may be forced into an unhappy marriage.'

'This is a turnaround for you ...'

'Not really. I've only done whatever I needed to help all of us survive,' Mallory said.

'How can I help?' asked Jas.

'Talk to Arven. Get a reprieve for them.'

Jas shook her head. 'It won't make any difference. But I'll try. He doesn't listen to me at all when I talk to him about politics. He has this annoying attitude that women don't understand things like that. It's like living in the dark ages. It's not how I'm used to being treated.'

Mallory watched Jas as she paced around the tent in agitation. 'Most of the women here are happy, Jas. You must know that?'

Jas stopped pacing and looked at Mallory. 'I know they *think* they are happy. But it's this place. It lulls you. Then you're alone and you realise it's not an oasis, it's a prison, and you are sex slaves to the gaolers.'

Even as she finished speaking Jas knew that what she had said wasn't strictly true, but she wanted to believe that Emin was hypnotic. That they were powerless to fight. Because then she could excuse her own lack of motivation in finding a way to escape.

'We're all kidnap victims, falling in love with our captors,' she continued. 'It's a psychological ailment that helps us cope. It doesn't make any of it real. I don't love Arven. How could I? We're too different. But when I'm around him I think I do love him.'

Mallory was shocked by her words. She had always admired the Emperor. He was far more a man than her snivelling ex-husband had been.

'The Arrak Nah Tiaman are better than human men,' Mallory said. 'But that doesn't mean they aren't flawed. Women are their weakness. All because they have this belief that they partner for life. But it is better than the alternative. They could have been rapists. We could all have been passed around and used as whores. Fundamentally, their beliefs have protected us this far.'

'Mallory. They are rapists. They justify it by marriage. Don't kid yourself that we mean anything more to them than a means to repopulate.'

'Do you really feel raped, Jas?' Mallory said, raising her eyebrow in disbelief.

'I …' Jas didn't answer.

She shrugged, then turned and left the tent without another word. She knew that Mallory's question was valid, and it was so hard to define how she really felt about Arven. She wanted and lusted after him but wasn't completely certain that this was coming from her own desires. Even so, the thought of him stirred her, and she quashed the feelings, forcing anger back into her heart and mind. She didn't want to be treated like a 'mere woman'. Emancipation was the cause for which her ancestors had burnt their bras back in the day …

Jas walked back through the streets, her Jinx guard following a few steps behind. *And I bet you hate that, don't you?* she thought, glancing back at the tall man. *You're subservient to me, yet I could so easily have become your wife instead of Arven's.*

As she approached their tent, Jas saw Arven greeting the council members at Kale's tent. Another meeting was taking place. Jas would have to take drastic measures again if she was to learn the latest news.

She entered her tent, then pulled the drapes around the bed and lay down. Dream-walking was becoming easier for her with every attempt, but her mind was in turmoil and she found it hard to relax. She felt for Jenny and Rosa, and all the other unmarried women in the camp who were still being forced into the auctions. *What is the point of being Empress if nothing I say matters?* She turned over on the bed. It was hot and humid in the tent.

She sat up, removed the top robe, then lay down again in her chemise. Her mind drifted around.

She remembered Andrew sitting quietly in class while Steinberg flicked chewed up bits of paper with his ruler. Her memory drifted back to Steinberg's cut knee, his ripped trousers and worst of all his terrified screams as the Jinx had ripped him apart. She curled into a foetal position. She found these memories hard to reconcile with the Jinx and their culture, even though Arven had explained it time and again. It was a rule of combat. You kill your enemy; that way they can't come back for revenge. They can't gather their own army and steal back the women – that was what it really came down to. But how could the human males even hope to do that? There was no way they could find them on another planet, was there?

Beads of sweat sprang up on her skin. She stretched out, wishing there was a fan in this godforsaken place. *What I wouldn't give for a little air-conditioning right now.* There was no denying that Jinx Town was hard for those that had to live and work in it. How were the bakers coping in this heat? How did the other women feel about washing their clothing in a pool of magic water, even if it was self-cleaning? Or cooking their food over open fires? True, they hadn't had much technology on Earth in the last few years, but if they were to return, couldn't they have everything back as it was?

The thought of the old world suddenly made her feel sick. Things hadn't been right, she knew that, and if she were to believe all that Kale said, then the Earth had been on a rapid decline anyway. But then, Kale could be lying. The truth was, if the women believed there was nothing to go back to, wouldn't they find it easier to accept their lot? She didn't trust Kale, never would.

Back on Earth, before her capture, Jas had known they were all living on borrowed time but had refused to admit it. Taylor would find the bunkers eventually – he had known all along that the government and key personnel were hidden there. He had told her once that it would be like Noah's Ark down there. There would be engineers, teachers, plumbers, carpenters and all manner of skilled people specially chosen to rebuild the world when the Jinx gave up. That was what the 'powers-that-be' were counting on. Then they would rebuild. Reform the population out of those that remained. And in the process the world would have been rid of surplus inhabitants. No longer would there be shortages of food and water. The government wouldn't have to pay out massive amounts of capital in pensions, either. The old, the infirm and any remaining single males would have been culled by the Jinx, or by each other in the final desperate hours of the end of the world.

Jas squeezed her eyes shut, pushing away images of the carnage she had seen over the years, some of which she had wrought herself in order to defend Andrew. If she ever did get back to Earth, she would make it her mission to really help Taylor find those bunkers, one way or another.

These thoughts are insane. I'll never get back. Never. Not unless I somehow persuade Kale to take me there.

'You can't leave it much longer, Lord,' said Kale. 'In the other encampments the Al Kuzemen warn of rebellion. There aren't enough females to populate our entire planet. We need to go back and find more.'

'There aren't any more. We looked, over and over,' said Councillor Barok.

'How has it come to this?' asked Arven. 'How have my loyal people turned so? We've done everything we could, all of it to save them and their bloodlines.'

Kale sighed. He felt irritated by Arven's naïveté. 'Jealousy, Lord. When you took your Empress there was hope for continued prosperity. Now they fear you are too blinded with love and no longer care to provide for the needs of your subjects.'

'That's ridiculous. You know the women were scarce. Jasmine was the last found in a long time.'

'We still have some marriages to take place. This might placate a few of the more outspoken men,' Kale said. 'But if those men don't make matches among the remaining women, then we may well have a mutiny on our hands.'

'What do you advise?' asked Arven.

'You must go to the other towns and reaffirm your commitment to the people. Preside at some weddings, show them you care about our race.'

'Of course I *care*,' Arven said, irritation coming through with the harshness of the words. 'A royal tour would be a good thing. Jasmine and I ...'

'Go alone,' warned Kale. 'Otherwise it might be seen that you are flaunting your Empress before those who have no wife.'

'This is insane. Haven't I done all that I could? Haven't I given my people all of the women, until now?'

'Yes. But the rumour is that you saved the best for last,' said Barok.

Arven shook his head; he didn't know what to reply to this because to him Jas *was* the best. She was perfect, beautiful, sexy; and despite the constant tug of war to gain her own independence, she was still a very good wife. The thought of leaving her behind, even for a few days, made his stomach churn. But maybe it would be good for her, to feel the pain of separation. He smiled as he thought about her. He knew about the dagger she kept under her pillow, and leaving it in the bathroom all those months ago had been a test of her loyalty and of the bond the marriage created. Never once had she attempted to use it on him, even on those occasions when his passion for her grew too intense. At those moments she would merely hold out her hand and ask for rest, and he would hold back, forcing his urges to cool.

Arven had never felt like this for Celin. The bond had been good, but not as strong or as intense as the one he had formed with Jas. He *loved* her. He really did. All they needed now was to produce an heir. That would settle things; bring about good feeling among the people. Until then, Arven knew the Al Kuzemen was right. He had to go and visit some of the other camps, and he had to leave Jas behind if he was to focus on rebuilding his relationship with his people. But what could he promise them when all of their last raids had failed to turn up females? Even the Al Kuzemen were no longer able to find the few still scattered across the Earth.

'I'll do as you advise,' Arven said. 'But I don't like to leave Jas alone. She will be lonely.'

'There are the other women in the camp,' Kale pointed out.

'She prefers male company,' Arven said. 'So perhaps you will be a companion to her while I'm gone?'

Kale felt his nerves prickle at the thought of being anything to Jas. Being around her made him feel uncomfortable, and always had from the beginning. He didn't know what to make of her. However, he couldn't refuse the request of his Emperor without it seeming strange. Any married woman was safe alone with the Al Kuzemen, or any other male for that matter. Their ethics were such that they could not interfere with another's wife. Kale wondered briefly why these thoughts even occurred to him, and as he watched the Emperor leave his tent, he felt a flush of guilt colour his cheeks. The truth was, he liked the thought of being alone with Jas, much more than he should, and that was why she made him nervous.

It would be a very good opportunity to observe the human closely. He knew of her dream-walking. Knew that even as the Emperor had come to him in privacy, Jas had been listening outside. It was hard to admit this to anyone, however. Kale didn't want to acknowledge that the human females had powers of their own, even as he had observed them. He thought again about how Mallory's was the first he had recognised. Her aptitude for languages, and her natural intuition, had clearly been a magic that had been latent in her own world. Once exposed to the Emin atmosphere, however, this dormant power had awakened. She had taught herself to communicate with all women from all continents of her world.

The artistry that the women displayed in all areas was also quite unique. They were creative and intelligent for the most part. Adapting rapidly to this environment, even singing when washing clothing in the streams and rivers and doing the harsh chores they were unused to. Emin women had been fragile in comparison with the humans. They had had one calling in life, to marry and to breed, whereas the humans females were so much more than that.

Kale reached for his jug of wine. The girl, Ailsa, who had been his servant for some time, had been taken that week to the arrivals tent. She was to be auctioned at the end of the week along with a group of women that Mallory still deemed 'unready'. Kale knew that Mallory's instincts were right on this. He had seen it in Ailsa's eyes when the guards had come to take her and he had resisted the urge to intervene. The girl was unmarried, and there were hundreds of males to every remaining female. Ailsa would have to be integrated, and that meant married and breeding as soon as possible. Even so, it hadn't sat well with him, and Kale couldn't help feeling that their behaviour was leading them all to impending doom.

Mallory was worried. She had felt this intense fear ever since they had brought the latest batch of girls from their camp duties.

Ailsa was crying in the corner, and despite her reassurances, Mallory couldn't get the girl to calm down.

'I can't have a Jinx bastard growing in my belly,' she wailed. 'It's a sin to have sex out of marriage.'

'Ailsa, the thing is, you will be married. It's just that your husband will be from this world, and under Arrak Nah Tiaman law your marriage will protect you.'

Mallory was afraid to explain the feeling she had that times were changing. There were a lot of good things happening in the camp. New births of both male and female children, the balance fortunately swinging toward female births. But this didn't stop the unattached males from becoming frustrated by their lack of companionship.

The Arrak Nah Tiaman might be warriors and murderers but they weren't rapists. It was the one major thing that set them apart from the men of Earth, and Mallory admired their high moral standing on bonding and the stock they set in the marriage ceremony. If there had been such a thing as adultery, then they would certainly have made it punishable by death. Fortunately, no-one felt the urge to commit the sin. Once bonded, the couples cared for each other, and divorce and adultery had no equivalents in their vocabulary.

Mallory understood better than most how reproduction was crucial to these people, and even more so since they had lost their entire population of women. Times were desperate, and there were still so many men left alone. Mallory feared that some males would change their attitude towards fidelity in their desperation to mate and reproduce. She was concerned that they would become like the men on Earth had, and change their policies to suit themselves. So far the women had all been well treated, but how would this go for such a reluctant wife as Ailsa, whose deep religious convictions meant she would never acknowledge the local rituals as legitimate?

Ailsa stopped crying and let Mallory show her to the pool room. She would bathe in the soothing water and sleep away the anxiety. In a week's time the girl might or might not be ready, but either way she would be married to the first man she bonded with.

Mallory saw Jenny and Rosa return. It would only be a matter of time before she was forced to separate them permanently. They looked at each other sadly across the room, then went to their newly-designated beds on opposite sides of the tent.

'I'm sorry,' she said to them both, but neither woman answered. Instead they lay down, tears in their eyes.

Two warriors arrived with another girl, this one taken directly from the nursery. The girl was only 15, and Mallory knew her well, as she sometimes worked in the arrivals tent providing food for the prospective wives.

'Oh no!' Mallory exclaimed. 'Absolutely not, she's way too young.'

The warrior met her eyes and glared at her with his shifting gaze. 'This makes ten,' he said. 'There are no others near the right age.'

'She's old enough and ready,' said the other warrior.

Mallory found his leer intimidating.

'I will bid for that one myself,' he continued.

'Get out of here,' ordered Mallory. 'Don't bring any more here until you have a direct order from the Emperor. It is him I answer to.'

The soldier towered over her, but a lick of fear flickered across his features, and Mallory realised that her instincts were right: the soldiers had been acting on their own and had no orders at all to bring the girl to the tent for auction. She had to see Jas and Arven as soon as possible. Things were beginning to change. She had never had cause to doubt the word of an Arrak Nah Tiaman warrior before.

17

Rajik

Gravil was looking forward to spending more time with his new bride. At the auction three days earlier, when they had bonded, he had known that he had won the best of the ten women available. She was pretty, even by human standards. Pale yellow hair, brown eyes, a natural smile. Plus she was younger than most of the others. He hoped this meant they would have many children together.

Once, before the plague, he had hoped to marry and have many sons. Now, he hoped mostly for daughters, but one son would be enough to carry on all of his family traditions. Gravil was an Al Hazim Rah, and he made daggers. These were powerful weapons woven with magic; a magic that could be recognised and wielded only by an Arrak Nah Tiaman hand. Gravil was among the best in his trade. He was valued by his guild, and one of his daggers even took pride of place in the Emperor's collection.

Gravil turned right at Al Kuzemen Hallim's tent and down the sandy road that led to his own. When he was younger, he had been drawn to the Al Kuzemen guild. But it had been clear to Hallim that Gravil had another destiny. Yes, Gravil could manipulate magic; it was in his hands, seeped from his pores and leaked out from his soul due to his lack of trained focus. But Gravil was a swordsmith. Hallim had *felt* it. So he had found the boy an apprenticeship with the master forger, and it had been the best thing for him. Gravil's magic had found the release it needed, and soon he had been making his own reputation and been rapidly promoted within the guild. Though still young, he had taken on the succession to the elderly master, Makier El Finis, and would replace him when he retired.

Anticipation at seeing his wife at the end of the day lightened his journey, and his speed picked up as he turned into the next street. Her name was Lucy and he loved the roll of it on his tongue. Gravil murmured her name, tasted it, enjoyed the strangeness of speaking so softly. The Earth language she spoke was so different from his own tongue.

'Loocee ...'

'Gravil?' said a voice beside him, and he turned to see his cousin Harmin stood outside the meeting tent.

Harmin had been socialising a little too hard again. He had drunk an excessive amount of wine, and Gravil could smell the sharp tang of Earth alcohol, which he recognised as whisky. Gravil had tried it once, but the potent liquid had burned his throat and made him cough until he was almost sick. He wasn't much of a drinker anyway, unlike his cousin, and even the smell of it on Harmin's breath brought back that feeling of sickness.

'Cousin, how goes your day?' Gravil said.

'Would be better if I had a wife to hurry home to,' Harmin said.

Gravil smiled. He was used to Harmin's gruff teasing and didn't mind it too much, as it reminded him how lucky he had been when he bid for Lucy.

'Yes. I'm a lucky man.'

Harmin folded his arms across his expansive chest. He was taller than Gravil, but not by much, and every bit as strong and broad.

'Too lucky,' Harmin said. 'You know I put a bid in for her myself. I remember seeing her when she first arrived, as I was on guard duty. Had I been as pushy as you, she might be my wife now.'

Gravil went very still. He didn't care for the harsh, jealous tone in Harmin's voice. His cousin could be mean when he drank too much; often he had roused others into unnecessary fights. Fighting among their people was rare, and forbidden except within the bounds of training. They were soldiers, they fought the enemy, not each other. That was the rule.

'I'll speak to you tomorrow, Harmin,' Gravil said, turning away.

The pathways were quiet. Most of the men were either in the social tents or home with their wives and children. Gravil continued up the path toward the street that led to his tent. He felt a twinge of concern at his cousin's jealousy. Maybe he could put in a good word for him at the next auction? Give him an opportunity to be first up? Although Gravil himself hadn't called in any favours that day; he had always seen it as something that was meant to be. Lucy was his, was destined to be his. Surely Harmin could see that?

Since his marriage, Gravil had been more aware of the unmarried men in the camp. They behaved differently toward him. Some, like Osias, his childhood friend, had asked personal questions about his wife and the seeding ritual. Gravil had brushed aside the questions, finding it all intrusive. He had no urge at all to discuss Lucy that way. Their coupling was beautiful, fulfilling and ultimately private.

Harmin rounded the street corner just in time to see Gravil enter his tent. He didn't see Lucy, but he imagined her waiting for his cousin, lying wantonly on their bed, or swimming in the bathing pool, all of her naked charms – those human mysteries he so desired to learn – blatantly available now to her husband.

Rage filled him. It wasn't fair! Gravil had always had the Al Kuzemen luck on his side, and Harmin wondered if he had used the magic he pumped into his daggers on the auction selector. Perhaps fate would have given Lucy to Harmin if he had been of a magical persuasion. He should have been up on the stage first. He should have pushed Gravil aside and taken the steps two at a time. Surely then Lucy would have bonded with him. Of course there was no saying Lucy would have bonded with anyone else at the auction. But Harmin had seen her looking at him. He was certain she had been admiring him the day she arrived in the camp. He also knew that the Earth women viewed marriage differently to them.

Harmin stared at the closed tent. His mind burned through the heavy fabric and he imagined Gravil seeding his wife as she gasped in his arms. Harmin had been married before the plague had killed the local women. He knew what passion a man could have for his wife, and he wanted it again. Gravil had never been married. Some would say that meant he deserved it more, but Harmin knew that meant he was less likely to miss having a wife.

He approached the tent. He could at least spoil his cousin's fun that night.

'Gravil!' Harmin called at the tent door.

The flap lifted and Harmin found Lucy before him.

'We're eating,' she said in stumbling Emin.

Gravil came up to the tent door. 'Harmin?'

Lucy went back inside, but listened as Gravil and Harmin talked.

'I want to come in,' said Harmin.

'Another time, cousin. We are just about to eat. If I'd known you were visiting I'd have asked Lucy to prepare food for you also.'

'It's all right,' Lucy said. 'We have enough, Gravil. I don't mind.'

Gravil stepped back and allowed Harmin entry. Lucy fetched another plate and goblet and placed them on the low table. Then she filled Harmin's glass with wine and began serving food onto all of the plates.

Harmin was taller than Gravil, a giant of a man as all of the Arrak Nah Tiaman were, and he made Lucy feel nervous. She hid this by sitting down at the table, and waited as the two men joined her.

'So you are Gravil's cousin?' Lucy said. On Earth she had always been a good hostess, and she fell into the old habits of politeness easily, even though the language was difficult.

Harmin said nothing, but his eyes devoured her, and as Lucy looked up, waiting for his response, she flinched away from the naked lust in his expression.

'I had a wife once,' Harmin said. 'She wasn't like you though. Earth women are very different from our kind.'

'Earth women are our women now,' Gravil pointed out.

'Well, for the lucky few they are,' Harmin said. 'I have never been blessed with the fortune of my cousin.'

Gravil frowned.

'Harmin, would you like some fruit?' Lucy said, offering a bowl. She could feel the tension in the air, yet Gravil appeared not to notice it at all.

Gravil watched Harmin as he picked up his chalice, slugged down the wine and reached for the jug to refill his glass.

'Maybe you've had enough for one day,' Gravil said.

Harmin refilled his glass, ignoring Gravil, but his eyes narrowed as he watched Lucy eat. Harmin reminded Gravil of an avaricious bird. Every mouthful that passed through his wife's lips brought a tightness to Harmin's face. Gravil had never seen anything like it before.

'Lucy,' Gravil said sharply. 'Leave the room.'

Lucy looked at Gravil, surprised by the sharp manner in his voice. So far, her new husband had been only kind and loving to her. The change in his tone scared her, and she stood immediately, leaving the main tent area to retire to the alcove that housed their bed. As she stood, Harmin jumped from his seat at the table.

'I don't want her to leave. I want to look at her. Surely I'm permitted that?'

'I think it's time you went home and slept this off,' Gravil said, his hand falling to his dagger belt. Jealousy surged up into his face. He couldn't explain why, but he didn't like Harmin watching Lucy. He felt somehow that his wife was in danger. *That's insane. We aren't animals. We aren't like the humans with their petty jealousy and ambition.* Gravil walked to the tent door and held the flap open, waiting for Harmin to leave.

Harmin stood in the centre of the room looking around. He could no longer see Lucy but his lust for her wouldn't decrease, and it burnt at his heart as well as his loins. He stared at Gravil, indecisive. Deep down, underneath the drunken haze, Harmin realised his behaviour was inappropriate, but he couldn't help himself. If he didn't know better he would swear that the woman had woven some magic on him. He knew this was insane though: women had no magic. They were for recreation and leisure, not power. But it still seemed to him that the men who possessed them had more than the rest of them.

'There used to be a pattern to life,' Harmin said as grief surged into his eyes, flooding them with moisture. 'There used to be hope. Now there seems like nothing is left for those of us who remain alone. Let me bond with her also. Haven't we always shared everything together? We've been as brothers, more than cousins, our entire lives.'

'Do you even know what you're saying?' Gravil asked. Fury made his voice harsh, and from the other room Lucy found the guttural tongue even harder to follow. 'You would break our most sacred law? Get out of here!

And don't come back. You aren't welcome in my home, Harmin. Stay away from my wife.'

Harmin rubbed his eyes. 'I can't help how I feel. She should have been mine. She should have a chance to bond with me.'

Harmin came to the tent door, and as he met Gravil's eyes, the young daggersmith knew that this wouldn't be the end of the matter. Harmin meant to steal Lucy away from him, and he would never have a moment's peace while his cousin still lived. A red rage came down over his eyes.

The dagger was in his hand. Harmin lay sprawled on the floor. The dark red stain around the body expanded out onto the rug and poured into the sand below. The red veil left Gravil's eyes and he dropped the knife.

'You had no choice,' said Lucy calmly from the opening of the alcove. 'He wanted to steal me away.'

Gravil had never before committed murder. He was a tradesman, not a warrior. The stain on his hands glared an angry accusation.

'This is what we are going to say,' said Lucy. Gravil had never noticed how hypnotic her voice was. 'He attacked me. You came home and found him here. He was insane with jealousy.'

'He attacked you …'

'Yes. He did.'

'I had no choice …'

'You killed him to defend my honour.'

18

'We're bonded. Being apart will give us physical pain,' Arven said. 'But the pain will lessen, or at least we will both learn to accept it for the short time we are separated.'

'Why do you have to go?' Jas asked.

'There are problems in the other towns,' he explained.

'What kind of problems?'

Arven was quiet. Under normal circumstances he would never discuss politics with a woman, but Jas was different and he felt she would understand and cope with his absence better if he explained. He had to admit he was surprised at how quickly she had settled into her new life on Emin. There had been no further attempts to escape, nor had she killed any more of his guards. He had expected her at least to try, but the fact that she hadn't gave him faith in their bonding. He knew her lust for him was genuine and thought that maybe she loved him also. Even though she never said the words.

'There have been a series of incidents. Things we could not have foreseen. My people have begun to … *kill* each other.'

'The lack of women,' Jas said intuitively.

Arven nodded. 'I had thought to give them hope. Now, instead of a dying race, we have become avaricious. Our faith, our covenants, have been shattered by these new sins.'

'Surely you had murder before?'

'No. Our faith does not permit the taking of life except in circumstances of war. But now the war is on our own land, and it is between those that have wives and those that want them.'

'I'm sorry,' Jas said. Her hand stroked his arm in that soothing way she had. A strange calm fell over him, and he turned in the bed, pulling her into his arms. Her head rested against his chest and it amazed him how well she fitted against him. How perfect the touch of her skin against his felt.

'But, surely jealousy isn't a new thing? There will always be someone who wants something that belongs to others.'

'There have been small outbursts of it, but a week spent in meditation with the Al Kuzemen usually eradicates these thoughts. Now, some men have resorted to attacking other men's wives. Such outrages are not our way. This we cannot allow.'

'You're becoming more human,' Jas pointed out. 'Maybe it is being around us that causes this?'

Arven shook his head. 'No. It is not the fault of your species, but a defect in ours. Patience is not a strong part of our psyche. We have never had need of it, because everything we want, we take. In a way that is what motivates these men now. They want a wife, there are few women old enough to marry, and so they are taking ones that belong to others.'

They made love again, and afterwards Arven left Jas sleeping while he went away to make preparations for his journey.

Later he returned to find her ready and waiting to escort him to the vortex.

'There's no need,' he said. 'We should say our goodbyes here.'

'I want to,' Jas said. 'I insist; and I'll even wear those Empress robes to make it look official.'

The pain began soon after she had watched him pass through the vortex, heading to the first town – a place that Kale referred to as Rajik. Jas had returned to her tent to lie listless in their bed, and the days had dragged after he left. She felt isolated. She rarely saw the other women, with the exception of Mallory, and so boredom set in while she spent the days alone.

A strange agony twisted her gut, night and day for the first week. She could barely eat. She felt like a lovesick teenager, and the whole thing annoyed her immensely. It wasn't enough that she was the sex slave to this alien Emperor, she also was cursed to pine for him as well. It went against everything she believed in, everything she had fought for. Even Taylor – and it was strange to think of him now in this context – had never brought these emotions out in her.

During the second week of his absence, Jas took to walking, and she learnt every street and avenue in Jinx Town. Her personal guard followed her at a distance, never interfering. She didn't interact with others, but as she passed the tents and workplaces, looking in on the bakery, standing by the pens as the animals were fed and watered, she learnt more and more about the workings of the town.

She found a stream that flowed through the sand just on the outskirts of the town, with a long stretch of grass running beside the occasionally tree-lined bank. There were fish in the stream. Odd looking creatures that were more mammalian than the fish on Earth. A shoal of cat-like things, with stumpy growths that looked like the beginnings of paws, bounced over the water, swimming upstream like spawning salmon. They had long whiskers and sharp-looking teeth and they snapped at each other as they flew through the air and plummeted back into the clear water.

Jas's scientific brain became fascinated with the new plant life that had sprung up around the water, and watching the fish took her mind away from Arven's absence. Sitting down on the river bank she picked one of the strange blue flowers and raised it to her nose. The flower disintegrated, turning to sand in her hand. Jas looked down at the sand on her robe, picked up a few particles and peered at them closely. *If only I had a microscope.* The sand appeared to be giving the plants life. Or else the magic of Emin moulded everything from the sand. But that explanation felt too biblical, and she was a scientist by nature, after all.

Sat alone by the flowing water, Jas was able to collate her thoughts. By the third week of Arven's absence she had began to feel more like her old self. The walking had helped to rebuild her fitness and she had taken up jogging again, even though she mostly did this in the privacy of Arven's tent: running round and round until she sweated off the fugue that had suffocated her for months. She realised that she had been lulled by Arven and their lifestyle together. She thought about her old values, the way her life had been on Earth. It had been hard, but she had always felt she had a reason to live, a reason to survive. Emin was safe for her. There was no imminent threat. It had made her lazy, and she no longer felt like the soldier she had once been.

Over the last few months her hair had grown, she looked and acted female, following the formula that was expected of her. She wore the clothes, did any duties that were given to her in her role as Empress, which often included visiting the nursery and the arrivals tent to support the women there. This had become second nature, even though she barely believed the words of reassurance she gave them.

What has happened to me? It had to be the magic. As always, she blamed Kale for the problem. *That damn magician put a spell on me so that I'd react to Arven and meekly become the wife he wanted. And I let that happen.*

Kale was to blame for everything. She was sure of it. Since Arven's departure, the Al Kuzemen had avoided her, and Jas had begun to wonder why. He was an odd man, not unattractive but somehow solitary and monk-like in his behaviour. She wondered if the Al Kuzemen could marry or whether, like Catholic priests, they followed religious codes that forbade it. She determined to speak to Mallory about him.

Jas walked back from the river and headed over to the arrivals tent. There would be an auction that evening, and she was expected to preside in Arven's absence. It gave her a good excuse to visit Mallory.

As she approached the tent the hollow feeling she had felt on Arven's departure was suddenly replaced by homesickness. She wanted to return to

Earth. She wanted to wind back the clock, and wished she had never met the Jinx Emperor. Her feelings for him were confused. She didn't know what was real and what was being imposed upon her emotions.

'Empress,' said Mallory, bowing as Jas entered the tent. 'I did not expect to see you until later.'

'Let's talk,' Jas said, and she indicated that Mallory should follow her.

They left the tent, walking out among the streets and lanes.

'How are Jenny and Rosa doing?' Jas asked.

'Good. Thank you for helping them. I don't know how you wangled a reprieve from the auction. It must have been a difficult thing to persuade the Emperor.'

'Not really,' Jas said. 'But I'm glad all is well. The girls in the tent look very young.'

Mallory nodded. 'Too young. But it has become necessary to placate the single men. This will be the last auction for some time. It will be well attended. Kale said he is having extra security there today. He fears an outburst of violence from the disappointed; and the order in which the men come up to the stage will be determined by a raffle instead of just how quickly they get in line.'

'Sounds fair,' Jas said. 'Can Kale ... marry?'

Mallory frowned. 'There is no reason I know of why he shouldn't be able to.'

'He's never put himself forward though, has he?'

'No. But that doesn't mean much. Quite a few of the Al Kuzemen don't ever marry. It's said their magic is their mistress.'

'I was just wondering about it. I wondered if there was any religious reason.'

Mallory shook her head. 'The people have an emphasis on reproduction. But Kale has shown no interest in any of the females so far.'

Unlike the arrivals tent, which was surrounded by quite a buzz, Kale's tent was calm. Jas imagined that the Al Kuzemen was in quiet meditation. Or maybe he was absent, on some mystery duty.

'Wait here,' she ordered. Her guard looked confused, but nevertheless remained in the doorway of Arven's tent as she crossed the few feet of sand to Kale's door. As she approached, the guard on the Al Kuzemen's door stood upright. He didn't salute – it wasn't the Jinx way – but the straightening of his spine was a mark of respectful acknowledgement.

'I need to see the Al Kuzemen,' Jas said, and the guard immediately lifted the flap to allow her to pass.

Kale was seated in a chair that resembled a cushioned throne. Jas had never been inside his tent while awake. Yet she had seen the furnishings many times while she dream-walked. She recognised the chaise in the corner, where the girl Ailsa had slept, but now it was draped in a red velvet cloth instead of bedding. A bowl of fresh fruit sat on the table where the maps of Earth had been strewn.

'Empress.' Kale stood and bowed. 'You honour me. But not for the first time.'

Jas nodded. 'I wanted your help. I miss Arven. But I'm sure you know that.'

'It is only natural after such a strong bonding.'

'In my world we called this feeling love. But I don't think it is a genuine emotion, Kale. I think it is something to do with the magic on Emin, and I want to understand it more.'

'Excuse me, Empress, but magic is not for women to wield.'

Jas's jaw stiffened. She was sick of this sexist view the Jinx had of women. So women weren't permitted to use magic, nor were they involved in the politics, and they certainly wouldn't be allowed to fight side by side with the men. They had to know their place, in the kitchen and the bedroom only it seemed. But Jas was having none of it. She had been muted, her faculties dulled, for almost eight months now. She wanted answers and she was going to get them, no matter what she had to do to make Kale talk.

'I don't agree. I wish to ask you questions about the magic. Are you refusing to answer?'

'Of course not. Ask your questions.'

'May I?' Jas asked, indicating the chair next to him.

Kale nodded and Jas sat down. They were so close that Jas could see the bead of perspiration that bloomed up on his brow. Instinct told her that Kale was nervous around her, but she didn't know why.

'Why aren't women allowed to use magic?'

Kale sighed deeply. 'It isn't that they aren't permitted, Empress. It's that they don't have the aptitude for it. There are no female magicians among our women.'

'Have there ever been?' Jas asked.

'The ancient scrolls tell us of great warrior women who were mages. There have never been any in my lifetime though. And among the Al Kuzemen it is thought that this is merely a myth.'

'Of course,' Jas said, 'the women you have now are from Earth. We aren't like you at all. Maybe we are different when it comes to magic too.'

Kale stared at her for a long moment. Was she revealing to him the fact that she had some power? Did she understand that Kale had seen something in the Earth women that indicated they might well have an aptitude for magic after all?

'What do you mean?' Kale asked finally.

'Nothing at all,' said Jas, and Kale could see no guile in her. 'This is all purely curiosity. Part of my wish to understand of your people.'

'I see. As Empress you should study our history.'

Jas nodded, but paused while she formed the next question. She wanted to know so much about the feelings she had been experiencing. She still believed they were somehow unnaturally induced.

'Can a Jinx love more than one woman?'

'We bond for life.'

'That wasn't what I asked you.'

'It's not possible to "love", as you call it, any other than your wife or husband.'

'Why?'

Jas looked into Kale's eyes and the Al Kuzemen blinked and sat up in his chair. His discomfort around her was obvious, even though he tried hard to hide it. Jas recognised the behaviour, lapsing naturally into her old mode of reading body language – a skill she had honed in order to identify any danger. She noted that Kale had pulled his arms into the chair tightly and was carefully avoiding touching her.

'The bonding is magic. It is a merging of the soul, as much as the body. It is impossible to love another.'

'Unless your partner is dead,' Jas said.

Kale nodded. 'We have had to adapt to this.'

Jas reached out and touched Kale's arm. The Al Kuzemen stiffened but didn't pull away, even though she had expected him to.

'Kale,' she said. 'Have there ever been any cases of adultery?'

19

Taylor's alarm clock beeped beside him but he was slow to wake. He felt a warm body pressed against him and tried to lapse back into his dreamless sleep and hold on to the feeling that Jas was beside him, snuggling her head against his chest and groaning gently as the alarm continued its incessant mewing. He felt her arm circle his waist, the warmth of her skin, sweat-damp, sticking slightly to him.

Without opening his eyes he reached out and hit the cancel button on the alarm. Silence, but for the breathing of his companion as she nestled against him. Taylor opened his eyes and turned his head. Dawn lay beside him. Sleepily opening her eyes, she turned and stretched. Then, realising he was watching her, she smiled.

Her smile was quirky and he liked it. She was a very attractive woman. Not beautiful, but certainly pretty, and Taylor wondered how he had been so blind to her until now. It was almost a year since Jas had gone missing and the occupants of the Trafford Centre had begun to rebuild their lives. With no more Jinx attacks, a host of new survivors had surfaced and joined the group. A community had been formed, and those of his men who wanted to were dating, or partnered.

Taylor smiled back at Dawn as she snuggled close to him, scrutinising his face. His head hurt; they had all partied too hard the night before, but it seemed only right that the birth of the first baby in their community should be celebrated. Donovan was the proud father of a baby boy, and it did signify something important to the survivors. Life was going to go on.

'I should get up,' Dawn murmured. 'Cows don't milk themselves.'

Taylor nodded. He didn't know what to say, and could barely remember how it had come about that he had Dawn in his bed. But he remembered the lovemaking and felt good about it.

'I need to get back to rifle training with the new recruits,' Taylor said.

There was a clumsy silence as they stood, fumbling around in the darkened room looking for their clothing. Taylor didn't know what he should say. He felt ill-equipped to deal with the morning after. It had been a long time since this had happened and he wasn't sure how Dawn felt. Maybe she only wanted a one-night stand? Or perhaps she was looking to pair up with him? Taylor wasn't sure he was ready for that, but he knew he didn't want it to just end either.

'So,' said Dawn finally. 'You ... erm.'

'I'd like to meet up later. That is, if you want to,' Taylor said, expelling the awkwardness from the air.

'Yes,' she said quickly, 'I would.'

She turned to the door, but he stopped her and turned her to kiss him. It felt strange, but good, and the need for her rose up inside his chest. Guilt quashed it and he let her go, but she was smiling now, and the embarrassment between them was eased. It was an awkwardness that had never arisen between him and Jas.

'Go milk cows,' he said. 'We could meet for breakfast?'

Her smile widened. 'I'd like that. Go teach some civvies to shoot straight.'

After she had left, Taylor went into the bathroom and splashed water on himself. His mouth felt dry and furry – definitely too much whisky – so he brushed his teeth twice and then headed off out into the mall.

The mall had become a city in the last six months, and it was thriving. That morning most of its occupants were sluggish, so Taylor found himself mostly alone as he walked toward the training bay. Inside, he unlocked the rifle stores and opened fresh packs of bullets, lining them up opposite each range. His head hurt and he wished he had taken some medication before leaving, but as he waited for the new recruits to emerge, he knew he wouldn't be the only one suffering that morning.

Andrew arrived first. 'Hey Captain. Mind if I get some practice in before the newbies get here?

'Knock yourself out,' Taylor said.

Taylor put on a set of ear muffs, and held out a pair to Andrew. The boy took them, collected a rifle and began to load it with professional speed. Taylor watched, silently impressed, as Andrew rattled off some well-aimed rounds at the wall, effectively disintegrating the target. He wondered how old the boy must be now. Sixteen? Seventeen? He wasn't sure, and it was difficult to tell, as Andrew was obviously tall for his age and the training had built his once weedy body into a toned and wiry frame. He never missed training of any sort, and Taylor wondered what motivated him still, when so many others had become lazy since the Jinx attacks had stopped.

Andrew put the rifle back on the stand and returned his unused rounds to the store. Then he took off his ear muffs and looked at Taylor awkwardly for a moment.

'Is something wrong, Andy?' Taylor asked.

'Do you think we'll ever see her again?' the boy asked.

Taylor looked away. 'I don't know. I hope so. But ...'

Andrew turned and headed to the door.

'Andy,' Taylor called after him. 'I think … I *know* … she's still alive. I feel it somehow. She's resourceful. She'll find a way back here if she can.'

'I know. I feel it too.'

As Andrew left, a few stragglers came in and began their tedious execution of the targets as Taylor yelled orders and made them load and unload over and over. His mind was elsewhere, though. He had started something now with Dawn, and why not? Despite his reassuring words to Andrew, he wasn't at all sure that Jas was still alive, and he felt it impossible that she would ever be able to find her way back from the world of the Jinx. No-one had ever done that to his knowledge. He had to think of the future now, not the past, and Dawn was offering him something that made that future far more attractive than it had been in the last year.

The farms were thriving. They had three functioning now, operated on a rota basis so that the work was shared out. And they had reaped the rewards for their first season of crops only a few days earlier. Lead was placed on the first rung of every fence, and so far the farms had remained unmolested. The biggest breakthrough had been the arrival of new refugees, mostly women, and this was thanks to Dawn and her crew, who had built up a network by sending radio messages out along the airwaves in the hope that more survivors would find them. It had taken six months of daily calls, but a small band had arrived, rapidly followed by a larger group.

Taylor's attention was drawn to the opening leading to the mall. Outside, the city was awakening. Men, women and children were rousing themselves and going about their daily duties.

'That's enough for today,' Taylor said, and the recruits packed up their weapons.

After he had locked up the store, Taylor headed toward the mess. He was hungry and was looking forward to the promise of fresh eggs and toast: all of the products of their labours were filtering now into the food chain. In two years there would be fresh beef, pork and chicken. But for now they contented themselves with the produce made by their animals. The breeding of them had only just begun to take root.

It's amazing what we've achieved in a year, Taylor thought as he entered the mess. It was still quiet, so he joined the short food queue. He glanced around to see if Dawn had returned from her milking duties, but he couldn't see her. He felt somewhat relieved, as he still wasn't sure how to handle their new relationship, or what it meant.

'Hey,' a voice said, and he turned to find Dawn behind him. 'I'm over there if you want to join me.'

She pointed to the other side of the water feature that looked like a ship's swimming pool, and Taylor smiled and nodded. He really liked her, always had. She was hard-working and resourceful, but very different from Jas. But then, there was no-one like Jas. At times, when he thought back to his discovery of her abilities, he wondered if he had imagined the whole thing. She had brought something into his life that he hadn't known existed. Magic. Taylor still found it hard to believe – it was impossible that she could have changed her appearance like that, wasn't it? Maybe he had been deliberately blind to her sexuality. Maybe they all had. It had been easier that way. But somehow that chink in her armour had appeared, and Jas had let him in. Let him see the real her.

He sat opposite Dawn and placed his tray of food down before him.

'Here,' she said. 'It's cream. I skimmed it from the milk this morning.'

She held out a small jug and Taylor added the cream to his coffee, stirring it in. The first sip was so luxurious that his palate almost didn't like the taste, but as he drank deeper the taste-memory of coffee and cream sank in. It was better than he recalled.

'You like it?' Dawn asked.

'Yes. Thanks.'

She looked fresh and pretty, despite the heavy night drinking, despite the morning working. She was more girly than Jas. But then, Dawn had never tried to be anything else.

'Penny for them,' she said as the silence between them lengthened.

'I was just wondering why it's taken me so long to spend some time with you.'

Dawn grinned. Then shrugged. 'Probably because I only just made a real effort to seduce you.'

Taylor looked up at her smiling over her coffee cup. She *had* seduced him, hadn't she?

'It's just as well you made the move,' Taylor said. 'I'm a little slow on the uptake.'

Dawn laughed. 'You are. But then, don't get worried that we need to be full-on or anything. I know this must be weird for you.'

Taylor shook his head; it was becoming less weird by the moment. He liked the idea of being 'full-on', and he wondered again what had taken him so long. Maybe the birth of Donovan's child had changed things, but now Taylor could see the future shaping up. Their growing community was more than just a ragtag band of survivors scrabbling for food. They were shaping their own destiny, rebuilding the world without the old hang-ups and politics; and unlike in any apocalypse movie he had ever heard of, forming a government was the last thing on their minds.

20

Jinx Town

Arven's imminent return brought a new state of confusion to Jas. She had been spending a lot of time with Kale and had grown fond of the Al Kuzemen, even though that fondness hadn't stretched any further than friendship. She suspected however that Kale's feelings ran a lot deeper than hers did.

'The Emperor returns today,' Kale said as they drank herbal tea in his tent.

Jas always visited him; he never came alone to the Imperial tent.

'Is that why you've avoided me the last two days?' Jas asked.

'I haven't. I merely had duties to perform. But I was receiving messages from the other Al Kuzemen, telling me of the success of the tour.'

'Arven has managed to calm things down then?'

'Yes. It is the particular skill of his leadership. Arven has always had a talent to inspire loyalty.'

Jas sipped her tea. She had grown used to the strange concoction, even though it was bitter, unlike the tea she was used to, and the Jinx apparently had no equivalent to sugar.

'You must be pleased that your husband is returning,' Kale said.

Jas said nothing. She let his words hang in the air and the silence answer for her.

She didn't realise that Kale hoped she would touch him again. It had been weeks since the time when she had taken his arm, looked into his eyes and said those strange words to him. His arm still burned from the memory of what he had felt there: her power, her strength, the magic that had pulsed into his skin from hers.

The Al Kuzemen had known all along that she was different, and now he knew the truth about himself too. Still, he was as a moth to a flame. He could not resist the pull she had on him. *Have there ever been any cases of adultery?* She had said the words in English, as there was no Emin equivalent for 'adultery'.

'What is that?' he had asked.

'Where a man or a woman is unfaithful to their husband or wife.'

He had needed further explanation. The thought had shocked and horrified him; the denials had been quick to his tongue. 'No. No. Such a thing is impossible.'

'Define impossible,' she had said.

'We can't love more than one person. It's not possible.'

'For a Jinx maybe, but I'm human. I can.'

They had never spoken of it again, but her words had gone around his head in a loop. He had felt the strangest urges. Feelings he had never experienced or thought he would experience. He had never felt the need to take part in the marriage auctions, though he had always thought that one day he would want a wife, and a son to pass his knowledge onto. Now all he could think was that Jas should be that wife. There was no woman equal to her, no-one he would rather bond with; but she was taken, and this was a boundary he couldn't cross.

'Tell me more of your culture,' he said suddenly. 'Tell me more of love among your people.'

Jas smiled. She had been waiting for Kale to make this leap once more, but the Al Kuzemen's resistance had been stronger than she had anticipated. The Jinx were very different from humans, not easy to seduce by all accounts; especially if seduction wasn't a skill you had honed. Jas knew she had no real aptitude for it. Her skills were in disguise, not lovemaking, although that always seemed easy with Arven, as everything she did pleased him. Kale was different. He was wary of her; but she felt his interest despite this.

What am I doing? Jas wondered. *This is like playing with fire.* But if she were ever to be able to return home, find Andrew and Taylor, then she had to do something other than be the plaything of the Emperor. If that meant seducing Kale, then she would do what she had to in order to free herself and help the other women on Emin. They didn't belong here, had all been subdued, lulled by something in the atmosphere that had made them all acquiescent. Since Arven's absence she had been increasingly certain that it was all just a spell, and the longer he was away, the freer she felt.

'It's time,' said Kale suddenly, and Jas wondered if he had read her thoughts and that somehow she had betrayed her true feelings of indifference to him.

'You need to go and prepare for your husband's return, Empress,' Kale continued, and he stood, bowed and held out his hand to her.

Jas took it, and she felt something ignite along her skin that sent shockwaves into Kale. It was like recognition. It felt corny even to explore and probe the feeling – any words she gave it were inadequate – but she had no lust or love for Kale. What she was feeling were his raw emotions and her own innate ability to translate and use them against him: just as she had used the sword on the battlefield and the dagger in the auction. Maybe her special talent wasn't just limited to her chameleonic ability to hide.

Kale felt guilty that he had contrived the moment, but he had wanted that feeling again. He had to know what the ripple of power he felt meant. She let go of his hand as she stood, and he was left with a feeling of excitement. It had to be her feelings for him; that same passionate need that had tortured his nights ever since Arven had left. He wanted her, but such thoughts were treachery against the Emperor. Kale was not treacherous by nature, and the guilt was crippling his ability to concentrate.

Jas walked away, heading toward the exit, but then turned and looked back at Kale. The Al Kuzemen was shaking, his face was white, his eyes burned with his inner torment. She reached for him, pulling him closer, her lips pressing against his. He froze. Jas pulled him nearer, moulded her body into his; but her mind was the adulteress, not her body. She felt nothing as she touched him, and this surprised her more than a sexual response would have. But she played the part anyway, made him feel she enjoyed his touch.

Her tongue pressed against his closed mouth until he opened his lips and allowed her exploration. Revulsion shivered down Jas's spine, but she didn't pull away as Kale crushed her to him. She revelled in the feel of his lust and magic though. It was as though his emotions were like words written in the air and she could read and understand every one as though they were in plain English.

'Someone approaches,' Kale said, pulling back.

His face was flushed with guilt and lust, and the two emotions fought with each other until common sense won. Kale released Jas, almost pushing her away.

'No. This is not right. It's not possible.'

'Ah. But it is,' Jas replied.

She turned and walked to the exit of the tent just as the council emissary, Yago, arrived to speak to the Al Kuzemen.

'Empress,' Yago said bowing. 'Al Kuzemen.'

'I must prepare for the Emperor's return,' Jas said.

Kale nodded. He appeared to be incapable of speech, and he looked away as Jas raised the curtain over the door and left the tent.

Later they stood side by side as the vortex arrived. It was smaller and less disruptive than the portals the Jinx had used to pillage Earth.

'Why is that?' Jas asked.

'Less distance to travel,' Kale replied. He was polite but quiet, and had barely spoken to her since she had arrived in her full Imperial robes. 'To pass through time and space, more power is required.'

'This power ... Where does it come from?'

Kale watched Jas through the corner of his eye. Her question was odd, but he could see no reason why he shouldn't answer.

'The power, the magic, comes from all around us. All that you see. Emin is made of magic. We are made of magic. It is a life-force energy that I channel and use to create the vortex.'

'Can anyone learn to channel this energy?' Jas asked.

'No, Empress. Only an Al Kuzemen, chosen in childhood, can use and wield this magic.'

'Those that have the power are indeed then invincible,' Jas said.

Kale didn't know what to say. It was a concept that had never occurred to him. He was the Al Kuzemen: he was born to serve his Emperor.

'Such power could give you anything you want,' Jas said. 'All you desire. Even the throne … It's just as well that you are so loyal.'

The portal opened before them and Kale picked up the magic, finishing the work started by the lesser Al Kuzemen at the other end. He pushed aside Jas's words, but they burned into his brain, ate at his heart in a way he would never have thought possible. There was no such word as treachery in his vocabulary, but he knew that Jas was right. His abilities made him strong. Hadn't his power been enough to bring Earth to its knees? Despite all of the strange science and technology the humans had?

Anything you want. All you desire.

For a moment he felt distracted, and the portal gateway slipped from his grasp. A backlash of energy whipped across the wasteland and smashed into the border tent beside him. It bowed and rocked, shuddering. The guards inside rushed out to see what had caused the disturbance. Kale forced his mind to keep control, pushing the current of power back in on itself.

The vortex took solid shape and Kale could make out the form of the Emperor and his escort inside. One slip of the mind could crush the occupants, turning their solid forms into bloody matter. Then, where would they be? The Emperor was their leader, the men and women of Emin looked up to him, believed in him. With no heir to take over, who would rule?

'What's happening?' yelled Jas, and Kale could hear the panic in her voice as the power fell again unchecked.

Kale pushed his treachery away from his soul and focused all of his attention, taking up the slack left by the other Al Kuzemen. His face relaxed as the energy rolled over and through him and he manipulated it with a mere flick of the mind; as simple as blinking if you knew how.

Jas gripped Kale's arm, but he was so deeply into his meditation now that he barely registered the gentle press of her fingers. There was a force riding him. Jas recognised the energy; it was the same feeling she had when she touched the Jinx weapons, but far stronger. It was like a sea rolling over a pebbly shore, or the feeling you get as you receive anaesthetic: a wave washing over your body as the drug sweeps away all thought and strength from your limbs. Only it gave strength. Experimentally Jas pulled on it. She felt the energy push back as though it was a flexible wall.

Her hand dropped to her side as the vortex opened fully and Arven stepped down onto the carpet-covered sand before them.

Kale came out of his trance and bowed.

'There was a strange moment inside the vortex,' Arven said, frowning slightly as Kale stood upright again.

'My Lord,' Kale said. 'I have no excuses. For a moment my concentration slipped. I throw myself on your mercy.'

'Old friend,' Arven said, placing his hand on his shoulder. 'All is well.'

Arven turned to Jas. She was swathed in a robe of maroon silk, and he could barely make out the boyish frame she had once had. Her hair had grown longer still and the dark waves that framed her face emphasised the deep blue of her eyes. She was frowning slightly, but she shuddered as he smiled at her.

'Jasmine,' he said, and Jas stepped forward, falling into his embrace. Her body trembled as he held her. *I'm home,* he thought.

21

'I have missed you Jasmine,' he said.

Jas resisted as Arven pulled her close, but as soon as his lips found hers she lost all thought of fighting, and the urge to return to Earth diminished.

They made love. Arven's passion was intense and Jas matched his lust with her own. Afterwards she felt strangely different. The seed had exploded, giving her the most intense orgasm yet; the abstinence had made her want him even more, and she had given herself to it without fear. But her doubts still remained. She still found it hard to accept that this was to be her life from now on.

As Arven slept, she thought about Kale and her feelings for him. There was no love or passion there, only friendship, and she knew deep down that she could never feel the same intensity for him as she felt for Arven. *How could I even consider betrayal,* she wondered, *when everything feels so right with Arven?*

It isn't about betrayal though, is it? An odd, cold fear sank into the pit of her stomach. She hated this feeling of dependency. She wasn't some robot – some prissy little housewife – and never had been. She was a soldier, and her independence had always been one of the things she had been proud of. When she was around Arven she became everything she hated, and she found it difficult to accept. It was an internal struggle that continued to rage. She couldn't just give in to it, recognising that she was happier now than she had even been. It was all too simple, too convenient.

This really isn't me. But did it matter? She wasn't the first woman to question herself and she wouldn't be the last.

Jas turned over in the bed, facing away from Arven. She could hear his steady breathing as he slept, but it was easier to clear her head if she didn't look directly at him. *On Earth this spell would probably be voided. I'd be able to think straight. I would know then how I really felt.*

Earth. Home. She thought of the mall, of Andrew and Taylor and all the other soldiers whose friendship she had held so dear. A distant pining clutched at her chest until she experienced real pain. It intensified.

For all the love and excitement she had gained through her contact with Arven, her old life still felt like unfinished business. It *did* matter.

I need to get away. Need to find myself again. I really don't know that Arven is what I want. I didn't choose this.

Arven turned over and draped his long arm over her hip, spooning his body against hers as though he could sense her thoughts even in his sleep. Jas lay still. The touch of his skin had a calming effect, and the pain in her heart diminished. But she fought against it. Resented his influence because of what it meant. She wanted her pain. It made her feel as though she still had the ability to make her own choices; and that was the crux of the matter when it all came down to it. Jas didn't feel in control, and that made her more insecure, not less.

This isn't love, she thought. *Love doesn't mean you lose yourself.*

Or did it? How many friends had been absorbed by their lovers' needs? How many couples gave up on other friends once they found each other? But Jas had always railed against it, thought it unnecessary and stupid to allow another person to consume your soul like that.

The weight of Arven's arm became unbearable against the bone of her hip, and Jas turned again, causing him to move. He rolled over back to his side of the bed, and Jas lay on her back, breathing deeply as the thoughts continued to pick at her mind.

The old world was gone, whatever way she looked at it. Earth wasn't the same. The Jinx had destroyed all that remained, and returning there was almost impossible. *Almost.* But there was Kale of course. Kale, already under her spell, could perhaps be persuaded to take her home. But on what pretext? He was fiercely loyal to Arven. *But not so loyal. He let me kiss him. I felt his desire.* Jas sighed, and a half remembered quote floated through her mind: 'Oh what a tangled web we weave, when first we practice to deceive.' She couldn't remember where it was from, or how she had heard it, but it brought back that feeling of nostalgia for her old life once more.

She glanced at Arven. The frown left her face, and her features softened as she saw his profile in the dim light of the tent. He was such an attractive man. The feelings she had ran deep, but not so deep that she could allow him to own her. She could never permit that, not now, not ever. That would make her weak, and weakness was something she couldn't tolerate in others let alone herself.

I do love you. But I don't know if it's real. That's perhaps the main issue, and there's only one way I can find out … Jas's thoughts stumbled. There was no way to prove or disprove her feelings; short of leaving Jinx Town. And that wasn't going to happen anytime soon.

22

'Tea is good for the soul,' Mallory said, pouring the greenish liquid into a cup. She held it out to Jas.

'Thanks.' Jas took the cup and stared down through the liquid, searching for the bottom. 'I didn't think I'd ever get used to this stuff. But it is somewhat addictive.'

'Like Jinx Town itself,' Mallory smiled.

Jas frowned but didn't answer, using the motion of sipping the tea to fill the silence.

'You must be delighted now that Arven is back,' Mallory observed. 'And now that things have calmed down in the outpost towns.'

'I suspect it will be only temporary,' Jas said, 'although Arven won't speak to me about it. The Jinx will have to find a new influx of women soon, as I'm sure the men won't remain patient forever.'

Mallory nodded. She heard the cynical tone in Jas's voice but chose not to acknowledge it. 'We have many girl children now. They'll grow and the men will have wives. They just need to realise there are none left on Earth for them to take.'

'Kale thinks there are many left on Earth,' Jas said, and then bit her lip. She didn't really want Mallory to know of her talks with the Al Kuzemen. 'I overheard him ...'

Jas bowed her head, sipping the tea once more in order to avoid meeting Mallory's inquisitive gaze.

'What else did you ... overhear?'

'Nothing much. Just that he *feels* there are more. Hiding out.'

'I suppose that means that Arven will send a scouting party again ...' Mallory said.

'Yes ... He probably will. I hadn't thought of that.'

As Jas left, Mallory sat silently in the now empty arrivals tent. Jenny and Rosa were long gone, married off to different men in different towns. She doubted she would ever see them again, but hoped for their happiness. She had begun to feel that there was little point remaining in her role as translator. She might as well put herself up for auction now. There were no women of marriageable age left, only girl children waiting to grow up to fulfil that role, many years from now. All of whom could speak the Emin language fluently. Even so, the thought of marriage, and all the joys and anxieties that it brought the women of Earth, filled her with a strange dread. Technically she was still married; unless Gerald was dead. Although, as she reflected on what had happened in those last days at the village, Mallory realised she might as well consider herself divorced …

She had suspected something was wrong for a long time. Gerald had been acting strangely. And ever since Jenny and Rosa had been taken by the Jinx, Mallory had felt fearful. It was an irrational hyping of the terror they already lived with: the day-to-day concern that the Jinx would return never changed; she had merely grown to live with the anticipation. But this anxiety was different. She was afraid of Gerald.

Mallory knew that Gerald had been drugging her and the other survivors. She sometimes found it hard to wake in the morning and felt sluggish all day.

'I think the tonic is disagreeing with me,' she said to him one morning.

'Don't be ridiculous. It's a harmless vitamin supplement. We all need it,' Gerald said. 'You'll continue taking it Mal. It's better this way.'

Gerald couldn't meet her eyes as she turned to stare at him.

That night he supervised her drinking down the medicine, and for the next few nights he continued to watch her closely as he gave the tonic out. There was a sedative inside, of course, along with a mix of vitamins, and some anti-depressant to keep the women calm. It ensured they remained placid during the day as well as asleep through the night. That way no-one challenged Gerald's decisions; they went along meekly with all of his instructions, doing exactly what he said. Mallory knew this for a certainty, but she didn't know *how* she knew.

One night, Mallory poured the tonic down the sink when Gerald wasn't looking. She needed to clear the fugue from her head. Gerald's face had scared her when he had said he couldn't find Jenny and Rosa. She knew he had been lying, and she had her suspicions why.

That first night without the tonic she didn't sleep well at all, and she felt even worse the next day. But she persisted, surreptitiously disposing of her dose of the liquid each night. She suffered sickness, some irritation and more than a little paranoia, but after a week she began to feel better. Her head had cleared. But she still played docile, and Gerald didn't notice any change at all in her behaviour. He had become very sure of his power over her and the others.

During the second week, Mallory confirmed her suspicions about Gerald's night-time activities. It was obvious what was happening really, but she needed proof, needed to see it with her own eyes, before she could fully believe that he had changed so much without her realising. Even though she had seen the monster lurking beneath his lecherous gaze as his eyes fell on various women among them, she had found it hard to believe that Gerald would act on those feelings. Surely he had no need to. She was a good wife and she gave him everything he needed.

Every night that week, Mallory listened to his not-too-silent tread as he left the door slightly ajar and went into Beth Turner's room. At first she thought that maybe they were having an affair; that Beth was complicit. The paranoia bit deep after that. Maybe the sedative was to keep her from knowing the truth? But what was to stop Gerald from killing her if she found out? *He's no murderer,* she thought. Then she remembered Jenny and Rosa, and wondered what had really happened to them. She couldn't get the thought out of her head that maybe *he had fed them to the Jinx.*

One night toward the end of the week, Mallory got out of bed after Gerald had gone and listened at the door. She heard the bed creak in the room next door, but no sound came from Beth. Her heart was thumping in her chest. She didn't want to see, but knew she had to. Gerald had changed. He had become unfeeling. Cold. Not like the man she had married at all. She wanted to understand why.

In the days before the Jinx, their marriage had always been strong. Even that time when he had told her the worst news she could possibly hear.

'I got the results back today, Mal. You're infertile.'

It had winded her like a punch in her stomach. Mallory had always thought they would be able to have a family one day. Gerald had told her so coldly, his voice bland and doctoral, that she had wondered how he felt about it.

'It doesn't matter. It's how it's meant to be. It doesn't change how I feel about you,' he had said.

He had refused to discuss it again, except to say that the idea of adoption didn't appeal to him at all.

After the Jinx arrived though, their infertility had felt like a mixed blessing. Who would want to bring children into this dying world only for them to be slaughtered by those monsters? Of course Gerald had never said how he felt about it, but maybe Gerald had wanted children; maybe that was what he needed from Beth?

She could hear his breathing, heavy and excited in that way that was familiar to her. The noises he made during sex. But the words that were coming out of his mouth she didn't recognise. They were filthy. Horrible.

'Open your legs, you stupid cunt. You're mine. All of you. And I'll fuck you whenever I want.'

Mallory pressed her hands over her ears, began to back away toward the bed, but something stopped her; a sharp noise that drew her out through the door and into the hallway. It was the sound of a slap.

'Wake up bitch. Wake up!'

Mallory could hear the tears then, the fear as Beth came round, the sting still on her cheek. Mallory's face smarted as though she could feel it too. A monster was in Beth's room, and it wasn't Gerald, it was something using his body.

Mallory stood at the door. Gerald hadn't even bothered to close it. He was so sure that they were all still asleep and under his control. Gerald carried out his rape unaware that his wife could see and hear everything. Mallory knew then that Beth wasn't involved, nor was she enjoying Gerald's violent attentions. Gerald was the image of everything that he said he hated. He had turned into the thing they all feared most. He wasn't human anymore. He was alien. He was the epitome of the evil that had befallen Earth.

As Gerald reached his orgasm, Mallory backed away and slipped back into their bedroom. Once back in bed, she forced her breathing to even out, and she lay still as Gerald returned to the bed, stinking of sex because he hadn't even bothered to wash the guilt from his skin.

Mallory jumped awake, shaking off the recall-nightmare that still hounded her dreams and haunted her days. Gerald's betrayal had been all the worse because she had become the wife that housed the serial rapist or murderer: there was nearly always a woman at home who saw the blood on her husband's clothing after he had murdered some poor innocent. Mallory felt the guilt of it sit on her shoulders. Even though her complicity had been only brief, she still regretted not stopping Gerald immediately. Even now she couldn't understand why she hadn't confronted him with her knowledge. Instead the torment had limped on for another week, until she had grown so angry that she had been unable to stay there any longer. It was better to die than live like that, better to walk outside and give yourself to the Jinx. The unknown was less frightening than the familiar.

She looked around the arrivals tent once more. Strange how the Jinx had turned out to be the ones to have morals, and the men of Earth to have so few once society had crumbled. She could put herself forward for marriage, but what would be the point? She was useless to the Arrak Nah Tiaman as a wife: there would be no offspring. And anyway ...

Her mind fell to the problem of Arven and Jas. Mallory's jaw tightened. *Jas the faithless.* Jas had become too interested of late in Kale, and had spent so much time in his company during Arven's absence that it was hard not to notice. Mallory found it difficult to ignore now: her feelings for Arven had never diminished, and she resented Jas's treacherous nature. Arven deserved better. He deserved a wife who would love him alone.

She shrugged. It didn't matter anyway. Kale would never take the bait: he was too loyal. Rules in Jinx Town were not made to be broken: unlike the fragile commandments of Earth.

23

The vortex opened in Jenus, and Arven's men poured out ahead of him into the sandy courtyard in two neat rows. Arven took a moment to adjust to the daylight. It had been night when he left, but Jenus was on the other side of Emin and the night and day time zones were opposite. He experienced a strange vertigo and paused for a moment before exiting the vortex. He shook away the sensation and stepped down onto the sand, striding confidently between the two lines of his guard toward the waiting town councillors and their Al Kuzemen, Haradin.

Jenus was much like his own town, Sharik, with rows of colourful tents set out under the bright sky. A city made of canvas and silk.

'Lord,' said Haradin. 'We are so grateful that you have come.'

Arven accepted the bow and lowered his head in respect of the Al Kuzemen's position.

'Where is Salvar?'

The Al Kuzemen looked confused but quickly recovered his composure. 'You weren't told?'

'Explain.'

'Salvar is dead. Last night there was an uprising, the guards didn't get there in time. Salvar died and his wife is missing. We've rounded up the culprits but nobody will say where Alicia is.'

'I was told a man had died. Why didn't anyone tell me it was Governor Salvar?' Arven said.

Haradin grovelled; his long moustache draped on the sand as he bent low. 'I don't understand, Lord. Our message was clear to your Al Kuzemen. I can only apologise if there has been some misunderstanding.'

Arven looked around. The Governor's tent was prominent on the horizon of the town: purple, large and decorated with ornate drapes of gold fabric and cord.

'Show me,' Arven said as he strode out ahead of the Al Kuzemen.

The armed soldiers moved along the street around him as the Emperor walked rapidly toward the scene of the crime. Arven was flanked by a constant guard of six soldiers who matched his pace perfectly while Haradin struggled to keep up. They reached the tent and two of the guards entered as Arven and the remaining men came to a halt outside.

As he crossed the threshold, the stench inside made Arven's normally strong stomach clench. It took a second for his eyes to adjust to the gloom, but soon he could see that the once ornate interior was splattered with rancid blood.

'We left everything as it was for you to see,' Haradin explained. 'I can weave a spell to make the smell more bearable. If you wish it, Lord?'

Arven turned his head, taking in the carnage. 'What happened here?'

'A small group of men attacked the governor's tent. They killed his guards. Then killed the governor. As I explained, his wife is missing.'

'What was their motive for this?'

'Motive?' Haradin said. 'We aren't sure but ... all of the men in question were ... unmarried.'

'That isn't an excuse for all this bloodshed,' said Arven, but his own words gave him a jolt. Hadn't that been their own motive when they had first opened a vortex on Earth? Hadn't they killed in order to rebuild their own future? Perhaps this was the message he had given his people. Maybe this was all his fault after all.

Arven distracted himself from this strange self-awareness by walking farther into the expansive first room. Around him he saw the usual furniture. The sitting area: a small chaise, comfortable cushions, ornate jars and a low table with a bloodied mosaic. The cooking area: small stove, hanging pots and pans, a teapot sat on top of the table. Broken cups strewn over the floor. Two wooden chairs, with velvet cushions. Red stains on the rug-covered sand. The sleeping area: a large bed, draped with closed curtains, small tables either side, both containing lamps and candles, a baby's crib.

'The governor and his wife had a child?'

'She is pregnant, Lord. Expecting any time.'

Arven lifted a curtain to reveal the house pool. Blood and gore were smeared on the tiled floors. A guard stepped forward and fastened the drapes back, revealing the full horror of the room.

'Have you seen this?' Arven asked.

'Yes. This is where we found the Governor's body.'

'So whose blood is splattered all over the tent?'

'We think it is mostly the guards'. A fight took place inside the tent. The Governor was bathing.'

'Where was his wife?'

'We don't know, but we think she was sleeping in the bed.'

Arven turned back to the bed; he lifted the drapes and stared down at the silk sheets. They looked as though they had been recently occupied. He pressed his hand down on the fabric. The bed was warm and slightly damp, as though from perspiration.

'Someone was here. Just now.'

'Impossible, Lord. The tent has been under guard.'

Arven looked around. The tent was certainly empty, but he felt uneasy. It was as though they were being watched, and occasionally he felt as though there was another person in the room, but every time his eyes tried to focus on the extra figure, he couldn't quite place it.

'Take me to the prisoners,' Arven said.

They left the tent and walked across to the square. The murderers were being held in the marriage tent, and as Arven walked inside he felt an overwhelming sense of *déjà vu*. It was so like the tent in Sharik that the memory of his wedding came flooding back. The happiness he felt was instantly overshadowed by this awful event. He felt a sorrow he hadn't experienced since the plague had destroyed the women of Emin.

Ten men were chained in a cage in the centre of the tent. All bedraggled and beaten, heavily guarded by Jenus soldiers. Murderers. Criminals against their own people. It was something that Arven had rarely had to deal with. The Arrak Nah Tiaman didn't kill each other; they only fought for survival.

Arven walked up to the cage and stared in. One man lay half unconscious against the bars, blood leaking from his mouth and nose. Another stood, arms linked around the bars, holding on as though he knew that if he let go he would fall down. The third man was sleeping across the floor, head resting on his arms. The fourth and fifth sat back to back, supporting each other. The remaining men were sleeping or unconscious, with the exception of one. He, Arven knew instinctively, was the ringleader, and he sat meditating in the far corner, his eyes closed, his mouth moving softly as he whispered his mantra over and over.

'Get him up,' Arven said. 'I want him out here so I can talk to him.'

The guards moved inside, pushing back anyone who dared move to protect the leader, and quickly grabbed the man. He didn't struggle, nor did he aid them; instead he went limp, so they pulled him out of the cage, feet dragging on the floor.

He fell at Arven's feet, then turned cold, arrogant eyes up to the Emperor.

'Why have you done this terrible thing?' Arven asked softly. 'Why kill the Governor? He was a good man. An excellent leader and provider for this town.'

The man said nothing, but his eyes glared into Arven's with a murderous light.

'Where is the Governor's wife?'

The man didn't reply. One of Arven's guards stepped forward and kicked him hard in the back, sending him sprawling before the Emperor.

'Murder is a crime punishable by death,' Arven said. 'You will die without honour. You could redeem yourself a little by telling us what you've done with the Governor's wife.'

The man spat blood down into the sand at Arven's feet.

'We don't know. She disappeared.' His voice was breathy.

The guard kicked him hard again. The sickening crunch of ribs cracking echoed through the tent. Arven looked up and saw the other prisoners had now all roused and were watching the leader.

'Please. He speaks the truth,' said the man who was still stood hugging the bars. 'She just ... vanished. We don't know where she is.'

'What did you do to the Governor's wife?' Arven asked again. 'She was heavy with child, you sick bastard.'

This time Arven kicked out, catching the man on the jaw. Blood and teeth burst from the prisoner's mouth.

'I swear we did nothing to her,' he spluttered, wiping the back of his hand over his bloody mouth. 'She was there, then she wasn't. We wouldn't have hurt her ...'

'Then what were you going to do? Why did you attack the Governor?'

The prisoner heaved in a ragged breath and gasped in pain as his lungs pressed against his cracked ribcage. He shook his head and refused to answer any more questions.

'Lock him back up. I want to go back to the tent.'

Arven turned to leave, then stopped. 'If I don't find answers soon, then we'll torture the truth out of them.'

Back at the Governor's tent, Arven raised the curtain on the bed again. The sheets were still ruffled, but now the place he had touched was cold.

'Where are you?' he wondered. 'What happened here?'

He couldn't stand the thought that his men had murdered her too; an innocent woman and her unborn child. It was a strange feeling for the warrior King. They had shed so much blood in order to give their world a second chance. He had allowed his men to slaughter all of the men of Earth that they came across. Now, he wanted to save an Earth woman, because she belonged to them, not Earth. She was a future mother, giving Emin the children they most needed and desired ... but that wasn't the reason Arven felt so concerned. Jas had mellowed him. Jas had made him see things differently over the last year, and part of him wished that he had not given the orders for so much bloodshed. Surely they could have worked something out with the Earthlings? Surely there could have been a compromise?

The curtain leading into the pool room was closed. Arven cast his mind back to his first visit. He was certain he recalled it being left open when they were last there. Stood beside it, he thought he heard something: a murmur, a catch of breath. But no. His mind was playing tricks on him. He pushed aside the curtain, glanced around the empty room, then turned away.

Ripples on the water. His head snapped back as he looked once more at the warm pool. The water was clean and clear – just as it should be. Steam came off it. It would be the perfect temperature and would never grow cool. There was no sign of blood spillage reaching the magical bath. He saw the ripples, though, the steady movement, as though a figure stood in the middle. He squinted at the spot, looking from the corner of his eye. He had heard tell of those who could hide, like chameleons. It was once a powerful magic, but was now long since lost among his people. An Earth woman couldn't have that power though. Not possible.

He shook his head. *I'm imagining things. There's nothing there. They killed her, buried her, and are too afraid to admit to this terrible crime, because that would be the worst thing they could have possibly done.*

'Lord?' said Haradin behind him. 'She … That's impossible.'

Arven turned back to the Al Kuzemen, then looked once more at the pool. Alicia was coming into view, the magic waning. A gasp burst from her lips as she clutched her stomach.

'She wasn't there. Now she is!' said Haradin.

'Magic,' Arven answered. 'She used magic to save herself.'

'She's a woman. Women can't use magic.'

Alicia cried as another contraction pulled at her stomach.

'Get her out of the water and send for a midwife,' Arven ordered with a sudden flash of realisation. 'This baby is coming and it's the only reason she's lost control of her power.'

24

'Leave me alone. Why do you come here to torture me?' Kale said.

Jas smiled sweetly and sat down opposite him. 'Shall I pour tea?'

'No. You mustn't come here anymore.'

'Kale. You know I need to talk to you. We need to decide what to do.'

'There's nothing to decide. You're Arven's wife. You've bonded. I cannot see you again.'

'I want to go to Earth,' Jas said. 'My life here … It's wrong. It doesn't feel like me, Kale. The decisions aren't mine.'

'What are you talking about?'

'This bonding magic … On my planet it would mean nothing. I'd be free to …'

Her words hung unfinished before them. Kale's heart was pounding at the sight of her, and it took all of his will not to reach out and take her in his arms and make her his.

'Please …' he groaned. 'You torture me. I know I can never have you.'

Jas leaned forward and took his hand. 'I agree that it is impossible here. I can't feel the same emotion you can. It's because of the bonding. But don't you see there is no magic on Earth? All of this … spell would be negated. I'd be free to choose you, Kale. And I would choose you. Don't you see? It's your children I want to have.'

Jas let go of his hand. She was almost at the door of the tent before Kale burst from his seat and caught her to him.

'You could take me back while Arven is away,' she said. 'We could test my theory that my feelings for him aren't real. Don't you want to know?'

'I can't betray my Emperor,' he cried.

Jas pushed him away, her face reddening with anger and frustration. Kale fell to his knees. He was a man destroyed. His magic was weakening by the day, and it was all because he couldn't concentrate on anything but Jas. Since the Emperor's return he had been wracked with jealousy while imagining them together once more. He had even heard her screams of pleasure as Arven … as Arven … He couldn't even think the words to himself anymore. Now he sobbed at her feet, expecting nothing but scorn.

'I can't …' he said again.

Jas knelt beside him, taking his tearstained face in her hands. She kissed away the tears and then lingered on his lips in that fascinating and sensual way she had done before.

'Don't worry,' she said. 'I'll soon fall pregnant and none of this will happen again. Arven is determined to have an heir.'

The meaning of her words, softly and lovingly spoken, sank into his envious heart, and he crushed her to him, forcing her back onto the rug. His hands roved her body. He felt the magic ripple over her skin, but not the one thing he wanted. Her lust remained silent. But still Jas kissed and stroked him, allowed him to explore her body through the fabric of the satin robes she wore. He had never been permitted such intimacy, and Kale loved the feel of her.

'Al Kuzemen!'

Mallory stood at the entrance of the tent, her eyes taking in the scene of Jas and Kale lying together on the floor. They were both fully clothed, but there was no mistaking the feelings Kale had for Jas.

Kale jumped to his feet holding out his hand to Jas, who also stood quickly.

'This isn't how it looks,' said Jas.

'Oh really, Empress? How do you think this looks?' Mallory said coldly.

'We both tripped over the rug …'

'Must have been some fall …' Mallory's lips were tight, her face blank.

'How can I help you, Mallory?' Kale said, recovering his composure far quicker than Jas had expected.

'The Emperor has returned. He was looking for you both.'

Jas stopped her just as she was about to leave the tent. 'This really wasn't how it appeared,' she said again.

'If you say so, Empress.'

Jas stared at the tent curtain as it fell back into place behind Mallory, then she glanced at Kale. The Al Kuzemen was quiet and thoughtful. He frowned and turned away from her.

'I must go and find Arven,' Jas said. 'Before Mallory does.'

But it was already too late.

25

'You have both betrayed me,' Arven said.

'No,' Jas denied.

'Mallory told me how you were rolling around with Kale, kissing him as you do me.'

'That isn't true. We tripped. We both fell down ... It just looked *wrong.*'

Arven's heart felt like shattered crystal. He wanted to believe her, but somehow he knew it was all a lie. Since his first trip away, and then his recent visit to Jenus, Arven had felt a wedge had been forced between them. Even when they made love, Jas always seemed to be somewhere far away from him. It was as though her mind constantly refused to follow her heart. They had bonded. It was real. It was love. How could it be even possible for her to contemplate betrayal?

'Where is Kale?' Jas asked. 'Ask him. You know he and I can't ... It isn't possible for me.'

Arven sighed. He could hardly bear to look at her, and now she was showing concern for Kale. This was worse than he had thought. At first he hadn't believed Mallory. He didn't know why she would lie, but his recent experience on Jenus had taught him that the Earth women were far more unusual than their mere physical differences. Some, it seemed, held a latent magical ability. What if Jas was one of those?

He remembered Kale's warnings when they first brought her to Sharik. She had hidden herself so well on Earth, using glamour to disguise her appearance. But Arven had only seen the loving woman in her from the day they married. She had dropped the boy persona, and even the warrior in her had seemed tamed. *How wrong I was,* he thought. *She is a powerful mage, but she really doesn't know it yet.*

Perhaps that was why she was so drawn to the Al Kuzemen? Arven looked at Jas again. She sat calmly on the edge of the bed, but her hands wringing in her lap gave away her inner turmoil. She was afraid of what he would do now that he knew of her betrayal. Arven, however, had no idea at all what he was going to do. There had never been a case of adultery in his generation, although there were rumours of such things having happened from time to time in the past. The old scrolls and commandments might help.

Arven went to the far wall of their tent and opened up the writing desk, where he often worked in his capacity as Emperor. Jas had never asked what it was he had to do, when he sat reading and signing those old-looking pieces of parchment, but she assumed they were some form of decree or judgement. There had been more of those moments in recent months too. Since all of the attacks started.

'What happened in Jenus?' Jas asked suddenly.

Arven ignored her; instead he sat down and unlocked his desk, taking out a thick, leather-bound book. He opened it and began to read.

Jas lay back on the bed and closed her eyes. She saw her old life on Earth flicking by like a black and white movie behind her eyes. She would never see it again. She would never know if her feelings for Arven were real. She considered telling him the truth about her insecurities, but the opening words wouldn't form in her mind. How could she explain that her attempted seduction of Kale was all a test? A test to see if her feelings for Arven were real.

She felt foolish suddenly. Her heart hurt as she realised how stupid she had been. She had lost him now, and real or imagined, the feelings associated with that loss brought about a physical pain in her heart, lungs and chest. Every breath she took hurt. Every movement of her limbs brought agony. She felt as though she were in deep mourning, and the grief that washed over her brought with it the realisation that she had ruined everything that was good in her life.

She felt his hurt emanating across the room, and this projection of his emotions suffocated her with guilt. She was hurting so much that eventually all she could do was close herself down. She could think no longer, so she pulled the blankets over herself and slipped away from her guilt into a restless sleep.

Arven turned the pages of the book, and the words fed into his brain. He had forgotten their old philosophies in the last few years. Life on Emin had changed to accommodate the Earth females. But now he recalled why they had searched so hard for Earth. It was because they had known that this was their only hope.

'Two tribes fought for supremacy ...'

Yes, there had been two tribes. Two sets of people that had lived on the mother planet over one million years before.

Arven glanced over at the bed. *They were the same, but different.*

'The first tribe believed in the old faith. They worked with the power of earth, water, air, fire, and worshipped the old gods who gave them their magic. The second tribe slipped away from the old ways. No longer did they worship the sun. Instead they set about to destroy it with their own magic, which they stole from the planet's core. The first tribe expanded their magic. They knew the Earth would be destroyed by the evil of the second tribe, so they found a doorway and they left the planet, setting out in search of a new, clean home.'

'You're mine,' Arven said, peeling back the covers. He took the dagger from his waist and began to cut away the robes that covered her still.

Jas came out of her restless dreams, her head muffled as though she had been drugged.

'What …?'

She was naked before him, and she watched through slitted eyes as he dropped his clothing to the floor. Then she felt the weight of his body as he climbed on the bed. There were no loving and tender kisses, even though Jas tried to wrap her arms around him. He pushed her touch away, positioning himself above her.

'Arven …'

His hand over her mouth silenced her words.

'I don't want to hear any more lies …' he said, pushing inside her so hard that she gasped in pain.

'Please …' she said.

'I love you, Jasmine.'

His lovemaking was rough and painful, but still Jas responded to him. Her body liquefied and shuddered underneath him, her legs wrapped around him as she welcomed him, her nails raked his back as he took her. When the seed exploded inside her, it was as though she had truly given herself to him for the first time. She seemed to open up, like a lily as the sun rises, and Arven felt a part of himself remaining inside her.

Afterwards she lay sated and quiet, but Arven climbed from the bed and drew on his robe. She watched him for a while as he sat cross-legged on the floor. He seemed to be meditating, or at the least he was in very deep thought.

'I'm sorry …' she murmured, then drifted off to sleep.

26

'Tell me the truth,' Arven said. 'Have you been with my wife?'

'No, Lord,' Kale said. 'But I'm bewitched by her. She has my heart and soul, despite my feelings of loyalty. I knew it was wrong, and I tried to stay away. But I couldn't.'

Kale knelt before the throne. The meeting was taking place in the marriage tent, but the Al Kuzemen and the Emperor were completely alone.

'I should take this before the council. You should be punished,' Arven said, even though he believed the Al Kuzemen had told him the truth. The man had always been incapable of lies.

'Yes,' Kale agreed.

'Kale, we have been friends a long time. How could you do this to me?'

Kale shook his head. He couldn't put into words the feeling of insane jealousy he felt whenever he thought of Jas and Arven alone together. It was as though some kind of fever had taken hold of him and it was leading him down a path of total destruction.

'How long has this been going on?' Arven asked. 'How long have you had illicit contact?'

Kale looked up, surprised. 'This has not been illicit, Lord. You asked me to keep her company while you were away.'

'So this is my fault then? Social contact, so that she wouldn't be alone: that's all I asked from you.'

Kale hung his head. 'It was all it was to her, Lord. She has never been able to feel the same for me.'

Arven's heart lurched with hope as he heard Kale's words. Was it true then, that Jas did love him and no-one else?

'I wish I could believe that,' Arven sighed again. 'I just don't know what to do with you – or her – right now.'

He felt confused and scared. If he involved the council, then all decisions might be taken from him. He was too close to make a proper judgement, and yet his heart insisted that he was right to wait. He had to see how this would all pan out.

From the day they had bonded, Arven had felt Jas's inner torment. He had never understood what it was, but he knew she needed her independence, and he had tried, within the realms of propriety, to give her some freedom. Even leaving her with the dagger, although he always knew she could use it on him at any time. He had hoped for a quick pregnancy. He knew that this would bond her closer to him and to his planet. Emin would become her home, because her children would be born there and all thoughts of Earth would diminish. It had settled all of the other women, and Arven was sure it would have helped Jas too.

'What did she want from you?' Arven asked Kale suddenly.

'Want?' Kale said surprised.

'Did she ever ask anything of you? Ask you to do anything for her?'

Kale lapsed into his own thoughts but didn't answer. How could he tell his much-loved leader that his wife wanted to leave him? That she believed her love wasn't real? That she had said she wanted to have Kale's children? He couldn't tell the Emperor the truth. It would only hurt him more. Best that he took the blame for all of this.

'Nothing. She wanted nothing from me. My attentions were unwanted.'

Instinctively Arven knew that this was a lie, and it surprised him. Did the Al Kuzemen love Jas so much that he would give his own life for her? At least that was a feeling Arven understood. Arven's emotions for her were bordering on obsession. Being apart from her had grown more difficult, not less, and often he had felt the urge to abandon his duty just to be with her.

Since Jenus he had been suffering with a deep sense of guilt. He had made so many mistakes, and had become aware of how he had killed an entire world to save his own: never realising that bringing the women to Emin would create other problems.

'On Earth we believed that there was a thing called karma,' Jas had told him once. 'It means that what you do to others one day comes back onto you. You suffer for your crimes.'

At the time he had found her words difficult to comprehend. It went against the beliefs he knew her society held, and it made him aware of how complex she really was. Or at least how her faith in science conflicted with her own superstitions. However, all of these philosophies were fed by the black book he had been reading. It was an old and ancient text. The basis for his people's faith. Throughout the generations, the magic had taken the religion from them, just as surely as science had stolen the faith of the Earthlings, the second tribe.

Once Arven had seen his race as superior to theirs, but the book had told him the truth. They were the same, but different. One evolved with magic, the other with science. It was that simple.

'Do you remember why we looked for Earth?' Arven asked Kale suddenly.

'Yes. They were the closest match to us. The two tribes.'

Arven nodded. 'I had almost forgotten the myth. Now I know that somehow it is more relevant than I had first thought.' Arven didn't elaborate, but part of him wanted to discuss karma with Kale. He had thought long and hard about their crimes against humanity, and now he wondered if the new rash of murders and infidelities was their punishment. The fact that his own wife's faithfulness was in doubt brought the thought of karma closer to home.

'Leave me. Return to your tent. You're to stay there until I decide what to do.'

Kale nodded and, as if they had been waiting for the order, two guards arrived to escort him back. He would be a prisoner in his own home, but at least it would give him time and space to think over his crime.

Arven watched him go but remained in his seat until the seven councillors entered the tent wearing their parliamentary robes. They seated themselves on the chairs before the Emperor.

'I have summoned you here to discuss a very grave matter,' Arven began. 'As you know, I have recently returned from a tour of the distant towns that were experiencing problems. Yesterday I was summoned to Jenus, where I learnt that Governor Salvar had been murdered.'

There was a collective gasp from the men before him.

'It seems there was a minor uprising. Ten men took it upon themselves, for reasons that are still unclear, to attack and kill the governor and his guard. Thankfully the governor's pregnant wife hid from them and managed to survive.'

'There have been several reports of attacks on married men,' Councillor Gallin said. 'This is merely the latest. It all seems to stem from avarice. It is unmarried men, attacking married ones. The women are generally left unharmed.'

Arven nodded. 'Yes, and in one case, a recently widowed woman was forced into a bonding with one of her husband's murderers. Her husband's blood was still on the man's hands.'

'Appalling!' said Councillor Mari, who was seated at the back.

'There have been cases of something the human females call "adultery",' Gallin reported. 'But it is uncertain whether or not the women in these cases have been complicit.'

Arven sat upright in his throne. 'What cases?'

'In Regenus, a man found his wife in the arms of another man. She said it was rape. Her husband didn't believe her and he killed them both.'

Several cries came from the assembly. 'Impossible! She had to have been telling the truth. A bonded woman couldn't willingly give herself to another man.'

'A bonded Arrak Nah Tiaman female couldn't. But as we are learning,

292

the Earth women are somewhat different from our own,' said Gallin.

'Just supposing it was true,' said Arven. 'How did the woman overcome her natural revulsion when accosted by a man not her husband?'

'I have a theory on this,' said one of the councillors and he stood up to address the others in the room. 'With your permission?' he said, bowing to the Emperor.

'Councillor Abeken, you may have the floor,' Arven said.

'As you know, I was given the task of examining and observing the settlement of the women. I was set an assignment to write a paper for future reference. The Earth female's mind works very differently from the Arrak Nah Tiaman female's. Their race has developed ideas of equality. Sexual promiscuity is something some of them enjoy. They consider it their right. As they do birth control. Some of them consider marriage and motherhood a burden. Or something to be scorned. Like fidelity. On Earth it was deemed acceptable for women to be lovers with other women. Such was also the case between some men: a strange practice that has never appealed to the Arrak Nah Tiaman. We've had cases were such female lovers have had to be separated; living in different towns in order to keep them from each other once they are married. But I digress. In short, the women are so emotionally different from us and our women that it is a wonder they have settled here at all.'

'I'm not sure this has answered the original query, Councillor,' said Gallin. 'Please explain why you think it is possible they could commit sexual acts with men other than their bonded husband.'

'Isn't it obvious? They *think* differently,' Councillor Abeken continued. 'It has less to do with emotion than you might imagine. They can love with their heart, but their mind will still rebel. And the mind rules the heart in this case, not the other way round.'

'Are you saying that it *is* possible for a bonded female to want to be with another man?' Arven asked.

'In theory, yes. Or indeed another woman,' Councillor Abeken said. 'It is part of their conditioning that they should seek to prove themselves free to do as they please.'

Arven fell silent as the council discussed the issues back and forth. It shed new light on his own personal circumstances. He still did not want to bring up the issue to the council, but knew he must act soon in a decisive manner. If suspicion was put onto his wife or the Al Kuzemen, and it was found that he had already known about their liaisons, he didn't know how the council would react.

'It makes a kind of sense,' Arven said suddenly. 'Are the faithless women in question mothers yet?'

The council fell quiet, and they waited as Councillor Abeken stood once more.

'My statistics haven't taken those factors into consideration. However, in all the suspected adultery cases of which I'm personally aware, there have been no children born between the bonded couple.'

'Then we must ensure we impregnate our wives as soon as possible,' Gallin said, and the council erupted into laughter.

Arven, however, did not join in the hilarity.

27

'Wake up,' Jas whispered, shaking Kale's shoulder.

The Al Kuzemen was so deeply asleep she struggled to rouse him.

'What …? Jasmine. Why are you here?'

'We're getting out of here. Now.'

Kale sat up, rubbed his eyes, and looked around his tent. 'I don't understand.'

'A few moments ago Mallory came to see me. She told me the council were meeting to determine our fate.'

'No. Such a meeting would never take place in our absence.'

'You think not? I don't agree. I think Arven can't decide, and he has passed the buck. Either way, you and I are dead meat.'

'Your talk is so strange …'

Jas tugged at Kale once more. 'We're leaving. You're taking us out of here or we're going to be executed. Is that clear enough for you?'

'No. Arven would never hurt you …'

'Hell hath no fury like a man scorned …' Jas said.

'I don't understand you.'

'He will execute us if he thinks us guilty. Don't fool yourself, Kale. We're leaving. Now move.'

He followed her, stumbling blindly as she led him not to the front of the tent but to the back. There she showed him the gaping hole she had cut through the canvas. Jas unsheathed Arven's dagger from the belt tied around her waist. As the blade pulled free, it began to sing and shine in a way that Kale recognised. Only a warrior could bring life to a blade in this way.

'Wait,' Kale said. 'I need my staff.'

Kale returned wearing a robe and carrying his magician's staff: a stick almost as tall as himself. Jas nodded and they stepped through the gap and slid along the back of the tent, weaving through the other homes as she led him out toward the wasteland.

'We can't survive out there,' Kale said. 'We need provisions. The desert is a harsh place.'

Jas held up a brown cloth sack. 'I have some provisions right here. Come on. This way.'

She slipped away from the oasis, passed a pen full of horses and began to run headlong toward the dunes. Kale paused at the pen, looking after her, then back at the town. He didn't know what was happening or if this was advisable, but he felt like he had no option. He would die for his Emperor, if that was the punishment Arven deemed fit, but he couldn't let them kill Jas. The thought sent agonising pains through his chest and stomach. And so he ran after her and they left the town, rapidly losing themselves in the raw landscape of Emin's desert.

By nightfall they were exhausted, but Jas refused to stop and make camp. The sand seemed to swallow her feet as she walked, making the journey laboured as they waded between the tall dunes.

'We need to get as far away as possible,' she merely said. 'They'll find us if we're too close to the camp.'

'I'll hide us,' Kale said. 'We won't be found.'

Reluctantly Jas agreed, so they settled down for the night in the valley of the dunes.

Jas opened the sack to reveal bread, cheese, fruit and a flask of water. They drank first, then nibbled on the bread and cheese, but neither of them had much appetite. Every little noise brought Jas to her feet, dagger ready.

'Sleep,' said Kale eventually. 'You have to sleep. I promise nothing will harm us this night.'

He knelt down and began to draw strange symbols in the sand around them. The air quieted. It was as though they were hidden in their own bubble, and as the sand began to whip around, a storm brewing, Jas lay down and slept within the boundaries of Kale's protective circle.

Arven returned to his tent after the meeting to find Jas gone. He didn't panic immediately as he hadn't restricted her to the tent: he hadn't wanted his guards to become suspicious. *She's probably visiting the nursery or talking with Mallory.* Even so, it was rare for him to come home and not find her there.

He stripped and bathed, washing away the desert sand and the grime of guilt that lingered in the deepest recesses of his mind. When he had first given the order to attack Earth, his thoughts had been only of taking the women, of rebuilding his own world. But recently his dreams had been haunted by the mounds of dead bodies, children, men and women. Stinking and rotting as the birds picked over their bones. He wasn't proud of the genocide he had committed, and the thought that his own world might be crumbling around him made the guilt and anguish worse.

Arven stepped out of the pool and pulled on a robe. Then he entered the main tent, looking around for signs of Jas. It was more than an hour since his return and she still hadn't come back. He opened her wardrobe, found everything in place. Then he walked back to the tent doorway and called for his guard.

'Do you know where the Empress went?' he asked.

The guard looked confused. 'Nowhere, Lord. I thought she was inside.'

'You didn't see her leave?'

The guard shook his head. 'No, Lord.'

Arven dropped the curtain back over the door and turned to look around the large tent with new eyes. Maybe she was sleeping in the four-poster bed? He crossed the room and hurriedly lifted the curtain, only to find the bed empty and unused.

It was then he felt the breeze. A subtle movement of air behind the bed. He pulled aside the back curtain and stared at the canvas wall. The tent had been slit in the middle. A space wide enough for the Empress to leave by. Arven lifted Jas's pillow and saw that the dagger and belt were missing.

He dropped the bed drape back down. He threw off his robe and quickly dressed in loose trousers and shirt, then affixed a cloak around his shoulders and headed toward the door.

The guard was surprised to see him lift the curtain and leave the tent, but he followed the Emperor as he turned left and headed toward the tent of the Al Kuzemen next door. This tent had a double guard on the door, but they stepped aside as Arven entered.

'Stay here,' he ordered all three guards.

By morning Jas was certain that Arven would have men on their trail. She had spent a tortured night, dreaming of his army pouring once more from a vortex. This time the army would have only one objective: to cut her treacherous head from her body.

'We need to call up a vortex,' she said. 'We have to return to Earth.'

Kale shook his head. 'There's nothing left on Earth. The planet is dying.'

'Are you with the Green Party or something?' Jas snapped. 'I know places to hide.'

They set off once more, weaving their way through the dunes, but Jas was slower that day. Her body ached from the previous day's exercise, as she was no longer used to running, and the sand sucked at her feet and legs, making the going so difficult that every step felt as though they were running up a flight of stairs. The planet was contriving to delay them long enough to be captured, or so it seemed.

'There's only one solution. They won't find us on Earth.'

'Wait,' Kale said. 'I shouldn't have agreed to leave last night. This only makes us appear guilty.'

'We *are* guilty, Kale. You want me.'

Kale said nothing, noting that she hadn't said she felt the same. He had always known of course that she didn't want him, but she would have allowed him full access to her body in exchange for something she did want.

'What do *you* want?'

'Excuse me?' Jas stopped walking and turned back toward the Al Kuzemen.

'It isn't me. What do you want?'

Jas said nothing. She was staring beyond Kale's face. He watched her features change as she looked behind them.

'They're coming. Oh my god! Kale, you have to raise a vortex. Now!'

Kale turned and saw in the distance an army of horses and riders heading their way. They were still some miles off, but it wouldn't take them long to catch up.

'We have no chance. We can't outrun the horses,' Jas said.

Kale floundered. He didn't know what to do, but his first instinct was to throw himself on the mercy of the Emperor. He didn't move; he was paralysed with fear.

'Kale? Can you hide us from them?'

He didn't answer.

'Kale!'

'No. All they need is another Al Kuzemen. My magic will be like a flare giving away our location.'

'Then the vortex is the only answer.'

Kale turned. 'I can't raise a vortex ...'

'Of course you can. You did it before.'

'It takes two Al Kuzemen. One controlling the destination, the other controlling the opening.'

'No. No, no, no, no! Why didn't you tell me this before?'

Kale shook his head.

'Come on.'

They ran as fast as they could, weaving in and out of the dunes, constantly aware that the horses were hot on their heels.

'We might as well give up,' Kale gasped, coming to a halt. 'This is useless. We can't outrun them, and even if we hide, the trackers will find our trail eventually.'

Jas stopped and bent over, her hands on her knees as she retched into the sand. Kale came to her side.

'You're sick?'

'It's the exertion,' she said once she could speak again. 'I'll be okay. I just need to rest.'

'Come,' Kale said, and he raised his staff. Thunder echoed through the mounds of sand. 'I'll create a diversion.'

28

When Arven discovered Kale missing he knew that Jas was the one who had taken the initiative to run, and he cursed himself for not anticipating her reaction. Now the whole of Sharik would know of her betrayal. Stupid. He could have kept this quiet. He had already decided to forgive both of them. He had planned to keep her by his side. She would travel to the townships with him, would never be alone again, or be in a position to become tempted to seduce another Al Kuzemen. Then, when the gods blessed them, there would be children, and Jas would no longer crave a return to Earth. Her family and friends would be established on Emin and she would finally belong to the Arrak Nah Tiaman.

Arven shook his head as he rode. Damn her. She was so headstrong, so determined. There were so many good outcomes that could have been. Now there would have to be a trial, or at the very least a meeting with the council to discuss the position. That of course was what worried Arven so much. Adultery was a new thing to the Arrak Nah Tiaman. How would the council deal with it? Of course he could pull rank, but that would only create bad feeling among the councillors. The only course of action he could now be seen to take was to catch Jas and Kale and bring them both to justice.

Arven's heart hurt so much that his stomach churned with nausea. It was a feeling he was unused to, and he resented it. Jas had made him weak. He had been a fool. All this time she had been waiting for a chance to escape back to that useless and dying planet she called home, and Arven hadn't seen it coming. He had been too besotted by her. If it hadn't been for Mallory he wouldn't have discovered her betrayal.

His mind stumbled on that day. She had met him as he headed to the assembly to give his initial report on Jenus.

'Emperor. I need to speak to you urgently.'

She had bowed before him. Normally he would have spoken to her in front of the guards, but something in her demeanour had told him what she had to say was for his ears only. They had stepped inside the marriage tent. Arven had seen the councillors waiting but had dismissed them, rearranging the meeting for later that day.

'Thank you for taking this seriously,' Mallory had said. 'Arven, I come to you with the gravest news. Your wife is faithless. She and Kale are having an affair.'

Her words had meant nothing: until Mallory had explained. She had described finding Jas in Kale's arms. She had told him of their many private meetings. She had explained what adultery was, and the word had burned into his brain like a heated knife.

'I don't know how far this has gone,' Mallory had said. 'But I couldn't allow her to ridicule you like this.'

Mallory had placed her hand on his chest. She had looked up into his face, her eyes shining, her lips damp and welcoming. It was a look he had seen on Jas's face so often: that slight offer of her pert mouth as it waited to be kissed.

'You deserve a faithful wife,' Mallory had said.

Arven had stepped back from her, and she had dropped her hand down at her side. 'You would turn me into a faithless husband?' he had asked.

'No, Lord. Of course not. Please forgive my familiarity.'

'I could never take another woman.'

'No. I didn't mean … Of course you couldn't. Not while your wife lives …'

Arven had seen the gleam of tears in her eyes as she had backed away, bowed and then left the tent. Human females were so complicated. He would never understand them or their motivations.

Of course he had taken it up with Jas, heard her denial. Listened to her lies. Still he had been unable to help himself from possessing her, and part of it had been proving to himself that she was his and his alone. Even now, he still believed that was true, despite the overwhelming evidence to the contrary.

Later, when he had discovered them gone, he had ordered his men to track them through the dunes, but at the last minute had mounted his horse and joined the search. He couldn't leave Jas to the fate of his men. If she fought, they would kill her, and Arven knew she would fight to the death if she was determined to escape.

Of course it was a fool's errand. Their flight was irrational. No-one survived for long in the dunes. The desert heat, the sandstorms, the lack of shelter and the sinking, heavy sand would pull them up before long. Arven had no doubt at all that he would find them. But what he would do with them then, the life-force only knew.

The dunes parted before Jas's eyes. A large doorway hollowed out inside the nearest mound, and Kale pulled her forward. Inside was a small cavern. It was cold and dark, but Kale struck his staff against the wall. It had the same impact as lighting a huge match, and it sent a spark of light up into the air above their heads. Jas looked around as the dune closed up behind them.

'We'll be safe in here. For now.'

Jas was surprised to find rocks inside the dune and sat down on one, heaving and gasping until her breathing slowed once more. She felt feverish. More sickness pulled at her stomach, but she hadn't eaten properly in 24 hours, so she knew there could be nothing left inside her.

'We need water,' she said, testing the near empty flask.

Kale nodded and once more moved his staff. The rock beside Jas parted and a trickle of fresh water poured out onto the sand, splashing her feet.

'How did you do that?' she asked. She unscrewed the flask and placed it under the flow. 'I assume it is safe to drink?'

'Yes. Natural water. It was already flowing within the rock. I just let it out.'

'So this place ... this cave ... it was also already here?'

Kale nodded. 'All magic is based on what nature already offers. We have just learnt to manipulate it to aid our needs.'

'How does that work with the vortex?'

'There are pathways in the universe that lead us to all times and all dimensions,' Kale said. 'The vortex is a pathway. I merely have to know the exit to which it leads.'

Jas thought about it as she sipped the water. It was cold and fresh and tasted pure. She held out the flask to Kale. The Al Kuzemen shook his head.

'Drink your fill first,' he said. 'How do you feel now?'

'Hot. Strange. It's nothing, though. Just tiredness. Tell me more about the operation of the vortex.'

'What do you wish to know?'

'You said it requires two people to operate it. How does that work?'

Kale waved his staff once more and a rock shifted, moving to a place opposite Jas. The Al Kuzemen sat down and looked into her eyes. His feelings had shifted. Here they were, alone. He could have her. She could be his. But he felt no attraction at all. Maybe he was tired also? Or maybe the spell she had worked on him had finally faded. *What am I thinking? She's a woman. She isn't capable of such magic.*

'The vortex requires the power and concentration of the trained minds of two Al Kuzemen. One of them will have memorised the final location. The other manipulates the main force to open the gateway.'

'These gateways. I think they are wormholes ... How did you learn to do this, Kale? Where does the magic come from?'

Kale smiled. It was typical of a human not to understand the simplicity of magic. The tribe that followed logic and invention had always been so close-minded to nature.

'Magic is everywhere, Jasmine. It is in the air around us, and the Al

Kuzemen train in the knowledge of its manipulation. I know it is hard for you to understand. You are, as I recall, a woman very involved with science. Your magic is not our magic. Your ways are so different from ours.'

'I have my own magic,' Jas said. 'It might well be closer to yours than you realise.'

Jas lowered her head and concentrated. Kale watched in fascination as her long hair shrank back into her head and her shape and body changed. She became a boy before his eyes, and even though Kale knew that it was an illusion – that this was merely a glamour she conjured – he could not deny the skill it took to create the spell.

'I'm not as useless as I appear.'

Jas dropped the spell, and the woman reappeared instantaneously.

'I think I can help you with the vortex,' she said. 'If you open the portal, I can give you the location. I know exactly where we can hide on Earth. I'm going to take you deep into the heart of one of those black spots that your magicians cannot see into.'

'We can't cross uncharted ground. It's not possible.'

'Yes it is. Now. Talk me through the magic. Tell me how the ritual of opening the vortex works. We're going to do this, and we're going to Earth.'

'The trail has gone cold, Lord,' said the Tracker. 'I can't find them.'

Arven looked out across the valley of dunes. There was nowhere they could hide, yet his men had covered every inch of the area. It was as though Kale and Jas had disappeared. Arven's heart beat faster in his chest as a fevered fear formed in his mind, sparked by the thought that Jas was gone from him and that he would never see or love her again. He knew then that, if they did find them, he would never allow the council to punish her.

After speaking to the council he had thought long and hard about Abeken's words. Maybe this was all part of Jas's conditioning. She had always found it difficult to accept the magical elements of their world. But she was his wife and she loved him. She just needed to learn it *was* the truth. But how could he teach her? How could he show her that her feelings were real?

Perhaps the only way was to let her go. The separation would teach her that she needed him.

But no. He couldn't stand the thought. His greed for her outweighed any and all needs she might have to be free, because that freedom would cost them both so much. She was like a spoilt, petulant child. Sometimes you had to punish children in order to teach them right from wrong. Jas would have to be punished. But Arven knew he wouldn't allow that punishment to be too harsh. The loss of her privileges would be enough. *When we find her, I'll …*

Arven shook himself. He knew the only thing he would do was hold her and kiss her. How can you hurt the one you love?

'Go back to the town, send for Al Kuzemen Haradin. Get him here as soon as possible,' Arven ordered, and the two nearest guards turned their horses around and set off back to Sharik. 'We'll set up camp for the night,' he continued, and those around him passed on the message to the rest of the search party.

29

Kale and Jas stood on the top of the dune, surveying the sleeping warriors below.

'There is no Al Kuzemen, but I'm certain they will have sent for one.'

'Good. Then we have time. We do this quietly and quickly.'

Kale hung his head. He felt sad and afraid. He didn't want to leave his home. He loved his Emperor, and now wondered how he could have been so foolish as to think he was in love with Jas. The feeling had dissipated. It wasn't true. It was merely an attraction his loneliness had fallen prey to. Alone with her, all he saw was another man's wife, and he no longer had the desire to taste her forbidden fruit.

'We could just walk down there, give ourselves up?' he suggested.

'Do you want to die?' Jas asked. 'Because that is all that awaits you down there. I've seen your people in action. They don't take prisoners that aren't useful, and you and I have outgrown our expediency.'

Jas wiped her brow. The fever was still raging. The sickness was churning inside her stomach. She drank some more of the water from the canteen. Somehow she had lost her grip on Kale. He hadn't made a pass at her when they were alone. She had expected he would want all that she had promised. Maybe fear had dampened his urges, but Jas thought it was more likely that the fascination had worn off. She wasn't worth losing his life for.

'I'm sorry,' she said. 'I got you into this, but there's nothing either of us can do now. We'd be fools to go back. You'd be executed for sure, and I'm certain I wouldn't be far behind you.'

'We don't kill our wives. That's a human trait.'

'They will make an example of us, Kale. Whether you like it or not, we humans live among you. Arven will realise he has to make us toe the line. Our deaths will ensure that no other women take part in extracurricular activity.'

Kale shook his head. She was again using words that didn't translate, but he got the gist of their meaning from the emphasis she put on them. He knew she was right: even though it went against all of their laws. No Al

Kuzemen had ever been put to death for treachery. It wasn't in a mage's make-up to be disloyal to his Emperor. But then, no Arrak Nah Tiaman wife had ever betrayed her husband either.

'We didn't do anything wrong,' Jas said, as though reading his mind. 'Not really. And it is my fault entirely. But they won't see it that way, Kale.'

Jas looked down at the piles of sleeping bodies. They were all wearing the same armour, but even so, she felt Arven's presence. It was as though that thread that held them together had shortened. It eased the sickness somewhat, and it angered her more than anything had ever done. That tug of magic caused by the bonding ceremony. The cord would snap when they passed through the vortex – she was sure of it. Then she would have her own will back and be in control of her body. She would be sure then that this was all some sedentary spell that kept her prisoner. Why else would she have gone along with it for so long?

The thought of crossing the vortex brought a dark infusion of pain and sickness to her stomach. She turned and heaved water and bile up over the sand while Kale watched her.

'You *are* sick,' he said.

'It's nothing. I'm fine. It's all the fear and this damn spell.'

'What spell?'

'The bonding. It's pulling me back to him.'

Kale was silent. He turned to look once more at the camp. 'He's down there?'

'Yes.'

'You love him.'

'No. At least, not really.'

'When will you believe it to be true? This is no spell,' Kale said. He sighed and stepped back from the edge and took her hand. 'It's time.'

There was only one way to show her now. She was a fool to them both. Her will had destroyed them, and Kale knew that she would never believe him. She had to learn the hard way.

They climbed down the dune, weaving their way through the valley until the moons began to dim behind them. The sand was stirring again, but it was a light shiver, not the hurried onslaught of a storm.

'If this isn't done right we'll die, or be lost in the vortex.'

'I'm sure I can do this,' Jas said, but her face was blank and emotionless. 'Besides, if we stay here we're dead anyway.'

Kale shook his head. She was so stubborn. He raised his staff and turned to face the brightening sky. Jas already knew what was coming, as the Al Kuzemen had explained that a vortex this size could be opened only as daylight dawned. She held his hand to increase the connection, and Kale slammed the staff down, opening the vortex up before them.

A violent wind whipped up before them.

'Concentrate Jasmine!'

She forced her mind to find the place where she had once felt safe. She looked down the centre of the vortex and found the theatre, but it wasn't what she wanted. She switched her mind. The safest place had been the mall, and she knew that she would find help there. She focused her thoughts, drawing on the same natural instinct she used to create her glamour persona of Jas the boy. It was, after all, the same magic and required the same level of concentration.

On the other side of the dunes, Arven woke and jumped to his feet as his men stumbled up around him. A vortex had been opened, he could feel it. It was a possibility he had never considered, as he knew that two Al Kuzemen were needed. Was Kale insane? This was surely suicide!

He ran to the makeshift pen and threw open the gate, mounting the nearest horse bareback while his men still stumbled around half asleep.

'Follow me!' he yelled.

He galloped toward the disturbance, with his men trailing behind. As they arrived, they saw Kale and Jas, hand in hand, walking into the vortex.

Arven's horse reared and bucked, throwing him off into the sand. He fell and rolled, striking his head on a piece of rock, but still he stumbled to his feet, staggering forward: just in time to see the vortex close.

'No!'

Arven fell to the ground, staring down at the scorched sand. It was the only evidence that a vortex had been there.

Inside the vortex Jas stumbled, clutching her chest as a fierce knife-like pain penetrated her. Kale pulled her upright, never releasing her hand.

'You're losing it! Concentrate!'

'I thought I heard …'

Jas forced her mind to reject the pain, even though it tore the breath from her lungs, and she pushed forward, projecting the image of the mall. She felt the vortex closing behind them and she drew herself up, swallowing down the bile that rose once more in the back of her throat. In front of them the gateway opened. She could see the mall now, and she could see daylight before them.

Jas heard someone say 'Fire!' and could make out the shapes of soldiers at the entrance.

'Don't shoot! Don't shoot!' she yelled. 'It's me! It's Jas!'

The vortex was so loud, she wasn't sure they had heard her. Then, she saw an impact grenade hurtle into the mouth of the vortex, landing at her feet as a rattle of gunfire burst around her. She grabbed Kale's hand and waited for the explosion to blow them both apart.

ABOUT THE AUTHOR

Award winning author Sam Stone began her professional writing career in 2007 when her first novel won the Silver Award for Best Novel with *ForeWord Magazine* Book of the Year Awards. Since then she has gone on to write several novels, three novellas and many short stories. She was the first woman in 31 years to win the British Fantasy Society Award for Best Novel. She also won the Award for Best Short Fiction in the same year (2011).

Stone loves all genus fiction and enjoys mixing horror (her first passion) with a variety of different genres including science fiction, fantasy and Steampunk.

Her works can be found in paperback, audio and e-book.

Also By Sam Stone

WITH TELOS PUBLISHING

THE JINX CHRONICLES
Hi–tech science fiction fantasy series
2: Jinx Magic (Sept 2015)
3: Jinx Bound (Sept 2016)

KAT LIGHTFOOT MYSTERIES
Steampunk, horror, adventure series
1: Zombies at Tiffany's
2: Kat on a Hot Tin Airship
3: What's Dead PussyKat
4: Kat of Green Tentacles

THE DARKNESS WITHIN
Science Fiction Horror Short Novel

ZOMBIES IN NEW YORK AND OTHER BLOODY JOTTINGS
Thirteen stories of horror and passion, and six mythological and erotic
poems from the pen of the new Queen of Vampire fiction.

OTHER TITLES

THE VAMPIRE GENE SERIES
Horror, thriller, time–travel series.
1: Killing Kiss
2: Futile Flame
3: Demon Dance
4: Hateful Heart
5: Silent Sand
6: Jaded Jewel (coming in 2015)

Other Telos Titles

THE HUMAN ABSTRACT by GEORGE MANN
A future tale of private detectives, AIs, Nanobots, love and death.

HOUDINI'S LAST ILLUSION by STEVE SAVILE
Can the master illusionist Harry Houdini outwit the dead shades of his past?

ALICE'S JOURNEY BEYOND THE MOON by R J CARTER
A sequel to the classic Lewis Carroll tales.

APPROACHING OMEGA by ERIC BROWN
A colonisation mission to Earth runs into problems.

VALLEY OF LIGHTS by STEPHEN GALLAGHER
A cop comes up against a body–hopping murderer.

PRETTY YOUNG THINGS by DOMINIC McDONAGH
A nest of lesbian rave bunny vampires is at large in Manchester.

A MANHATTAN GHOST STORY by T M WRIGHT
Do you see ghosts? A classic tale of love and the supernatural.

BLACK TIDE by DEL STONE JR
A college professor and his students find themselves trapped by an
encroaching horde of zombies following a waste spillage.

FORCE MAJEURE by DANIEL O'MAHONY
An incredible fantasy novel.

SHROUDED BY DARKNESS: TALES OF TERROR
edited by ALISON L R DAVIES
An anthology of tales guaranteed to bring a chill to the spine.

TIME HUNTER

A range of high-quality, original paperback and limited edition hardback novellas featuring the adventures in time and space of Honoré Lechasseur. Part mystery, part detective story, part dark fantasy, part science fiction … these books are guaranteed to enthral fans of good fiction everywhere, and are in the spirit of our acclaimed range of *Doctor Who* Novellas.

THE WINNING SIDE by LANCE PARKIN
THE TUNNEL AT THE END OF THE LIGHT by STEFAN PETRUCHA
THE CLOCKWORK WOMAN by CLAIRE BOTT
KITSUNE by JOHN PAUL CATTON
THE SEVERED MAN by GEORGE MANN
ECHOES by IAIN MCLAUGHLIN & CLAIRE BARTLETT
PECULIAR LIVES by PHILIP PURSER-HALLARD
DEUS LE VOLT by JON DE BURGH MILLER
THE ALBINO'S DANCER by DALE SMITH
THE SIDEWAYS DOOR by R J CARTER & TROY RISER
CHILD OF TIME by GEORGE MANN and DAVID J HOWE **SOLD OUT**

TIME HUNTER FILM

DAEMOS RISING by DAVID J HOWE, DIRECTED BY KEITH BARNFATHER

Daemos Rising is a sequel to both the *Doctor Who* adventure *The Daemons* and to *Downtime*, an earlier drama featuring the Yeti. It is also a prequel of sorts to Telos Publishing's *Time Hunter* series. It stars Miles Richardson as ex-UNIT operative Douglas Cavendish, and Beverley Cressman as Brigadier Lethbridge-Stewart's daughter Kate. Trapped in an isolated cottage, Cavendish thinks he is seeing ghosts. The only person who might understand and help is Kate Lethbridge-Stewart … but when she arrives, she realises that Cavendish is key in a plot to summon the Daemons back to the Earth. With time running out, Kate discovers that sometimes even the familiar can turn out to be your worst nightmare. Also starring Andrew Wisher, and featuring Ian Richardson as the Narrator.
An adventure in time and space.

Order direct from Reeltime Pictures, PO Box 23435, London SE26 5WU

ART BOOK

ALTERED VISIONS by VINCENT CHONG
Vincent Chong has provided cover artwork for authors such as Stephen
King, and has worked with publishers all around the world, as well as
providing illustration for record covers and websites. Now some of his
incredible artwork is collected in *Altered Visions*.

TV/FILM GUIDES

DOCTOR WHO

THE HANDBOOK: THE UNOFFICIAL AND UNAUTHORISED GUIDE
TO THE PRODUCTION OF *DOCTOR WHO* by DAVID J HOWE,
STEPHEN JAMES WALKER and MARK STAMMERS
Complete guide to the making of *Doctor Who* (1963 – 1996).

BACK TO THE VORTEX: THE UNOFFICIAL AND UNAUTHORISED
GUIDE TO *DOCTOR WHO* 2005 by J SHAUN LYON
Complete guide to the 2005 series of *Doctor Who* starring Christopher
Eccleston as the Doctor

SECOND FLIGHT: THE UNOFFICIAL AND UNAUTHORISED GUIDE
TO *DOCTOR WHO* 2006 by J SHAUN LYON
Complete guide to the 2006 series of *Doctor Who*, starring David Tennant as
the Doctor

THIRD DIMENSION: THE UNOFFICIAL AND UNAUTHORISED GUIDE
TO *DOCTOR WHO* 2007 by STEPHEN JAMES WALKER
Complete guide to the 2007 series of *Doctor Who*, starring David Tennant as
the Doctor

MONSTERS INSIDE: THE UNOFFICIAL AND UNAUTHORISED GUIDE
TO *DOCTOR WHO* 2008 by STEPHEN JAMES WALKER
Complete guide to the 2008 series of *Doctor Who*, starring David Tennant as
the Doctor.

END OF TEN: THE UNOFFICIAL AND UNAUTHORISED GUIDE TO
DOCTOR WHO 2009 by STEPHEN JAMES WALKER
Complete guide to the 2009 specials of *Doctor Who*, starring David Tennant
as the Doctor.

CRACKS IN TIME: THE UNOFFICIAL AND UNAUTHORISED GUIDE TO *DOCTOR WHO* 2010 by STEPHEN JAMES WALKER
Complete guide to the 2010 series of *Doctor Who*, starring Matt Smith as the Doctor.

RIVER'S RUN: THE UNOFFICIAL AND UNAUTHORISED GUIDE TO *DOCTOR WHO* 2011 by STEPHEN JAMES WALKER
Complete guide to the 2011 series of *Doctor Who*, starring Matt Smith as the Doctor.

TALKBACK: THE UNOFFICIAL AND UNAUTHORISED DOCTOR WHO INTERVIEW BOOK: VOLUME 1: THE SIXTIES edited by STEPHEN JAMES WALKER
Interviews with cast and behind the scenes crew who worked on *Doctor Who* in the sixties

TALKBACK: THE UNOFFICIAL AND UNAUTHORISED *DOCTOR WHO* INTERVIEW BOOK: VOLUME 2: THE SEVENTIES edited by STEPHEN JAMES WALKER
Interviews with cast and behind the scenes crew who worked on *Doctor Who* in the seventies

TALKBACK: THE UNOFFICIAL AND UNAUTHORISED *DOCTOR WHO* INTERVIEW BOOK: VOLUME 3: THE EIGHTIES edited by STEPHEN JAMES WALKER
Interviews with cast and behind the scenes crew who worked on *Doctor Who* in the eighties

WIPED! *DOCTOR WHO*'S MISSING EPISODES by RICHARD MOLESWORTH
The story behind the BBC's missing episodes of *Doctor Who*.

TIMELINK: THE UNOFFICIAL AND UNAUTHORISED GUIDE TO THE CONTINUITY OF *DOCTOR WHO* VOLUME 2 by JON PREDDLE
Timeline of the continuity of *Doctor Who*.

THE COMIC STRIP COMPANION: THE UNOFFICIAL AND UNAUTHORISED GUIDE TO *DOCTOR WHO* IN COMICS: 1964 — 1979 by PAUL SCOONES
Your comprehensive guide to *Doctor Who* in the comics.

THE TELEVISION COMPANION: THE UNOFFICIAL AND
UNAUTHORISED GUIDE TO *DOCTOR WHO* 1963 — 1996 by DAVID J
HOWE and STEPHEN JAMES WALKER
A two-volume guide to the classic series of *Doctor Who*.

ROBERT HOLMES: A LIFE IN WORDS by RICHARD MOLESWORTH
Whether writing scripts for the far-flung fantasies of *Doctor Who* or *Blake's
7*, or for the more everyday gritty reality of *Bergerac, Shoestring, Juliet Bravo*
or *Public Eye*, Robert Holmes was one of television's most innovative,
creative, respected – and least lauded – of talents from the '60s, '70s and
'80s. Now, for the first time, this book examines his work in detail.

50 FOR 50: CELEBRATING 50 YEARS OF THE DOCTOR WHO FAMILY
by PAULA HAMMOND
50 previously-unpublished interviews covering all five decades of the
show's history.

TORCHWOOD

INSIDE THE HUB: THE UNOFFICIAL AND UNAUTHORISED GUIDE
TO *TORCHWOOD* SERIES ONE by STEPHEN JAMES WALKER
Complete guide to the 2006 series of *Torchwood*, starring John Barrowman
as Captain Jack Harkness.

SOMETHING IN THE DARKNESS: THE UNOFFICIAL AND
UNAUTHORISED GUIDE TO *TORCHWOOD* SERIES TWO by STEPHEN
JAMES WALKER
Complete guide to the 2008 series of *Torchwood*, starring John Barrowman
as Captain Jack Harkness

24

A DAY IN THE LIFE: THE UNOFFICIAL AND UNAUTHORISED GUIDE
TO 24 by KEITH TOPPING
Complete episode guide to the first season of the popular TV show.

TILL DEATH US DO PART

A FAMILY AT WAR: THE UNOFFICIAL AND UNAUTHORISED GUIDE
TO *TILL DEATH US DO PART* by MARK WARD
Complete guide to the popular TV show.

SPACE: 1999

DESTINATION: MOONBASE ALPHA: THE UNOFFICIAL AND UNAUTHORISED GUIDE TO *SPACE: 1999* by ROBERT E WOOD
Complete guide to the popular TV show.

SAPPHIRE AND STEEL

ASSIGNED: THE UNOFFICIAL AND UNAUTHORISED GUIDE TO *SAPPHIRE AND STEEL* by RICHARD CALLAGHAN
Complete guide to the popular TV show.

THUNDERCATS

HEAR THE ROAR: THE UNOFFICIAL AND UNAUTHORISED GUIDE TO THE HIT 1980S SERIES *THUNDERCATS* by DAVID CRICHTON
Complete guide to the popular TV show.

SUPERNATURAL

HUNTED: THE UNOFFICIAL AND UNAUTHORISED GUIDE TO *SUPERNATURAL* SEASONS 1-3 by SAM FORD AND ANTONY FOGG
Complete guide to the popular TV show.

CHARMED

TRIQUETRA: THE UNOFFICIAL AND UNAUTHORISED GUIDE TO *CHARMED* SEASONS 1-7 by KEITH TOPPING
Complete guide to the popular TV show.

THE PRISONER

FALL OUT: THE UNOFFICIAL AND UNAUTHORISED GUIDE TO *THE PRISONER* by ALAN STEVENS and FIONA MOORE
Complete guide to the popular TV show.

BLAKE'S 7

LIBERATION: THE UNOFFICIAL AND UNAUTHORISED GUIDE TO *BLAKE'S 7* by ALAN STEVENS and FIONA MOORE
Complete guide to the popular TV show.

BATTLESTAR GALACTICA

BY YOUR COMMAND: THE UNOFFICIAL AND UNAUTHORISED GUIDE TO *BATTLESTAR GALACTICA* by ALAN STEVENS and FIONA MOORE
A two volume guide to the popular TV show.

A SONG FOR EUROPE

SONGS FOR EUROPE: THE UNITED KINGDOM AT THE EUROVISION SONG CONTEST by GORDON ROXBURGH
A five volume guide to the popular singing contest.

THE AVENGERS

BOWLER HATS AND KINKY BOOTS: THE UNOFFICIAL AND UNAUTHORISED GUIDE TO THE AVENGERS by MICHAEL RICHARDSON
This is the most in-depth reference work about the show. It covers all aspects, going through the production episode by episode, with full behind-the-scenes details.

FILMS

BEAUTIFUL MONSTERS: THE UNOFFICIAL AND UNAUTHORISED GUIDE TO THE *ALIEN* AND *PREDATOR* FILMS by DAVID McINTEE
A guide to the *Alien* and *Predator* Films.

ZOMBIEMANIA: 80 MOVIES TO DIE FOR by DR ARNOLD T BLUMBERG & ANDREW HERSHBERGER
A guide to 80 classic zombie films, along with an extensive filmography of over 500 additional titles

SILVER SCREAM: VOLUME 1: 40 CLASSIC HORROR MOVIES by STEVEN WARREN HILL
A guide to 40 classic horror films from 1920 to 1941.

SILVER SCREAM: VOLUME 2: 40 CLASSIC HORROR MOVIES by STEVEN WARREN HILL
A guide to 40 classic horror films from 1941 to 1951.

TABOO BREAKERS: 18 INDEPENDENT FILMS THAT COURTED
CONTROVERSY AND CREATED A LEGEND by CALUM WADDELL
A guide to 18 films which pushed boundaries and broke taboos.

IT LIVES AGAIN! HORROR MOVIES IN THE NEW MILLENNIUM by
AXELLE CAROLYN
A guide to modern horror films. Large format, full colour throughout.

TELOS MOVIE CLASSICS: *HULK* by TONY LEE
A critique and analysis of Ang Lee's 2003 film *Hulk*.

APE-MAN: THE UNOFFICIAL AND UNAUTHORISED GUIDE TO 100
YEARS OF TARZAN by SEAN EGAN
Guide to *Tarzan* in all the media.

STILL THE BEAST IS FEEDING: FORTY YEARS OF *ROCKY HORROR* by
ROB BAGNALL and PHIL BARDEN
History and appreciation of Richard O'Brien's *Rocky Horror Show*.

HEALTH AND SPIRIT

CELTIC SPELLS by ALLISON BELDON-SMITH and MARY BAKER
A year in the life of a Modern Welsh Witch
This attractively-presented book, illustrated with full-colour photographs
throughout, celebrates the beauty of the Welsh countryside, and the
pleasure of life and nature in balance. The spells and meditations
contained within are designed to be simple to carry out and will enrich
your thinking and appreciation of nature, of friends, of love and of life.

ROMANCE

CATHERINE: ONE LOVE IS ENOUGH by JULIETTE BENZONI
The first book in the international best-selling "Catherine" series of
historical romances, back in print in the English language for the first time
in decades!

EROTICA

AWAKENING JESSICA by ATHENA MICHAELS
A powerful and arousing rite of passage, passionately mixing the sensual and sexual themes of 9 1/2 WEEKS with the mystery of THE PHANTOM OF THE OPERA.

BYTE ME by ROBERTA STEELE
Sexy and intriguing, it explores the world of control and vulnerability, trust, desire and betrayal.

CRIME

PRISCILLA MASTERS
WINDING UP THE SERPENT
CATCH THE FALLEN SPARROW
A WREATH FOR MY SISTER
AND NONE SHALL SLEEP
SCARING CROWS
EMBROIDERING SHROUDS

MIKE RIPLEY
JUST ANOTHER ANGEL
ANGEL TOUCH
ANGEL HUNT
ANGEL ON THE INSIDE
ANGEL CONFIDENTIAL
ANGEL CITY
ANGELS IN ARMS
FAMILY OF ANGELS
BOOTLEGGED ANGEL
THAT ANGEL LOOK
LIGHTS, CAMERA, ANGEL
ANGEL UNDERGROUND

ANDREW PUCKETT
BLOODHOUND
DESOLATION POINT
SHADOWS BEHIND A SCREEN

ANDREW HOOK
THE IMMORTALISTS
CHURCH OF WIRE

TONY RICHARDS
THE DESERT KEEPS ITS DEAD

HANK JANSON
TORMENT
WOMEN HATE TILL DEATH
SOME LOOK BETTER DEAD
SKIRTS BRING ME SORROW
WHEN DAMES GET TOUGH
ACCUSED
KILLER
FRAILS CAN BE SO TOUGH
BROADS DON'T SCARE EASY
KILL HER IF YOU CAN
LILIES FOR MY LOVELY
BLONDE ON THE SPOT
THIS WOMAN IS DEATH
THE LADY HAS A SCAR

OTHER CRIME
THE LONG, BIG KISS GOODBYE
by SCOTT MONTGOMERY

A STINK IN THE TALE by EVGENY GRIDNEFF
A RIP-ROARING comedy-thriller replete with intrigue, adventure
and unexpected twists and turns.

NON-FICTION
THE TRIALS OF HANK JANSON
by STEVE HOLLAND

To order copies of any Telos books, please visit our website where there are full details of all titles and facilities for worldwide credit card online ordering, as well as occasional special offers.

TELOS PUBLISHING
Email: orders@telos.co.uk
Web: www.telos.co.uk

To order copies of any Telos books, please visit our website where there are full details of all titles and facilities for worldwide credit card online ordering, as well as occasional special offers.